THE
ORCHARD
KEEPERS

THE
ORCHARD
KEEPERS

R. PEPPER-SMITH

NeWest Press

Library and Archives Canada Cataloguing in Publication

Pepper-Smith, Robert, 1954–, author
The orchard keepers / Robert Pepper-Smith.

Issued in print and electronic formats.
ISBN 978-1-926455-90-7 (paperback).   ISBN 978-1-926455-91-4 (epub).
ISBN 978-1-926455-92-1 (mobi)

1. Title.

PS8581.E634O73 2017   C813'.6   C2016-905880-8   C2016-905881-6

Editor: Thomas Wharton
Book design: Natalie Olsen, Kisscut Design
Author photo: Anna Atkinson

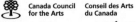 

NeWest Press acknowledges the support of the Canada Council for the
Arts the Alberta Foundation for the Arts, and the Edmonton Arts Council for support of our publishing program. This project is funded in part
by the Government of Canada.

 #201, 8540–109 Street
Edmonton, AB T6G 1E6
780.432.9427
NEWEST PRESS www.newestpress.com

No bison were harmed in the making of this book.
Printed and bound in Canada   1 2 3 4 5 19 18 17

This book is for
Anna and Deane

PART I

THE
WHEEL
KEEPER

THE
WHEEL
KEEPER

From the late 1800s on, many left Roca D'Avola in southern Italy to work in the orchards and vineyards of the Argentine and of British Columbia. Every season they would go and many would return. They were called the *golondrinas*: the swallows. Often, with false papers or with an illegitimate child, they saw their way under the eyes of the authorities by cunning, disguise and quick flight. They learned the illusion of promises: a 1908 brochure advertising land grants and work on the Canadian railroad flaps on the mayoralty walls and on the door of Tommassini's café in the Roca piazza. It shows a verdant valley, a river called the Illecillewaet. When you examine the brochure photo closely, you see a forest of black and grey spires, the green and blue fronds painted on.

Often, survival for the golondrinas depended on a recognizable sign: boots made by Giacometti on the Via dei Mutaliti; a yellow accordion, a word or an accent carried under your tongue. We offer this *signo* to our children, to make it easy to see where we're from.

The Italian-Canadian Association of R.

Driving over the rise of the new highway, I see below me the long grey reservoir that was once the K. valley. Wet flakes scatter from the cloud cover that has settled between the mountains, and a wind — leaping like a cat — raises a steely shimmer near the shore, then farther out. Except for the wind in the spruce and firs, and in the abandoned orchards above the takeline, there is no sound on the reservoir, and I recall with a shock that as a child of five I saw this grey mass long before the valley was flooded. I recognized it and I felt it recognized me.

Below the surface of the lake is the village where I was born and lived till I was fifteen. I slow the car and turn off the highway onto a grassy track that leads through an overgrown orchard to the shore. There I climb out of the car with my young son. I try to tell him about the village of ninety houses that once stood below us on a riverbank, show him by the trace of mountain peaks and avalanche tracks where it once was. Yet all he can see is the grey water staring back at him and he looks up at me, his face blank.

I can't see any of that, Daddy, he tells me.

Still he's happy to be out of the car — we've been driving for over an hour — and he pulls a branch out of the high grass and goes to poke at some wind fallen apples under an old orchard tree.

This I remember: in the village, the house my family shared with nostra nonna was called "the castle" because it was built of Italian stone to last. Now its hallways are currents, with the fish we call redfish in them. Before the dam chutes were closed for the first time, before the water crept into the felled orchards and torn-up vineyards, many of the village houses were burned and plowed into their cellars or moved to a new site above the takeline. That site was soon abandoned because of the dust storms that rose from the reservoir bed when vast amounts of water were let down during *the summer to feed American dams. A railway bridge with a cedar catwalk under it crossed the river from the village to a far hillside. It too was dismantled. It crossed below me, and on the far shore stood the Pradolini house where my aunt Manice and my cousin Anna lived briefly.*

So many years have passed since that time. Now I have a child of my own, a boy who is seven. He has no memory here.

I'm cold, Daddy, he says coming up to take my hand, the wind ruffling his hair. Let's go!

We climb back into the car. We are driving to my cousin Maren's wedding in the Butucci orchards. She, too, lived in our village for a brief time, and we shared a love and the hardship of those days.

I have a gift for her that is quite unusual, a gift that I hope will remind her of how much we once mattered to each other.

1

In our family a story is told of a child who went through the wheel of Roca D'Avola and was returned into the arms of her mother.

Many infants who went through the wheels of southern Italy died within a year.

So it was remarkable that Manice lived.

And only because of the help of the wheel keeper — a Scottish slater of eighteen, my grandfather.

Children vanish. They vanish through doors, under stairs, in the branches of apricot trees. They can be seen on the railroad bridge, on a catwalk of wooden planks, the river far below.

In a dream I have my mother rises from her bed, floats away. I grip her by the ankle to pull her down. In another dream my father is absorbed into the alcove wall of our apartment on the street of the grandmothers. The wall takes him in like water.

The night my cousin Anna — ill with appendicitis — was brought by ferry across the river, I was standing on nostra nonna's porch roof. Anna was my aunt Manice's daughter. I'd parted our kitchen curtains to climb out. I could smell smoke from across the river. Less used, the doors. You take a heap of stone and planks, you put it together and you have a house.

What is a house that goes as far as a breath?
It's for human beings to live in, Anna.

I had heard the village cars and trucks first in the street of the grandmothers and then farther away, quiet in the way they came together on the potholed road that led south of our village. Asleep, I was dreaming of the way Our Lady of Sorrows rings to announce an avalanche or a fire and when I awoke the bell's ringing became the low idle of the village engines, first in our street then farther away. Cars and tractors were coming in from the vineyards onto the road to light up the runway on the southern flats.

Wait, my uncle would say: that's how he would announce a riddle for which he'd immediately supply the answer.

Why is our road full of potholes?

Nests for the fishes!

I'd climbed through the kitchen window onto the porch roof to watch the long string of headlamps, the bright glare of the aircraft lights on the tractor my uncle used to hunt night deer in his vineyard on the Georgia Bench. I heard a rustling in the chestnut tree by the porch.

The train station was lit up and behind it the shadow of the mountain, the glaciers above the treeline. Long gashes in the mountain forest, the tracks of avalanches. And in our garden by the cedar fence, the madonna's cart in grape leaves and ribbons, the odour of dill torches.

This house had been built by Albert Murray, my grandfather, over forty years ago. In the village it was called "the castle" because it was the only house built of stone with two kitchens, the summer one downstairs, the winter one upstairs with its iron stove. The year Anna was born we moved into the castle's upstairs apartment. After months of no work, my father had gotten the job as captain of the river ferry. He was also the deckhand and the ticket collector. To signal that you wanted to cross you rang a bell. There was room for three cars to be taken to the road on the other side of the river that went south into the valley orchards and vineyards. I remember his first uniform: the grey pants with the long black stripe, the blue jacket with provincial crests for shoulder patches, the grey cap with a peaked visor.

Those who know the river, he said to my mother, those who know the river!

He was standing in the doorway, wearing the same smile as when he brought home a redfish or, one fall, a pair of deer antlers and a bloody skullcap — food on the table.

On the porch roof, I saw fires across the river near the rail-road bridge: the Pradolini house and the Swede's barn. The drone of an airplane shimmered above the fire, the house turned to breath. I felt like running to warn the grown-ups. I can still feel panic fluttering in my stomach at the memory of those fires, always at night, always on a warm night when the air was still.

Wait, my uncle would say, how does the Hydro take the heart out of us?

They burn our neighbour's house. Their machines trample fences.

A little grape syrup in their tanks, he suggested, to stop them.

The night the call came for Anna, my father, getting out of bed to answer it, touched my ankle. I was asleep in the cot by the big stove we called the iron monster. As black as a loco-motive, it darkened half the kitchen wall.

Anna's not well, my father said. I have to bring her across the river.

In the foyer at the top of the stairs that led down to the first floor he was putting on his ferryman's jacket and cloth cap.

My mother who was with him said, We'll be back soon.

I felt then that they wouldn't be back soon. How can you count on such hurried promises? When Anna was born ten years previous to that night she was not expected to live. I was told that, born prematurely, she was kept in a shoebox on my aunt Manice's stove. I don't remember the shoebox. I do remember my fear that she would vanish, though I felt responsible for protecting her. She lacked the bones that would weigh her to earth.

I was also told, She will be like a sister to you. I understood that to mean: carry her like the madonna under your coat, a bird in your hands. And yet I who was to protect her had been left behind.

2

In our family the *ruotaro*, the wheel keeper, was used to threaten us. He was said to ride a horse with wicker saddle-baskets for l'*innocenti*. His infants came from the Roca D'Avola *ospizio*. In wicker baskets he took them to the ospizio in Napoli. Some died on the way. *Innocenti, esposito*: children of the wheel. In my dreams he's a small, slight man with willowy ankles who rides a plowhorse. I was told that he always left for Napoli after dark; that you could hear the hollow clop of horse's hooves in the Roca D'Avola streets and if you listened, cries muffled by the baskets.

Once, climbing into an apricot tree in nostra nonna's garden, I broke a main branch. She chased me with a cedar stake used to hold up a vine. From the swaying young tree I'd watched her walk among the high vines in her backyard garden to a barrow. She picked a few peas, shelled and chewed them to a paste. She uprooted a few of the dying stalks and laid them across the path. As she moved the barrow to the end of the row, the wheel shrieked. She opened the faucet near the coal chute and a plume of sprinkler water swept across the pea vines toward the apricot tree. To avoid the water I climbed out on a branch to lower myself to the ground. It snapped and she heard it.

Beyond the backyard gate rose the stucco wall of the Community Centre. A blind wall on that side, with a rickety flight that climbed to the one fire door, high up.

I hid there.

She called for me and I hid behind the railing, laughing behind the wooden slats.

Come down, she shouted. Or I'll send the ruotaro for you.

That was the summer of 195_. I was five years old.

A week later, the St. Leon hospital called to say that my aunt Manice was about to have a baby. There are complications, the nurse said over the telephone. We — my father, nostra nonna and I — took the south road through the orchards on the other side of the river. The gravel road led through cherry and peach orchards and there were tall, grey-boned ladders in the peach trees. Though it was dusk, through the car window I could see the pickers on the ladders and at the roadside bins, emptying the fruit into them. The cloth sacks they carried were round and full. A strong odour of ripe peaches came through the backseat window that I'd opened. The pickers wore long-sleeved shirts and blouses to protect themselves from the peach skins; I could see them in the trees at dusk on the ladders, the white shirts and blouses among the masses of dusty leaves. Ten or twelve, but there always seemed to be many more. That came from their voices, from the languages I couldn't understand welling through the leaves. Portuguese, Italian, high up in the trees on the grey-boned ladders. I remember the smells and how they carried the ladders slung on a shoulder, golondrinas flown in for the harvest. The white shirts were coming out of the orchards then toward the road, going to tables under lanterns hung in the trees. Women at the tables were canning the fruit too ripe to sell.

The car was raising dust billows behind it, gravel rattling on the floor panels. We had taken the gravel road because of the call from the hospital and my father was driving the same way he piloted the river ferry — with the intent searching look of one who watches below surfaces.

We went over the crest and below was the river, much wider here. Though it lay far away between the hills, it seemed to fill the windshield with its own soft light. The sudden smell of winds reminded me of melting snowfields above the village. We were going down the St. Leon road toward the river. The tug toward the mass of grey water was so strong that I knew we would not live. Because of my fear I no longer heard the gravel that was rattling against the floor panels. The hurry was Anna's birth; nostra nonna, sitting by my father, urged him on. Watching the roadside for deer, he was not paying attention to the turn in the road.

I had to put down an anchor. I slipped off a dress shoe that smelled of nostra nonna's cellar where it had been stored on a shelf above the floodline, maybe for years. Nostra nonna had placed it in my hands for Anna's birth. I balanced the shoe in the open car window, then pushed it out.

By the time my father understood what had happened, we were a mile down the road.

Without saying anything he pulled over, got out of the car and walked away alone. His bowed shoulders and stiff walk said, You can't show up for your cousin's birth in one shoe!

Nostra nonna sat in the passenger seat without turning round. She wore a kerchief and beads of sweat had gathered on her neck. "*Bambino piccolo*, we won't be there on time."

High branches over the trampled grass beneath the trees, three-legged ladders propped against the trunks. By then it was dark; nostra nonna had spread the dress she'd brought from the car in the grass, for me to lie down on.

Go to sleep, she said.

The canning fires lit up the pots hung over them and the trunks. I could see gleaming knives as the women worked. A woman with a long ponytail brought us some food from a table. Later I'd learn to call her the Calabrianne.

Boy, she smiled. Where is your shoe?

I dropped it out the window.

Why did you drop your shoe out the window?

Grandmother said we were going to drown.

Nonna looked at me out of her astonished eyes.

That we were going to drown, I nodded.

She reached over to grip my shoulder, as if to silence me.

I remember that the first time I saw my aunt Manice was in late summer of the 195_ harvest, a few weeks before Anna was born. Because nostra nonna was ill that summer, she had crossed the river to help with the harvest.

I was sent across the room to Manice.

Head bowed, she sat alone at the end of the breakfast table.

My father had placed something cold in my hand, folded over my fingers. "Take that to your aunt." It was a two-year-old piece of her wedding cake wrapped in tinfoil. It was his way of saying, *I know your marriage is finished.* Without opening it,

Manice slid the foil package into a patch pocket on her loose, ash-grey dress that had four wooden buttons up the front of it.

Your aunt Manice. I stared at her, open-mouthed. Till then, I'd known nothing about her. Her dress was that of a poor fieldworker. Her black blouse was also very loose and had old-fashioned wooden buttons. She had a broad, gentle, almost shy face with clear brown eyes. Her hair was tied up in a kerchief, like a village grandmother's.

I went up to her. I pressed my hand on her belly.

After her hip operation nostra nonna once said to us, I pinched myself to make sure I was awake. As the effects of the anesthetic wore off, she wasn't sure whether she was dreaming or awake. Now I placed my five-year-old hand on Manice's belly, to make sure she was real.

You're my sister's son, she said. Your name is Michael Guzzo.

Yes, I nodded.

Do you know where I live?

I shook my head.

I live south of here on the St. Leon road. You should come to visit me. I have my own orchard where the dam is being built.

Caught by her clear brown eyes, I'd forgotten my hand on her rounded belly.

Kicks, I said, like a rabbit.

Yes, she nodded, a rabbit. I'm going to have a baby who will be your cousin.

She told me she was married to my uncle Paolo though I'd never seen them together. I had no idea that he was twice married and had two families, one at each end of the valley.

To keep his secret he had forbidden Manice to visit us. Now everyone knew though nothing was said.

Manice and Paolo sat at opposite ends of the table and did not look at each other. Or they looked through each other and spoke as if the other were not there. My uncle spoke loudly and cheerfully. He had seen my father return the wrapped piece of wedding cake to Manice and from that moment on his voice was loud.

I knew several of the golondrinas at the breakfast table, but Manice I did not know and I kept my eyes on her. She didn't say anything. She ate little and put down the knife and then the fork with its tines on the plate rim.

In those days of light dew we began early and picked till midday. To lift the dew, my uncle Paolo who had raised a glass, said, We are people for this harvest; we are people for seven harvests from now! We all knew this Aconcagua saying of his that broke in during the meal. He was from the Aconcagua in the Argentine. His family had worked the vineyards there, and when he was twelve they emigrated to Canada. My uncle worked on the trains. He'd been a train-man most of his life, a fireman shovelling coal till he became an engineer. Paolo I'd see almost every day, and at night I'd hear his engine that we called the Sentinella. From every train came the long whistle followed by a short blast. But each was as individual as a voice, and from as early as I can remember I'd learned to identify the Sentinella's whistle on the mountain, our sleep, the dark village. Now it was whis-pered that he had another family in Field and that the girl who sat beside him — the girl who had arrived in the cab of the Sentinella — was his daughter Maren from there.

Maren is with me, he told me, leaning across the table. He didn't say that she was his daughter, only that she was "with him."

I was hiding the fried egg I didn't like under the rim of my plate. When I saw that Manice was watching me, I slid under the table to crawl away. The tablecloth hung down on both sides, making a kind of tent with legs and boots tucked under the walls. The new cousin had slid down beside me.

What's your name?

Maren Pradolini, she said. She had green eyes and a slender chin.

Long neck she called me then. Like a horse.

My uncle caught me between his boots. He lifted me to touch the rosette of sculpted fruit and birds around the ceiling light. "Is it damp?" A damp rosette meant wasps in the vineyard.

No, I said. I looked out of his strong hands at that girl who had crawled into the chair beside his. Slender chin, green eyes, a mocking smile.

He was telling the girl about Bennello's new plane. On the side my uncle sold dynamite to mines in the mountains, and he and Bennello flew it in.

We'll take you up tomorrow, he promised her. Then I heard him whisper, Go to your nonna, sit by her. She's rich in vineyards and houses. She doesn't know you well yet.

Wait till the dew has lifted. After the breakfast, we stood at the vineyard gate by iron scales used to weigh grape bins. The pickers had brought the wooden bins on high-wheeled carts. The fence posts were already warm and the dew had gone from the wire fence. Some of the pickers had strings looped in their belts to tie the legs of netted birds for their soup.

Smell the sugar! my uncle shouted.

Empty bins scrubbed with sulphur water at the gate — the first morning of the harvest. Men and women from Italy and Portugal wore rubber gloves against the wasps.

Do you hear?

When I nodded, my uncle smiled.

He opened the gate and to safeguard our luck I darted among the vines. As soon as they heard the clatter of stones under my feet, the birds struggled.

Caught wing and neck, one tried to fly through the nets over the ripe grapes.

The bird weighed nothing and it throbbed like a bell. I covered its eyes to pretend night. Yet it's our smell that overpowers them. I was still young, without the odour of the soup makers. Freed wing, the gaping beak. I cupped it for a moment, the throbbing bell of damp feathers, then tossed it over the vines.

A few weeks later, because of the call from the hospital we were going to Manice's house. The car parked on the shoulder of the St. Leon road, I was unable to sleep on the dress that my grandmother had spread in the grass by the canning fires. I remember feeling that days had passed, though my father had hardly been gone an hour for the shoe. To avoid nonna's anxious, impatient eyes I hid under a smokey blanket that the Calabrianne had brought.

When my father had returned with the pushed-out shoe, he threatened, If you throw it out the window again you'll walk for it!

Nonna had fallen asleep in the front seat. Driving south along the river, I could hear her head knocking against the door window. I wanted to wake her up: such sleep was reckless, too trusting. I didn't know what she was dreaming, why her head knocked against the window like a doll's.

We turned into a lane that led through Manice's orchards to a house that was dark, silent. It was one of those small wooden houses built during the war, so strong that Manice had had it moved here from St. Leon and put on a stone foundation. Behind the bedroom curtain that my father drew aside stood a high brass bed with a carved headboard. Nostra nonna opened the window that looked out over the orchards and the road lined with canning fires. I watched the three or four wasps chewing on the sash outside the flyscreen while my father lifted my suitcase onto the bed.

What have you brought, he joked. What have you got in there, bones? You plan to stay forever.

Nostra nonna took my hand. I buried my face in her midriff that smelled of oranges placed to dry under the stove. Manice was in the St. Leon hospital.

I slept in Manice's bed with nostra nonna. Anna was born that night. I awoke to my father's voice returned from the hospital, his words turning over in the darkened room. Through the still window curtains I could see the dark shapes of the trees. The warm night air smelled of dry grass and smoke. I heard a truck passing on the gravel road. The darkness weighed like a breath on my cheek. There was a dull gleam on the sash, where the wasps had fed.

The murmuring of two voices. Yes they were speaking but I hardly heard anything: the words breathed in and out, distant and strong, voices that enter and leave and just before you fall asleep echo in a tin pot.

While she and my father talked, nostra nonna gripped my ankle. I felt that without gripping my ankle she would have drifted from the bed, from the sheets, from the warmth of the canning fires that burned all night. Her hand was cold, she was warming her fingers where her skin touched mine. My blood fled to warm hers; and at the same time the soft murmur of the voices fell round me, to the sheets, on my lips and eyelashes.

The heart has a peculiar past; everything that has affected it is present to it. My grandmother was telling my father how she had once climbed through the orchards of Roca D'Avola in Italy with her first child in her arms. Around the baby's neck she had tied with a red silk string a picture of a saint torn from a calender, the *segno di riconoscimento*. Before she could marry the baby's father, he had died on the road to Napoli. He was taking baskets of fruit and nuts to the Napoli markets and, drunk, he'd fallen from his horse. "Unmarried, I must *make the gesture* of giving up the child."

The ospizio she was climbing towards had a wooden box that rotated in the wall facing the village. She placed the infant in the box which was called *the rouota*: the wheel. To awaken the wheel keeper, she tugged on the bellcord. A clear night: above, a swath of stars, a high warm wind booming through the trees. She touched the rolled picture of the saint, the two closed eyelids. "Then I turned the box into the wall."

By signs of recognition we say, We'll come back for you; we'll bring you home soon. The shred of cloth, the piece of ribbon, a picture torn from a calendar – all catalogued, preserved. Images of saints, foreign coins, torn pieces of coloured cloth: segni di riconoscimento, signs of recognition. That night, the ruotaro takes the baby into the village. The mayor examines l'innocenti, checks her sex. She is healthy, well-fed. He opens the registry.

He asks the wheel keeper if the mother has made the required payment.

I never saw her, he replies.

What name have you given her?

Manice Esposito.

The village mayor checks the registry, running his thumb down the entries.

The next morning nostra nonna is at the ospizio gate posing as a wet nurse. "The mayor of Roca D'Avola has sent me to nurse l'innocenti."

The wheel keeper – a young boy of eighteen, our grandfather – looked at her, laughed.

You're the mother, he said.

I am the wet nurse hired by the mayor.

No, you are the mother who pretends to be a wet nurse.

How do you know?

By the smell of your milk, he says lightly.

The blood trusts, I heard nonna say to my father, still I carried a knife. He led me to my child.

Here is Manice Esposito, he said.

Then it was my turn to laugh. Who says Manice Esposito, who gave her that name?

I did, said the ruotaro.

It was already written in the wheel keeper's book:

Manice Esposito, born August 11, 1920 with
a picture of San Giovanni Neponani tied around her
neck with a red silk string.

The day nostra nonna brought Anna home, I was helping my
father fork up potatoes in Manice's garden.

Who is getting born? I asked.

Your cousin is getting born. My father laughed, straight-
ening his back.

Your cousin is born, he said, but you say she is getting
born.

How long does that take?

He looked at me out of his amused eyes. His eyes were
shaped like those of a sparrow and they had the same dark
colour.

You and she will be friends, he said.

I was made to sit on the porch steps while nostra nonna
got out of the car. She crossed the yard, to place the bundled
baby in my lap. I remember feeling that they'd wrapped the
cousin Anna to hold her together. Only the screwed up face
showed through the swaddled cloth. A face with scratches on
it, the pale blue eyes, the fringe of thick dark hair.

You will be friends, nonna said. She will be like a sister
to you.

Anna weighed almost nothing in my lap and I felt like
pushing her off. I was instructed not to free her arms, not to
untie the mitts from her hands, "because she could scratch
her face."

That fall I hunted in the orchards and in the outbuildings for bones. Something to hold you together, was the feeling I had. I didn't want to see a lot of Anna, only I was afraid that out of sight she would be taken away somewhere. "You and she will be friends. She will be like a sister to you." Then began my mistrust of words, of pronouncements. Even at that young age I felt that such relations couldn't be made by what people said, by words. Anybody could see that she could easily drift away, that she lacked weight. To make the cousin whole I hunted for bones: pellets from an owl's stomach, a heap of burst calf skulls by the roadside, the hawk skull on a shelf in the barn.

That child slept in a shoebox. There was goat's milk with her, an eyedropper. Her legs were no longer than a man's finger. How those stories get told in families, with laughter. "No longer than your finger," "in a shoebox kept on the stove," "not expected to live," "by the smell of your milk."

We called you "the baby" till Manice returned from the hospital with a name for you.

I followed nostra nonna up the flight to Anna's bedroom. Nostra nonna had found the path with the fewest creaks; I remember her milky, carefully placed ankles, the way her hand glided along the banister. With twigs and a wood chip my father had demonstrated how they rolled this house, lifted from its foundations, on logs across the tracks in St. Leon. It seemed strange that it could have been moved here, many miles away. When nostra nonna's cellar flooded, I felt that her house would float away, that one morning I'd find only water lapping the cellar walls.

Nostra nonna showed me Anna in her crib. Slept in a shoebox people say, not expected to live, but I remember that even then she was too big for a shoebox and that her eyes were open to look at us when we came in. Only her head and face peered out of the blanket that she was wrapped in. She sucked milk from an eyedropper while I held the dish with the goat's milk in it. She never seemed to sleep. She was always wide awake with those wide eyes, now grey now slate blue, and I tried to get her to look at me: I rapped softly on the crib railing. Her hand like a wrinkled water flower: touch the palm and it closes, draw out your finger and it opens. To make her whole, to give her weight, I placed the sack of bones under the crib.

Paolo called the next morning.

How's the bambina piccola? Does she have all her toes and fingers? What's her name? I remember that the forced cheeriness of his rapid-fire questions astonished me. "You tell the grandmother I'll be down soon. In the Sentinella!"

For three or four nights in a row I listened for the Sentinella's whistle on the tracks by the river. Once I heard the clatter of hooves in the gravel outside the house and I imagined that the ruotaro had climbed through the cousin's window to place her in a wicker basket among others. In my fear I sat up in bed to listen for the cry of the basketed little ones. I realized the cousin had no name and nothing tied to her, *nothing to say she was ours.*

A week after my aunt Manice had returned from the hospital, I was riding the bicycle that nostra nonna had bought for my cousin Anna. The lane climbed through Manice's orchards, and I was on the crest. Below was the river, placid that morning, a glittering ribbon that reflected the hills on the far shore. The bike rocked as it went downhill. Nostra nonna had raised the training wheels with a wrench from her pocket. Soon I was going faster than I'd ever gone before. The wind rushed into my mouth, drying it. I crossed the river road at the foot of the orchard to fly over a stone embankment.

Nostra nonna found me in a heap under the bicycle. She took me to the same hospital in St. Leon where Anna was born. She stood at the foot of my bed, cowling her head with her kerchief, so that only her eyes showed through.

Nonna, what are you doing?

I am the ruotaro, she said, changing her voice into a man's that made me laugh. I've come to take all the little boys who are never home for supper.

She made the sound of hoof beats on the painted radiator under the window, rapping it with her palms.

No, I remember saying to her. It's the cousin you want.

3

Birds feel the death in our hands. As a young girl nostra nonna was the bird-freer in the vineyards of Roca D'Avola. These vineyards were below the padrone's pine forest with the rare stock dove and the skylark in them. Before the harvest could begin she would go among the netted vines to free entangled birds. Otherwise they'd make the pickers' soup, which the padrone considered to be very, very bad luck for the harvest. Nostra nonna freed them without harm; she had delicate, patient fingers, yet there was no physical reason for her success. In her hands a bird stilled while she covered its eyes with her palm.

She would cover our grandfather's eyes with her hands to make him sleep. Her success, he said, had more to do with the smell of her calloused hands than with their warmth. Your hands smell like stone, he told her once, Anjou stone.

The story begins in 1920. My grandfather is riding a bicycle from Dundee Scotland through France to Italy. His father was a master slater in Dundee, his mother a weaver. I see him pedalling south to Italy on a bicycle with low-slung handlebars. In the bag strapped over the rear fender he carries a slater's hammer and a coil of copper wire. He is going south from the twenty-four hour jute factories of Dundee where there is no work for young men, to the village where his father had once cut and packed slate for the roof of the Lelands courthouse, a pale sea-green slate to set off the dull brick of the building. His father and mother — my great grandparents — had met in the village near the Italian quarry; she was a sharecropper who worked in the orchards and vineyards of Roca D'Avola. When he left for Scotland with the slate packed in straw in crates, she accompanied him.

From his mother my grandfather had learned the dialect of the region; he was fluent in Italian. When he told her of his plans, she asked him to see to a debt that she'd left behind: a few lire owed to Tommassini, the owner of the trattoria in the piazza. After so many years that debt would have to be paid in a memorable fashion, perhaps with a goat.

Wet snow was falling in the streets of Roca D'Avola, an event for the village. He rode under snow that fell out of the heavy low sky and when he looked up the flakes themselves turned grey. In France, he'd stopped at a hillside inn of Anjou to notice the town roofs, patterns of metallic slate for the sun's reflection:

Comme les cheveux d'une jeune fille, said the innkeeper.

Where the *albero* — the festival pole — was usually planted outside the village church of Roca, a moon-tugged boulder had shouldered its way through the earth over winter, to lie hidden beneath the cobblestones. Men with pickaxes and shovels were digging a hole for l'albero. They'd uncovered a dun-coloured boulder that now wore a little cap of snow, impossible to go on.

We dug here last year, one of them muttered. And it was good digging, too.

Albert Murray heard the priest in the church doorway say *Festa paesana* in his little voice of disgust.

One among them turned to a young woman, very pregnant:

Lucia, bring us some water to drink from Tommassini's, in a voice that had the authority of a father.

Albert Murray leapt onto the back of the stone. He felt its back, a gentle brushing of the fingertips. He had such fine, strong hands at eighteen, grey stone dust under the fingernails. One nail, split, was bound with string tied in a knot.

Lucia, he said to the pregnant girl, a glass of Tommassini water.

This he poured into the fine cracks in the stone. He knelt down to listen, to feel for the exhaled air with his lips.

He knew in accepting the glass the trace of her elbow, of her lips, the trace of her voice like stone dust on a sill. Where are you from, she'd asked. You speak like us.

Dundee, he told her, All the way from Scotland. Hopped onto the back of the stone, he who had brought a goat to settle an old debt. The gentle tapping over the stone: here he said, here and here. Listen to how the voice changes. That kind of talking takes awhile, it goes behind and underneath. And with a few quick blows the boulder is broken up.

The priest who had watched from the church doorway hired him to repair the ospizio's northern wall that had been damaged by a mudslide. He could tell this boy who spoke with the accent of the region knew how to work stone. Presently the ospizio housed no innocenti. They had been sent into the hills to wet nurses, their names in a book. And it was not a thick registry for a village.

Lucia was not used to it, thick about the shoulders, to bind the hair under the scarf, how to twist and curl the mass. She felt its weight as though it were not her own as she carried her child, only a few days old, through the orchards behind the village, to place her in the rouota: because she was unmarried, it was the demand of the priest. Her hair had grown long since her brother had left for Canada, and she'd left it uncut. Sky bright with stars; a booming wind in the trees. I'll cut it when I see you again, she'd told him.

That night Albert Murray was the ruotaro. Usually this task was given to the wet nurses of the ospizio, closed down now because of the damaged northern wall. He drove sheep out of the ospizio orchard with handfuls of snow. When the snow pelted one of the sheep, staining its coat, the animal would trot for a few feet and then stand gazing straight ahead with darkened eyes as if listening. He remembered the priest's instructions: Now that you're repairing the ospizio wall, he'd said, it is possible that a mother will use the wheel. Try to get a payment from her before she vanishes. If there is a signo attached to the baby, carefully record its details in the book of the wheel keeper. Preserve the signo, no matter how tattered and worthless.

Before entering the ospizio the slater rolled his long trousers above the bird-thin ankles, rolled the trousers so as to make no sound as he went down the corridor with its plaster walls, by rooms open to the hills. Much later that night, while he was reading by lamplight, he heard the creak of the turning wheel, then an infant's cry.

A week later she lay beside him to listen, as when you strain every nerve to hear a cry baffled by the wind. I describe him precisely as she described him to me: he disappeared into his hands. Asleep, he wrapped himself in his hands as in wood; the milk from her breasts wet his shoulders.

In the morning he sat at the empty table and he said, conjuring an imaginary breakfast with his fluttering hands, I myself generally have some porridge and milk, a little tea, a slice of bread and ham, and, as far as I can afford it, a little steak. For dinner I generally have broth; sometimes potatoes and milk; and I generally take tea at night, with bread and cheese, or bread and butter, with a slice of toast.

She smiled, shaking his conjuring hands that placed the imaginary porridge and milk at the empty table as if to awaken him.

What is toast? She blew gently in his eyes, Full of smoke she said, we have no toast here.

Where are you going? He had felt in the way she looked at him and in her smile her plans to leave.

Vlanmore in Canada, she told him. Or I'll lose my child to the priests.

Another time: Sanmore, the word a blur in her mouth, dream smudge. All the months of letters from her brother, then the invitation: the money order for passage. The extravagance of paper, printed land brochures with coloured reproductions of a painting that showed the Illecillewaet river with a boat on it, a mountain forest.

What does it say?

He looked at her.

I can't read, she said.

He traced out the words, blotting them: the cracked nail. "What's the stone like on this river the Canadians call the Illecillewaet?"

The stone?

Yes, he whispers in her ear. The slate.

For the infant Manice he gouged the skin of a North African plum, the pit a lump of yellow ice. He licked the juice from her belly and tossed her in the air, Manice Tomorrow he said, Manice Tomorrow, see what tomorrow may bring and he laughed flashing his bright little teeth while he tottered around the room on his bird ankles, tossing the laughing child into the air with her plum-sticky belly. He tossed her up and up with her fat little arms spread and the fingers spread to grip the air. To you he said. To your mother who is going to Sanmore, Vlanmore. And I am yours, yours in the big light of this place, with its big booming orchard winds.

See my teeth, he smiled. You have no teeth all you have is a dirty chin, wiping her face with his shirttail.

We will play emigrants now.

The bed is our boat, or hide under the bed till your momma comes home.

The whole village smelled of oregano. She was out cutting oregano on the hills, to be brought to Napoli in sacks on horses. She spread it to dry under the eucalyptus trees. The money her brother had sent wasn't enough to cover passage to Montreal and a train ticket to the village beyond the Rockies called Sanmore or Vlanmore, where her brother had set up a bootmaker's shop. While Albert Murray repaired the ospizio wall and tended the child he'd named Manice, the child who was not his own, she cut oregano on the hills to make up the difference.

Her fingertips, glistening with oil, made tracks on the wall by the bed. The ospizio wall of rough plaster, in the hillside orchards.

Vine stalks blackened with philloxera among the trees.

From each room with its windows flung wide open came a wind carrying the earth odour of oregano. He walked with her down a long corridor booming with wind by old plaster walls. She carried a sack of her clothes under her arm.

His breath was between a sigh and a whistle as he followed her down the corridor, and she always stayed with him till he slept.

Or sometimes till she slept.

Touch my lips she says to him and his touch is the air.

Touch me she says and his touch on her cheek is like breeze. All of a sudden she is asleep, head on his chest. He takes in the track of fingerprints on the wall, and through the window the tall trees that border the ospizio, the various shadows that have laid open the orchard. He takes in the fluttering, the wild fluttering of ribbons tied to the tree marked for the albero and the wind that rushes to them is a good dry wind from the hillside: it smells of winter stones the size of oranges.

There is honour in local stone.

It honours the soil and the light and the moderating effects of the valley. It allows you to distinguish between what is foreign and what is kin to you. It makes you feel that you are growing from the inside outwards.

It's time, she said, rising to dress him.

Once a terrified bird flew through the window into her hair.

He was looking at her, laughing, he had seen it before she had. The laughter on his lips like a light froth; who knows how long he had lain there, watching her sleep.

She shook her lifted head, flaring her nostrils, remembering the smell of his hands on her face.

The baby, too, had touched her and she held its face near hers. She swaddled Manice and stroked her forehead till she

slept, humming whatever came to mind, words that drifted
in and out of meaning and sometimes she would laugh low
at what she heard herself sing:

There are those who uproot and those who plant
There are those who plant and those who uproot
On the priests lightning and thunder
Lightning and thunder upon the priests
Not a hoe the sickle
And the sickle is not a hoe
Not egg the lemon
The lemon is not an egg

How strange their night laughter sounds! The soft laughter
of the low-lying ice mist that has crept into the orchards.

They remember: the cut-up olive and amandier branches,
firewood stacked by the door.

I did that for you, she reminds him.

And their faces in the winter, so warm.

The shadows of her arms fall across the window slats as
she measures with her fists the size of the moon, one atop
the other. They can smell the low-lying mist that climbs on
its knees into the lower orchard like a planting drunk, late at
night, so late at night under such a moon that the earth lows
and drifts, dark and dank. The three-fisted moon throws
slats of light across her shoulders, her hair and she listens for
the priest's footsteps as she does every night, hardly able to
sleep. She says, If he hears about us, he'll come for my child.
To take her to the ospizio in Napoli.

I will *dress you, I said to him. If I leave now I'll be noticed and
caught.*

No, I will do it.

No, I said. Don't you see? To fool the priest's eyes, you must be dressed in a woman's clothes with a woman's hands.

The next morning, in an oregano cart, Albert Murray leaves for Napoli with my child.

Segni di riconoscimento: in the ospizio the slater led me by the hand into a room of cluttered wooden shelves. It was like a shop, but of the strangest things: foreign coins, a shoe with a missing heel, a strip of cloth torn from the hem of a dress, rolled up pictures of saints, all tied to infants that had passed through the wheel.

Where are they, I asked.

Figlia della Madonna, the ruotaro said, in the hills with wet nurses.

4

Albert Murray arrived in R. on a train from Montreal. It was early autumn, that's to say the autumn of 1921 or 1922. In the Rockies he saw mountainside after mountainside of black and grey spires: fires had climbed through the trees in the railroad's right of way. He arrived to find a river village surrounded by burnt forests.

He went to stand in the village fountain, to play the chanter he'd learned to play while working on the Montreal docks. He'd saved enough for his train ticket and a little more. Then his haversack had been stolen on the train. A young woman he recognized was kicking up road dust as she pushed by a barrow full of rags for the midwife. It was one of the last hot days of that year, dry, and the sun bowed her shoulders. She held her proud, shy head to one side listening to the reedy chanter.

Do you see this? It's not mine.

He had stepped into the fountain, chanter in hand, motioning to the water. An orange floated there.

Do you think I've forgotten your name?

Lucia, she reminded him. The shy, curious glances between them said they had not seen each other for months. While he had remained in Montreal to work, she'd travelled to R. with the child Manice, to join her brother.

No Lucia, you can't have the orange to eat. Who knows how it got there, and she, walking toward him said, So what? As if how it got there mattered now that she, Lucia, was about to climb into the fountain to press into him.

He stood in the water, pants rolled to the knees, and played on a single reed that made the frantic sound of birds she'd never heard of. It was his way of saying he'd lost everything, that he had no savings with which to begin their life here. Even his boots had been stolen on the train, and now he was cooling his feet.

I put the orange there, he confessed. It was all he had after the months of absence: something quickly pocketed in the dining car.

Where did that come from?

From the train.

You bought it? her eyes wide at the extravagance.

I stole it for you.

On the riverbank below the village, he was tapping a slate face with a hammer, spread his hand on the grey face of the bank.

He tapped once between thumb and forefinger, then pressed an ear to the stone. A keen smell of snow in the air seemed to come from the stone itself. In its song, the way healthy stone sings when you strike it, was a kind of soft laughter.

A muted light played on this stone that already smelled of winter; it shimmered in indistinct colours with grey edges. He tapped along the riverbank, listening and humming.

The slate face that went for a hundred yards in both directions hummed back.

High on the bank above stood Our Lady of Sorrows with its cedar shake roof. At his feet, a wide river. The slate he'd stacked on the sandbar was so sharp that it had split the rotten calf gloves he'd found in an alleyway.

The river frothed ice crystals. His fingers were going numb.

And there, the wide grey sky between the mountains, lean with snow, any day now. How the hammer's small voice rang against the cloud mass.

In his hunger, he rested against the slate face. A few grains of snow fell on his sleeve. The coat he'd borrowed from Lucia's brother was tight at the shoulders, his left hand numb.

What does rain sound like on the wooden roof of Our Lady of Sorrows?

On a wooden roof rain does a tap dance. On a slate roof it sings.

Here now, the booming grounds. Taunt ropes, three fingers thick and lashed to iron rings driven into the bank, shivered like violin strings. On the far side of the log boom he could see the D. Street sawmill at the mouth of the Illecillewaet. Through the clapboards, the gleam of the sawblade.

A storm was blowing down the valley, and the grey-backed logs began to rock at his feet.

By the mill, three men and two horses were dragging cedar logs ashore. Now the men began to strip the logs. They raised their arms high and the bark came off with the sound of tearing paper.

Lucia had taken him to her brother the village bootmaker. She walked ahead, eating the orange while he wheeled the rag barrow. She crushed the peel in her hands to perfume her hair, a childish gesture of happiness.

When they caught the extravagant fragrance, people in the street turned to her. She chewed on the crushed peel. A bell rang as she opened the shop door.

In the narrow shop with its odours of leather and beeswax, more like a darkened corridor than a room, boot moulds lined the sidewall shelves. They were waiting on the shelves unmoving. A pair were taken down. They rested in the bootmaker's hands like fat pigeons the colour of milk. They were asleep.

The bootmaker ran his hands that glistened with beeswax over their wings. They were like birds that slept in wells. At the bench he covered the boot moulds with a leather sheet. The leather was soft, subtle, indistinct in colour: it had been worked to exhaustion, and it shed the pale colour of buried asparagus shoots.

For the field inspector's wife, he said.

From a shelf behind the workbench he took down two or three pairs of boots. Try these, he said. The men who paid for them died in last winter's avalanches.

When does it rain here? the slater asked.

In the fall.

And how long are the roof icicles?

Long, long, said Lucia. From the eaves to the snow-banks! Though he had only arrived that day, she could tell by his questions he was already thinking about work, about the pitch that a slate roof would require in this new village under the mountains.

He walked across the logboom to the mill. The mill was silent. Rather than follow the shore, he walked straight across the two acre booming grounds. Hungry, he touched some wild potatoes in his jacket pocket. A light snow was falling. Before setting out across the logs, he'd strung his new boots around his neck on copper wire.

Where the bark had been worn off the log felt slick underfoot. He used his toes to grip it.

You put the only food you had at your feet and you pointed to it. He hadn't kept the orange for himself. When he saw Lucia with the barrow he immediately took it out of his shirt and placed it in the fountain.

There it was, floating, a poor joke for you.

And then he took out the chanter.

> He made the sounds of strange birds, I tell you. Though he was very hungry he did not eat. It's there, he said of his only gift now that his haversack had been stolen. Help yourself.

He went across the logs toward the mill. Sometimes only shadows were visible in the slanting snow, a short coat that flapped at his waist. In the mill the giant circular saw, choked with sawdust, gave off a soft grey light between the clapboards. When he fell on his hand, pain stabbed into his left elbow. How could he have fallen — hunger dizzy? He gave a cry, more of vexation than hurt. The three near a slab fire on shore stood up. He could see their gloves drying on stakes tapped into the ground.

You see he's fallen in, he heard one say. That was the boss Gio who the day before had refused him work.

The three left the fire to come to the shore, good. Now they would see what he could do: walk hunger-faint across the sleek backs of the logs as though they were the perlins of Our Lady of Sorrows. Yes, they would see that in his agility and confidence he was the one to replace the church's wooden roof with slate.

Asleep out there, the boss Gio shouted.

Now he was going toward the workers on shore, the short coat flapping at his waist, the slant snow blurring his eyes and lips.

They were stripping cedar logs for street light poles. While they rolled the poles onto the drey, he carried the bark to the fire in his one good hand, his left hand curling in pain and going numb from the fall.

Who will pray in your church? he asked slyly. Under a wooden roof? Who will do that for you?

He reminded the boss Gio of the dangers of a wooden roof in a valley where sparks from the locomotives regularly set off forest fires.

On a wooden roof rain does a tap dance, he observed. On a slate roof it sings.

On the veranda steps she was dealing out cards she had collected by the tracks. Men played cards on the station platform waiting for a train, in the roundhouse at night, and she'd gathered those dropped on the tracks or flung by the wind.

Yours is the king of hearts, she said, watching him swing an axe in his good hand to split firewood. It has one torn corner like a dog that's got its ear chewed in a fight.

And who is this? she said wide-eyed, mocking, taking another card from the deck, A lady? And look how she stands, proud! Why don't you offer her your arm? But no, the king of hearts with his chewed ear, what does he do? He slips back into the pack and there he hides, too proud to ask for food.

She had said this while watching Albert Murray go into the cabin he'd rented from her brother, promising to pay later. To have been robbed of everything he'd saved angered him, and he wanted no help.

Crows flapped overhead while he gathered chestnuts. Lucia had shown him the abandoned field with the two trees in it. The chestnuts were wet in the dark grass and he had to feel for them with his fingers among the long tufts that were stiff with frost. This field, too, had gone a little way and then been abandoned. The potatoes he gathered were wild potatoes, bleaching along a ditch that had not grown over. Take that spade, she had said, her words ringing against the flinty ground as obstinate as he. Someone had planted the two trees, the field, and then gone on, who knows where.

He's dreaming of Lucia's lips, said one of the sawmill workers in the drey. He spoke of the slater who had fallen asleep stretched out on the snow-covered poles, his head lolling against the sideboards. The street had taken a turn to follow the high bank, the river below frothing with ice. On the seat Gio stood with the reins in his hands. He was gazing with pursed lips at the silvery roof of Our Lady of Sorrows. He had supervised the building of the church and now he had doubts.

Her lips touch you, said the worker to the sleeping figure and the others smiled.

At a dug hole in the street, they awoke the Scottish slater to roll out a cedar wood pole for the street lights. Soon all the storefronts, lit up with kerosene lanterns, would have electric lights. It looked ready to spread the light in its newness, the tea-coloured pole stripped of bark.

He was no longer able to uncurl the fingers of his left hand. And yet he must work to live. In their cabin on Second Street, Lucia drew up two chairs and they sat face to face. He looked frightened and defeated, his nostrils pinched white from the pain. Their daughter Manice was asleep in the only bed.

What are our most beautiful birds here? she asked in a soothing voice. Two yellow finches came early in the spring, with bright yellow throats. Too early because the snow had not yet melted. Come outside they called, empty your pockets. They had shrill voices like two tin pipes played against a wall.

I said to those birds, what do you want?

Threads, they piped, threads for our nest. They were in the chestnut branches by the King Edward Hotel. High up, two yellow stains, I heard them piping against the wall.

I said, What do you promise me? They had the voices of dripping icicles. Thaw pain, they said.

From a high shelf she lifted down a cedar plank with the nest on it. Of woven threads and feathers it looked like a watch satchel and it weighed nothing.

They worked hard those birds. She looped a thread through the nest mouth and carefully tied it to the fingers that Albert Murray was no longer able to uncurl by an effort of will.

The nest of threads hung from your fingers. What is held in there? Let its weight thaw your hand.

Already, an ice skin in the river shallows. He stood in the cabin doorway, a pair of antlers cradled in his arms. That must have been the autumn of 1922, their second in the village. She could smell the blood on the skullcap. The antlers looked like those dwarf oaks that, no taller than your waist, grow out of crevices and hollows near the treeline. The cabin was filled with the odour of her cooking. And through it all, like a bitter thread, the smell of the animal's blood. It must have been huge to bear those antlers. She imagined its eyes and the mist of its breath in its nostrils. He talked in his pride of winter meat, more than enough for seven families. He'd already give some to Mrs. Canetti down the street.

Those antlers, moss-covered, were heavy. He had them cradled like a stone in his arms; the points were spread by his face like splayed fingers. She had dreamt of this creature. In the dream the creature had come out of a forest of lodge pole pines in which the night slept out the day. It was very old. Two young deer walking alongside supported its head with the gigantic antlers. She remembered the two deer had milky blue eyes for they were blind. And now the creature's antlers had appeared in her doorway, spread in her lover's arms. She felt then he was unlucky. Something was going to happen to him. Maybe what he lacked was not luck but guile, the sly slipperiness some golondrinas have, those who smell trouble from a distance and who, when it arrives, have long disappeared.

The burnt-out spires that surrounded the village disturbed him.

"Where will we build our house?" Near the CPR tracks so that during the next fire they could run to the station, where a train just might happen to be waiting? Near the Western Canada Wholesale building, that, surrounded by its shipping yard, looked like a place of refuge?

In the hills of Roca, she told him, there were often earthquakes, mudslides. You had to be careful where you built your house. To find a safe place, she said, you went into the church at night when the priest was asleep and cut from the hem of the alter cloth a little square this size, and she pointed to her thumbnail. This you put under your tongue. Then you walked your land. At the safe place to build the alter cloth would warm your tongue. It would signal: Build here!

She went out into the snow hissing under the new street lamps. For the first time, the street that led past the storefronts to Our Lady of Sorrows was lit up after dusk. The after-dark light reminded her of a magic box that she'd seen in Montreal: you gazed through the peephole into a candlelit world, a street scene like this, with figures in windows and doorways, passersby. There is a man in an alley chopping wood; another is crossing the street to the movie theatre, with his lady. He wears a cloth cap and the woman has black gloves painted on her wooden hands.

Mackenzie Avenue lit up at night reminded her of a magic box, only she was in it. Light quivered on the faces of a passing railroad crew and it gave their eyes a fevered glitter. Their foreheads shone like mirrors; their voices sounded tinny and hollow, as in the Illecillewaet canyon. Outside the dome of light loomed the mountain. A locomotive's lights flickered way up in the high pass.

She felt a terrible unease as she withdrew to stand in the doorway of the Modern Bakery. She remembered how the magic box owner had signaled her time was up. He'd brought his hand between the candle and the lens that illuminated the street, a suffocating blackness. How pale and waxen the passersby on Mackenzie Avenue looked as they strode arm in arm through the falling snow, now laughing now transfixed by the electric murmur of the street lights and the cascade of light that filled the street. She felt like running, to claw her way out of the glittering light that settled on her eyes and lips like flour.

Albert Murray was at work on the church roof. He'd stripped the cedar shakes for kindling. Below, by the church doors that Lucia was painting green, were stacked slates from the Illecillewaet valley. He had not been satisfied with river slate. It was too soft, he'd told her, will only last for sixty years. So he'd taken trains into the mountains, jumping out here or there on a high grade to walk up a burnt-out valley, an avalanche track, till he found stone good for a hundred.

A dark green streak on her hand, from painting the church doors ferried upriver from St. Leon. The St. Leon boat builders had made these nail studded fir doors a good ten feet high, to hang on steel hinges forged in the roundhouse at night, when the stewpot was bubbling. The doors were laid out in the churchyard on sawhorses. Three coats of paint for the summer heat and three for the knife-edged winter cold.

The mountain billowed over Our Lady of Sorrows in a blue, milky haze. The snowcap, thawed and refrozen, flashed like a mirror. There was blasting going on above the village, to lay a second line of track. A puff of smoke, rattling windows, sometimes the aftershocks and salvos shook the churchyard. A section of new track near the village had already been laid. She had walked on it. To the side were slabs and blocks of blistered rock, with scored dynamite tunnels. The raw stone, covered in blasting dust, smelled like stagnant water.

Now, many years later I imagine hearing that young woman say, How quick things are done here! The frenzied building was like her decision to leave Roca, to get away overnight. She sees the swagger of the laid track, but also its fear, the inner trouble. The fear of remaining among the burnt spires that surround the village, the unsure place.

5

At dusk, the three-car ferry tied up in its moorings, my father cast for the redfish long after they had settled into the deep currents.

I was sent to find him.

Supper! I called from the landing.

I could hear the line hiss as he made a cast, the lure strike the surface. A warm, still night, the air clear, flicker of village lights on the river. I climbed under the padlocked barrier, walked up the ramp to the deck that smelled of oil and iron rust. Off the stern, the shadow tip of the rod flicked like the willow wand Anna used to knock chestnuts out of the crowns of the trees.

You're going to have a sister.

Is Anna here? I said. I thought she must be asleep in the wheelhouse. I remembered how, since she was born, it was said she would be like a sister to me. I was five or six years old then, now I was thirteen, and I hadn't seen her often. Paolo didn't like his two families to visit the village: he kept them away from us. The stillness that I felt came not from the sky nor the mountain nor the river, but from my father's face under the peaked visor, his body a long shadow that goes rippling along the rod.

Anna! I called.

No, he smiled. Your cousin Maren is coming to live with us.

Hands under my arms he pulled me to my feet.

We walked up the road through the village orchards. My father had placed the fishing rod and the tackle box in the wheelhouse. Anna was not there.

For a few steps he turned on the flashlight that he carried in his pocket.

Better, he said, turning it off, his hand on my shoulder. He'd heard the Hydro was going to build a dam south of Burton. In a few years our village would be flooded. We would have to move, and he was talking of building a house in the orchard above the takeline. The village houses and buildings would either be trucked to a new site or burned.

We could say we won't go.

We have to go, he said, resting his hand on my head. They take what they want in the end. And we will get what we can from the Hydro, he assured me.

Still I remember something in his voice I'd never heard before — a far dark drifting like someone speaking out of a dream.

How will you trick them? I was remembering nonna's story of how the slater, dressed as a woman, had escaped under the eyes of the priest with the infant Manice.

I won't have to trick them, I'll show you.

The road went between slate banks then through orchards to the takeline. With his flashlight, my father pointed out orange ribbons hung from surveyors' stakes, the heap of peach trees torn up to make room in the orchard for our new house.

Nostra nonna will be angry!

I remembered how she once chased me with a cedar stake when, climbing into a apricot tree, I'd broken a main branch. I tried to measure her anger from one branch to twenty or more trees and looked at my father in alarm.

Nonna gave us this land, he said.

For Anna's birth I was given new shoes. For Maren we were given land. I sensed his happiness, yet all I could feel in myself was alarm. The wide gap in the trees was darker than the mountain, and the churned-up earth smelled of broken roots.

I don't like it here.

You will, he smiled, When you have your own room.

Those words seemed to float without meaning: takeline, reservoir at full pool, own room. All I could think of was the castle, the village, the railroad bridge and the Pradolini house across the river flooded. I imagined the reservoir foaming across the stump hills we used to call orchards, through the vineyards to touch the trees outside the promised bedroom window.

What if we drown?

This will be our orchard, he reassured me, above the takeline. Now that Maren is coming to live with us.

That's all I could do, ask questions, and I felt his grown-up impatience; I was only trying to call him back. We asked a lot of questions in those days, questions for grown-ups who were off somewhere in some dark water, trying to think out where to go while our houses were trucked away or burned.

It was two days before the village *festa* that was to last a week. My father read a letter from Maren's mother. Before taking his early train to St. Leon, Uncle Paolo had slipped it under our door. I'd found the envelope, Don't Show To Nonna written on it—the thick letters scrawled on the envelope with a carpenter's grease pencil, in capital letters built out of lines that crossed, or leaned against each other like timbers.

Don't show to nonna. Yet she knew nothing and everything.

Before I could open the letter, my mother took it: Not for your eyes, either.

The letter lay tucked in its envelope on the kitchen table that my father pushed against the window as he said: Maren must come for the festa. My bed had been taken out of the laundry room, put by the big stove that we never used, the iron monster that clicked its teeth at night. She must have her own room, my mother said. A boy doesn't need his own room; a girl does. By my bed my father had also made a shelf for the books I read in those days: adventure books, boyhood mysteries, stories of people who lived far away. One had a picture of a sacred lake in a volcanic crater, where the Maya said clouds were born, and I loved to imagine what that would look like, the birth of clouds off of water.

The letter on the table pushed to the window to make room for Maren. Later I saw it among the copper-bottomed pots on the shelf above the stove. I wanted to read it, to see why the cousin was coming to live with us.

But in a way I already knew. Three days before, my uncle had arrived to sleep downstairs. Through the laundry room window, I'd heard him talking.

Good morning, Mother, he murmured.

He spoke softly on the porch below. They'd brought out chairs for their coffee. Nonna's would be half milk, warmed in a separate pot. I could hear the legs scrape as my uncle drew his chair in, to lean against the wall below my window. The porch, this house listened to you. No radio chatter, no ticking clock, the light and the smells listened to you.

I heard nonna say, So *she* has left you too? And what about my granddaughter?

Years later I found out for certain what my uncle was bargaining for that morning with a shy smile in his voice:

a granddaughter in exchange for the Giacomo house in our village.

I'll have to take her away, he'd threatened. To the Aconcagua. *You give me the Giacomo house and we'll stay.*

It was then that it was decided: Paolo would get the house that Nonna owned across the street. Because he was often away on the trains, Maren would come to live with us.

I didn't know then he was losing his eyesight and he didn't either. Macular degeneration, the doctors would later call it. I took the way he looked at you out of the corners of his eyes as a kind of slyness.

My parents made Maren's bed in the room off the kitchen we called the laundry room. It had a double washbasin in it, a washing machine, a big window that swung open, with the clothesline outside. It used to be an open porch, with wooden stairs that led up to it. The trainmen used to leave their overalls and jackets on the stairs for Nonna to wash. That's how she made some of the money to buy the Giacomo house given to my uncle. Now the porch was glassed in, with a window in the kitchen wall that looked into it.

In the laundry room my mother was standing behind my father.

Maren is coming to live with us, she murmured. Who will work when the valley is flooded?

He turned to her, a brief glare of anger in his eyes. We'll have the peach orchard above the takeline.

Who knows if you can ripen peaches on the side of a reservoir, she complained. She went into the kitchen, to pour a cup of wine. We should move to Westbank.

Westbank, my father echoed. He spoke again of the Hydro's unwillingness to pay anything but the "going rate" for our village land. It was worth much less than the orchards and vineyards of Westbank. I felt then that my parents' voices were adrift, that they'd slipped away into the place of their leaving.

We don't have to move I told them, my voice uncertain.

And we'll end up paying taxes on lake bottom! my father shouted. His angry words rushed through by body as though I were transparent air. I crept behind my mother, a sound shadow.

I drove with him to the bus depot. It smelled of floor cleaner and old newspapers. Though the waiting room was empty, I knew with a child's logic that Maren was behind the photo booth curtain, by the twenty-four hour lockers that you paid to use. She waited for the whirr of the machine to produce the strip of photos before she drew aside the curtain. Maren's bags were already by the glass doors: two suitcases with big metal locks. Because we were late, Maren was the only one left. Pushing aside the curtain she smiled when she saw us.

Her hair was cropped short. "I asked my mom to cut it!"

At the ticket counter, while my father carried the two suitcases outside, Maren asked the price of a return ticket to Field, wrote it on her palm.

She held up the strip of photos. Who is that? she said, pointing not at the wet photos which she held pinched at a corner, but at herself. Maren, I said. I remembered the green eyes, slender chin, I had no trouble recognizing her.

Once again she went to the counter, to verify the price of a return ticket to Field. When the dispatcher spoke, she looked first to his lips, then to her palm, like nonna checking an address on a letter, number by number, word by word.

My father drove down an alley, through puddles from the heavy rains, by rain-stained cedar fences and metal garbage cans on stands to keep them away from the dogs and above the snowbanks in winter.

Maren's dim eyes; she reached for the door handle, lifted it. A twelve button accordion rode in her lap.

You used to play in the Field *bassa banda* I said, remembering.

We were riding in the back seat; my father had put the two suitcases on the seat beside his. Maren had been on the bus for most of the day.

I had a long day to get here, she said. On the bus she had sat across from a boy and a girl. At a rest stop she had seen the two, the boy, the girl lean across a cafeteria table with their chins propped in their hands to kiss. They had leaned across the cafeteria table smiling and had kissed smiling with their eyes wide open and it wasn't the kiss but what they exchanged with their open eyes that she remembered.

My mother has a room for you, I said, my voice full of resentment: she was to have my room, the laundry room. Now I remember the oiled floor boards, with cracks between them. If you put your ear to one, you could hear what was going on below. I used to listen to my uncle's voice. I had learned to predict when he would ask our grandmother for money.

Her hand was on the lifted door handle. My father, who had heard the click of the latch, drove as if a load of firewood had shifted on the car roof. He explained that at the last minute the station dispatcher had ordered uncle Paolo to take a train to St. Leon. He drove past the Giacomo house that nostra nonna had given Paolo; she twisted in her seat to gaze over her shoulder at the darkened windows.

A low murmur, Maren was singing to herself.

She had lifted the door latch. She could have leapt into the alley, the price of a return ticket written on her palm. Instead, Maren told me she'd never had her hair cut so short, that the cut had given her a different face. I remembered the last time I'd seen her, under the table during the grape harvest. She was four years old then. Between those table-cloth walls, I'd felt I was in my kingdom. A pale light shone through the cloth. On the roof, rain was the clatter of knives and forks. Voices the voices of people in the street. She had slid out of her chair under the table. You have a long neck, she'd told me. Like a horse's. She smelt of cinnamon and diesel oil. She'd arrived in the cab of the Sentinella, perched on the sacks of cinnamon that my uncle used to dust his vines against mildew. I remember that her mocking smile made me feel trapped, no longer left to myself.

At fourteen Maren wasn't tall for a girl. She had angular features and a downcast look under bushy eyebrows; she looked as though she felt singled out. She had the waist and hips of a young girl and so with her wrists. But she had a woman's hands and she hid her breasts under my mother's loose-fitting blouse. She'd begun to walk as though others had a *reason* for noticing her. That evening when I saw her coming out of the laundry room, turning to close the door, I thought she was a stranger, a thief maybe, for she closed the door like a stranger's door.

So that she wouldn't sit alone in her curtained room, she was made to do her homework at the table cleared after dinner. Papers spread on the table, textbook open, my father explaining a math problem, writing quickly as he spoke.

I'm one of those people that are no good at math, she said. The night before the festa, she wanted to talk about the albero: prizes hung at various lengths from the top of the pole; you kept what you reached and carried down.

My father looked astonished at what she was talking about. "We stopped that years ago." He turned away as though trying to recall something.

Well, you're from Field.

The next day, to announce the beginning of the *festa campestra* it was custom to visit others in disguise. My uncle dressed up Maren as a man, with a tape-on moustache. She wore a plaid shirt open at the collar, baggy sleeves with rolled-up cuffs. Pant legs tucked into the big work boots she had on, so they wouldn't get caught in the bicycle chain as she rode beside my uncle, pressing the moustache to her lip. Her hair piled up in my grandfather's hat from the cellar, with yellow tobacco stains on the rim.

This is my brother Antonio from the Aconcagua, announced Uncle Paolo. He had put a cap gun in Maren's pocket ("You're a dangerous character!"). They were visiting Mrs. Canetti, Maren's godmother.

Your brother, so young and handsome. And from the Aconcagua!

He's a tough customer, my brother; he's going to take over my business.

The *commare* was setting out plates of gnocchi, two bottles of beer.

Your business, what business?

I sell blasting supplies on the side, commare; and Antonio here is telling me to be on my way. He wants to fly Bennello's plane, too!

Maren laid the cap gun on the table. Under the moustache, she burst out laughing. That day in the village she was the dangerous brother from the Aconcagua. For once Maren seemed free, in her element. Now and then she pressed the moustache to keep it stuck on, over her eager laugh and wild gestures with the cap gun.

Once, to calm her, my uncle placed his hands on her shoulders: You behave yourself here. Stay by your nonna, who is rich. And then, with a puzzled look: When I look at you straight on, you seem blurry. When I turn my head to the side I see you better.

That night — the night before the madonna was brought out for the parade of decorated fruit carts — there was a fire and music on the Illecillewaet sandbar. Maren and I went out there. We were tolerated by the older teenagers who were making plans of mischief for the evening.

Who would you like to go out with, one of the older boys asked me. His girlfriend was toying with his idle fingers in her lap. Others laughed: He's too young.

Maren, I said.

All of a sudden the stillness in their looks, the cedar crackle in the fire throwing off blue flames.

A joke I blurted out.

The next morning, my uncle pulled Maren by the arm down the alley.

Don't you shame me, he said, and he lifted her hand to see if any of the painted hand prints on the fences matched hers. You behave yourself here!

Once after school Maren and I happened to walk home down an alley of high fences of weathered board. It was as though we were walking in the Illecillewaet gully with the strong sunlight reflected from the wind polished boards and the smells of rotting garbage from the cans on wooden stands by gates that, taller than a man, were always closed. Maren tried to remember the houses on the street-side, to figure out whose we were walking by. In those days she was a liar. She told me she had a knife her father had taken after she'd buried it in the head of a dead raven. Or that her father, who had moved to a different town, was going to send a picture of this woman he lived with. At the pink stucco wall of the Community Centre, I pushed her down: My uncle is your father. Everyone knows.

Okay, she said. And this, too.

She would go into my parents' bedroom, to look through the dresser drawers. She took out my mother's jewellery box, the folded bills hidden under it, the old razors, the railroad watch that no longer worked, the folded ferryman's shirts, the panties, the one crumpled tie. And replaced them as they were.

Once my mother watched from the doorway.

Later I heard her say to my father, when she thought I was asleep: She wants to belong here.

Dressed as a clown Maren wore my grandfather's slouch hat, a taped on moustache.

On that bicycle, she pedaled past looks that said: The daughter from Field.

They made her eager to play the fool. Once she sang in a hurried, breathless voice:

Girl guide dressed in yellow

This is the way you treat your fellow

The next morning — the third or forth of the festa — nostra nonna said to me, Bring the dill for the madonna's cart.

All winter the dill was kept in the cellar. On the cellar stairs I saw that water, glittering with coal dust, had welled over the first three steps to meet me. After the heavy rains of the day Maren arrived by bus, nostra nonna's cellar had flooded. Now as in previous years, when the water vanished I'd find salamanders in the mud and shrimp that lived in underground streams, translucent with pepper grain eyes. Crouching, I made glittering trails in the coal dust on the surface of the water. A raft of grape lugs and cedar bolts had floated from under the stairs where I'd built it in the winter.

The echo of wine bottles under the light by the furnace. I pulled the raft in, untied it, poled with a broom handle along the wall. Ripples slapped the stone walls, water came up between the slats as I poled the raft over to the shelves. Reach down the dill fronds from rough cedar shelves above the high water mark.

The house is dying, I imagined saying to Maren. Already it refuses us. .

At night I hear waterfalls in the cellar. I see smoke stains on the windows.

The house had settled during the night, creaking like the ferry in its slip. That morning my father's shirtsleeves and hands were covered in shavings that had the odour of cinnamon and old oak. He was planing the doors stuck in their frames.

My father called from the top of the cellar stairs: Anna is here.

She came down to the step above water in a dress with patch pockets, a sunhat. Don't worry I won't kiss you she said and then she did — a cousin's kiss. Under the plaited brim of the sunhat, I saw dark eyes, flashing teeth, someone over winter who had grown almost as tall as I.

Maren's living here. Where is she?

I said she was with the priest, to get ready for the parade of the madonna and the trip to bless the new graveyard above the takeline.

I haven't seen her in a long time! Do you think she'll recognize me?

Yes, I nodded, uncertain.

What if she doesn't remember me?

Just say your name, I said. Just say, Anna Esposito.

We climbed the stairs into the kitchen. I laid the dill on the table. My father was sitting by nostra nonna, brushing wood shavings from his hands. They were discussing the land buyers sent by the Hydro.

Try always to have a friendly witness around, my father recommended. Offer wine, our braided bread.

My uncle, his voice full of anger, was talking about the

Hydro machines in the vineyards last evening: Their drivers say, Sorry. We weren't sure about the fence line. They trample fences!

A little grape sugar in their tanks, he suggested with a sly look.

Talk about everything under the sun except the business at hand, my father countered. Never allow two of them to discuss business with you alone.

He passed to Nonna a Hydro brochure that showed holiday cabins on the shore of the future reservoir, which was advertised as a recreation area.

They lie like the priests, she said.

That day of the madonna, of the trip upriver to bless the new graveyard, we stripped the window frames to paint them for the festa. My father was on a ladder scraping the blistered paint with a tool shaped like a claw; a snow of heavy flakes fell into my hair, my eyelashes. The different clothes I put on, the various colours of my hands: green of the church doors, pale violet of our windows. The dust, the paint flecks in my hair like flakes of many-coloured slate, chalky dust smeared across my forehead as I wipe away the sweat, holding the ladder for my father. He was two storeys above me, and I couldn't look at him.

They say not to paint, he says, hooking the clawtool on a rung. That painting our houses for the madonna won't bring us more Hydro money. This isn't for money; this is for honour.

All these years later I can still smell the burning dill. It had a sweet smell, the grey smoke that drifts on the river while my uncle plays his yellow *zerocetti*. The dill torches hiss as they strike the river among the flowers sent out for the festa.

My grandmother said, You come with me. I had never seen her look so determined; her cheek was white, as if she'd received a slap. She'd slipped a pair of kitchen shears into the pocket of her black dress. This was after I'd brought the dill from the cellar and after she'd slid the Hydro brochure across the table.

At the foot of my uncle's house across the street I knelt to peer into the madonna's shrine, the size of a birdhouse made of slate. My uncle had found her in the 1923 avalanche. Twelve years old, he'd brought the madonna down the mountain under his coat: She's the only one I saved. Orchards south of the village were being cut down for the new dam and a pall of smoke rose there. The madonna wore a blue robe that draped her arms above the upturned palms. Her high, rounded forehead. I tried to imagine the eyes under the lids, once pressed in snow like flour. A pale plaster showed through her chipped fingers.

While nostra nonna knelt to clip a square of silk from the hem of the madonna's blue robe, she muttered under her breath:

> And the sickle is not a hoe
> Not a hoe the sickle
> There are those who uproot and those who plant
> Those who plant and those who uproot

For you mother, she said. A song from Roca. My gift for your gift. It was the song she used to sing in the ospizio to the

infant Manice. She would sing it at night to calm the baby
against the priest's footsteps, full of whispered hope to get
away. Now she struggled to her feet, the square in her fist. I
wanted to know what it was for. For you, she said, raising a
finger to her lips to say quiet, no more questions. From down
the street we could hear the creak of the picker's cart, many
voices.

A red silk thread tied around her wrist, Anna carried
long dill fronds that quivered as she walked. In the street of
the grandmothers my uncle wheeled a picker's cart with the
madonna on a bed of straw and grape flowers. Others joined
from behind their gates as he walked to the ferry landing.
He'd slung his yellow accordion with its buttoned bellows on
one shoulder. The Canetti family waited behind a gate and
by custom it was the grandmother who opened it.

Come place a gift: a handful of grape flowers, a ribbon
in the cart, a loaf that smells of saffron. My father was waiting at the landing, the low rumble of the ferry's engine. Six
girls of the village, Maren among them, carried dill fronds
and lit candles along the gravel river road. The gravel clattered in the heat. The fronds above them, like pale sputtering
flames. Maren had powdered her eyebrows and fingers with
grey ash. In her open shirt she smelled of sweat. Green eyes
and slender chin — she walked at the side of the priest. I saw
her eager smile. With the five at the side of the priest she was
far from Paolo's silencing glance. She wouldn't look at me.
She wanted to be left in her element, the ceremony itself.
She looked like she belonged. Anna with her lit candle was
behind; she was talking excitedly to the candle bearer at
her side in a loud, cheerful voice that I could tell was meant

for Maren who wouldn't turn around. I could tell each was aware of the other, though nothing was said between them.

Out on the river, we passed below the railroad bridge. I remember that we were going to the new graveyard that the Hydro had made above the takeline. We were going to hold a ceremony over a plaque for the seventy-six who had died in the 1923 avalanche.

Wait, my uncle said: Once their mouths were full of snow, soon they will be full of water!

My father's ferry had turned upriver into the strong currents, among whirlpools capable of drawing a log to the bottom to release it. At middeck, tables from the firehall were laid out with salads and gnocchi, roasted ham and braided bread. The accordion music went out like smoke, awake and dreaming, travelling low across the water. To have a feel for the currents, to feel your way along as a blind hand glides up a bannister.

We passed beneath the railroad bridge, and Paolo brought nonna a plate of salad and gnocchi.

I won't be eating with you, our grandmother said very brusquely. I've burnt my throat with tea.

Anna looked at her, sensing there was more to it, and said nothing.

Go see a doctor, my uncle advised, if you've burnt your throat like that. He placed his accordion on the table, offered to drive her to the clinic when we returned to the village.

She pushed away the plate he'd brought her. I'm fine.

She stood to walk to the stern.

You come with me, she said, biting her lip.

Off the stern we could see the churning prop water, the railroad bridge with its catwalk of cedar planks, the green haze of the Pradolini orchard on the far shore.

You are my only grandson.

Yes, I nodded. I bought the Giacomo house for you. It was meant to be yours.

She had bought it from Mr. Giacomo, a logging contractor who had recently moved to our valley. It was a narrow two storey house that he'd lived in temporarily with his wife, while he looked for land north of our village. He wanted to plant vineyards beyond the takeline. Nonna had wanted it for me as a promise and as a symbol of success — the house of a rich man!

Much later I would learn that he had sold it to nonna to buy a judge's house in Burnham, to float on a barge across Olebar lake for his wife. His wife had dreamt of the judge's house and he'd wanted to make it hers. In those days I wondered at the way we move towards dreams and the deft way we handle them, as though light and memory could be manipulated in our desire.

Now nonna pressed the blue square from the madonna's hem in my hand. When you go to look for your new home, put this under your tongue. It will protect you. I could see shame and bewilderment in her eyes-she had meant that house for me when I was older and now she'd been forced to give it to Paolo, and she didn't know where I'd end up. I didn't know then of the secret negotiations between nonna and my parents, to keep Maren near. Yes, Paolo would get the Giacomo house, a home to share with his daughter. To my parents nonna would give an orchard above the takeline, in compensation for my loss.

Where would I end up? The ferry was advancing upriver, against the current. Under my feet I could feel the reassuring iron deck, I could smell the cottonwoods onshore and I could see the inviting, wide, slow pace of the river ahead. The water behind us frothed white then spread in widening ripples to the far banks. Yes, all was well. And yet, I sensed in the solid weight of the iron beneath my feet a lie: we were going and yet we are already gone.

Maren had joined us. Nonna wet her kerchief with spittle, to quickly rub the priest's ash from Maren's nostrils and from under her eyes, those round peering eyes that smiled at the old woman. You two look after each other, nonna said.

I saw Maren draw back then, flushed to her hair. She gave me a quick, bewildered look. She took Anna's hand and the two walked away to the middeck tables where Paolo was uncorking wine bottles.

Now I see our grandmother's words had named a distance between us we were unable to cover. Our automatic reaction was to fly from each other. The cousins at the middeck tables were laughing and whispering, and I had the impression they were making fun of the way I stood rooted at the stern, embarrassed and exposed by the old woman who loved us. I had no idea of how to look after either of those cousins and yet I was drawn to them both. From where I stood, rooted by our grandmother's words,

I could see that they were watching me, mocking and distant.

Later, Paolo would take me aside to ask, What did nonna say?

Nothing, I said then, turning quickly away.

Now that he'd bargained for the Giacomo house, he always wanted to know what the grandmother had to say outside of his hearing.

The metal railings shook as the ferry slowed to turn ashore. Once landed, Anna strode away and stood on a high sandbank.

I'm going to see the new village, she said, turning to look over her shoulder.

It was hot where we had landed. There were some cottonwood fibres caught in Maren's hair from trees over the sandbar. A path led up to the new graveyard. I remember trying to search for mocking laughter in Anna's eyes, a reaction to our grandmother's words. She said to no one in particular: Me and my sister are going to see the new village.

Maren hoisted her shirt to show me a bottle of wine she'd taken from the crates under the middeck tables and in her knapsack a carton of ice cream from the icebox.

Me and my sister aren't going with the others to the new graveyard.

In the new village I saw Maren sprawled on the curb outside Beruski's store, which was on the blocks used to move it there. Over the past days the Hydro had moved buildings and houses from our village to this site. Soon many would live here.

Got to get up, Maren said, but she didn't.

Anna was propped against a chestnut sapling. The street was empty, the windows of Beruski's store sheeted in cardboard. As she went to pass Maren the carton of ice cream, she scraped her knuckles on the bark.

I saw then she was drunk. Because of the wine, she didn't seem to feel the pain of the scrape nor did she notice the blood welling on her knuckles.

Why don't you get down from your bicycle, she said with a wave of her hand, and help us.

Maren, who was on the other side of the trunk, roared with laughter.

Jumping bean, she cried, wiping the tears from her eyes. Jumping bean get a grip. She was no longer wearing her loose-fitting blouse; she was wearing Anna's cowgirl's shirt braided up the front, with studded cuffs. Maren had gone over the fence to Beruski's, to take a wild rhubarb leaf that looked like a star cut from wet tissue paper spread in her lap.

First off your bicycle, Maren repeated as a kind of joke. I had walked here as the cousins had from the ferry. Why are you staring? Did you follow us?

The ferry is loading, I answered. Time to go back to R.

Those places are from R, pointing to Beruski's store, the Fuscaldo house, the Swede's house. But this isn't R.

Not R, Anna echoed, the corners of her mouth trembling with mirth.

And then she imitated our grandmother's voice: You two look after each other.

He can look after himself said Maren, turning red.

A clear mid-afternoon light had settled on the pavement, clean as a pressed sheet. When I knelt to lift her, Maren shut her mouth and tried to compose her look, yet her lower jaw trembled. She smelled of wine. She dragged a wisp of hair across her lips and bit it, to keep calm. Only, her eyes had begun to water.

I have to pee, she said.

Crouching, Anna lifted her. We went down the street, past houses from our condemned village that were still on blocks in the air. There was a high flush in Maren's cheeks and a brightness to her eyes. Anna was almost as tall as Maren. When she laughed there was a certain gladness in her voice. Walking back to the ferry made her stop laughing, made her wipe the tears from her cheeks. My sister, she said.

I saw Maren didn't like being called *sister*: she gave Anna the look of someone slapped, as if she, too, felt the distance between *sister* and what we really had; between *new village* and a site strewn with uprooted houses and stores, blind windows sheeted in cardboard. It gave me a giddy feeling in the chest, the sense that we could float away anytime.

Early the next morning, all the laundry room curtains were drawn. To call Maren, I rapped softly on the laundry room glass. I carried a chair across the floorboards to the iron stove, to reach down the letter hidden among the copper-bottomed pots.

On the cellar stairs I crouched above the water stirring against the walls.

The letter said:

For one thing she is too lonely.

I felt her breath.

Maren had come down behind me.

Why do you want to push me in? Turning to look over my shoulder, I shoved the letter into my pocket.

I felt her breath. I don't want to push you in. I can't sleep here; it's not like I remember. What were you reading?

A salamander had surfaced at the foot of the stairs, its head a dark aspen leaf. I reached for the net tucked by the stairs, made out of a nylon stocking strung on hanger wire.

Nothing for you.

The cellar light held it to the surface, wide black eyes. I turned the net inside out to free the struggling body with its flame-coloured belly. It thrust its snout into the little hollow between the curved thumbs of Maren's cupped hands.

From the cellar stairs, we could hear my uncle's accordion in the street of the grandmothers. He was the bassa banda. He played "The Dolphin," "Grass," "The Black-headed Saint."

That's your father, I reminded her. It was the third or fourth morning of the festa campestra and he was waking everybody up.

She told me what she remembered from six years ago. She remembered the albero hung with prizes: salami, mortabella; money and toys disguised as bunches of leaves; and at the top of the pole the grand prize, a young lamb that had been slaughtered and dressed for cooking.

I haven't seen that in a long time, I said.

We took the salamander to the river. We went down the alleys to avoid my uncle's cheerful accordion. She had opened the gap between her thumbs to look into its glittering black eyes.

Listen.

Cranes were flying over the village to the southern flats; their wings made the sound of slowly revolving helicopter blades.

Maren had stopped in her tracks.

Cranes, she said.

There were hardly any songbirds, although crows flew restlessly from chestnut tree to chestnut tree. We went down the river road patched with gravel. The cranes were dropping into the river like an uncoiling braid of hair. On the Illecillewaet sandbar, while she slipped her hands into the river,

I stood back to read:

> She ran away to Nakusp last week. If she had had enough money, she would have gone on to Vancouver. We believe there is no point in forcing her to stay with us any longer; it will only make her more miserable.

To prepare for the last days of the festa, we children were gathered in the church basement. A nun in a black and grey habit described all the toys in heaven. She was directing her remarks to the younger ones — ages five or six — who, wide-eyed, heard about the dazzling, irresistible toys of heaven. Maren shook her head in disbelief. She bit her lip, glanced from side to side. Later, when it was discovered that money collected in the madonna's plate had been stolen, the nuns put us in a line, palms up.

Hold out your hands.

When the ruler struck, Maren made a fist, more in panic than in anger; she refused to let go. The nun tried to shake the ruler from her fist. Maren's eyes were full of wild panic. Turning to flee she tripped over a chair and split open her chin. I remember her look of helplessness as she examined her bloody hands. She ran to a door that opened onto a staircase leading outdoors. The nuns rushed after her. I saw that, expecting me to follow her, she'd stopped at the door. I edged behind the rushing nuns and the taller children who were staring in disbelief at the blood pouring from her chin.

I climbed around her in the high branches.

Hi! Fine!

She told me she was fine before I asked her.

You have to go to the St. Leon clinic, I said.

Crouching below me, shirt pressed to her chin, she said, Sometimes I have this feeling I shouldn't be alive.

My father's shouts guided her down. Call the doctor!, he shouted, though he knew it wasn't the doctor's day in our village.

I slept on the way down and woke up in the streets of St. Leon. I don't remember the doctor who arrived to unlock the clinic door, turn on the lights. In the operating room there were pads of blood-stained gauze in the sink, implements scattered across a metal tray on the counter.

Climb up then, his voice full of sleep. He spread a clean sheet on the table. He quickly draped a sheet over Maren's chest. He wrapped her arms in the sheet, then tucked the ends under her back. When he sponged her chin she began to cry, staring at the ceiling.

I'm ordered to hold down her knees.

The doctor, impatient to return to bed, doesn't wait for the injected anesthetic to work. For the first two stitches she winces, lips clamped between her teeth, her face bathed in tears. Her knees, trembling under my hands, feel like wood.

I didn't question what the doctor demanded of me; I held down her knees. There was nothing else I could do. By her amazed, staring eyes and her reproachful look, I felt my stomach hollow to the shame of that betrayal. Now, many years later I understand these things: to hold down her knees, *to jump to that order*, was to make myself less than I was. When he missed a stitch the doctor swore, pushed through the sickle-shaped needle. He wiped away the disinfectant, dabbed on antibiotic cream, then taped on a dressing that had to be replaced every day. As he gave his instructions, Maren, free of the wrapped sheet and sitting on the table, continued to stare at me with astonished, reproachful eyes, the look of someone who sees you as you've never been seen before.

She doesn't do her chores because she's unhappy. She lies about it so she won't get into trouble. Then we bawl her out; for that she builds a wall around herself so it won't penetrate, and so she won't get hurt. After it's over we all hate each other, and the work still isn't done properly.

Under an open window through which I could hear the trains, my father reworked his house plans. He was sitting at the kitchen table, drawing by lamplight. I was in bed: a fold-up cot that my mother brought out at night, made up. I watched her step over the low sill, to sit with her bare feet outside on the warm porch roof shingles.

My father got up to rap on the laundry room window. Through the drawn curtains you could see the light from Maren's reading lamp.

He rapped again softly: I've something to show you. His finger traced across the house plans.

This will be your room, he said, on the first floor.

She was wearing my mother's flannel pyjamas and her feet were bare. Her hair that had grown longer was tied at the nape, and she had a gauze dressing taped to her narrow chin, under the wide, green eyes. She smelt of cinnamon and disinfectant.

She had her new look: cheerless, resigned. From my bed I heard her say, I can't stay here. Of course you can stay with us, my father said with surprise. You're tired after the shock of your fall. You need to rest.

Through the window over the sink I could see that across the tracks the train station was lit up: the passenger train was arriving. It would stop for an hour then go on to the coast. My father called it the Vlanmore train. Italian immigrants once took that train from the transatlantic docks of Montreal. Where are you going they asked each other. Some were going to Vlanmore, others to Sanmore, others to Windamore. But they all got off here at the same village, my grandfather among them.

Sometime in the last days of the festa campestra Paolo came into our upstairs apartment from the roundhouse, with the yellow zerocetti on his shoulder. That accordion was made in Castelfidardo in 1910. It was tuned slightly sharp for the sake of brilliance. In his arms he carried a copper brazier from

St. Leon. It's cold in the Giacomo house! To warm his room at night he'd burn almond shells in the brazier. There was a little metal shovel to stir the coals.

He asked for nothing, though now and then he gazed at Maren. He touched the dressing on her chin — a caress that was also a reproach.

Maren had never heard of the Aconcagua.

"It's a mountain in the Argentine." He described the vineyards of his childhood watered by the melting snows, the vast grasslands. He spoke of peach trees that grew so quickly they were used for firewood, of the Barletta wheat and how you had to plow not three but six inches deep so that the rockless soil would retain sufficient moisture. I saw Maren's eyes squint, as in a glare.

He carefully unfolded a map before her, tracing a railroad from Rojas to Mendoza.

You take the Rio Cuarto from Mercedes.

Maren refused to play "The Red Rooster" on his accordion. A pale light shone through the window onto the table where my uncle had placed the copper brazier.

Play Carpani's "Moonlight." Once again she shook her head, eyes lowered.

She won't play for her father!

And why so often then did he say "she"?

Look at her, how she is eating!

Look who she is asking.

He pointed in her science book and laughed: How do you know—?

Well because ... and Maren explained. She held the book open before his hands.

You can do all kinds of things, leafing the pages to show him.

I can't see those blurry lines.

Maren hated math but she knew more chemistry than any of us and this made her proud; she spoke hurriedly.

Paolo said she was "showing off."

He touched the side of her plate: Your mind is elsewhere.

"Thank you!" In the midst of his words, her mind *was* elsewhere. She was wearing a light blouse that my mother had given her, full at the wrists.

I could tell by Paolo's composed expression that he had something to tell us and now he spoke: Today I lost my job on the railroad. My eyesight is going.

Do you hear me, he repeated, Do you hear me? He had the yellow accordion on his lap, still buttoned, and at his elbow on the table the copper brazier that glowed dully in the late afternoon light.

My parents rose from their chairs. My father placed the science book before him: Show us.

I turn my head to the side, he said, I can read fine. I look straight at the page, all I see are blurred lines.

I didn't believe the shy, faraway smile in his voice. I was sure it was another trick of some kind, something to do with money.

Anna Esposito. When I think of that name, my mind wanders. Nine years old, she was the only girl left on the school field. A late afternoon under a cloudy sky, long shadows on the field. In order to keep her attention, but to show that she would not be let in our game, we made up names for ourselves.

Vince Berutchi called himself Ochi.

Peter Alfi; Scusso.

I was called Tulip.

The game went faster and faster; we played without looking at her. That was on the school playground, under a cloudy sky in 196_.

Anna called out, Who is looking at you?

You're looking at us, I said.

I'm not looking at you.

Then who is?

Tulip is looking at you.

What's your name, Vince asked.

Tulip! she said, and I felt singled out by the laughter of my two friends.

While her influence over us grew, she remained quiet. Even our words sounded blurred; we talked too fast. I remember her standing at the edge of the school field, always with that mocking flicker that never left the corners of her mouth. Her wide, quiet eyes reminded me of a salamander's. Now she had a worried look as she twisted a finger in a lock of hair behind her ear.

Come with me. Tulip wants to talk to you, she said. I followed her off the field, to stand by the playground swings.

I went over to the Giacomo house today, she said, to look for Maren. Paolo was in the kitchen talking to the land buyers and I was on the porch. I heard him say he'd sell the house, that he's going back to the Aconcagua with his daughter.

The swing chains were creaking in the wind that came up from the river. The seats cut from truck tires turned and weaved like driftwood under the bridge.

Did you tell nonna?

Yes, she said. But Paolo told her he's not going anywhere. You gave me the Giacomo house, he says, and we're staying.

6

A few months passed and though I watched Paolo carefully nothing seemed to change. Maren continued to live with us, and once I asked her about my uncle's intentions. She shrugged, said that he was looking for work in town, which meant they were staying. Still she looked confused and uncertain, as if not sure of what he'd do next.

Then that fall Manice lost her house. It was around the day my father took the ferry across the river for winter firewood. He carried his two axes, his chainsaw and gasoline can to the landing, early enough so that the Cancelled Sailing sign hung on the padlocked gate wouldn't bother anyone. We were going for cedar on the other side, burnt-out spires from the 1930 fire that had leapt the river, burned lower town.

I don't see how it could have happened. I look at the river, wide with the colour of a sky massed with snow — and I say, How did the fire cross?

There used to be a shake mill in the cedar grove on that side, I remember my father saying. In the summer of 1930 a fire started in the slash near the mill. It was so small no one paid any attention. The village was more worried about the forest fires to the south, which had filled the valley with a haze that turned the sun blood-red. One afternoon the wind picked up. Within minutes the fire had spread from the slash into the mill yard. Wind-driven, it roared from the storage sheds to the mill, and it flung burning shakes like handfuls of leaves across the river into lower town.

Anna and I left my father in the pilothouse. We ran from bow to stern, coats flapping in the unusually warm wind. Anna high-stepped as she ran, to make the clop of a horse's hooves on the deck.

The ferry landed, my father walked into the cedar hollow. Anna and I climbed through nostra nonna's orchards to clean out the Pradolini house for the golondrinas who would arrive later in the day. I found a broom to sweep the leaves from the porch; we carried out a kitchen table that had collapsed on its legs and boxes of newspaper and wine bottles from the cellar. In the yard by a chestnut tree was a bathtub of tea-coloured water, streaks of rust on the chipped enamel rim. We played that game Anna liked, travelling from room to room on the counters, abandoned bedframes, and furniture without touching the floor. Anna loved to climb. She was sent into the crowns of the old chestnut trees, to knock down clusters with her willow wand. My uncle would guide her down with his shouts.

Now, climbing over a bedframe, she asked me, What are we going to do to help Maren?

She's not going anywhere, I insisted, though I was surprised at the hollow feeling in my chest that now, many years later, I recognize as a love I would not admit to myself.

Do you trust Paolo?

No, I said. He only says what he thinks you want to hear.

83

And in my confusion over what felt like a sudden breath of fire in my chest, I could not think of what to do.

That afternoon the golondrinas moved into the Pradolini house. For the harvest they crossed the river at dawn, on a catwalk under the railroad bridge. After the last ferry run, they'd use the same catwalk to return to this house. Because she was worried that one of them might fall in the river, my mother gave them watered wine at supper — late supper at dusk at tables of planks and sawhorses under the trees outside the vineyard gate. They ate, drank, carried hurricane lanterns over the river. The Calabrianne was among them. I remember her vigorous strong face, the tight braid of grey hair at her nape, the way she laughed when, under the peach trees where nonna had spread a black dress for me to lie down on, she'd heard of the shoe I'd pushed out the car window.

Sometimes my father offered a ride on the ferry which, out of politeness and deference, the golondrinas refused. Sometimes ten or twelve lived in the old Pradolini house, workers nonna had hired for the harvest. While they ate supper at the plank tables I would listen to their Québécois French, their Italian and Portuguese. Once I heard the Calabrianne sing in her high plaintive voice:

Blessed virgin
I met a man and a woman
bound in a ball of yarn
water flow thaw pain

Later at night from my bed I saw lanterns on the railroad bridge.

The river brought their voices that I heard clearly without understanding, voices brought close with a ringing and an echo in them like the sound of a bell way down the valley or up the mountain.

That autumn, the autumn of 196_, the Hydro took Manice's orchard at the south end of the valley and bulldozed the house into its cellar. Beneath her orchard the hillside was gouged into levees for the new reservoir. The earthmoving machines had cut terraces to her fences. Though she was paid valley prices for her land, the word we used was "taken."

After a rainstorm, I remember watching her peach trees sway and tremble as though trying to walk. At first I thought they were wading through the earth till I saw that the earth was moving with them, yawing in deep cracks to the pit below.

My uncle had brought out the madonna to stop this, a little blue doll with chipped fingers. He carried her among the half-buried trees. I remember the silence — all the birds, terrified, had fled. He placed her in the branches of a young apricot tree, reasoning that at least to save herself, she would not let any more trees go over. Among the apricot leaves her eyes were the colour of fir pitch. When you tapped her side she sounded hollow. We could feel the low murmur of the earth and how Manice's house had begun to tremble; you could hear stones falling from the cellar walls.

Terrified, Anna climbed into a chestnut tree near the house. High in the branches, she clung to the swaying trunk. My uncle had to climb after her to bring her down.

Why did you sign? Why didn't you make up an excuse? Why didn't you say you couldn't write or that you hurt your wrist! screamed my uncle.

Manice held out the court order the land buyer had brought: my uncle snatched it from her to read that she had to be out within a week.

The day Manice moved to the Pradolini house, we crossed the river to help. Ears white with calamine lotion, Anna took my father by the wrist to show him her garden, a small fenced garden with a magnolia tree in it that smelled of warmed olive oil. She said she didn't want to move to the Pradolini house, the house of the golondrinas.

Where will we go from there? she wanted to know.

When my father had nothing to say, he wore a kindly expression to mask his worry and lack of knowledge. A wind was flowing down the banks among Manice's orchards, carrying the smell of the warmed land at dusk. All the lights in Manice's house were off, and a lot of the furniture was heaped on the porch. Nighthawks, diving over the river, made a hissing sound with their wings.

Nighthawks he said, to take Anna's mind off the house of the golondrinas, the house she was going to move into. They hunt by sound!

Anna went to bicycle around the house that was to be burned down, and she sang:

I don't want to go.

Me and my sister don't want to go!

Anna's words touched a worry that I'd been living with for months: that it was only a matter of time before Maren, too — like this house — would vanish. That what she or I wanted, even if it was not yet clear to us, didn't matter.

Stones falling from the cellar walls made the hollow clop of a horse's hooves. Anna rode swinging a rope through the dangling clouds of mosquitoes till she came into the porch-light flushed, licking the salt on her arms. Sand crusted under her nose as she drank water from a baby food jar — all the glasses were packed.

Let's run away together, she said to me, then went to sit on the porch to pulp some berries, a lavender hand trail dotted with seeds. "We used to make money from these."

Anna what are you doing?

Turning on the lights.

No, not in the middle of the evening, Manice said softly from the porch table. Anna don't interrupt us. Go play now.

I remember my Aunt's pale, anxious expression, the way my father knelt on the steps to listen.

Go play now.

One light off and one light on, Anna said in the kitchen, turning on the light over the stove, the alcove light.

I'm the ruotaro, she said brightly, watching her mother. I've come to take all the people who are never home for supper.

As long as we're here, I said, the machines stay away.

Today, many years later, I remember how things would go. First the drivers of the earthmoving machines would splash the house walls with diesel fuel to set them on fire. Then they would use their machines to push the smoldering wood and stone into the cellar and blade it over with earth. They were powerful, those Hydro people. They had machines that tremored the earth under your feet, a schedule of things to do that took all the light of recognition out of their eyes.

I remember the land buyer at the kitchen table, tugging at his cuff-linked sleeves to straighten them, the flash of the tiny gold links over the court order. He talked of land values in the valley, of what land like Manice's had gone for in St. Leon and in Renata. And when Manice asked where she'd find orchard land elsewhere for his price, he smiled, spread his hands to say, That's for you to decide. We've bought from others you know: Beruski's store, the Giacomo house. He walked through the house, measuring rooms; he counted the trees in her orchard; he saw money in all that, underwater.

That autumn, after she moved into the Pradolini house, Anna started school in late September. Lost in the hallway, she wandered into our class.

I pretended I didn't know her. I was afraid she would shame me.

Isn't that your cousin?

I shook my head, bent over my desk, gazing at the wood grain till I became absorbed in it, all forehead. Dimly I could hear their laughter. Others had turned in their seats to say, Don't look at us!

Anna stared at people. Lost in looking, my father called it, or *gathering wool*.

What is your name? asked the teacher Mogliani.

Mumbled words.

Speak up child, what is your name!

An-na es-*pisi*-to!

General laughter; to hide her face in her hair, she lowered her head. Our teacher took her by the hand to the office.

When he returned, he wrote on the board:

figlia della madonna

He told us of the famous wheel of Naples, through which many, many children were passed. I remember his words: And what were these children named?

Innocenti. Esposito.

Our teacher Mogliani was from Naples. He told us how lucky we were, that almost all of the infants who went through the wheels of Italy died in the first year, many thousands of them.

You are as rich as kings, he said.

Rich because alive? When people say things like that to you, you don't know where you are. Many laughed. We knew most of what we had was to be taken by the Hydro.

I never knew when one of the cousins would show up in a way unconnected with my life. By appearing in our class doorway, Anna had singled me out for ridicule. I can still hear the mocking laughter of my classmates who saw my unwillingness to acknowledge her. She was four years younger and I didn't want to see her in school. I felt she was from a different life, that she didn't belong there.

That day after school I saw her crouched in the alley behind the Community Centre. With a stick in her hand, she was prodding thoughtfully at a grey cat under the Centre's fire stairs. In shadow, the cat glared at her, its tail twitching. She didn't look at me even when I crouched beside her.

You can come with me to nonna's I said.

They all laugh at me!

Not if I'm with you, I promised.

7

I awoke before dawn for the festa campestra.

My mother was making coffee at the gas stove under the narrow alley window. From my bed by the stove we called "the iron monster," I watched my mother make coffee before she left to deliver the bread by cart horse in the street of the grandmothers.

Uncle Paolo is ashamed, I said.

Yes, she nodded.

In our village, when a man for some unknown reason didn't show up for work, we would say he was "ashamed." Now that he'd lost his job on the railroad, Paolo delivered bread by carthorse in the village alleys. She'd seen his dogs outside the King Edward Hotel, where he drank at night. She delivered the bread when Paolo was ashamed, in order to make money to buy land in Westbank.

I must have slept through the baker's call. I stayed in bed, half-awake and through the open window I could hear the whistle of the yard engine as it put together cattle cars for St. Leon.

The Sentinella was in the roundhouse. My uncle used to take the Sentinella to St. Leon, for the zucca melons.

From the river I also heard the whistle of my father's ferry that announced the first morning trip from the far shore.

There was a ringing in my ears, like a voice in a tin pot

when someone dies. I sensed that my cousin Maren was still in her room. I had awakened from a dream, the print of her kiss on my lips. And the music: the distant wail of an accordion in the orchards under the mountain, a ribbon of her tone that, lifted from the vineyards and the orchard floors, brings the odour of dusty leaves and ripe fruit. With the imprint of her kiss on my mouth and the taste of cinnamon, I draw the sheet over my head.

I struggle against the odours of wax and bread, of violets and horse dung.

I feel my mother's hand burrow under the sheet to find my shoulder, my cheek that she touches with her fingers that smell of coffee.

Paolo is ashamed.

I see his two dogs outside the doors of the King Edward Hotel where he drinks at night.

The warm fingers that touch my cheek make the kiss vanish.

I heard my mother leave through the backdoor in the laundry room to pick violets in the garden, to tie to the horse's halter before she harnessed it to the bread wagon.

The last time Paolo was ashamed, I'd helped my mother package the bread in wax paper that you folded around the loaves and then there was a machine in the bakery to seal the ends with heat. It left wax on my hands so that they gleamed as though polished as we loaded the bread crates into the wagon. We went down the alleys early in the morning, when the air was heavy with the smell of dew from the mountain, heavy and still.

My mother wore a broad-rimmed hat of plaited straw.

She would bring the horse to a halt by drawing her hands together, or turn it up the alley by drawing the rein gently along the neck. Once she said, Would you like to learn music?

In exchange for our looking after Maren, my uncle had offered accordion lessons.

I'd heard him play during the first night of the festa. Outside the Giacomo house, I'd heard him play "The Rooster."

To save our condemned village, the St. Leon fishermen had brought a fishing scow upriver, their papier mâché San Calogero with its great almond eyes at the bow. At the head of the procession walked the Calabrianne. As she walked by the Giacomo house, Paolo struck up "The Rooster." He was sitting in his second-storey window, lit up by a lamp at the far wall.

For her, he played "The Rooster."

The paper San Calogero followed behind on its bed of grape leaves, a mantle flung over its stiff, outstretched arms.

The Calabrianne smiled as she passed under the music, and she made a dance step. Then she returned to her solemn posture, and the coil of knotted hair at her nape no longer trembled.

I went out to decorate the Butucci orchards. A withered apricot struck between my shoulder blades, and I knew that Maren and Anna were in the trees. A warm breath stirred around the trunks, with its odour of leather and rope. Now and then, far off in the alleys, I could hear the voice of my uncle's accordion. I heard Maren's laughter in the crown of the trees, a track of gleaming prints that vanished. Nonna was at the trestle tables, where women were spreading the

gnocchi, the braided bread. She came over to touch my forehead:

You've a fever!

Once again I felt the press of Maren's dream kiss on
my lips. My worry that she would vanish had turned to an
icy feeling that flowed through my veins and made my legs
tremble.

Nonna made me sit in the grass beneath an apricot tree.
From another table came the Calabrianne. She opened a
blanket that smelled of smoke from the barbecue pits for
me to sit on. Her breath tasted of the young wine they were
pouring at the trestle tables.

Are you staying for the dance?

In the long hours before the dance the Calabrianne
wore a Calabrian dress embroidered at the chest. She spoke
to Nonna in Italian I couldn't understand. She said she was
one of the golondrinas.

That bird, the insect eater that you often saw on the river
at dusk, skimmed the water and dipped to drink. I had never
touched one and now I touched her inner elbow. I had often
caught the finches we called the grapeaters, to toss them
high over the nets. How could she be one of those birds?

Will your mother dance?

Paolo is ashamed, I said. My mother would have to
deliver the bread and help the baker later in the day. Maybe
she'll be too tired to dance.

Even now I'm not sure of her name but we called her the
Calabrianne.

I'd climbed into an apricot tree to tie festa streamers in
the crown. In branches and leaves that were coated with dust

from the new reservoir, I'd fallen asleep and dreamt of the wail of the Sentinella on the mountain, of Maren leaving on that train, her hand slipping out of mine.

You come down out of that tree, our grandmother called. You forgot to drink, she said, touching my forehead. Why do you look so worried? Go home to bed. Fell asleep! What if you'd fallen? Nonna stood at the trunk. She pressed a wet cloth to my lips.

Go to bed.

On the street of the grandmothers I kept under the chestnut boughs, by surveyors' ribbons that marked trunks to be cut down for the new dam. Were it not for the weight of my hands and eyelids, and that of the strange buzzing in my ears threaded by the voice of my uncle's zerocetti, I felt I'd float away, vanish over the high-beaked snowplows by the roundhouse. While I climbed the steps in the castle to our apartment, the voice of my uncle's yellow zerocetti grew stronger.

I'll teach you to play.

I didn't like the accordion's harsh unpleasant voice, tuned sharp for the sake of brilliance. He left it on the kitchen table, to lead me outside by the wrist. We sat on the wellhead. He smelled of the cement he'd mixed to cap the village graves. Now that he no longer worked for the railroad, he'd also taken the job of cementing over the village graves. He'd made a plank keyboard, with whittled hollows for the bass buttons. The plank between knee and chin, this one up and this one down he said, tapping his fingers on the wood.

You try.

I could tell that he didn't want to teach me. He spoke in a low voice about the vineyards of his childhood, the ox skulls that were used for chairs in the workers' huts, of ox carts whose wheels were solid wooden discs as tall as a man.

Do you think Maren will come to the Aconcagua? The worry in his slumped shoulders and the fear in his glance made me draw away from him.

She wants to stay here, uncle.

With his thumb, he was rubbing the dried concrete from his palm.

Is the zerocetti grey or is it yellow?

Everyone knows it's yellow.

One of my eyes says grey, he said. The other yellow. You tell my daughter that.

Why?

I need her to go to the Aconcagua with me. To see the place where I was born.

You tell her, I said.

Anna danced before me like a cat. For the festa she was wearing one of Nonna's dresses from the cellar that smelled of coal dust and cedar. She had a dark green streak of church door paint on her hand.

Who's behind me? Anna asked.

In Maren's room the yellow zerocetti cleared its throat. I could smell its bellows of strong manila cardboard and its soft leather gussets. It was dusk. My parents were still in the orchards.

Go on, Anna said, look through me.

In the laundry room doorway, she danced before me like a cat. I felt the low bass chords in my chest and in my fingertips, and I could smell Maren's odour of cinnamon.

Try to go through me, she said.

Anna wore my mother's lipstick on her bright, fixed smile and mascara smudged under her eyes. When I went to touch her she was not there and then she was. "He wants to take her to the Aconcagua." When I pushed through, I heard her whisper, She doesn't want to go.

Maren made the accordion say I had a long day to get here; I walked from the Butucci orchards. She was playing the accordion on her cot.

Did Paolo give this accordion to you? she asked me. She made it wail like the Sentinella and laughed.

For as long as I could remember I'd heard that whistle on the mountain, usually at night, when Paolo used to take a train to St. Leon for the zucca melons.

It woke me up; it was like a familiar footfall in the stairwell and a voice I knew.

We're going to the Argentine, she said. Do you want to go with us?

Yes, I nodded.

Thank you, she said. Thank you for saying that.

She talked of the Aconcagua till her eyes shone. Her laughter was like a track of wet footprints on warm floorboards.

They don't have a real San Calogero in St. Leon, she said. Just a papier mache one. Do you want to come to the Aconcagua?

I want to go with you.

There isn't enough rain there.

How do you know?

Paolo told me. Why won't you look at me?

In truth I couldn't look at her. In the presence of her quiet stare, her excited patter, I felt my throat tighten at the thought of her leaving.

Through the window I could see girls peeling zucca melons on the platform of the canning factory across the tracks. She made the whirr of many wasps, then a bird's flapping in the vineyard nets. She played and the Sentinella was in our room — I felt its whistle vibrating in my chest. Last night the Sentinella had whistled on the mountain and I'd heard the clatter of my uncle's boots in the street of the grandmothers as he went to meet his favourite engine. Even today I think of how she was playing at going to the Aconcagua, playing a child's tune on the accordion. Anna's saying she wants to stay here was echoed in the song Maren played, and in the mascara smudged under Anna's eyes, the worried, tight smile.

That night in 196_ was the last night of the festa campestra. In the Butucci orchards, my uncle had come into the firelight. "Where's Maren?" To turn a trussed lamb over the barbecue pit he wore a leather apron and a bright red handkerchief tightly bound about his head. You could smell the grease burning on the coals.

On the street of the grandmothers, walking to the Butucci orchards, I'd heard her tone that filled my head with the scent of her skin. Soon, I was no longer sure it was Maren; maybe it was the wind in the river alders, under the bridge, the chattering catwalk, the streamers in the crowns of the apricot trees. As he stood in his greasy apron, staring around, Paolo did not seem to see me there. In the firelight he had the wide-eyed look of someone peering underwater.

I climbed through the branches near the barbecue pits. I sensed that Maren was in that tree. Her hair smelled of cinnamon. She had tied streamers to the crowns of the trees. From there, under the street lights I could see buildings that used to be in town had vanished: Beruski's store on Mackenzie Ave, Mallone's café. This place that was ours was rapidly vanishing. The streets, the lights, the orchards with their odour of ripe peaches and the smell of the canning fires — all that expressed what I now recognize as the temper of our life was being removed, before my very eyes.

I heard her voice in the leaf shadows: I don't want to go to the Aconcagua. Her voice among the leaves was plaintive and wide awake.

Are you going to St. Leon tomorrow? I asked her. On the Sentinella?

I edged along the branch, to kiss her on the mouth. I felt the softening of her lips, their acceptance, then she pushed me away. In her anger-filled eyes there was a memory. Her look reminded me of how, while the doctor sewed her chin, I'd held down her knees.

I don't want to see you anymore, she said.

I don't want to see you again! she screamed at me, then dropped from the branch to the ground.

When you're in a room I'll leave, I shouted down at her. And when I'm in a room you leave. With both hands I gripped the branch. I could have fallen when she pushed me. I hadn't chosen to help the doctor I reminded myself. Yet my shouts rose from the hollow feeling of being seen as less than I wanted to be.

She went off to stand among three girls near the canning fires, Anna among them. They had some kind of game going, kicking a hard green peach like a ball, and soon they were running among the trestle tables in the fire light, kicking the peach back and forth till the women who were canning fruit at the tables told them to stop or go elsewhere. The others, Rose and Lacey, were girls from north of our village, and I really didn't know them then, although they came into my life later in a way that took me far from this valley.

Sitting on the branch, I wondered whether Maren was telling them about the kiss and my betrayal, and I felt a burning sense of shame.

I'd seen Rose and Lacey picking fruit in the Butucci orchards. They were on Alberto Braz's crew and slept in the same shack and worked together. Once, Rose had asked me if Maren was my girlfriend and I'd only laughed. She had clear brown eyes and the strong wrists of someone who worked with horses — she'd told me that her parents were horse loggers on the Big Bend. She'd smiled after asking about Maren and then looked at me in a measured, intent way that years later I would learn to love.

Later that evening I found Maren standing in our garden by the house. She was carrying the twelve-button accordion slung on her shoulder and a small cloth knapsack. I'm running away, she said. I don't want to go to the Aconcagua.

Why don't you just stay here?

I don't belong here.

Across the street, I could see a light flickering in the second-storey window of the Giacomo house. That room faced the mountain and was cold even in midsummer, with its walls stuffed with newspapers and sawdust. To warm his room, my uncle had lit a heap of almond shells in the brazier he kept there.

I'm going away now. Do you want to come with me?

Yes, I nodded. I'll go with you. I felt that I would do anything to regain her trust, and I took her hand briefly before she backed away.

Standing under the chestnut tree near the porch, she gave me a tired smile. On the accordion, she made the low wail of the Sentinella on the mountain.

Soon we heard the clatter of my uncle's boots in the street of the grandmothers, on the way to the roundhouse.

You wait here, she said, and watch for Paolo.

She went into the Giacomo house, climbed the stairs to the room with the flickering light in it. I remembered Anna saying in the school playground, He's going to sell the Giacomo house to by tickets for the Argentine. And I also remembered his promise to our grandmother: *You give me the Giacomo house and we'll stay.* In Paolo's bedroom Maren found a trestle bed of faded green deal boards, the rolled-up mattress at one end. On the floor a copper brazier was burning. It gave off the bitter fragrance of almond shells.

Do you think he'll try to take me with him soon? I imagined her asking while I stood outside under the tree near our porch.

I don't know, Maren.

She fingered the carved headboard. She wasn't often in that house. Now I see her draw the brazier to the bed by one of its looped handles wrapped in cord, to tip out the burning almond shells. At first nothing happens, the heap glows dully on the wooden floor. Impatient, worried that Paolo might return at any moment, she searches the room for something to add. There's a stack of music sheets on a sideboard that she crumples onto the fire and soon the green deal boards are catching, the mattress begins to smoulder.

When she returns to me, I see dull orange flames and long shadows climbing in the window.

I'm going now, she said. I'm going to hide on a train that will take me away from here.

I'll come with you, I said then. I will.

Hi Anna!

In her anxiety she called me Anna as I climbed into the cattle car. Frost gleamed on the rails in the shadow of the canning factory. Last night we'd found this place for her to hide and I'd gone home to bring her a blanket. Maren sat on a mattress of burlap sacks. Light streamed in through the cattle car slats.

Where is my father, she asked. Is he looking for me?

Paolo says when he finds you, you're going to the Aconcagua. Are you running away to Vancouver?

Yes, she nodded. Nearby, girls were peeling zucca melons on the cannery platform. Inside the cattle car I could hear drawknives make the melon skins hiss like split stone. The tasteless juice glittered on the knives and on the fingers and elbows. There was ash on the tracks from the Giacomo fire.

Everybody's looking for you.

You're going to tell them where I am, aren't you.

Once again I felt my throat tighten at the thought that I had not regained her trust.

Though I had brought a blanket to the cattle car, she had not slept under it; all night through the cattle car slats she'd watched the red glow of the Giacomo fire.

We slipped by the factory platform heaped with melon rinds where the drawknives flashed. Crossing the tracks I saw Lombardy poplars glittering behind the train sheds and the wide beaks of the snowplows.

Through a side door we crept into the roundhouse. Maren went in and I followed. A pot of stew was bubbling on the stove by the door. High above the wooden beams were covered in dust; light streamed in from banks of encircling windows. A worker was pressing a flat metal bar to the grinder at the far bench. Sparks flew under his goggles. The Sentinella stood by another engine that we called "the Tall Musician" because its whistle sounded like a deer bone flute.

That morning I felt I was seeing everything for the last time. Dawn streamed through chinks in the roundhouse walls, through the banks of dirty windows. Arc lamps blazed over the tracks, lighting up the empty cattle cars.

The roundhouse windows had turned the colour of river stones. To let out the Sentinella, the doors would swing open and the big engine would creep into the yard. Through the windows, you could see the shadows of empty cattle cars that smelled of sulphur water.

In the cab of the Sentinella, Maren explained the many levers. I didn't really listen to what she was saying. For the first time, I felt what it would be like to leave that vanishing place of my bones, my hands and touch.

"I've been in here lots," I heard her say. Between us there was a strained smile. She talked in a low solemn voice of the Aconcagua till her eyes shone. She spoke of how in one year twelve sets of twins were born, of the wide river Plate, of the Mendoza earthquake that the French geologist Bravard had predicted.

That's not you, I told her. That's Paolo.

You're going to tell them where I am, she said with her resigned look. Aren't you?

In her eyes I was still the doctor's boy.

8

Rattling and swaying, the train crossed the railroad bridge and climbed into the Pradolini orchard. Through the cattle car floor I heard the voice of the wheels that asked for nothing, a reassuring clack. On the ridge track that led south through the valley orchards, I smelt canning fires and windfallen, rotting fruit. Through the slats I could see across the river the glittering tin roofs of our village and the D. Street Mill at the mouth of the Illecillewaet.

I had never been south of Burton. Yet I could smell the Kootenay lake, the packing crates on the St. Leon wharf, the rail car barge that brought in Renata fruit, all things that my aunt Manice had told me about.

I can walk all the way around Paolo, Maren was saying. She wore a pleated, cream-coloured blouse that had no warmth in it. I can walk all the way around him like this, tracing a circle in the cattle car straw with her toe to show the limits of his sight.

In our apartment, she'd pocketed a handful of peppermints that my mother liked to keep in a blue bowl on the kitchen table. I'd filled my pockets with *ciambelle*.

Now she gave me a mint: Put it under your tongue to make it last. We hadn't had anything to eat since the afternoon before the Giacomo fire, and she hadn't slept all night. Peppermint on her breath; I felt her lips tremble under mine. She'd drawn near to kiss me and in the softness of her lips I felt a welcome but also a lingering doubt. All around us, the smell of dry straw and urine. She'd made a mattress of burlap sacks among the straw bales that were used to pack the zucca melons.

Under my tongue, at the root, I could still taste the burnt house. I'd watched the flames climb out the second-storey window to curl into the eaves. I'd waited till the roof shingles began to smoke and then ran. Too breathless to yell, I went up to my mother who danced in the Butucci orchards and pointed to the red glow above the village roofs.

The clang of Our Lady of Sorrows' bell and then the fire truck's siren. My father drew the hose from the fire truck bed as though he were casting wildly for trout. I could hear the shouts of men over the fire's roar. At the yellow and red-painted hydrant on the street of the grandmothers my uncle spun the brass hose coupling. I heard the cough and purr of the fire truck generator as arc lamps lit up running figures in front of the Giacomo house.

Paolo knelt to connect an attack hose to the main line, dragged it to wet the smoking walls of the adjacent houses. I heard windows popping, glass shivering into the Giacomo yard. Now my uncle and my father carried the attack hose through the front door, only to be driven back by the smoke and heated air. I saw my father, head ducked, raise his hands to cover his singed ears.

I can still smell that house. It stank of charred wood and saw-dust, a bloated mattress dragged into the street, burnt plastic and linoleum.

I'd taken a bottle of drinking water from the fire truck, filled my pockets with ciambelle at our kitchen table.

You haven't slept all night, I said to Maren. You rest then.

I sat cross-legged, to cradle her head in my lap. The gleam and dim of her fingerprints on the water bottle. Through the cattle car slats I could see the river.

I listened for her slowing breath, felt the heartbeat in her fingertips. I stroked her hair, her minnow features. To breathe, our grandfather had cupped his hands before his face as the avalanche snow flowed like flour around him. Clawing to break the suffocating ice that his breath made in the little cavern around his nostrils and mouth, he wore his fingers to the first knuckle.

I wondered what death I might bring her. It's not only birds that feel the death in our hands.

Wait, my uncle once said to me: What does a man have for himself when he has lost himself?

A fist in the mirror!

At five, Anna had drawn a picture of the ruotaro, a gap between the black hat and head and between his body and the horse. My hands repeated that gap above Maren's closed eyelids, her throat hollow with the locket in it; now I dared not touch her. I felt then that we were unlucky somehow, that it was not only houses and orchards that were vanishing, but a tenderness that needed a place of its own. My head resting against the slats, I heard the thrumming of the train wheels. On a high grade they slowed to a clack. Through the slats I saw familiar trees: peaches and apricots pruned by her hand, the light between the branches as distinctive as a signature: that was Manice's orchard above the tracks. She let no one touch her trees and did all the pruning on her own. There were the trees I'd known since the age of four and they were always pruned that way. Where Manice's house used to be, smoke trailed from the bladed earth. A ground-moving machine stood in the clearing; its raised blade, dirt-crusted and as long as a wall, gleamed like a weapon. I heard my uncle's low voice: A little *grape syrup in their tanks.*

I felt then a flash of anger. Yes, I said to myself, a little grape syrup in their tanks. I thought then with a child's logic that if the machines could be stopped the destruction would stop.

9

Many years later Anna told me how she heard the story of our grandfather's death. She heard this story two days after the Giacomo fire, when Maren and I had disappeared. She and Nonna were in the castle's backyard garden. Our grandmother was telling her how the slater had gone to help dig out the seventy-six buried in the snow. While he and the other rescuers were in a trench they'd dug to open the tracks, an avalanche began on the mountain opposite. It could have been started by a shout when another body was discovered, that of a Chinese cook. The face of the mountain fractured. The slide quickly turned from white to black as it ripped up soil and flung timber spears, filling the rescue trench.

The village heard its roar from thirty miles away.

Nonna had crept into the street of the grandmothers, into a stillness that said they already knew.

Now, a plume of sprinkler water travelled across the back yard porch at her feet. She cranked down the faucet handle. The hose vibrated shrilly, stopped. She told Anna she wanted to see who was out on the downtown sidewalk that evening. A familiar dip of the head, the right sort of cloth, a step that vanished in a crowd. It was strange how the slater was beginning to return to her in this way: the glimpse of memory in the way a hand rested lightly on a child's head.

That morning she'd been to the doctor about the burning in her throat, the dull old coin in her cheek. Folded in her pocket a medical report that talked of the surgical removal of bone and muscle, at her age.

At her age!

Returning from the clinic, she'd seen someone who looked like Albert Murray standing in front of the theatre, cap pulled low over his eyes and one hand resting on the head of a young girl. The child was wearing a sundress with patch pockets. The man's clothes were not Albert's, she would tell me later. He was Albert in build, in the set of his shoulders. He reminded her of how young Albert Murray must have been when she knew him. He must have been very young.

The gate unlatched, she and Anna stepped into the alley.

She touched Anna's forehead with the back of her hand. You seem hot! Head bent, with dull glazed eyes, the cousin was listening to something inside herself. She had not left our grandmother's side since the Giacomo fire.

Where are my cousins?

The police called, our grandmother told her. They're down in Burton. They were hiding in a cattle car, they'll be back tonight.

The yard engine was pushing box cars together: the clang of the warning bell as the engine backed down the track, the metallic echo as the box cars engaged. Hand in hand they walked down the alley. She wondered if she would see the slater again. Not all the cedar wood fences were as high as hers, and she compared gardens, looking for something new: today a child's wading pool, the evening sky reflected on its surface. Passed the bowling alley, then boarded up, turned by the King Edward Hotel.

She and Anna went to rest in a park by the tracks. A strong light was spreading across the snowfields, high on the mountain behind the train sheds. She watched Anna hop over the tracks, to a young boy who was sucking water from a squirt gun handle. That was the Butucci boy. He was five or six.

Anna said to him, bent over, If you eat seeds and swallow lots of water, a garden will plant in your bones.

The children had walked beyond the tracks to the station platform. And there he was again, a figure on the platform. She remembered when he'd got a job painting the station. That was the last day she saw him, over forty years ago. He'd come banging through the screen door with two paint tins hidden in burlap sacks the train crews used to wipe down the engines. Isn't it a pretty yellow? He pried the lid from a tin of station paint. He went into their house. He started moving the little furniture they had in those days into the centre of the room. The walls were a dull whitewash they'd lived with for over a year. When they could no longer see how the paint was going on, they laid down the brushes and went to sit on the porch to drink wine, passing the cup back and forth. It was an unusually warm evening — like early summer. He cupped his hand on her belly, waiting for the kick of their second child. She heard the wail of the D. Street Mill calling the night shift to work. The alley gate had been left ajar. From the porch steps, they could see the Community Centre, all lit up. Women in groups of two or three were strolling by the gate, to follow a snow path to the *Gioco De Lotto* at the Centre. The air was still, and as they passed beneath chestnut trees, shadows streamed down their fine cotton coats. How elaborate their hair had been done up for the Lotto. There were no men. The men were in the bars or working.

Some women had stopped at the gate.

I've found work, Albert said.

Give us your luck, they said arm in arm, laughing. Come and touch our cards with your luck.

He had the fine nervous gestures of a small man trying to make room for himself and she was not used to them yet. She took his head in her hands, held him in her gaze, seeing him again for the first time. Such a fine lovely man she'd breathed then.

From the park bench, she watched Anna and the Butucci boy pass below a lone figure on the station platform and disappear into a hollow near the train sheds. She stood to follow, to see where they were going. The fading light was turning the gravel between the tracks a deep blue. There were so many rails, narrowing and confusing her steps but the pleasing colour of the gravel and the figure on the platform drew her on. She heard the warning bell of a yard engine backing down the line, but paid no attention. The strong vibration at her feet told her something she was too tired to understand.

Earlier that evening the Burton police had called to say her grandchildren had been found in a cattle car.

Now there was a man crouched near the platform. When he looked up at her, she bent to touch the yellow streak on his lip.

In the end, she tells the ruotaro, I've not been able to escape you.

I've not been able to keep anything.

10

Two nights after we got back from Burton, I was standing on the castle's porch roof. I was watching the procession led by my uncle's tractor with its aircraft landing lights. All the village cars and trucks were lining the dirt runway south of the village. My cousin Anna, ill with appendicitis, had to be flown to the hospital in Naramata. The cars and trucks were shining their headlights on the dirt runway, so that Bennello could see where to land.

I saw a fire across the river near the railroad bridge. First my aunt's house, then the Giacomo house — and now the Pradolini house had been torched by the Hydro. Through my father's binoculars, I could see Manice's and Anna's belongings heaped under the the orchard trees beyond the garden and the yard. In the yard stood one of the earth-moving machines. It would wait till the house collapsed and then push the remains into the cellar.

Behind me I could hear Maren draw the curtains in the laundry room. Since we'd been brought home she stayed mostly in her room. Once she told me that she didn't leave her room because she didn't know what to do anymore, and that she was waiting for Paolo to take her away.

Earlier that night, the night of the Pradolini fire, my father had come over to my bed. "Anna's not feeling well." I'd felt the grip of his hand on my ankle to awaken me. He was wearing his ferryman's uniform: the grey pants with the black stripe, the blue jacket with the provincial crest on the shoulders, a cap with a peaked visor.

Do you want to come?

I shook my head.

Better, he smiled.

I had gotten out of bed to watch him polish his shoes in the foyer, a few nervous passes of the cloth. Nonna is downstairs my father reminded me — as he always did when he knew Maren and I would be alone. "If Paolo calls, you get him to speak to her."

My mother was going with him: "Anna has a high fever."

I could hear a shower drumming on the metal roof. I knew that Nonna was downstairs, but each time they went out at night my parents told me this.

Now and then people called after hours from the other side of the river.

If my father knew them he couldn't refuse. "They wait for me. How can I sleep?"

Usually he was in bed by ten o'clock. I could hear the radio, a reassuring murmur and no light from under their door.

A call about Anna had come from the Pradolini house after midnight. It sent out a stillness into which we awoke, listening. My father got out of bed to answer.

Never once did I see him angry at an after-hours call.

Though once he refused to start up the ferry.

Sleep in your government car, he shouted to the agents who, on the other side of the river, were sent to demand the Pradolini house.

I was watching the cars and tractors on the flats south of the village. With their headlights on, all the cars and trucks from our village were driving onto the southern flats; the brightest were the aircraft landing lights on my uncle's tractor that he used to hunt deer at night on the Georgia Bench. Overcast sky, no stars. From above the low drone of an airplane. Bennello dropped through the clouds, circled overhead, then skipped onto the lit-up runway.

Anna was so ill that she needed to be flown out. And across the river I could see the Pradolini house on fire, flames lifting in the windows and in the eaves. Panic in my throat, I climbed through the window into the kitchen.

I rapped on the curtained laundry room window. When Maren opened her door I said, We have to stop that machine across the river. Who is next?

She helped me to find an old pair of work boots in the foyer, gardening gloves, a torn pair of my father's pants bagged for the Salvation Army, a plaid shirt from the back of the closet, our grandfather's cloth cap from the cellar.

We have to disguise you, she said. In case you're noticed.

To make the boots fit, I stuffed newspaper in the toes.

I won't go with you. She knelt to roll the pant legs past my ankles. Two they'll notice for sure.

I looked down at her. No one in those days would have called my cousin Maren beautiful: she had Roca D'Avola features, the look of a peasant girl from southern Italy. and when Mrs. Canetti stopped her on the street of the grandmothers to comment on her looks, she'd say, From Roca, and laugh because Maren's bushy eyebrows, her widespread eyes and the shape of her mouth made it easy to see where she was from.

Last night Paolo had tried to come for her. Through the laundry room window, we could hear my uncle's voice on the porch below. I no longer have the Giacomo house, he bargained with our grandmother. You give me money for the Aconcagua and maybe she can stay.

Nothing more from me! our grandmother shouted at him. You want to take her away from me in my hour of prayer! She must have pushed him, because we heard his boot stumbling down the steps. Go away from here!

In our kitchen I filled a sandwich bag with sugar. For the earthmoving machine outside the Pradolini house. Maren was waiting by the foyer door. When I went up to her she smiled, touched my cheek. I felt then such a deep sadness and anger, not only at the way I'd betrayed her at the doctor's, but at the way our orchards had been felled, the way our houses had been strewn with diesel and torched or trucked away like toys, that I sank onto the foyer bench. I felt her warm breath on my lips then, the slightest brush of a kiss: You have to go.

I wanted to ask for her forgiveness but I couldn't find the words.

They'll be back soon, she said. You have to go now, and she pulled me to my feet.

Walking down the street of the grandmothers to the railroad bridge, I pretend that everything I see is already gone.

Pretend that everything is lost, nostra nonna urges us.

Only then will you see the true face of things.

I take off my boots to feel my way along the cedar catwalk on the bridge. For luck, I touch the sugar bag in my pocket. Up here the river's breath feels cool; the bridge smells of creosote and old steel.

What was that sound?

A nighthawk, I imagine Maren telling me. So close, a sudden whir in my ear.

I hear my grandmother murmuring:

> Not egg the lemon
> The lemon is not an egg
> There are those who uproot and those who plant
> There are those who plant and those who uproot

Below me, the river shimmers like a dragonfly wing; its own breath a mist that hovers over the sandbar and on the village flats where all the trucks and cars are lined up.

In the foyer, Maren had led me to the door, her warm breath heavy on my lips.

Hurry, she'd said. Some things needed the two of us to find them; we two are the reason they're felt.

Above me, the creosoted ties, steel rails. On the catwalk I was halfway across the river. Already I could feel the heat of the Pradolini fire as I walked toward it. One by one I saw the village houses, shimmering like breath. I heard popping windows, the fire's roar in the Pradolini eaves. I saw the gleaming blade of the earthmoving machine raised high in the trees. It had to be stopped before it pushed in the house of someone else that I knew or loved. Behind me in the shadows on the castle's porch, the scarred chin, gentle green eyes: Sometimes I feel I shouldn't be alive.

Not that many years ago there was an unusually dry winter in this valley. Hardly any snow dusted the mountain forests, and in summer the reservoir retreated to the clear river channels. To prevent dust storms, the Hydro seeded the valley bottom with fall rye, and I walked out in the green fields between the river channels to find the village foundations. Here you can see the foundations of the Giacomo café, there the crumbling, silted walls of "the castle." It's all there and in memory I trace the streets, the gravel river road, lines in my palm. I only see Anna or Maren now and then, at weddings or funerals.

This summer I saw Maren at her own wedding feast. She'd married one of the Fuscaldo brothers. I remember the boys of the Fuscaldo family, they were so polite and wanting to please. By the end of the wedding feast the father had tucked his chin to his chest, asleep, almost drunk. But it was the sons, the three of them who kept up the chatter at the wedding table for the girl who had married the youngest. And you could see where she was from, in the shape of her face and lips. Maren stood tall above her seated husband though she was no taller than a girl, her slender arms covered with freckles, and on her wrist she wore the bracelet her young husband had given her, a thick band of gold. She wore it as though it were a leaf that had fallen on her wrist and that she'd tied there with a strand of her own hair, some girlish game she'd forgotten, so that the leafy wrist went up and down in the conversation, knocking wine glasses on the table as she reached in her laughing for some plate to pass among the boisterous brothers.

The girls the two older brothers had with them were as polite as they were. They didn't laugh boldly with their mouth open. If they laughed at your teasing or your jokes it wasn't laughter at all and they weren't going to lean half over the table to pass you some plate you wanted, not at all the kind to get out of their chairs and display themselves like that, with that gold bracelet negligently banging around things.

Then she calmed the Fuscaldo boys with a Roca D'Avola song. She sang a few words at the end of the wedding table and they sat listening, quiet in their chairs, astonished looks on their faces: where did *that* come from, that song, and they felt the thrill of it growing on them in their chests.

My son and I were sitting at the far end of the table. His mother and I no longer live together, though in writing this I imagine I'm trying to keep her near.

What we don't forget is like distant music. It stays with us, a song in the air to thaw pain. The valley bottom is no longer the place of certain words that have abandoned us. I offer this signo to our children; may it guide them under the tongue.

PART II

HOUSE OF SPELLS

HOUSE
OF
SPELLS

I get paid to watch mountains and forests. From the fire lookout on Palliser Mountain I've memorized the peaks, the avalanche tracks, the bends in the river below, the logging roads and cut lines. When anything looks different I see it.

The tower cabin is a standard one-room with a seven-foot ceiling and four walls of four-foot-tall windows, no curtains, the chrome-legged kitchen table and chairs under the east window. My bed is under the south window and my books line the north sill. In the west corner, a sink and a small counter with a bar fridge under it, run on propane. Only the fire finder, a circular table with a topographical map and two sighting apertures, stands above the sills.

I go outside to place my pots of basil on the catwalk banister, watch clouds build over the eastern ridge, beyond the outhouse and the patch of grass the Forest Service calls a garden. Below I can see three horses at the foot of the mountain, a grey and two buckskins, the ones Mr. Giacomo lost earlier this summer.

Sometimes in that morning light an avalanche track can look like a column of smoke. Golden conifer pollen drifts over the Slocan gorge, wisps of river fog rise off the hidden bend of the Palliser.

Low clouds blow up over the eastern ridge like water flowing uphill.

Now that I'm alone, memories float in and out of my mind. I've assisted my mother at two births, one in the spring of 1969, the other this year. Mrs. Giacomo's was the first birth. Her son was born blue, couldn't be made to breathe. While my mother tried for a long time, her mouth over the baby's nose and mouth, I held Mrs. Giacomo's cold hand and she turned to the wall.

I remember the baby's puckered, bruised eyes, glued shut with a sticky film and its limp, tiny hands. Finally Mrs. Giacomo reached for her child, to take it out of my mother's arms. She could see there was no hope. She took it under the blankets next to her chest and then she drew the blanket over her head.

Even though I was only sixteen years old, I couldn't leave her there alone. I crawled under the blanket to rest my head against her shoulder, and my arms around her felt so weak and useless. She felt like she was covered in ashes. Over her shoulder I could see the face of the still one in her arms. His tiny brow looked puzzled at not entering the living world. His limp hands were delicate, hollow-boned and the skin at his temples pale blue.

Later Mrs. Giacomo would blame my mother for the child's death. She would say that my mother had not done enough. That was the end of a long friendship.

Then this year Rose's child was born; I was there too.

My name is Lacey Wells and I've got a lot to tell you. I know who the father of Rose's baby is. His name is Michael Guzzo. He left last winter before Rose knew she was pregnant, when the Odin Mill shut down because of the snows. He left to travel in Central America.

I know why Mr. Giacomo wants Rose's baby and why he can't have him. And I want to make sure none of this is forgotten.

1

One night in the winter of '68, over a year before Mrs. Giacomo lost her baby, Rose wanted to see if there was ice on
Olebar Lake. She liked to skate and she was waiting for the
lake to skin over. She knocked at my window, and we rode
bikes in the dark through falling snow to a beach that was
packed with fishing huts.

We'd met the summer before, picking fruit in the
Butucci orchards. The Portuguese Alberto Braz would get
us up at 5 AM, hammering at the bunkhouse door. He would
drive us into the orchards in the back of his truck, the bed
bumping and jarring on the potholed road with a grassy
hump up the middle of it and Rose curled up and still trying
to sleep, head in her arms on one side of the truck bed. He
would really yell at us when we left ripe fruit in the branches
that we missed or that was too hard to reach. Sometimes
when he wasn't around, we played soccer on the river road,
using a hard green peach for a ball.

Now we rode bikes in the dark to Olebar Lake. Onshore,
Rose knelt to put her hand in the ripplets that were washing through the beach gravel. Surprised, she said the water
was warm. I'd heard that there were hot springs in the lake
bottom, and that sometimes, on nights like this, warm water
was pushed ashore by the wind.

She went out wading, trailing her hands, the snow driving in around her.

I took off my boots and rolled up my pants to follow, the
lap-lap of water that smelled of fish around my knees, grop-
ing over stones with my toes. Skin ice was splintering way

out, but near the shore the lake was quivering like a mirror that had nothing to reflect. Hissing snow was drawing over it in wide curtains.

"Let's go out as far as we can," I heard Rose say, laughing. "This water is as warm as a bath. I want to dive in!"

"You'll freeze biking home," I warned her.

"I don't care. This is really wonderful!" she said, the snow collecting in a grey cap on her hair and sticking to her eye-lashes.

I could hear the low chug of a barge coming across the water. A house appeared in the issuing greyness and in a gabled second-storey window I could see Mr. Giacomo peer-ing out in lantern light as if watching the shore for drift logs. The pilot cut the engine and I could hear the rattle of the anchor chains. The house drifted quietly on the barge before us. I could see Mr. Giacomo quite clearly in the second-storey window. His father was an Italian stonemason from the valley and his mother was Japanese. Though he was in his fifties, in the lantern light his skin looked smooth and clear, like a young man's, and I liked him for it.

"Ah," Rose said, standing beside me, "that house is for Mrs. Giacomo."

The window was drawn open and he was standing there with his hands gripping the sill, looking out for a long time. The barge rocked and I could hear the crackle of the old floors and walls. Sometimes I, too, have felt that anxious need to make things better: if only this would go right for me, I might get what I want. There was no house like that in the village. He had bought it in Burnham for his wife who had come from Burnham. She had always dreamt of that house being hers. When she was a girl, the owner of the house, a judge, used to hold Saturday night parties for people in Burnham who had money. She'd stand outside at night while the doctor, the mayor, the logging contractors and their wives passed by the uncurtained living room window in some glorious dance. Later they would settle at the brightly lit dining-room table, the women smoothing out their fine dresses. I've always wanted a life like that, she'd told my mother.

When the judge died the house stood empty for a long time. There was a dispute over his will. Then it went up for sale, and Mr. Giacomo bought it with its Burnham memories for his wife.

Now Rose asked the question that our village always asked: "Where does he get his money?" He told people he made his money logging in the Nachako country after the war but some people said he'd come home from occupied Japan already rich.

Though we were still and all you could hear was water rummaging along the shore, Mr. Giacomo called out,

"Who's there?"

Rose gripped my hand, touched my cheek and pushed me to the beach, trailing her palms to quiet the water around her knees. Sometimes she could be like that: shy and wanting to get away before she was called out or recognized.

2

More than anyone else in the village, my mother could heal birds and other animals. Once I brought her a robin that I'd scared out of the mouth of a village cat and she set its wing.

When she left to work in the canning factories of Westbank, she left the bird in the care of my father, and when she
returned to find it dead, she was furious. My father told her
that he'd done everything he could to keep the bird alive.
He'd fed it worms from the compost and he'd placed it in a
straw-lined cardboard box near the stove in his one-vat paper
mill and still it had died. I believe the missing ingredients
were touch and voice. When my mother attended a birth,
she would stroke the woman's back and belly and she would
sing in a strange, low way, not really words. Mouth music she
called it, sounds that entered the woman's body as the touch
of palm and fingers enters the skin of a drum. You felt that
whatever she was singing came from inside you, from your
belly and knees.

Once when I was ten or twelve, Mr. Giacomo called out
to me: "I need your mother! One of my horses is ill."

He was calling to me from an upstairs window in the
Blackwater Mountain Lodge. It was spring and I was coming
down from the Illecillewaet snowfield with my father's paper.

He got me to come up to the upstairs room. On a plain
wooden table there was a clay bowl. With pride in his voice,
Mr. Giacomo told me the bowl was from the seventeenth
century, Tokugawa period. He said that a dress spread on
bamboo on the north wall was a Shikoku kimono, things
he'd brought back from the war.

I'd heard that he'd bought the Blackwater Lodge and that
he ran a summer trail riding camp and that he kept Savona
river horses up there. In late spring and summer he took
groups of girls onto the alpage, and they were often accompanied by priests from their parish.

The Blackwater Mountain Lodge was built in the twenties by Italian stonemasons from Friuli. They were hired by the railroad to repair the stone trestles in the pass. For the lodge they used shards of mountain stone, and the walls were two feet thick. In winter they used to ski there, Mr. Giacomo's father among them. After two winters he married Susan Tanabe, who came from the Yokohama prefecture in Japan. They went to Vancouver to live on Powell Street, and just before the war they returned to Japan. Mr. Giacomo, their only son, stayed behind in Vancouver. He was sixteen or seventeen then, and on his own.

The sick horse was tethered in the courtyard. "There was a storm last night," Mr. Giacomo said, "and a large oak branch fell in her corral. She ate the new leaves." He asked me to check her pulse and then to hurry down the logging spur to fetch my mother. He asked about the wooden rack I had on my back and about the paper tied to it. He smelled of new wine and lavender soap, and he began to walk the mare around in the courtyard, talking to her.

The logging spur leads from the Illecillewaet snowfields through a pine forest to the railroad tracks and then it's a two-mile walk to the village along the grade. The paper I carried weighed twenty pounds and I kept watching the weather, which was uncertain. Above me stood the Dawson Glacier across which storms came into our valley, changing the weather suddenly. My father had made paper for the internment camps in New Slocan and Bay Creek, and now he sold to the artists of Baltimore and New York. Some of his paper was snow-bleached and some of it was sun-bleached. I would carry my father's paper into the

Illecillewaet snowfields, to bury it in powder snow. The light filtering through ice crystals bleached the paper, and it acquired a pure, enduring whiteness that made it rare and valuable.

I liked being up there on my own. My father would only let me wander on the gentle slopes just above the treeline where there was no chance of an avalanche and if the weather was bad he wouldn't let me go up there at all. I loved standing at the edge of the treeline, looking out over the snowfield and listening to its stillness. I loved the weight-less feel of the snow that I heaped on the paper, the way it sparkled and flashed in the sunlight. And it made me feel important that I was helping my father in that way.

Bright early morning, the western sky full of stars. My mother and I had walked up the logging spur to the lodge, the wind over the forest an unpacked sail. The mare stood tethered in the courtyard among girls from the east who were enrolled in Mr. Giacomo's riding camp. She must be kept walking, my mother said, and she must not lie down. I remember climbing a stone flight to the balcony where Mr. Giacomo sat as the girls, one by one, led a horse from the stalls. The courtyard with its flapping geese and many cats was bordered on two sides by high stone walls and on one side by horse stalls under a slate roof. Mr. Giacomo poured out a glass of cider for my mother. Below, the girls were being directed by the priest who had travelled with them from Montreal.

Mr. Giacomo poured out the cider with its sharp, frothy smell of windblown apples. I was watching the priest lift the last of the girls into her saddle. The most patient horse had been chosen for the youngest. It stood there unmoving with a drooping head, both ears alert. Last night, the riding party had slept in the attic. At breakfast I'd watched them climb one by one down a ladder into the dining room, the bread and bowls of hot chocolate set out on three long tables. Those girls didn't even look at me; I envied their chatty excitement, the way they laughed and carried on over their bowls, their privilege.

"Something big, something big," Mr. Giacomo was saying and his opened hands on the balcony table were a question. The riding party had gathered under an oak outside the courtyard, waiting for the priest. In his brown cassock he rode out among the scrub oaks.

"I've got something big planned," said Mr. Giacomo, opening his arms. "I want to plant vineyards south of the village, Italian vines." My mother looked at him with questioning eyes. They walked along the icy balcony strewn with sand that the sun never touched. He said that the weather was changing in the valley, winters were milder. It was now possible, he believed, to plant wine grapes. Did my mother know, he asked, of any land that might be available?

"I've been wanting to ask you this," he told her. "You're a midwife; you hear things that other people don't hear. Maybe you know a family that's thinking about selling its land."

"I'll ask around," she said.

She and the Giacomos were friends in those days, years before their baby died. She and Mrs. Giacomo had been friends since high school.

3

About a year after the Burnham house arrived by barge, my mother and I drove to Mrs. Giacomo's in Mr. Giacomo's car. I was stretching out my legs in the back, on a seat that smelled of wine lees and green alder shavings. Big flakes were sticking to the windshield. Mr. Giacomo had turned on the wipers. When we left our yard, the Columbia Avenue street lights had come on and I could see fresh prints that horses had left in the snow in the street. There was the Mallone café, the shades pulled. I watched the snow drift under the street lamps and gather in the corners of the darkened café windows. Above the street lamps and above the rooftops you could feel a cloud had come into this valley and the snow fell in silent ripples. There was hardly any wind. Mr. Giacomo told us he hadn't changed over to winter tires and now and then I could hear the summer tires slip on the icy street and the engine revved.

My mother was quiet tonight. Usually she would be chattering on about this or that. But she didn't turn around to look at me. She was holding herself still, not looking to the right or left. I couldn't hear her breath over the wash wash of the wipers. Earlier that morning she had delivered twins in the Palliser valley. She had been up all night with Mrs. Sandez and the twins were born in the morning, one after the other, around 6 AM. She'd had only a few hours to sleep before the call came from Mrs. Giacomo. While we were waiting at home for Mr. Giacomo to come for us, she poured well water from a small stone pitcher into clay cups the size of thimbles and she said, Drink up Lacey, Mrs. Giacomo's baby will be born tonight. I saw her hands tremble when she packed the rubber sheets, the thermos of pepper tea that she'd left to simmer for an hour on the stove to make it stronger.

Sometimes when I wake up I feel unsure of myself, too. I just look around before dawn, no bird chatter, and the night table and the wardrobe and the mirror in my room at home don't have their shapes yet, and I feel their wanting, as if in my sleep I haven't given them the smile or touch that calms them; and I feel sometimes that things, too, are afraid in their passing, cowering a little.

Mr. Giacomo drove into a tire-rutted yard in front of the Burnham house. Grey for want of paint, the house that had crossed Olebar Lake on a barge now stood on a high bluff above the Palliser River. It was too tall for our village, with peaked brows over the upstairs windows. A harsh light shone in the downstairs windows, as bright as the arc lamps in the train yard.

We walked up springy planks to the front door.

Inside, my mother didn't say much about how unprepared the house was for a birth, not even when she heard the roar of the propane heaters inside the front door, glanced at the arc lamps casting sheets of light on the drying plaster walls. The water in the kitchen was a garden hose stuck through the window, the stove to heat water and to warm the pepper tea was a camp stove.

This was one of Mr. Giacomo's biggest plans — to present a fine home to his wife — and the lack of order in the hallway and in the kitchen frightened me. It made me feel tired just to look at the kitchen shelves covered with a fine plaster dust and the stacks of labelled cardboard boxes. I wanted to go home.

Bothered by the lack of preparation, my mother spoke to Mr. Giacomo in a clipped, flat voice: John, she said, when she walked into the kitchen and saw the garden hose stuck through the window and all the pots still in boxes, I need pans and hot water.

Yes, he said, I'll get those for you. You go ahead and check on my wife. He moved boxes around on the floor, reading their labels.

The pots and pans are in here somewhere, he said, hurrying now. I'll find them!

When she climbed the stairs to the bedroom, her hand gliding along the varnish-flecked banister, I saw my mother slow and turn to me with a look of disbelief, for the upstairs, much disused, still smelled of mould and rat droppings and the ammoniate smell of squirrels' nests. She shook her head, kept climbing to the bedroom.

I think Mrs. Giacomo was in too much pain to even notice me; the contractions were coming on full. Her head rested on a green cushion, a cushion from the sofa in the hallway downstairs. She looked at my mother, her mouth a small round O of pain and her fingers clasped on her belly. Her eyes were the colour of the bloom on ripe plums.

I was helping John to move in, she apologized, in the way that people do when they feel they're being inconvenient.

It happens, my mother said. You can't always be exactly sure when a baby is due. She went about hooking the rubber sheet on the mattress corners. She told me to go downstairs for water and towels.

In the kitchen, Mr. Giacomo, pulling open boxes, asked me how things were going. He placed two clay bowls on a shelf above the counter.

When our baby is born we'll drink from these!

Those bowls looked as lumpy as cooking apples.

I was eager to help, and even now I wonder at how helpful I wanted to be, thumbs pressed on a pot lid as I carried steaming water up to the room, by the drying plaster walls. I wanted to show my mother that I could be useful. Still, I felt something was wrong and I kept busy in order to ignore the feeling.

My mother's voice was sharp and bitter, and I kept asking what can I do and I didn't mind when she snapped at me, I can't keep telling you, placing towels under Mrs. Giacomo's hips, her back propped with pillows, and Mr. Giacomo calling from the foot of the warped stairs, What do you need?

I went up and down those stairs to fetch towels and water, by the shadowless flare of light on the muddy-smelling walls. When I climbed the stairs for the last time, my mother called out of that hot, steamy room with its painted-shut windows, her voice calm now, and I thought to find some delightful baby that you lift in your arms to feel its struggling, wailing life.

I walked into the room and my mother turned the wrapped infant towards me. I saw it take two gasps like a trout drawn onto ice, and then it lay still in her hands. All of a sudden that room smelled of the winter lake, of the warm, lichen-coloured water that sometimes welled to shore, spreading out from the deep hot spring.

She just leaned over this baby, quiet, as if listening for some far, piping tune, her eyes wide and still, without reflection.

Later she would tell my father that she had immediately brought the baby to her mouth to breathe for it, but that was after Mrs. Giacomo had shouted at her, Do something!, to shake her out of a dream. And even then she had to think of what to do, like someone who has awoken and doesn't recognize where she is.

I don't think she even heard Mrs. Giacomo shout at her. She just stood there at the foot of the bed with the still one in her arms, just stood there. I could see by the bewildered look in her eyes that she had suddenly lost all confidence in herself. I could feel her cold grief creeping into my belly and along my inner arms, and I clapped my hands to startle her.

4

A lot of trains pass through our station at night. The westbound trains carry grain, coal and lumber to the seaports. The eastern trains bring freight from Asia. I remember the very first train to pass through our valley delivering Japanese cars to Ontario. It was delayed at the station that spring and a lot of people went out to look at it.

That train carried Toyota Celicas, Nissan Skylines and Datsun 240Zs. They were all kept unlocked. I'd never seen so many cars stacked like that before. They looked like ornaments; a trick of light had raised a metallic glow on them.

Rose and I climbed the double-decker car flats to sit behind steering wheels that smelled of vinyl and oily metal.

We were really becoming friends that spring, a few months after the Giacomo baby died. She climbed quicker than I could, like a raccoon, and now and then she'd look down at me to laugh encouragingly. I could smell on the cars an odour of oil and diesel smoke. I climbed into one and sat behind the steering wheel just to pretend I was driving past the 4th Street girls at the village fountain who were tossing water at each other from cider bottles, past Bruce Hiraki who was the son of my father's friend Mr. Hiraki. He was a little in love with Amy Mallone, whose father owned the café Mr. Giacomo was to buy, and rather than kiss her, he scooped water from the fountain to toss at her. I sat there, the train at rest, and Rose called down to me,

Want to drive a Nissan Skyline? To the coast?

Want that one down there?

She climbed with ease, her arms strong from working horses in summer. I'd seen her walk Clydesdales down our main street, when she brought those horses out of the forest for the fire season. Rose's family were horse loggers on the Big Bend where our river turns round, flowing south instead of north. In the fall of '67 they'd sent her to our village to attend school, and she'd stayed on Mrs. Beruski's farm south of town. She was around sixteen then, with those big horses walking beside her past the Columbia Bakery. They followed her like two obedient dogs. She was feeding them cider apples from her pocket. Now and then one would nuzzle her shoulder, snuffle the lank hair at the nape of her neck.

Those horses were the size of a full-grown moose. Their iron shoes rang out on the pavement. She liked to look in their serene eyes then. Had one of those animals misplaced a step, it could have crushed her foot. Up close they seemed to dwarf the cars parked along the sidewalk, blocked them from view. That fall — the fall she went to live with Mrs. Beruski — her family used them to haul logs out of the forest, to the shores of Olebar Lake. She whistled to make them lift their head to look at her, then they went back to nuzzling her pocket, pushing her along so that she laughed. She was taking them to Mrs. Beruski's farm on the flats south of our village; they'd stay there till the fire season was over.

Do you want to drive to the coast, Rose was saying, in this one? She was calling down to me through the open window of the car she was in.

Not really to go to the west coast. She was already pregnant then and she needed a friend. I wasn't sure of her, maybe because I felt her need for a home where she'd feel safe, a need that I didn't know how to answer. Still, I liked her laughter that was an invitation to cross the distance between us.

Sure, I'll go to the west coast with you, I said then. You drive, I'm coming up there.

Well, come on then! and I heard her voice settle and grow more assured. Maybe it was then that she began to trust our friendship.

5

Later in the summer, Rose and I were lying on our bellies on Michael Guzzo's raft off Olebar Beach. Michael Guzzo wasn't with us then, he'd left to go travelling months ago.

He was Rose's boyfriend. She'd got to know him in New Slocan. When she described him, his unkempt sandy hair, the green logger's vest that he always wore, his mild, chestnut-coloured eyes, I knew who he was. I'd seen him one summer in the Butucci orchards. He'd climbed into an apricot tree after his cousin Maren and when she came down out of that tree I heard her shouting at him that she didn't want to see him again.

And I'd seen him in the Grizzly Bookstore from time to time, going through the second-hand books. Before he left for Central America in the winter of '69, he gave me a carton of books for safekeeping. There's some interesting ones in there, he said, you can read them if you like. He took out one to show me: A *Catalogue of Unrecovered Items, Volume Four: Pottery and Clay Figurines.* He'd said that it was from the end of the Second World War. It showed photographs of items that were stolen by the Japanese army and navy during their retreat and that were never recovered during the occupation of Japan.

Rose and I were kicking the raft through the still water at dusk. I heard voices from the picnic tables under the bone dead oaks near the point. I heard two voices — a man's and a woman's — arguing and hushing each other. Rose said, That sounds like your mother.

When Mr. Giacomo shouted, You girls must be cold out there!, I recognized his voice, and he went to the barbecue pit to build us a fire. Whoever was with him had left.

I wondered what he was doing there. It was the first time that he seemed really interested in us. I thought then that the woman he was arguing with could have been my mother, but I couldn't tell. She had stayed away from the Giacomos since their baby's death and I didn't understand what she could be doing talking with him on Olebar beach.

Later in the fall, I'd find out why. At our kitchen table, my mother would spread adoption papers before Rose, and then I'd understand that she and Mr. Giacomo had been planning this all summer, that they'd met on the beach to talk about the adoption of Rose's child.

Rose was at the mast and I was in the water, kicking along the raft. By then it was almost dark, though I could see the oaks on shore that had died in the winter of 1968. I told her that I'd got a summer job working relief in a fire tower and that I'd be gone maybe weeks at a time. She looked at me then, and I saw sadness draw into her eyes, as if she'd miss me. I was surprised at how she felt; we'd only been friends for a few months. She turned on a flashlight secured to the mast with duct tape. The beam swept the beach, picking out Mr. Giacomo sitting on a drift log.

Rose, don't shine people, I said, embarrassed.

Well, at least I'm not flashing him, she replied.

We dragged the raft onto the gravel and went to sit by the fire, shivering in towels. We had stayed out on the water too long, and because the lake was rimmed by mountains on the western side, darkness had fallen suddenly.

Girls, it's too dark to bike home, Mr. Giacomo said. I'll give you a ride.

He owned the only taxi in our village, and he'd driven to the beach in that car. We loaded our bikes into the trunk. The whole time Rose was laughing, because to fit two bikes into the taxi was like trying to cram nine feet of trellis wire into a tin can: jumble of handlebars, pedals in spokes, hands black-ened with grease and road dust, a smear on Rose's cheek.

She had never actually met Mr. Giacomo before.

She was laughing out of shyness and not wanting to look at him.

Amused, he stood watching us. When the bikes were in the trunk he cinched down the lid with rope. The pouches under his eyes looked bruised and his strong hands that worked the rope were as small as Rose's.

I'd known the Giacomos for years, though Mr. Giacomo had never really talked to me till now. He had never really seemed to see children.

His wife and my mother had been friends since high school. My father had worked with Mr. Giacomo when he was a young man, delivering mail to the internment camp near New Slocan during the Second World War. He and my father bought vegetables grown in the camp to sell in our village.

At his feet were a small grey satchel and a sketch pad. He took some papers out of the satchel to show to Rose. Then he looked at her, seemed to change his mind, and put them away.

The car that he drove us home in, this "Johnny's Taxi," a 1964 Chevrolet, used to belong to my mother. One summer she'd worked in the canning factories of Westbank to make the money to buy it, and then she went for her driver's license.

It turned out that she was afraid to drive that old boat of a car: the pedals confused her and sometimes she stepped on the gas when she meant to brake, the car surging, and she'd pull over to the shoulder gravel in a sweat.

And then there weren't a lot of births in the valley, so she couldn't afford gas or repairs. She got the Italian truck farmers to pick her up when their wives were in labour. In the spring of 1967 she sold that black Chevrolet to Mr. Giacomo, and he made it into "Johnny's Taxi," the letters stenciled in white paint on the front door panels. This was just one of his money-making ideas. He owned vineyards and orchards south of our village; for a while, he was even a trail guide with horses.

Rose, shivering in the back seat, her shirttails wet and stuck to her swimsuit, a striped terrycloth towel draped over her knees and bunched under her so that she wouldn't wet the vinyl seat, asked who Johnny was.

"Johnny" he told her, was his first name: John Giacomo.

We looked at each other and laughed: he was no Johnny. Just as the village called the priest "Father," so they called Mr. Giacomo "Mr. Giacomo." It was just the way people talked about him. He did all kinds of jobs and dressed like any working man. Looking at him you'd think he was poor, but we all knew he was rich.

We drove through the Palliser valley past the Italian truck farms, past Mr. Pradolini's house and Mrs. Hiraki's house, both two-storey clapboard WWII houses that had been moved up from Renata after the dam was built.

Down there, nobody bothered with curtains, so you could see deep into kitchens and living rooms and the barns were wide open, lit up, with someone bedding down the cows, and I saw Mrs. Hiraki look up from her kitchen table at the car on the gravel road; she came to the window to watch us go by.

She looked out in a peering, alarmed way, as if our lights meant an accident or a death. I saw her raise a hand to shield the kitchen glare so she could see through. Now on her own, she came from a valley family that had been here since before the war. Her husband had died of a heart attack, after he retired from the Odin Mill, and her son Bruce Hiraki had recently died in a logging accident south of the Big Bend. He was felling a cedar when a root-rotted fir on the edge of the clearcut tumbled and caught him on the side of the head. I remembered my mother telling me about the accident. News travelled quickly in our village. I remembered seeing him toss water at girls at the village fountain, the way he looked at Amy Mallone with a merry glint in his eye. And I felt a stillness settle in me then, a deep ache in my chest.

I was there when the tree hit him, Mr. Giacomo told us. I helped lay him out in the truck bed and we took him to the hospital in Naramata, but it was already too late. He was bleeding from the ears and he'd already stopped breathing. We had to drive for miles along the reservoir before we could turn west below the dam, towards the hospital.

Mr. Giacomo was quiet for a while. Then he said, That dam was built ten years ago. Before it was built, in winter we'd get a week of twenty or thirty below. Six feet of snow fell. Now the weather has changed, he said, because of the reservoir behind the dam. You can even plant grape vines here.

I thought to myself then, I've never seen that dam. My parents had told me that it had flooded the entire Renata valley, that many people had lost their land, that whole forests had drowned. Though I have never seen it, I dream of that water sometimes, pressing down on a forest and I'm swimming over stripped trees that have lost their needles and that peer up at you like miles of ghosts.

These were all dirt farms we were going by, and the car lit up corn or sweet potatoes, or a tororo field, a quarter-acre vineyard, the nets furled and bunched on an overhead wire. You could smell manured soil and the sweet, heavy scent of grape flowers that, early for that time of year, spread through the valley on still evenings.

He told us he was the one to start winegrowing in our valley and where once there had been alder copses, scrub-land, and apple orchards there were now vineyards. He had even gone to Italy to buy Veneto vines that would grow on the village slopes and produce grapes that would ripen here in autumn. Over the years he'd bought up over fifty acres south of our village.

Whenever he'd come by our 4th Street house or my father's paper mill, not often over the past years, he never said hello to me. Once when I was standing right in front of him — was I eleven then? — holding out a roll of paper that he'd just bought from my father, he took it out of my hands and gazed right through me.

Now he was looking at me in the rear-view mirror, studying me, and for the first time in my life I felt a little afraid of him. I sensed he wanted something from Rose, and maybe he had already begun to suspect I might get in the way.

As we drove along, he explained that he was redecorating the downtown café he'd just bought from Mr. Mallone with things he'd picked up on Shido Island during the war and that he was bringing in ash wood tables and chairs that would need to be varnished. Afterwards there would be regular work, serving.

You girls have finished high school, he said. Do you want to work for me?

What will you call it, Rose asked, Johnny's Café?, and in her high spirits, in her not having to pedal home in the dark, she burst out laughing.

He didn't turn round to look at her. He kept himself still, maybe listening to her laughter. Rose, wiping the tears from her eyes, was suddenly quiet. She looked at me and shrugged, though I was sure she felt the change in him, too, and it confused her, made her unsure.

After his stories and his offer, he was quiet. Maybe he was hurt by her laughter or maybe he was just amused; I couldn't tell by the expression in his eyes when he glanced at me in the mirror.

We drove into the village past the roundhouse, the doors flung open and spilling out light. We stopped in front of Mr. Giacomo's house on 4th Street. On his porch, he showed us a 30 power telescope and a drawing board lit up by a battery-powered reading lamp. He told us that he was sketching the basaltic areas south of Vieta and the Imbrium Sea on the moon, difficult because of the way the light passed quickly over the Crisium plains.

He had to sketch quickly, he said, because the moon kept slipping out of the telescope's viewing area.

Ten degrees of brightness for the peak of Aristarchus, he said, the highest degree of brightness on the moon. It could only be expressed by the purest white paper. Five degrees for the walls of Argo, expressed by slight shading. He drew on paper my father made; it got whiter as it aged.

Rose smiled at the drawing he showed us, her teeth chattering.

You girls are cold, Mr. Giacomo said then. You'd better go home and change.

When we had closed his gate behind us, Rose turned and said, Thank you for the ride!

He called out to her, Pioneer E is going to pass by the moon on its way to the sun tonight, and take photos of the face of the moon we never see!

Who cares, Rose said under her breath, and she glanced at me in a way that made me laugh.

I turned round to see if Mr. Giacomo had heard. He'd given us a ride home, offered us work in his café. He had been kind to us. Yet I also felt that what Rose had said was her way of keeping to herself. Maybe even then she sensed that his kindness had a cost.

On the walk home, pushing her bike and shivering in her wet towel, Rose told me how she got to know Michael Guzzo. He was working in the Odin Mill in the fall of '69, and she used to bring lunches to the scaler Mr. Beruski on night shift, when she was living at Mrs. Beruski's. It was one of her duties for reduced room and board, to take those lunches to Mr. Beruski who measured the logs as they came into the mill, calculating board feet. The scaler would thank her as he unpacked his hot meal, gnocchi sometimes, or a chicken wing pasta with a flask of diluted wine.

Michael Guzzo was a sandy-haired eighteen-year-old boy who drew lumber on the chain and he wore doeskin gloves that were too big and loose on his hands. The cedar they were cutting raised welts on his arms, so the scaler had called to say bring some salve along with my lunch. It was a night shift in early October and the snow she walked through had changed to fine powder, heaped on the stacks of logs that reached to the river and collected in the chain-link fence that surrounded the mill. The crew was gathered around the wood stove in the scaler's shack, under a forty-watt bulb, and this boy was at the table, his sleeves rolled back. The scaler took his flask and the metal canister of warm pasta. The others in the green chain crew smiled at Rose, standing around the stove. Their wool jackets steamed and smelled of cedar, machine oil, and the winter cold.

And when she brought out the salve from her pocket they said, From your hands, Rose, challenging her, a smile in their eyes, gentle or mocking.

She sat across from the boy, poured some salve into her hand to warm and spread on his enflamed forearms, but her hands were cold! So, elbows propped on the table, he cupped her hands in his and gently blew on them, eyes laughing at her. His eyes reminded her of her father's, so mild and chestnut-coloured. Two shy people who couldn't talk to each other. He wasn't even a year older. He wasn't particularly cute: his hair was long, sticking out from under a toque, his eyes reddened by the cold, and when he stood to rebutton his sleeves to go back to work, she saw that he was thin and a little taller than she.

He had built the raft that we'd kicked along off Olebar Beach. On weekends he used it to fish for landlocked salmon with a hand net.

I knew who he was. I often saw him in the Grizzly Bookstore, rummaging through boxes of books that people had left or forgotten on the trains. Once he said to me there is no other bookstore like it in the valley, because of those train books that came from so far away and from lives so unlike our own: *Anna Karenina*, *Cannery Row* and Spinoza.

Sometimes he'd hold a book just for the weight of it, for the feel of it, as though, if he were sufficiently still and watchful, it could communicate to him its own life. And sometimes he sat there for a long time in a disused chair in the back, an unopened book in his hands. He seemed sad then and little inclined to talk. Once he held out to me the collected dialogues of Plato; the paper in that book was like a Bible's, tissue-thin and almost transparent.

There, too, you could find treasures, clothing abandoned or left on the trains. He showed me a rack of such castoffs in the back.

Who owned these things, he asked me then, smiling. Doesn't it make you wonder?

He asked me if I wanted to try on any of those clothes — a pair of jeans that looked like they would fit me, a paper raincoat from Japan, a plaid scarf, a siwash vest that was almost in style — but I shook my head. I could see a sadness in his eyes that I didn't understand.

I asked where he was from because he wasn't from our village.

He said he was from south of here.

South? I asked. Where?

Nowhere in particular, he said. My family's land is under the Hydro reservoir.

I touched his arm, shocked.

Jesus! I said.

He laughed. What can you do about it? he said. They took our houses, our land, gave us some money and told us to move on, go live somewhere else. And there's nothing we could do about it.

I felt sick, the colour draining from my face. I didn't know what to say.

Maybe that's what I feared most: to have the place where I was cared for and loved taken from me. It made me feel dizzy to think about it. If our village were wiped out, who would I even be?

It's not your worry he said, smiling and gazing at me.

All I could do was look at him.

Then he said, The dreams are the worst. Sometimes I wake up at night with a crushing weight on my chest, I can hardly breathe. It feels like the weight of all that water.

6

A few weeks later, I went to my father's one-vat paper mill. I didn't often go there because he didn't like to be disturbed when he was working. That day he wanted to show me a windsock made for a newborn. I touched the painted eyes of the trout on it. It was made to swim in the wind on a long pole and he said it was for Rose's child. He had learned to make windsocks at the internment camp near New Slocan.

That was during the war, when Mr. Hiraki taught him to make paper. Mr. Hiraki and others had raised flying fish and paper horses over the camp on long poles.

"They remind us this won't last forever," Mr. Hiraki had told my father, watching the figures in the wind over the rows and rows of wooden shacks. "They give us courage."

Papermaking required my father's total attention: he'd settle the wave of pulp on the bamboo screen with a slight shift of his fingertips on the mould handles. I felt shy around my father when he was at work, yet I wanted to ask how he knew Rose was pregnant.

He said she swayed on her hips as though wading in a strong current, gripping her way over stones with her toes. Besides, he'd noticed her thick wrists and the loose clothes she wore.

Did I know who the father was, he asked me.

I was surprised at his curiosity. It wasn't like him to ask about other people's secrets, though in some ways our house was the clearing house for village secrets and stories. My mother was often away in other people's homes, there for grief or joy, birth or death. People often dropped by my father's mill to review their problems. His work was seen to be either odd or useless and therefore worthy of interruption. Sometimes, when he heard a truck or a car drive up, he'd go out the back door to sit among the river poplars and wait till the driver left so he could get on with his work, fretting over the thought that the paper in the press was spoiling.

Did I know who the father was, he asked me again. I shook my head, though Rose had told me his name.

I wasn't sure how much Rose wanted me to tell others then. I felt like I should protect her secret. On the raft she'd told me the father's name, Michael Guzzo. On the walk home from Mr. Giacomo's, she told me how she'd met him and that he'd gone travelling in Central America.

I was watching my father make washi paper. He was sprinkling hibiscus petals into the pulp, a pale mauve that was my favourite colour and that reminded me of the shadows under Mr. Giacomo's eyes and at the corners of his lips.

"What?" he was saying, he thought he'd heard me say something, but I'd said nothing, my mouth pressed into my rough sleeve and my gaze following him. I kept still because I was remembering a story I'd heard from several different people. Around here it's hard for an interesting secret to stay secret, and I've thought of it many times.

One summer in the '40s my father and Mr. Giacomo worked together. In those days, a young man starting out on his own, Mr. Giacomo delivered mail in the valley. He took rice, letters and packages to the Japanese internment camp near New Slocan. My father went with him, to buy vegetables and eggs in the camp that he sold to the railroad cooks.

Mr. Hiraki was interned down there. He was my father's friend from before the war. They'd worked on a section crew together, repairing track in the Odin pass, and when Mr. Hiraki had earned enough he'd bought a small farm in the valley south of our village. My father used to drive down to his farm in summer to buy vegetables.

Mr. Hiraki grows the best vegetables in the valley, he used to say, and soon he was taking orders from the village wives and the railroad cooks.

After the Pearl Harbor attack in December 1941, all Japanese-Canadians were identified as enemy aliens. Mr. Hiraki spoke out against the forced evacuation of Japanese-Canadians from the coast. Many times he said to anyone in our village streets who would listen that the war was against Japan, not Japanese-Canadians. "And what about you Italians," he'd ask the Pradolinis, the Staglianos, "Why are you not being arrested? It's because of the colour of your skin!"

He and his family were sent to the New Slocan camp. Before the RCMP came for them, the Hirakis asked their Canadian friends to store household goods. They thought they'd be back on their vegetable farm within a few months, that the forced internment was only brief. My father was a young man then and he was building his first house on 4th Street. They didn't ask one Canadian family to take all their belongings, they asked three or four. My father hadn't finished the second floor, so they asked him to take the piano and a big record player.

One day my father went to look for his friend in the camp. He found Mr. Hiraki doing what he always did, hoeing soil to receive rain and to trouble the roots of young weeds that he pulled by hand. The garden earth smelled musty, like an empty chocolate box and it had flecks of eggshell in it. Under dark, shiny leaves my father could see the bulge of beetroots and under feathery leaves carrot tops the colour of the lichen you sometimes see on the north side of cedar trees. He saw that Mr. Hiraki loved every plant, every little tree, and he gave them tender care. Still, something was wrong, something in the way his friend moved from row to row said he was afraid of being singled out and attacked.

Mr. Hiraki gathered sacks of beets and potatoes, carrots and lettuce for my father. Then he raised a trout on a barbless hook from his well. It was as black as charred wood and its eyes had skinned over from a lack of light. It struggled on the hook.

"The fish tells me the water is still pure," the farmer said. Then he let it down on a rope tied to a bucket, the trout circling and nosing the sides. It lived on insects that fell into the well and it was healthy and strong.

Mr. Hiraki said that he expected the well would be poisoned by people who attacked at night; he stayed awake at night, listening.

When they went into the shack for tea, Mr, Hiraki spoke of ripped-up camp gardens, of young fruit trees snapped at the trunk or torn up and laid on the ground with their roots exposed as if by a windstorm.

"Do you know who is doing this?" my father asked.

"People from the village," he replied. "They drive away before we can get to them, teenagers mostly. I've recognized a few."

"But it doesn't stop there," he went on. "The government sends us moth-infested rice. The shipment of seed potatoes that arrived last week was full of rot."

The shack that his family shared with the Kitagawas was divided into living sections without walls: a kitchen, two sleeping areas, a small altar in the main room. Lumber was expensive in the war years, so there were no inner walls.

He wouldn't accept money for the vegetables.

"What do you want, then?"

"Mulberry bark," he said. "So that we can make strong paper."

He explained that the paper would be used to make screens to divide the shack into smaller rooms for privacy; here the two bedrooms, he said, there the kitchen.

"Paper walls," my father said, intrigued.

"If you're interested," Mr. Hiraki said, "I'll show you how."

On the drive back to the village Mr. Giacomo left the camp mail sack in the back of the truck. They went through a rainstorm and when my father insisted they pull over to bring in the sack, Mr. Giacomo drove on. He said there was no room in the cab for the sack. "Besides, everything they write is censored, torn up, misplaced, forgotten."

My father shouted at him to pull over. Mr. Giacomo looked at him, surprised, and drove on. "No one deserves to hear from them," he said.

When they got to the village, the mail was a sodden mess, a pulp of cheap tissue paper and glue.

Later that summer, Mr. Giacomo went off to a war that the Japanese were about to lose. Because his mother was Japanese-Canadian and he knew the language, he was taken to Shido Island off Korea. High-ranking prisoners of war were kept there. He interrogated officers of the Imperial Fleet, a captured prince of the imperial family. He was told to ask about artifacts and bullion that the Japanese had stolen during their occupation of Asia and their retreat.

Mr. Giacomo was proud of what he had done on Shido Island for the war effort, and he often spoke about it.

My father stayed behind. He was too young to go to war.

Instead, he learned to make paper from Mr. Hiraki almost by chance.

He delivered a truckload of mulberry branches to the New Slocan camp and stayed on to help Mr. Hiraki cut the branches to length, steam them in a steamer made out of an old dairy tank. He was ashamed of how his friend was being treated, forced off his farm to live in a shack.

My father learned to peel the green and black bark from the white bark, as if he were peeling a stick-on label off a bottle.

He scraped away bits of clinging bark with a knife.

He washed the white bark in the Lemon River, to free loose specks of black bark, and in the New Slocan camp he hung the strands to dry.

By then, the Custodian of Enemy Alien Property was selling off the inmates' belongings for a song.

The inmates made records of their possessions. They wrote on the new paper called washi that Mr. Hiraki made. It was so tough you could hide it in the well. They wrote letters to Canadian friends, instructing them to sell a fishing boat or a house on paper that could not be pulped in the rain. These letters had to be delivered by hand; any mail sent through the post office was censored, and the sale of unconfiscated property was illegal.

Now, after asking about Rose, my father was making paper that he knew I loved. With no decoration, it could be cut and folded into greeting cards. The hibiscus petals, stuck in the fibres, were an attraction, and the cards I made from the paper sold well in the Giacomo café. I was watching the petals fall from his sifting hand onto the deckle, pale rose colour of the Illecillewaet snowfields last evening, light that I'd seen torn into a spreading grey that vanished.

To concentrate, he kept his back to me as the sheet formed in the deckle over the vat.

He was watching the pulp settle on the bamboo screen and now I could see what the petals had made, a leaning girl with her arms out. He could feel my stillness, my gaze, and he heard me stir and get to my feet and say, "I'll bring the lanterns in for you." He didn't turn to see me go, waiting for the fibres to bind. One slight tremble of his hand would send out a wave that would thicken the fibres at one end and ruin the sheet.

When I returned with the lanterns, I could tell he liked this one; he was smiling over the sheet.

The swirl of petals made me think of Rose, one arm a gentle curve for balance as if she were leaning to place a glass on the floor. I remembered how she used to walk her family's Clydesdales down our main street, the reins draped loosely over her arm, a lightness in her step.

All of a sudden I felt that the figure in the paper showed me who she was.

That's *you*, Rose, I would have said to her, if she'd been there with us.

Some thin flicker of light to touch down, a lightness of spirit, tentative and apologetic. Later on, when events began to wear her away, to bear her down and push her to earth, when I'd need the courage to help her, I'd remember that figure in the paper.

Now my father was lifting the bamboo screen from the sheet draped on the post. I could smell snow in the air that had drifted in when I went outside, not that it was much warmer in the mill, too warm and the paper would spoil. He rubbed his hands in warm water on the stove; his fingers, thin and arthritic, ached so at night that sometimes he drank grappa to sleep.

"Why doesn't Rose go back to the Big Bend," he asked me then, "to stay with her parents?"

"She has no friends up there," I said. "And her mom's mad at her for getting pregnant."

He shook the water off his hands, dried them on a towel by the sink.

"We'll have to help her, then," he said.

7

Today I got out the homemade ladder and caulked the eavestroughs in a few places, hammered a few nails in the frost-heaved catwalk. A storm was building over the eastern ridge, and I tracked a harrier working its way above the pines. Harriers are pale grey long-tailed hawks with black-tipped wings. Usually they keep to the valley grasslands. They hunt rats and mice by quartering the ground, buoyant and tilting to clear the Palliser valley fences.

Warm southwest winds climbing the ridge met colder winds from the glacier and I watched as clouds were born. Out of clear air, mare's tails appeared and rose into the mass above them. When it began to rain and sleet, I went inside to build a fire in the woodstove with chunks of subalpine fir and pine that lit like paper.

Outside, the trees bent over, the rain came in torrents, sheets that swept through the trees like hundreds of ghosts marching north.

What happens when you begin to lie to yourself?, I say to my ghosts. My mother remembers helping the young one to breathe. Yet I saw her paralyzed by grief and indecision. So it is not events themselves that make us, or what we remember of them. It's what we choose to forget, what we just can't stand to remember, that leads us by the hand down a road we can't recognize.

It would be so easy just to give up, to not try to fathom what I was beginning to feel. Last night I dreamt of the old judge's house. I felt that someone unseen had taken my hand, to lead me through its many rooms. In the dining room, a meal had been laid out on a big table lined with chairs. In another room men and women were dancing, all the furniture pushed to the walls. There was an aliveness to the house that came from the fullness of its memories. It felt cared for, and its memories reached out to hold up those dancing men and women, to give them the space of their laughter and desire.

When I awoke, I remembered how good I'd felt in that dream house, so welcomed. That feeling seemed to promise so much: that Mr. Giacomo would really help my friend Rose; that the Giacomos would overcome their grief and find the acceptance they wanted in our village.

And then I remembered how the house now stood, grey with neglect, in a bladed clearing with scarred fir roots sticking out of the earth. I remembered how it smelled of mildew and squirrels' nests. I felt then that Mr. Giacomo's kindness would have a terrible cost.

7 AM, the sawmill whistle blows. They are cutting yew, you can smell it. It smells like wet cinnamon. Through the fire tower binoculars I watch geese rise through the heavy mist on the river, lifting off the sandbar. The clouds above the village are heavy with rain.

I don't eat much. I don't like to cook and there's nowhere to go out. You could make a pie or jam out of the huckleberries on the *east slope of the Slocan Gorge, and sometimes I walk down to eat a handful for something to do. Huckleberries taste bitter and sweet at the same time and they have tough skins. This morning a flock of bushtits flitted in the bushes, eating them; cheeky, they scolded me when I got close and made me laugh.*

Some days there doesn't seem to be a clear distinction between myself and the cabin and the cedars, especially the birds. I feel well when this place is in bloom and they are chattering in the bushes. Because there is never any hurry, because I can take my time, even the raggy towel I use to dry the dishes has become something like a living thing.

Sometimes I feel people are like those dappled shadows you find under a summer peach or apricot tree, growing steadily and then fading as the light fades, say when a cloud passes over the sky. Then they grow bright again and they fade, not all at once, in their own time and when they show strong light they share their warmth and when they dim they're afraid and often alone and there is no pattern to it and no ultimate reason.

8

At the end of the summer, Rose and I went into the village bar to phone about a room; she needed a place to stay for the winter when her baby would be born. Mr. Giacomo was sitting alone in one of the booths and he turned to watch us come in.

Rose led him into the talk of his loss, her eyes shining and serene.

"The baby was a tiny thing," he said, weighed almost nothing in his hands. He had made the coffin, spent an afternoon in his workshop finishing something that was no bigger than a wooden shoebox, with a cross that he'd carved in the ash wood lid. He worked the lid with some fine chisels he'd found on Shido island, tempered and old, wanting the afternoon alone in his grief and in his fear of what might come next. "A blow close to home — to the heart — " he said, "for us to lose a child like that." He was wearing fingerless gloves and he was gazing at his hands wrapped around a coffee cup that smelled strongly of grappa, his face worn and drawn.

For the first time, Rose really looked at him. I had never seen her look so caring before. She'd overcome her shyness, which she usually expressed through laughter. It was unusual for her to be so quiet, and you never knew when she might turn what she heard into a joke, even a man's grief. Maybe because she was going to be a mother herself, she looked touched by his story.

She led him on in her quietness; he could have been talking to a mirror the way she looked at him, composed and quiet and touched his hand to listen. I wasn't sure of her friendship then; sometimes when she talked with Ian Beruski or Danny Moyer, older boys, there was a sparkling brightness in her voice, and she laughed quickly and eagerly at their jokes, when she wanted them to like her.

She brought Mr. Giacomo a plate of almonds from the bar. He hadn't eaten since morning, up in the vineyards pulling leaves to expose the fruit to the weak sun, and he was drinking grappa and coffee to warm up, he said. In his café there would be food all day but here the kitchen didn't open till five. When he looked at me his eyes were full of grief. He drained the cup, placed the taxi keys on the table.

Rose helped him to his feet.

"Where do you want to go?" she asked him.

He said, "You girls drive anywhere you want." He walked like he was wading in thigh-deep water and Rose supported his arm.

"We'll go down to Mrs. Hiraki's, then, to look at a room she has for me."

She looked at me and smiled.

I wouldn't touch him. He smelled of coffee and grappa, and I was afraid that if I touched him he would fall over or crumple. Rose had trouble guiding his steps. She warned him about the raised threshold, worn oak. She had the patient voice of a nurse. When we were outside, he couldn't button his sheepskin coat. She buttoned it for him.

"This is a marvelous day," he said, sniffing at the air, eyes shining. "You girls drive anywhere you want," and he stretched out in the back seat. He rolled down a window. To clear his head, he said.

Rose drove down main street, past the Giacomo café and the swept granite steps of the town hall. "I don't have a license," she announced and we looked at each other and laughed. We left town, went under some roadside willows in a hollow by a cattle pond, trees that were always the last to put out their leaves in spring and the last to lose them in the fall, and I could smell sap where an early frost had pried into the bark. Some Charlois were standing at a pasture fence, their dark eyes turned to the taxi and behind them a field of meadow grass that reached to the foothills.

"What will you girls do," he said from the back seat, "now that the summer is over?"

I could hear him sit up, pull at his coat, his voice thick and gravelly. And I wondered, how do you get to talk like that, deliberate or knowing, I'm hardly confident in anything I say. I heard him ask what kind of place Rose was staying in, and already in his asking there was some kind of promise.

"You're staying in a summer trailer?" he asked. "There's no heat in Michael Guzzo's trailer on the Palliser. There's no phone for when that baby of yours is due, no way to call." And the promise in his tone was, Oh now, we'll find something else for you soon enough.

I was surprised he knew Rose was pregnant and so was she; she looked at me with widened eyes then shrugged. The curiosity of our village was always on the alert, and now we knew that talk had been going around about her.

I thought about Mr. Giacomo's offering to help her find a place. Oh we'll help you find something soon enough, I murmured, trying to feel the weight of his words, find the feeling behind them.

Rose drove in a startled manner, pulling the wheel to the right or left as if she felt we were drifting to the gravel shoulder or the yellow centre line. It felt like she didn't trust her sense of distance. I'd seen her knock glasses and café spoons to the floor, reaching for them. Oh, she would cry in frustration, looking at the shattered glass on the café floor, why won't things stand! She walked like a dancer, all of her weight carried in the small of her back, but when she sat at the small linoleum table in her cramped trailer, she bumped the centre pole with her knee, spilling things.

"This is way too far down in the valley," she kept saying. "I can't live this far down!"

"You don't want to live way down here all by yourself," Mr. Giacomo agreed from the back seat. "You need to be close to the village and the hospital."

She was looking at the farmhouses and the orchards with increasing worry, as if the farther we drove the more the fields and the vineyards she didn't know made her feel alone and vulnerable.

I could have told her that Mrs. Hiraki's was miles out of town, but I didn't know that it would worry her so.

In summer we often bought vegetables and eggs at Mrs. Hiraki's farm. She would talk about the problems she was having, blighted tomatoes or rats in the pea crop. During our visits she talked just to keep us there a little longer, and she would show my father rows of withered leaves blackened with mould.

She's lonely by herself, my father told me once, driving back to the village. And she's having trouble managing.

Mrs. Hiraki was standing at the kitchen window when we drove into the yard, peering out. Rose parked under an old apple tree that had water wands rising out of its unpruned branches like the tines of a hayfork. Mr. Giacomo stayed behind in the taxi. "You girls go on in," he said. "I'm comfortable here. I'll just be in the way."

"They sell strong grappa in the village bar," he went on. "If I get out of this taxi now, you'll have to do my walking for me."

Mrs. Hiraki met us at the door. She took up Rose's hands and patted them between hers. She led us upstairs, glancing at Rose with a wary look, a tremor in her lips.

She showed Rose a room at the north end of the house under a sloped roof that made it feel small and cramped. She had washed the walls so that they gleamed and smelled of Lysol; under the single window there was an unpainted wooden table with a vase of dried flowers. The mattress creaked when Rose sat on it, on an iron frame that looked like it might have come from an internment shack outside of New Slocan. There was a porcelain basin where Rose could wash her hands and a tall wardrobe in one corner that just fit under the ceiling.

"Thank you!" Rose said. "Thank you for showing me this room." She gave me a quick, frightened look.

"There's more space here than in the trailer," she admitted.

Still, she couldn't stay. Later she said a smell of cooking came through the floor grate, the kitchen was directly below. A lot of food smells made her sick in the morning. She hated the smell of miso soup and Mrs. Hiraki had been heating miso soup.

We went downstairs, stood in the doorway to say good-bye. Rose couldn't say no to the old woman's staring, pleading look. You could tell that she hoped Rose would stay on, to help her with the farm, to keep her company. All Rose could say was, "I'll call you tomorrow."

The wind was picking up on Olebar Road when we drove home.

"When I find a place, will you help me to move?" she asked me. I knew she was only talking about a few boxes of clothes and some kitchen utensils.

"We will help you," I heard Mr. Giacomo say from the back seat. "My wife and I will help you get settled." I felt that he was testing her, to see what her reaction would be, to see how much help she would accept. Something in his voice worried me, something I couldn't make out then.

"Maybe you could move into Mrs. Camozzi's on 2nd Street," I said. Mrs. Camozzi's house had been built for the Stagliano family and now there was a sign in the window that said EIGHT BEDROOMS, and some trainmen stayed there, but maybe she didn't board girls. The hotel on Columbia Avenue was a two-storey brick building with a veranda that ran all the way around it. Road crews used to stay there, but now the rooms were rented out to old people mostly.

Why don't you come and live with us Rose, I wanted to ask her, to give her an alternative to the Giacomo's offer. We had two bedrooms, a small kitchen, and a mudroom in the back, a tiny living room that we called the parlour in a place on 4th Street people called the miner's cottage. Sometimes my father talked of building an addition but he never got around to it.

In her fear of being alone that winter, Rose did most of the talking on the drive home and mostly about herself. Her hands on the wheel looked as delicate as a child's, the skin under the nails a pale blue. Once, she leaned to peer through the windshield at apple bins at the side of the road, surprised to see them so late in the season.

Mr. Giacomo said the apples in those bins wouldn't ripen, that they were culls for the cider factory in Westbank and the jam factory in Sandon.

"I'll help you find a place," I said, turning to her. "When I'm in town I'll look after your baby for free when you get a job."

Mr. Giacomo said he could see the last of the fruit in the orchards, apples that the pickers had missed in filling their sacks to move on rather than climb for the one or two out of reach. His voice was gravelly, sleepy. It felt like he was talking just to stay awake.

"Gleaners stay into October before going to Burton," Rose said, "to cull what's left. They stay in a drafty bunkhouse where you have to light a fire at night to keep warm, burn vine cuttings or peach wood."

I could tell that she was avoiding asking for his help and that he was waiting, quiet, letting his offer settle in with all this small talk about apples.

"I don't want to live downtown," Rose said then. "I want a small place, with a sunny kitchen and a bath. I want a yard where I can plant a few flowers and grow some stuff. I want to make my own baby food and I want a porch where I can sit outside with him in the summer and nurse him without people looking. I want a plain wooden bed, not some old iron thing. And I want to be able to open the windows so the rooms smell fresh."

Her trailer had thin metal walls and an uninsulated floor. It had a propane heater under cupboards she'd painted red, but already that fall she could feel the chill of the floor through her slippers. The bed was the tabletop with the centre pole taken out and the top fixed between the bench seats so that it was like sleeping on a train bed, with your legs drawn in so that you could fit by the metal wall near your knees.

The trailer she lived in was too small for a girl with a baby. Where would she put the crib?

I couldn't tell whether Mr. Giacomo in the back seat was asleep or listening.

Now, driving back to town, I realized she was close to panic. I didn't realize that not knowing where you're going to live, that the prospect of a room like Mrs. Hiraki's, could scare a person so. An early snow was falling through the street lights and the tires creaked down Columbia Avenue, making the sound of your hand in wet hair after a shampoo. Flakes swirled over the taxi. Rose's hand darted out to snatch one from the air, to lick it from one of the wool mitts she'd put on because her hands were cold. She said that the mitt tasted of soap. There was hardly any traffic and all the store windows were dimmed. I could see tracks that horses had made and the fishtail track of a log that someone had towed to the Cowan St. Mill.

Mr. Giacomo was asleep. That night it felt like we could take him anywhere or even leave him in the back seat and maybe he'd awake, startled or afraid of where he was. Nothing more I could do, not even a blanket to cover him with. He looked so small there, curled up and asleep, his hands pressed between his knees.

"Where are we going to leave Mr. Giacomo?" Rose asked.

She was driving cautiously down Columbia Avenue, turned up 4th Street, unsure of what to do. She left the car running in the street outside his house, hammered on the door, and when she heard approaching footsteps, ran laughing toward me, saying, "Let's go!"

9

"You're working too hard," my father said. "Relax."

"Bend your knees and back. Get into a rhythm."

I was holding the two mould handles attached to the deckle; I scooped some milky water from the vat to send a wave across the mould that jumped off the far side.

"Let me show you." He was only using his fingertips to hold the handles. "Let the rigging carry the weight. If you lift it and force it, you'll be exhausted in four sheets."

I gritted my teeth and tried and tried but I couldn't make the even waves or splashes.

I'd spent all morning watching him, the relaxed rolling of the stock across the bamboo mesh in the paper mould, arms, legs and back bent, body bouncing and nodding with the mould and splashing stock.

"Be loose. Be gentle. You have to roll and work with the bounce. Stop forcing it." I laughed. He was using the voice of Mr. Hiraki to instruct me, bits of paper fibre on his apron, in his black hair, on the window over the vat.

When I watched him, there was never a pause or a dead moment in the forming of a sheet.

Every fall my father drives about three hours from here to an abandoned goat farm in the Illecillewaet valley, to bring out truckloads of mulberry branches. Someone had tried to grow mulberries in there, to feed to goats. He steams the branches, to strip the white inner bark that he pins under large stones behind a weir in the Palliser River, strands as long as a girl's hair. From a truckload he gets twenty pounds of bark that he makes into paper so precious that it's sold in the art markets of New York and Montreal, to water colour artists and printmakers. His paper has almost no smell and it has the sheen of new snow.

After the paper-making lesson, I went with him to help draw that bark out of the river.

We took it into the Illecillewaet snowfields for snow bleaching. The snowfields were retreating. When I was younger, I could walk to them. Now we drove.

We spread the bark in thin layers on the snow, covering it with snow. Every day for several days we'd drive up there to turn the bark over.

He looked the fibre over carefully for flecks of black bark. Sound carried far up there and from way below I could hear the scree of a merlin hunting in the pines. Above us in the bright light the sky was almost black in the saddle between two peaks.

I loved watching my father then. The fibre was new and held many possibilities. Who knew what kind of sheets it would make? It was healthy and strong and slowly bleaching in the snow and he handled the fibres carefully, spreading them over his palm as he turned them.

"Why is your mother spending so much time with Rose?" he asked me.

"She's thinking about giving up her baby to the Giacomos."

"The fool," he said. "She doesn't know what she's doing."

He gently stroked the fibres as if they were a cat's fur, turning them in the brilliant light.

"I want you to think about everything you've known. Has it ever been good to separate a family? Ever?"

He laid the fibres out in light so strong that it hurt my eyes and covered them with a layer of powder snow that sparkled and glowed, scooping it with his bare hands.

He refused to work with gloves.

Once I asked him why and he said because the strands were like new skin — they needed to be touched, caressed, to make them receptive, sensitive. In this way, he said, the paper will acquire stability, coherence.

"Do you like Mr. Giacomo?"

He looked up at me, surprised.

"Your mother and Mrs. Giacomo have been friends since they were girls. We get along okay."

"But do you like him?"

"It's not that I don't like him, hon. I don't trust him. He was a poor man when he left for the war, scratching up a living delivering mail and selling vegetables, just like me. Then after the war he came back rich. I don't know how. It just doesn't make sense to me. "

"He says he made his money logging in the Nachako country after the war."

"That doesn't feel right to me. I've worked with him, re-member? He's always dabbling in things, never quite making a go of it. A man like that doesn't make a fortune overnight. And now he wants to dabble in being a father. What about your friend Rose?" he asked me then. "What are you going to do for her?"

I felt a flash of anger. "Why is that up to me?"

"You're right," he said. "Hon, it's not up to you."

"We're in a very bad place," he murmured to him-self, absently spreading handfuls of snow over the fibres.

"Your mother thinks she can repair the damage done to the Giacomos, though that baby's death wasn't her fault! I don't think anyone could have saved their child."

"We'll help Rose," he said, "when the time comes. I'm just not sure how yet."

Still, I felt angry. Maybe I was being selfish, but I wanted to ask, What about me? Who was I supposed to please? You can't please everyone when you're put in the middle between people you love. When they're tugging at you from various directions.

10

When I was four, before the dam was built, we lived in a grey board and batten house on the Palliser River. The aquarium was in the back room, lit by a 100-watt bulb with a black lacquer shade over it. I remember lifting the lid and emptying a jar into it: crayfish, legs and pincers spread, drifted to the pea gravel. The water smelled of lichen. Here and there on the bottom were pot scrubbers of woven plastic where the young crayfish hid. It was a 20-gallon aquarium. The bottom was littered with potshard hideouts and in the middle a broken concrete block for the female with eggs on her belly. My father showed me the female's eggs by lifting it and turning it over. The crayfish's tail and legs were thrashing. Her young were used to catch winter trout.

I went with my father to catch crayfish in the Palliser, an empty mason jar tucked under my arm. His fingernails, whitish, were very thick and domed. His hands, so long in the water, showed the pale colour of winter fish. Already ice laced the shallows. He was flipping over river stones and cowling his hand to trap crayfish that were as long as my thumb, almost transparent, with pepper grain eyes and trout-coloured pincers.

"You're too small to fish on your own!" he warned me. Even at that age I had a reputation for going off on my own to catch trout. He had never seen such a child for fishing, my father told me, quick, darting hands in the Palliser shallows, flipping stones. I used to trap minnows in a nylon stocking I'd taken from my mother's drawer, laid out lines on the lake bottom. I walked out on the thin ice near the stream mouth, tapping my gum-boots and calling, "Fish, fish, I'm on your ice roof!"

I had a lot of confidence then, when I was younger. Later, it would help me get in the way of Mr. Giacomo and his plans.

Alberto Braz had told me that the fishing was best at night. You took out a flashlight and a jar of crayfish, the hand line wrapped on a yew wood reel and you shone a light into a hole chopped in ice. The rim ice, holding black, oily water, glows from the inside and the water at the side makes lace crystals the colour of ash.

All this I was told and wanted to try.

Calling from shore, my father got me to walk into the bay, then follow the point to the fishing huts where the ice was firm.

He weighed too much to come out after me.

Sometimes I've been afraid like that, too. One winter when I was eight or nine my mother was very sick. She'd worked herself to exhaustion and caught pneumonia, was so weak that she couldn't get out of bed. Even when I went to change the sheets, she could hardly move. And when I sat there listening to her watery breath — she was asleep — I was afraid that I would discourage her, so I went to the bathroom mirror to stare the fear out of my eyes, to practice a look of composed silence and hope. When I returned, my face a cheerful mask, the sheets tangled around her legs and chest were soaked through and smelled like cold toast. She'd drawn her head back on the pillow to breathe, her throat a pale white, wet hair plastered to her ear.

She opened her eyes then, and she must have seen the look on my face.

"Don't worry, hon, I'll get better. I am getting better. You don't have to pretend everything's okay."

It was the strangest thing: I felt the mask that was my face crumple and I heard a sob in my throat.

"I don't know how to take care of you."

"But you *are* helping me, hon. You are."

11

About a week after the trip to the snowfields, in the middle of the afternoon, I found Rose in our kitchen. I'd been down in the yard outside my father's one-vat mill, spreading paper on yew boards to dry in the sun.

You've made the right decision, I heard my mother say.

Rose was sitting at the kitchen table and I saw her nod. Then she turned to me and smiled and I saw panic in her eyes.

Are you sure this is the right thing? I heard her ask and I heard my mother who was standing over the stove making tea say, Yes dear, I'm sure.

There were papers spread out on the table, by a small grey satchel. That satchel was the one Mr. Giacomo had at his feet when he'd helped us pack our bikes into the trunk of Johnny's taxi, back in early summer.

What are those? I asked.

Adoption papers, Rose said.

I understood then that all summer my mother and Mr. Giacomo had been arranging this, planning this.

I sat beside Rose and she took my hand. Hers was sweaty.

You sure? I asked her.

Of course she's sure, my mother said, and she gave me a look meant to silence me. The Giacomos are a fine couple. I've known them for years. They can afford to raise and educate a child.

She brought Rose a pen and then she went quickly about making tea at the counter, not looking at Rose, as if her signing or not signing was a small, everyday matter. She wanted to make the thing seem quiet and small, because Rose looked like she was ready to bolt.

I watched Rose bite her lip, pick up the pen, and sign her name. She wrote out her name slowly, her face distracted, as if she were waiting inside herself for some sign.

Well, that was easy, she said.

How do you feel, I asked her.

Relieved.

That's right, said my mother, gathering up the papers. The last thing you need at your young age is a baby.

But Rose didn't look relieved at all. She was looking around the kitchen as if she couldn't believe where she was, as if she were looking for someone – or something – to tell her what her own heart wanted. All her lightness and confidence had left her; I could see her eyes welling with tears, which she quickly wiped away.

Well, that's that, she said, smiling bravely at me. I have to head off now. Mr. Giacomo wants to talk to me about working in his café.

I'll come with you, Rose, I said. I could feel pressure building in my chest like an expanding balloon. My hand in hers had gone cold.

No, no, she said. I need to be by myself for a bit. And then she left.

That evening I was helping my mother peel carrots for supper. She had been quiet since Rose left, thoughtful. I was surprised when she asked me to help with the dinner. Usually she liked to cook on her own.

When Rose was born, she told me, she was a small baby with these bright black eyes like a thrush's. I brought her home that night wrapped in a towel because her mother was exhausted and needed to sleep. I put her in your crib beside you.

Her voice was soft, distant, as she gathered up the carrot peelings from the counter.

Rose's will be my last birth, she told me. I can't go on like this. I don't have any confidence left.

It wasn't your fault that the Giacomo baby died, I said. Nobody could have saved it.

When I think about what happened my heart freezes, she said. My hands still shake! I feel that if I'd only acted more quickly, I could have saved that baby.

This really is best for Rose, she went on. She's too young to raise a child. She's still just a girl, with a girl's future ahead of her. She can't grow up overnight. It will spoil her life.

12

One rainy afternoon in the fall, my mother brought Rose into our house. Out in the street, in her winter coat, Rose had felt a rush of warm fluid. She sat beside me for a minute at the kitchen table to touch her inner thigh. Her eyes were so still that I could see the reflection of the kitchen window five feet away.

She unfolded a list of names that she showed me. I noticed that Michael's name wasn't in the list of boys' names. In our village, sometimes the son was named after the father. Michael had been away since last winter. At first there were a few letters that she couldn't answer because he was always on the move, then nothing. She had stopped talking about him.

"I'm not really going to keep it," she said, "but it was fun to choose names for something to do."

My mother got Rose to stand and began to help her undress, saying, "And now here you are, so young!" She helped her into a loose nightgown.

As the contractions deepened, her face crossed by brief waves of pain, Rose took my hand.

I saw that my mother's lips were drained of colour when she placed a jar of almond oil in a pan of warm water on the stove.

Her cloth bag was by the kitchen door and her birthing shoes and that loose cotton apron that she always wore that said MODERN BAKERY.

"You're in pain," my mother said.

"A little."

She led Rose to the bed, to spread almond oil on her belly. Smooth as lake water! my mother said as she massaged the oil in, her trembling thumbs pressing and rounding.

"You remind me of when I was young." She smiled. "You learn to sit on your hands, delivering babies. You learn patience."

I was sent for tea and when I returned she and my mother were laughing over the names Rose had chosen from the village telephone book. Still, there was a tension between them. Rose looked scared, unsure, and the glances she gave my mother were full of doubt. She must have felt my mother's trembling hands on her belly, their lack of confidence.

My mother was spreading a rubber sheet on the mattress, her face quiet and determined.

"I'm setting up the mattress," I heard her say to herself, "then I'll get the towels and pans of hot water," as if she were talking herself through the steps of a birth. Step by step, so that she wouldn't forget anything important.

When my mother said it was time to lie down, Rose shook her head impatiently, walking the room with her hands on her belly. When I brought her a wet cloth for her dry lips, she dropped it to the floor in a sudden wildness that made me think she'd run, vanish.

My mother took a firm grip on her hands and said, "You can't run from this. You'll only hurt yourself and the baby. Try to relax, be gentle with yourself. Breathe."

Even when her contractions were less than two minutes apart, my mother could not get her to lie down. Rose gave birth squatting over blankets heaped on the floor, holding onto the back of a chair. I held her from behind, pressing my knees into her lower back when she asked me to, my arms under hers and wrapped around her chest. I was so scared for her; I felt my own breath high in my chest, almost a sob.

"Here we go," my mother said, crouched beside Rose. "I can see the head." I could feel Rose pushing, her belly tight, and the baby slipped out. My mother caught it, held it up before us, a skinny body smeared with white mucous, a crumpled face with a pushed-in nose, two fists no bigger than my thumbs waving in the air.

With shaking hands, I put the infant in a towel after my mother had suctioned its mouth and nose and cut the cord with scissors. I gave him to Rose, who had climbed into the bed. My mother massaged her belly, to help with the after-birth.

"You've done so well," my mother said. "So well." I saw flashes of relief in her eyes. She straightened out the pillows behind Rose's head, brushed a strand of hair from her fore-head. For a moment, tenderly, she placed her palm on Rose's brow.

With one hand Rose held the baby across her chest. She lifted one of its tiny legs.

"He's a boy," she announced. My mother covered his chest and legs with a towel.

Her hand slipped to the sheets beside her, curled and list-less. I put my hand into hers. It felt damp and cold. Though I was composed and still, my heart was racing.

My mother leaned over Rose, lifting the wad of cotton between her thighs. For a moment, before the blood welled, I could see marbled fat under the torn skin. My mother threaded a needle and then drew up an injection of anesthetic.

She told Rose, "His head was a bit too big for you." Rose smiled at me with a defeated look that I'd never seen on her before.

I felt then that she was drifting away from me, far away, and that I'd failed her somehow. Her defeated look asked, Can't you help me? but I didn't know what to do.

There are two telephones in our house: one in the bedroom on the nightstand by my parent's bed where Rose held her child, one in the kitchen. My mother went into the kitchen to call Mr. Giacomo, closing the bedroom door behind her.

Rose kissed her baby.

"It's like kissing a stranger," she said. He was just staring at her. She moved her head around and he followed her with his eyes.

She closed hers. Her lips were pale with shadows underneath them. Her breath quietened and her hand gripped mine suddenly, then relaxed. The baby on her chest wrinkled his lips, curled his toes that were sticking out from under the towel.

"Don't fall asleep, Rose," I whispered. "Let's get out of here," a cold grief that I didn't understand pooling in my belly. I wanted to carry her away from there, the two of them.

My mother returned with towels, a bowl of warm water, and a handheld scale to weigh the baby. When she laid him out on a towel to wash him, he started screaming. After she'd toweled him dry, she asked Rose, "Do you want to hold him again?"

She put the baby in Rose's arms and he stopped crying right away. I didn't know that a baby could recognize its mother just by smelling her, just by knowing it's her and no one else.

Rose unwrapped the towel to count his fingers and toes. She checked his ears, the shape of his head. He was normal, looked normal.

"He's cute," she said. "Don't you think?"

I nodded, touched his little fingers that curled warm and surprisingly strong around mine.

We heard the front door close, the clatter of boots in the foyer. Mr. Giacomo was outside in the kitchen. My mother went out to greet him.

She brought him in, and he made a point of not getting too close. He waited till my mother asked if he wanted to hold the baby and he nodded, went to sit in the rocking chair by the window.

It looked like he couldn't quite believe what he had in his arms. I could tell he'd never held a baby before. My mother had to show him how to nestle its head in the crook of his elbow, and it just stared up at him, wide-eyed and quiet.

"It's okay," he said. "I'll look after you."

"You'll have a good life with us," he went on, looking down at the baby. "You'll see the house I've bought for us." Your window is on the south side. You can see the river from there. We're planting a lawn where you can play.

"My wife wants to meet you. She doesn't believe you're real yet, and she's waiting to greet you."

I knew that Mrs. Giacomo hadn't come with her husband because she didn't want to see my mother.

He was talking as if the rest of us were not in the room, as if we'd already left.

My mother was gathering up the stained blankets from the floor, lingering there. She kept her back to Rose and Mr. Giacomo, listening but not turning round so I could see her face. I wanted to clap my hands to turn her around. I wanted to know how she felt.

I squeezed Rose's hand hard to make her do something.

Rose watched Mr. Giacomo for about another minute. He didn't once look at her. He was smiling at the baby.

"You'll like your life with us," he said. "You'll have a good life."

"Will I get to see him?" Rose asked.

He didn't answer. Even then, he kept looking at the baby, but he looked startled by her question, as if it had never occurred to him.

Rose sat up. "I'm about to lose everything I've always wanted. That just hit me."

"I'm sorry," she said. "I didn't know I'd feel this way."

She drew back the blankets, wincing. In her nightdress she turned on her bottom, swinging her legs over the floor. Before she could stand up, my mother put her hands on her shoulders, saying, "Lie down. You'll tear your stitches."

"No!" Rose shouted then, shrugging off my mother's hands.

She got out of bed and stood in front of Mr. Giacomo. "Okay, give him back."

Mr. Giacomo looked up at her, his eyes full of amazement. But she wouldn't go away, she just stood there in front of him.

After a minute, his face as pale as a whitewashed wall, Mr. Giacomo gave her the baby.

"I'll let you rest," he said. He touched the corners of his eyes; he looked bewildered, almost ashamed.

My father called then, to ask how Rose was doing. I picked up the phone by the bedside as soon as I heard it ring. I heard him say to Rose, "Congratulations!" Then he asked to speak to my mother and she went out into the kitchen, to pick up the other phone.

"You hang up when you hear me on the line," she said, and Mr. Giacomo followed her out.

I sensed she didn't want me or Rose to hear what she had to say to my father; her lips were tight and she had that determined look she always wore when she anticipated an argument.

Four or five nights later, after she was rested and beginning to heal, Rose came into my room to wake me up.

"Are you going to help me pack?" she asked me. "It's time to go."

"Yes," I nodded, rubbing the sleep from my eyes.

"Hurry," she said, a false cheeriness in her voice. "I don't want to be out there in the kitchen by myself."

"I'll get dressed," and climbed out of bed.

'You're my friend, right?"

"Yes I am, Rose," I said. "I'll be there in a second."

In the kitchen, Rose showed me the bag she'd packed with dried peaches, provolone and a cold omelet wrapped in butcher paper. "Train food is expensive," she told me, widening her eyes. She walked slowly back and forth, the click of fastened suitcase locks.

My mother got me to sit cross-legged on a chair and she laid the baby across my lap.

"That's Mr. Giacomo at the door," she said, and she went out.

The baby's breath smelled like watermelon.

What's this in my lap? His eyes followed my finger: Hey, little fellow. It felt like he was waiting for me to do something, quiet. Maybe take him out and show him the village, introduce him to folks. He had the curious look of someone who wants to be shown around.

Sometimes hikers climb to my cabin, amazed to find it here, amazed to find a girl so young living alone. I invite them in. I feel cautious, but the Forest Service expects me to welcome visitors. They touch the fire finder, finger the lace ruffle on my pillow case, touch the washed plate by the sink, touch my little row of books on the south sill, turn to look at all the landscape through the wide windows. And often they say nothing, then they thank me and they go.

I watched Rose spread the snowsuit my mother had found for her on the chrome-legged table. The metal zipper that she opened made the sound of an angry hummingbird. There was a sack for the newborn's legs and a hood with two pink ears.

In the bedroom, we'd talked about where she was going. She was going to Field, the next stop on the train into the mountains, and she thought she might find work there.

A cousin who worked in the hotel up there had said he'd help her out.

"What if you don't like it in Field?" I'd asked.

"We're not going to *stay* there," she smiled.

"We'll come back when it's okay to come back."

Now she opened her blouse, the child's greedy, wrinkled mouth at her dark nipple. "It's time to go," she said, but she still sat there as if listening, her blouse open.

Mr. Giacomo came into the kitchen. He looked away when he saw Rose breast-feeding. He asked whether the baby was healthy, and my mother, who had followed him in, nodded.

"I can do nothing more," she said, gazing at him.

He gave her a scared, little smile, as if to say, "Once again you've failed us."

And he said, looking at my mother and then at Rose, "Well, thank you for everything you've done."

Yet I could see him ask himself, What mistakes have I made, that have led me here? The crinkles at his eyes had deepened and paled with shame.

My father had walked up from the one-vat mill. I could hear him kicking snow off his boots in the foyer.

When he came into the kitchen, rubbing his hands that were inflamed from the cold water in the pulp vat, Mr. Giacomo turned to go.

"On your way then, John?" my father asked.

"Yes," he nodded.

"Come to say goodbye?"

"Yes," he nodded again.

"How's that house of yours coming along, the one down by the river?"

"I haven't been there in awhile."

"Not here to change Rose's mind, I hope?"

My father went over to the kitchen sink to run warm water over his hands, his shoulders tight with anger. "You're not a man to respect other people's needs," he said then.

Mr. Giacomo looked puzzled, almost frightened. "I don't know what you're talking about."

"Look," he went on, "I'm only here to help. You don't have a car to take Rose to the station. Take the taxi," laying the keys on the table. "I can walk home from here."

"Thank you," he said to Rose again. "Thank you for considering our offer." He bowed slightly to her and then he turned and walked out of the kitchen without looking at my parents.

When we left the yard in Johnny's taxi, the Columbia Avenue street lights had come on. There was the Giacomo café, the shades pulled. I watched the snow drift under the street lamps and gather in the corners of the darkened avenue windows. Rose was quiet. Usually she would be chatting on about this or that. She didn't turn round to look at me. My mother had tried to convince her to stay for a few extra days, till she was completely healed, but she had refused. I don't feel safe here, she'd said then, a glare of anger and defiance in her eyes. Now she was holding herself still with the newborn in her lap, not looking to the right or left, absorbed by the street ahead.

My father called this taxi "the boat."

"I'm taking you to the train in a boat!" he said. He didn't want to say, I'm taking you to the train in Johnny's taxi.

I could feel he didn't want to acknowledge a debt to Mr. Giacomo, however small.

That 1964 Chevrolet convertible felt like a river scow, solid and slow. Now my father was turning up 2nd Street towards the tracks, taking the hill in a wide arc, hands climbing on the wheel as he leaned to the left to make the car more stable.

We passed by high-peaked houses with darkened verandas. I knew who lived in those 2nd Street houses, in every one. The Camozzis and the Sandezs, the Staglianos and the one-armed yard worker Danny Ote. I knew their lives, their memories; I'd known them for as long as I could remember. I felt held by those memories, held where I belonged. In our village, I knew I'd be cared for when the time came for me to be cared for. That's what Rose didn't have, and that's what she was looking for, I felt, starting with that baby in her arms.

I'd always felt that Mr. Giacomo didn't have the sense of being welcome in our village either, though he and his wife have lived here for many years. It's hard to say how I knew this. Then I realized many people in the village shared my feeling: there was a wary deference in the way people chatted with him in the street or in his café. Everyone called him Mr. Giacomo.

While Rose went into the lit-up station to buy tickets, my father carried her suitcases to the platform. I saw her under the yellow light of the station's tall windows, walking to the double doors that let out a vapour when they opened. I could hear the squeak of her suede boots in the new snow while she tried to walk in a normal, unaffected way. Carrying the newborn wrapped in a blanket, she stumbled once, tripped over her own feet.

My father gave me a twenty dollar bill. "Sweetheart, you look after her," he said. "Help her get settled." He wrote our phone number under the chin of the queen as if he thought that, once out of town, I'd never be able to remember it, then folded the bill twice before my eyes and drew my sleepy, half-frozen fingers out of my coat sleeve to close them over the folded bill.

All the anger and fear that I'd seen in his eyes when he'd found Mr. Giacomo in our house had faded. "You're right to get away," he'd told Rose in the car. "Mr. Giacomo isn't one to give up. Stubborn as a mule in the beginning, but he spoils everything he touches." Then he asked me to go with her, to help her get settled.

Now he said, "Call me from Field." He was such a quiet man; usually he hardly said anything.

Soon after the Giacomo baby's death, my mother told me that she didn't know what to do with herself. All the joy had gone out of her work. Standing there on the platform, I felt her entire desolation. I understood then that trying to replace that lost baby with Rose's wouldn't heal my mother. I was torn between going with Rose or going home to her. You can never tell how much you really matter. The kind of difference you make.

My father, watching Rose return from the station, said, "You *have* to go with her." He must have sensed my hesitation.

Carrying that baby, she was hurrying, and she looked at the same time vulnerable and alone, determined and scared.

She took me by the hand down the train corridor. We climbed into a narrow bed behind heavy curtains. I raised the blind to the lit-up platform that was rolling past at a walk, the clacking of the wheels and she on her side. Rose combed her hair while the newborn nursed at her breast. She had a nightshirt for me in a marbled green suitcase, warm from the stove where it had hung drying. Lying beside her I touched the little hollows in the small of her back that were the colour of pips left on raspberry canes after you pick the fruit.

The bed was narrow, and I felt pushed against the metal wall. The heavy curtain smelled of rug cleaner. Rose's feet were icy cold on my ankles. She said, "We're going," and I could sense her smile in the dark. She was going away to her new life, eighteen years old. People talk about responsibility, being mature, but they don't know what they're talking about. Mostly they mean, Do what I tell you. Outside I could see the dawn over the mountains through the flickering snow and when we went over the Palliser Bridge I saw my father's mill upriver on the bank, snow-covered ice in the shallows.

Rose handed me her sleeping baby and said, "Walk him a bit for me, won't you? I need to sleep."

I climbed through the curtains with the little one in my arms.

He hardly weighed more than the winter blanket I'd wrapped him in, and I felt his toes wriggling. I was worried that he might wake up and that I wouldn't know what to do. So I kept walking in the corridor, afraid that he would cry.

We were standing on the metal plates between cars and I was watching the mountains through a window opening that had no glass in it. Snow hissed over the face of the mountain. We were slowly climbing out of the valley and I drew the blanket loosely over Sen's face to keep him warm.

In the train bed she'd told me she'd decided to call him Sen.

I felt afraid without knowing why. In the village museum there are school photos from the 1920s: dirty-haired boys with wide, still eyes and girls with prim smiles, all out there in their faces – they had gone on to work in the saw-mill or drugstore, marriage, the house on 4th Street, the kids, a trip to Scotland or Italy, piling up experiences like money deposited in a bank. Then a car accident or a heart attack, a funeral and a mossy stone, mostly the usual thing. It all made me feel so tired.

But maybe a class photo, a bit of a second, was more than enough in any life, if you just paid attention to what you already have in your arms.

In the winter of 1964, when I was eleven, I sneaked out at night to go ice fishing on Olebar Lake. I took a flashlight and a yew wood reel. I had a mason jar of crayfish in my coat pocket. It was so cold that the ice hummed like a vio-lin string and stars glittered like a thousand miles of mica. Alberto Braz had marked the hole he'd chopped in the ice with a bundle of sticks tied with a ribbon that shimmered in the starlight. It was a long way out there and quiet and once I heard the huff of a moose in the dark firs along the far point. No one else on the lake that night, all the fishing huts closed up. I cleared ice out of the hole with my bare hands; I ran around in circles to attract fish by underwater vibrations. I laid the flashlight down, set my line, and soon I was hauling in trout after trout, little things with a blue and green speckle on their sides and the smell of archival water on them. Soon I had a heaped pile at my side with the ones on the outside beginning to freeze. Hungry, they just kept taking the bait.

There was no one else out there to see how lucky I was that night.

I kept looking around for someone to see what was happening.

And then, all of a sudden, I saw myself and what I had at my feet: way too many, too quickly and without much effort. Looking at the poor little things, I felt my stomach turn. I cleared away the frozen ones, the light had already gone out of their eyes. Five or six in the middle of the stack were still alive. Heartsick, I let them go.

Now I heard the car door slide open and Rose was standing beside me. To stay awake, I'd rested my forehead against the metal wall. The wind in the window opening was numbing my ears. The forest ran by and clefts in the rock peaks above were just beginning to show. After a while she said, "Give me him, I can't sleep."

When she returned to the sleeping car, I felt the train slow between high, sooty banks. We were climbing into the mountains. I walked through the dining car past linen-covered tables with flower vases bracketed to the wall and on each a peach in a silver bowl. An unripe peach is hard and sounds like an empty wooden box. The skin of a ripe one bunches under your thumb. I was hungry and tucked one under my shirt.

Then, thinking of Rose, I felt she was in trouble.

I hurried, almost ran back to our sleeping car.

I was remembering how in the fall of '68 Mr. Giacomo had paid us to find his horses that had come down from the alpage. I remembered that in the Slocan Gorge we could smell their grassy breath: his two buckskin horses were on the path. I could hear the clop of iron shoes and the suck of heavy shoes in the mud. They were coming down slowly, unsure, because the Palliser Range was buried in snow. In those days Mr. Giacomo was a trail guide, and he often took them into the mountains. They were coming down to their winter stables in the first snow.

"Lacey," Rose said then," it's Mr. Giacomo's horses."

To let them approach we stood by the path under the pines. I felt a warm muzzle brush my shoulder and arm. On their breath I could smell the sweet range grass that crackled when you walked through it. I could hear snow melting in the bearded moss that hung from the pines. The air had turned warm and it smelled of rain. Suddenly the horses tore away.

The clouds we'd seen south of there had gathered overhead. Hailstones raked through the pines. Shadows rolled over the mountainside and the air, suddenly cold, smelled like breath out of a well. We heard splintering wood in the trees across the ridge, then thunder heaved the forest floor.

I ran into the forest to press my forehead against a pine trunk. Whimpering, I locked my arms around the tree. Rose unlaced my fingers one by one.

"Look at me," she said, backing down the path, gazing into my wild eyes and holding me steady in her gaze. My hands clutched hers like old roots.

And now on the train I felt the same way, and I went looking for her.

When I got to the observation car, I heard Rose talking. She was sitting on the carpeted platform under the glass dome at the rear. Until I was beside them, I couldn't see that it was Mr. Giacomo she was talking with. He was wearing his sheepskin coat and riding boots. He was in one of those tall, cloth-covered observation chairs, his hands clasped between his knees. He must have walked to the station to get on the train before we did.

"You belong at home," he told Rose, adding, "Honey, you're leaving a good place behind."

"You really don't care about us," Rose said.

"What will you do away, in Field?"

"I'm going to work in a hotel." Rose looked at him defiantly.

"But who will look after your baby?"

Rose handed me the baby and unwrapped the cold omelet that she'd brought. She hurriedly and silently tore it to pieces to give me some. I could see her wrinkled brow and I saw her begin to hesitate.

So little warmth came through the blanket, it was almost like the baby wasn't there; a hand floated up to touch my cheek. He reminded me of an owl I'd found on the Palliser road, stunned by a car. I'd covered it with a beach towel to carry it to the gravel shoulder, wings tucked under my arm next to my rib cage so that it couldn't push them out. Though it was bigger than a cat, it weighed hardly anything, all feathers and hollow bones.

"We have to keep going," I told her. "It's what you wanted, remember?"

I could see that all her excitement at leaving for a new life was fading, worn away by her fear of being alone. There was a sudden desolation in her eyes. She was wrapping up the pieces of omelet that she'd left untouched, wrapping and unwrapping them as if not sure what to do with the food.

"Field is too far away," Mr. Giacomo nodded, watching her fumbling hands and mocking her gently. "Farther than Mrs. Hiraki's."

I hated his know-it-all patience then. He was trying to turn her around, turn her around with his mild confidence, his answers for every problem that she might have.

He was telling her that she could have the apartment above the Giacomo café and that she could work for him there. "Just a few afternoons a week to get you settled, then we'll see from there. You can stay with us as long as you like. Lacey here can visit when she wants."

"But he can't have two mothers," Mr. Giacomo advised her. "*Don't take away his good fortune.*"

He smiled and leaned in to touch my knee, as if to tell me that he was right or maybe to show that I agreed with him. I pulled away, shrank back in my seat.

"All right," I heard Rose say. "All right then. I can't do this on my own. I'm too scared."

"Thank you for helping me," she said to me. "Thank you! We're going back."

When I crawled under the blanket to hold Mrs. Giacomo after her baby died, I felt how icy cold she was, shivering, and now that cold grief flared through me.

Now, when anyone touches me, I pull away without thinking. Have you ever felt that way? It comes to me like a spark of static electricity, as when you barefoot it across a carpet on a dry morning and touch a door handle.

In the winter of '69, a few months after Rose met Michael Guzzo, I saw him in the Starlight Theatre.

In those days, my mother bought theatre tickets so she could sleep in the theatre. We'd go up the side aisle to where there was hardly anyone and wrap ourselves in blankets. She said she slept best in places where sleep surprised her, in the depot waiting for the bus to Naramata, on trains or in farm trucks returning home after a birth, jarring down the valley roads with a towel bunched on the rocker panel for a pillow, sleeping while the sun climbed over Odin Mountain, a dusty, rosy light flaring over the windshield. She slept a dreamless sleep and she awoke reluctantly, touching her dry lips and rubbing her eyes, looking around in all innocence or startled by where she was. Till all the worries rushed in, she briefly looked young and she had all the mussy-haired sleepiness of a little girl. Then she'd remember the Giacomo baby's death, but there was a moment or two when she didn't remember and I imagine the world was as it was, the flare of light on the Illecillewaet snowfields through the truck window, the long face of Cary Grant on the screen, the Palliser Valley orchards spreading by the bus window, and she was momentarily okay.

One night we were sitting below the prow, a little raised platform in the theatre where the sawmill crew usually sat.

Michael Guzzo had come in. My mother was asleep and I watched him take short steps down the aisle, feeling his way in the blinding screen light, turning to look over us. He smelled of cedar sawdust, and the sawmill crew called out as he went past,

Keep your head down, Guzzo, we can't see!

Where's Rose? someone in the crew called out.

Is she here?

He raised an embarrassed hand to brush away their laughter and to shield his eyes.

Yes, she was here somewhere.

They were showing *North by Northwest* and in the light of Mount Rushmore's face and Cary Grant's frantic running, I saw Rose reach up to take his hand and I heard her whisper:

It's you!

She took his hand to draw him down, and he put an arm around her to muss her hair.

I felt jealous then, watching how they sat so close together, and I wondered whether a boy would ever hold me like that.

How did he go from her life?

That winter he was only in town to earn money to travel. His uncle Paolo Pradolini, almost blind and no longer able to work, had bought an interest in the Odin Mill. He said he could get Michael a job there. I'd seen Paolo Pradolini now and then in town. He walked the sidewalks peering at you as if he thought he should recognize you in a smile of greeting, but you could tell that he wasn't sure, that faces were difficult for him. Finally, tired of the effort of recognition, he'd sit at a table outside the Giacomo café and play songs from the Aconcagua in the Argentine on a yellow accordion. Then he would smile.

He had a daughter my age — Maren was her name. I'd met her the summer I'd first met Rose, working in the Butucci orchards. We worked on a different crew and Maren and I never really became friends, though from a distance I liked her ability to climb and the way she teased the boss Alberto Braz. She tossed green peaches behind him as he walked the orchard floor, then climbed high in a tree before he could turn in his anger and locate the one who had thrown the unripe fruit. Later I heard that she'd run away, and I heard a rumour that she'd burned down the Giacomo house to stop her father from taking her to the Argentine. I never saw her again that summer.

The mill hired Michael as a family obligation, though he turned out to be a good worker, reliable, and even when they were cutting edge grain cedar for the Vancouver boatyards, he showed up for work, forearms bandaged because the oil in the dust raised welts on his skin.

Rose told me that he'd left to travel in Central America before she even knew she was pregnant.

The mill was going to shut down because of the coming snows, and he couldn't see sitting out the winter idle. He promised her that he'd be back in the spring, when the boss said they'd be rehiring.

Why are you going, Rose had asked him. They were sitting together on the narrow, cushioned seat by the linoleum table in his trailer on the Palliser, and she'd drawn away to look at him carefully.

She could see that this wasn't the whole truth. There was a sadness in him that she couldn't touch or hold or lessen, and it confused her.

He told her that he'd been drifting since his family had lost their land, their village, that he couldn't find a place to settle down in.

But you are coming back?

Yes, he reassured her.

There was a lake in Central America he wanted to see, in a volcanic crater where the Maya said clouds were born. Once in the Grizzly Bookstore he'd shown me a photo of it: there was a lone fisherman on a shore of pumice stones; bundles of sticks with ribbons tied to them showed against the water, and the sides of the crater, covered in pines, rose steeply all around. He had found this photo in a book at the back of the store, among the second-hand volumes he called train books.

What's so special about a lake? I asked him.

He closed the book then, touched its cover, a childlike, fragile look in his eyes that I felt drawn to.

Who knows what I'll find there? he said with a smile.

A sacred lake that he wanted to see. Have you ever felt that, amazed at what people do? That the wanting was enough for him to go? What are "wants"? And do they really matter that much, "I want this" and "I want that," and therefore I shall go. Doesn't it get a bit tiring after a while, wanting things? Don't you get worn out? What if you didn't want anything at all, what would happen to you then?

13

This morning I weeded the herb beds, painted the outhouse. I got a call from a lookout in the Asher Valley and went out on the catwalk to watch a narrow, boiling mass of clouds send bolts, some of them visible for seconds, into the ridge at my feet. I could hear the electricity zinging around the aluminum eavestroughs, crackling and sparking. Curtains of virga swept across Leon Creek.

Because maybe the cabin would be hit by lightning I knelt trembling on a stool with glass insulators in the bottom of the legs. Helicopters were in the air to the south, tracking three fires that I'd spotted. Every time I finished taking a bearing from the fire finder I'd look up to see another tree explode into flames before I could finish filling out the last message.

Later this evening, the unmistakable smell of wood smoke. I sat up in bed to look north and made out in moonlight a column rising straight up, thick with burning fir or pine pitch.

Because it was night, no one could be flown in to that fire in the Bremmer Valley. The road in was switchbacks through canyons, so it would take three or four hours to drive to the scene. High, strong winds, I write in the log book.

In the Bremmer Valley there's a wet hollow of alder saplings. I don't know how they got in there. The valley is narrow and dark and only gets a couple of afternoon hours of light. A raw wind must have carried in alder seeds, all at once, so that a field of them grew young and springy, their trunks no thicker than my thumb. Someone had tried to farm in there once, leaving only a fence line of rotten cedar posts grassed over, a scattering of lichen-covered apple trees that looked crouched and huddled in themselves, like cats moved into a new house, and a hollow for a root cellar.

A few weeks before Sen was born, I walked from the fire tower to the Bremmer Valley, to lay out an armful of alder saplings to dry in the field among the apple trees, shaking the soppy earth that was full of shale from their roots. A week later I took in a saw to cut off the root balls and I stripped the canes of withered leaves, carried them back to the cabin to weave into a crib. I wasn't sure it would ever be used but I wanted it just in case Rose needed me to take him. I'd offered to help her and I wanted to be sure I could. I laid in towels for bedding in a frilled pillowcase and tied to the side a mobile of painted pine cones that I knew would make her laugh, so that he'd have something to look at. I even made rockers out of bent saplings tied with fishing line and I placed it under the north window and moved my little collection of books to the east sill. Those were warm days, maybe the last of the season, and the fireweed was in second bloom along the Palliser Ridge. When I sat out on the catwalk for hours, it felt like midsummer and I could smell the heat in the cedar siding, waiting.

Whole days and nights went by, billowed in time, and I didn't know what was happening to her.

Now I see headlights on the dust roads, crews driving in to take out weekend campers and river runners. By now the fire is in the pine and fir, trees torching off like matchsticks on the slopes of Bremmer Mountain. Burning debris tumbles and ignites more fires across the Palliser Ridge.

Later this morning a cold front is supposed to move in, bringing sleet and rain.

14

When I had a few days off, a month or so after we returned on the train, I went down from the fire tower to see Rose in her new apartment and to serve at the parish supper. It was hard to see her, after her decision to return. She always looked tired, as if she wasn't sleeping well, worn and quiet.

Though she had her own place now, though she was still in our village, every day she grew more distant, more unreachable.

Yet when I asked her how she was, she'd say, Fine! and look at me defiantly.

It grieved me to be around her. All the lightheartedness had gone out of her step; she no longer laughed in that quick, bright way that made you feel good. Another time when I was in town I didn't even go see her. I told myself I was too busy.

On the first morning of preparations for the parish supper, I got up early because my mother was up: I could hear her in the kitchen. She was making toast and coffee though it was still dark outside and the birds were asleep. She was dressed as I've never seen her before, in loose, light blue cotton slacks and a plain blue blouse. She looked younger.

"Where are you going?" I asked, wondering at the brightness in her eyes. All the worry had gone from her face. Though she was no longer dressed as a midwife, I asked, half-asleep, confused, "Is someone having a baby?"

I looked around for her midwife's bag that she usually put on the kitchen table to check through before leaving.

"I've given that up," she said. "I've another job."

And in my astonished silence, she added:

"Cleaning rooms in the Mackenzie Hotel."

I'd never seen her smile like that. She looked wide-awake, as if she'd just come from a swim in the lake. She was making herself a bag lunch, slicing bread and laying lettuce and sliced tomatoes and shredded ham on it, her hands light and quick. She took a couple of apples out of the refrigerator and a handful of raisins. These she put in a paper bag and she took a thermos of tea.

In her old job, she never had time to make food to take with her. When the call came, she would just get up, check the contents of her bag and go. Usually the family would feed her. Now she had time to sit and drink coffee before she went to work. She got up early, to sit at the kitchen table and listen to the awakening birds. Sometimes, she told me, she even read a newspaper or listened to the radio. There was no hurry, no emergency.

She called her new job—cleaning toilets, she said: "I clean toilets in the Mackenzie Hotel"—the work of nonemergencies. She had no disasters to anticipate. No one was turning to her, full of pain, with a look that said, You're the only one here who knows what to do. Do something.

Lunch bag in hand, she said Mr. Giacomo had called to ask me to meet him by the river.

"He wants you to show him where to fish," she said. "For the parish supper."

On the Palliser banks, he asked me, "Do you think we'll have any luck?"

I said I didn't know.

We left the shore in his boat. I knew the deep pools under the bridge, where the sturgeon sleep like old dogs.

I remembered how he'd tried to touch my knee on the train and how my body had drawn away from him without even thinking. I didn't feel that I was myself around him anymore. It slowly settled in me that I was growing even more afraid of him. His smile was calm and inviting, the friendliest thing about him, but it made me afraid.

The metal line he let out had thread woven over it the colour of the shadows that flowed along the river bottom. The tip of his fishing rod was as thick as his thumb. The river was littered with alder leaves, so many coloured with a blue bloom, like ripe plums.

I counted eight boats on the sturgeon pool under the bridge. Every year at this time the village fished the river. By agreement only one sturgeon was taken, and it was offered to the priest.

"Since the death of our boy," he said, "my wife and me are like old people." He laughed. "We must look like we're cut out of cardboard! I believe people here see us that way," touching the corners of his eyes. When he looked at me his eyes were full of shame.

"Mrs. Giacomo hasn't left her room for weeks. Do you think Rose is going to keep her child? It must be so hard for her."

His face showed the same quiet patience that I'd seen on the train.

The sky had settled over the river and already a few flakes were falling; almost like night the way the light had faded, the snow beginning to cling to the sandbar. The jacket he handed me smelled of wood smoke, of the campfires the village had lit on the sandbar while we fished for the new priest and of the gasoline he'd poured into the outboard motor tank. He draped the jacket over my knees with raw hands touched by the cold, his knuckles swollen. He was massaging his knuckles and I wanted to give him my mitts but he said no, he was fine.

"Of course she's going to keep the baby," I said then. I'd put on a look of complete confidence. "Your helping her isn't going to make any difference."

For awhile he looked at me quietly. "Well that's it, then," he said. "I guess there's nothing more I can do."

He looked at me again and in his eyes there were still flashes of hope. "Rose has changed her mind before," he said. "Maybe she'll change it again."

In the stern at his feet there were paper lanterns with cut-outs pasted to them: horses and stars, half-moons, birds. Those were lanterns for the parish supper. Mr. Giacomo had brought them along for me to repair. I reglued the curled arms of foil stars, horses' heads, crumpled birds' wings that the Grade Twos had made from construction paper, finger-tips numb in the river wind that came up in the morning.

He asked me if we should pull up our lines to try another pool, but I didn't know for sure, and briefly his face looked sad. He couldn't fish in one place for fear the fish might be caught in another. I really don't know the river that well: a lot of easy and broken water, light and dark places.

He touched the corners of his eyes. I wondered then why he did that so often, then I felt it was the nervous gesture of a man who was no longer confident in himself. His face was almost grey in the cold mist rising from the river.

I thought about what he'd said: about how he thought people in the village saw him and his wife in their grief. Like old, used-up people, he'd said, like cardboard cut-outs.

He wanted a place of honour in our village. He'd always wanted to be among the best people, to fit in that way. Yet his wealth had not been enough to guarantee the health of his family, the respect of our village. You could see he felt he'd come so close, with his son and then with Rose, and now, in his confusion, he didn't know what to do. Maybe it's okay to have goals in life. But maybe you'd better accept they're unattainable, so that all you can hope to do is get a little closer.

"I'm sorry," I said to him then. "It can't be helped."

It was not Mr. Giacomo's boat that caught the priest's fish. Mr. Beruski caught it. Early afternoon, by way of a gaff-hook in its jaw, Mr. Beruski pulled the sturgeon onto the sandbar. It was lying on its side, gasping, and I covered its black eye with my hand.

"Over one hundred pounds," said Mr. Giacomo. He walked its length, prodding its belly full of roe, a disappointed look on his face.

Sometimes I look for a change in my luck too. The morning before I came down from the fire tower to serve at the parish supper, I saw three crows fly by the north window, each making the point of a triangle and I said to myself that's a sign things are going to get better for my friend Rose. I was that desperate for encouragement.

Later that afternoon, pulling handfuls of soppy rotten leaves from the rain gutters on our house, I saw my mother hurry across the street. She'd been working at the hotel, lost track of time, and wanted to be home waiting for my father who was down at his one-vat mill. On the ladder I saw what she hadn't noticed—that he, too, was in the street. He had stepped behind a transport truck so that she wouldn't see him under the street light that had just come on. This was a new game that they played, the waiting for each other. For the pleasure of seeing you. If she had slipped and fallen in the icy street he would have run to her. Her new life of nonemergencies was making her happy again, and so he was happy.

15

Four men carried the fish to the priest. With the sturgeon wrapped in a black tarp, they stood at the church doors. They had brought it up a river path, then along 3rd Street to the church. Although Mr. Giacomo was at the head walking with Rose in her waitress outfit, the others did not allow him to carry any of the weight. He might as well have been carrying air. He pretended for the onlookers, but his arms were slack. I saw this, standing on the corner of 3rd Street and Columbia Avenue.

In our village, when people make up their mind that you're generally more trouble than you're worth, the hints at first are often subtle. There was this drifter who took a job on the green chain at the Odin Mill. Things started to go missing: gloves, work boots, a sandwich from a lunch pail.

One day he sat down at the lunch table to pour tea from his thermos. What spilled out into his cup was bunker oil. No one said anything, the whole crew was there at the lunch table, watching. He quit within the week, took his pay and left.

People could see what was happening with Rose, I wasn't the only one. People could see how worn and tired she'd become, that a wall had been put up around her. I sensed this in the way others looked at her in the café when she was serving.

Earlier in her room above the café I'd brought Rose the rust-coloured paper raincoat I'd found in the Grizzly Book-store. I told her that the procession was about to start and that Mr. Giacomo was waiting for her by the river. I said she could wear the paper raincoat in the procession. On an unpainted wooden table there were roadside cornflowers in a slender vase, their leaves curled and withered. She had changed into her waitress clothes to go to work in the Gia-como café and was combing out her hair that clung to the brush with static.

Along the sill, light played on small pieces of driftwood she'd collected. On one she'd painted, bright blue, the eye of a fish because it looked like a fish and on another she'd painted a horse's mane. She'd sanded the pieces and polished them with beeswax. Light spilled over them as the shine spilled on her combed hair. After I picked one up, my hand smelled faintly of honey.

She said, "Early in the morning before shift we go along the river to find new pieces he can play with. I like to make my own things for him."

"I couldn't see myself in Field," she said. "I felt scared thinking about it. Still, I've got to figure out a way to get my life back."

She had no dresser, so her clothes were carefully folded in the two open suitcases she had taken on the train to Field. The baby's clothes were stored in bins under the second-hand crib my mother had bought for her, and he was asleep in there. Because the apartment was above the café, she only had to walk downstairs to work, and she would call the bar telephone and leave hers off the hook so that she could hear his cries should he awake while she was working. She hadn't put up curtains because she didn't know how long she would be there. After her shift she'd carry up a plate of leftovers to make baby food – whirred squash or peas and pabulum – in a blender that she'd take apart and leave to clean in the sink. There was no music or radio and all you could hear was the traffic in Columbia Avenue or the crackle of the frost melting on the east windows when the sun came up over the alley at midmorning; she had a towel bunched there to collect the dripping water.

The place filled me with silence, the silence of waiting and of being unsure of yourself. It made me feel quiet and expectant and I didn't know what I was waiting for. Even the creak of the floorboards sounded loud and edgy, maybe because there was hardly any furniture and the echoing ceiling sloped on two sides to join the walls at shoulder height.

I'd bought the paper raincoat for her, thinking she'd like to wear it, but she laughed and said no, turning down my gift.

She held the raincoat up to herself to check the fit; it had the luminescence of corn snow. It had been waterproofed with persimmon tannin.

"No," she said again, stroking out a sleeve to flatten it along her arm, "Honey I don't think so. Mr. Giacomo won't like it. He wants me to show up in my waitress things, to represent the café."

"Why don't *you* wear it?" she asked.

I thought that she would have been bold enough to wear it in the procession, to stand up to him, but I was wrong. Her laughter had sounded sharp and false.

"Do you like this place?" I asked her.

Now she looked at me thoughtfully. She picked up her brush and wrinkled her brow.

"You're my friend, right?"

"Yes, Rose," I nodded.

"No, I don't like this place. It doesn't feel right."

"Why not?"

"It doesn't feel like my home. I always feel we're being watched. I can't go anywhere without Mr. Giacomo asking, Where are you going? When will you be back? I try to pretend that we're okay but we're not."

At that moment she had lost her defiant, determined look. It no longer felt like she was pushing me away, and I could see how lonely and vulnerable she had become. I felt then that I could help her, and a memory came to me.

"Do you remember the night we went wading in the lake in the snow, when that house came out of the mist?"

She nodded, smiling.

"And Mr. Giacomo in the window?"

"Yes."

"Do you remember how anxious and worried he sounded when he called out to us, Who's there? Can't you hear Mr. Giacomo saying to your boy, Where are you going?, When will you be back?, while he grows up in that Burnham house? And where will *you* be?"

"Why is he that way?"

"I don't know," I said then. "I feel he's always trying to hide something."

She was sitting at the table by the window, the hairbrush in her hand. I bent down and gave her a kiss.

16

Each year I have to climb farther, a little farther, a few hundred yards or so, to bury my father's paper in the snowfields. Everywhere there is reflected light.

The morning of the parish supper, before I loaded the truck to drive up to the snowfields, my father laid out a two-by-three-foot sheet on his work table. You could see the impression of the grain of the yew wood drying board on it, under a powder snow luster. It smelled like straw.

Lacey, he said to me, running his hand over it, not one flaw, not one impurity. It's like a new human soul.

I drove up to the snowfields to lay out the paper and cover it with snow. Those sheets were translucent and they had a fine satiny sheen. Because of their purity, they'd last maybe hundreds of years. They were so strong you could pass them through a finger ring and they wouldn't shred.

They would outlast me.

I thought of all those trout I caught when I was eleven years old. I knew the ones on the outside of the pile were already dead: all the light had gone out of their eyes. No light, no life.

When I got back to town, I went over to the Burnham house. I'd heard that work had stopped there and I took along *A Catalogue of Unrecovered Items, Volume Four: Pottery and Clay Figurines*, a train book that I'd found in the carton of books Michael Guzzo had left with me when he went travelling. It was published by the Allied Powers after the war. In the introduction it says that the catalogued items, some of them identified by insurance photographs, were never recovered during the occupation of Japan, and the purpose of the catalogue, in several volumes, was to pass on the work of recovery to future generations.

The kitchen was still filled with unpacked boxes, the green cushion from the sofa in the downstairs hallway was still on Mrs. Giacomo's bed. I could hear the garden hose dripping in the kitchen sink. I ran my hand along the plaster walls, smooth as a yew wood drying board. They gave off a soft glow and they smelled like chalk. There were footprints up and down the hallway in the plaster dust, some of them my own. The propane heaters stood collected at the doorway. The camp stove still had a pot on it, a thin skin of dust on the bottom of the pot. The two clay bowls that Mr. Giacomo wanted to drink from in celebration were still on the counter. I leafed through the book, found the photo I was looking for. Those bowls were from the Tokugawa period, just as Mr. Giacomo had said, the potter's mark incised in the base. His wealth hadn't come from logging in the Nachako country. His wealth had come from artifacts he'd stolen at the end of the war. He had worked as a translator on Shido Island and used his knowledge to profit from the war.

I hated him then. I hated his lies, the sham way he'd gone about making a place for himself in our life. I hated him and Mrs. Giacomo, too, for the way they were trying to wall Rose in with their grief.

I pocketed one of those bowls. I stayed for an hour or so, lit candles that sputtered and crackled. I looked through Mrs. Giacomo's dresser drawers for her clothes and I looked under the foyer bench for any sign of recently worn shoes. I found out later she had left, maybe soon after the birth, moved back to their house on 4th Street, where she stayed alone in her room.

I went to look for Rose in the Giacomo café. She was disinfecting the kitchen counter where the fish would be prepared; her hands and arms, flushed to the elbows, smelled of bleach. Mr. Giacomo asked me to help him carry glass panes and the winter door up from the café cellar. We unhinged the sidewalk shutters, unscrewed the hinges from the cedar sash and fitted in winter storm panes and the pine wood door. Watching us, some passersby stood for a moment under the awning, under a darkening sky.

All the storefronts were lit up and the sky had turned a dark grey. Trees on the mountain stirred. In the café washroom, I folded and rolled an evening's fresh towels and placed them in the v-shaped rack by the sink.

When I came into the dining room, Rose was standing by the bar.

"I'm going back to the Big Bend to live with my parents," she announced.

"Oh, you'll not be leaving," Mr. Giacomo said and he touched her ducked head, laughing and smiling at me. "This is where you belong."

I couldn't imagine Mr. Giacomo touching me like that; it just seemed impossible that you'd allow him to touch you.

All of a sudden I felt very tired, and I went to sit in a chair by the window. It smelled of varnish because Mr. Giacomo had varnished the sill. I was wearing a loose-knit sweater that I'd bought in the Grizzly Bookstore. It felt like the weight of an extra blanket, because in one pocket there was a folded page torn from A Catalogue Of Unrecovered Items and in the other a Japanese bowl.

Rose came up behind me, to drape her arms over my shoulders. I couldn't see her eyes and I couldn't imagine the expression in them. I could feel the light weight of her forearms on my shoulders, the stillness of her gaze. I could see the freckles on the back of her hands and on her wrists that smelled of bleach. Under her resting arms I felt like a bundle of tense sticks.

To free myself, I leaned forward to rest my fingertips on the sill. The varnish gripped my fingertips when I touched it, like frost on a metal door handle.

I have to get ready for the supper, Rose said, and she went back to the kitchen.

I went over to Mr. Giacomo's table. I laid out before him the book page from my pocket and the Japanese bowl. I placed the bowl very tenderly, gently before him, quietly, like in the stillness when the hawk comes. I smoothed out the page with the photograph on it as though it were a precious sheet, pure washi. I felt that something inside me was just about to break. He stared at them, and then at me.

I didn't want him to have the whole book, just that page. Maybe he had other things that were in that book. But I only knew about the bowls, so that was all I could accuse him of.

The crinkles at his eyes deepened and paled, but he smiled.

"So you know," he said, and I nodded.

"They had lost the war," he smiled, "the ones we interrogated. The crown prince, the naval officers. We only took from them what they'd already stolen during their retreat."

He paused, and a shadow drew into his eyes. "That happened so long ago," he said, a softness in his voice. "It's not something I think about often."

I started yelling at him then. I told him not to waste his confident smile on me. It might look like he was trying to help Rose, but he was just hemming her in with his deceit. And nothing he had to offer was worth one touch of her freckled hands, one moment of her dancer's grace.

Just then Rose came out of the kitchen. "What's going on?" she asked.

"Nothing!" and he quickly balled up the sheet and pocketed it, put the bowl on a glass shelf behind the bar, by the upturned wineglasses.

That was almost the last time I spoke to Mr. Giacomo.

I left, didn't stay for the parish supper. I was shaking, exhausted, and yet I felt a kind of joy. I walked down our main street towards the tracks, hating his complacent smile, hating the fact that he didn't seem to care about what I felt.

He was going to have his family his own way, at whatever the cost. But I wasn't going to let him.

What if Michael Guzzo found out that he was a father? With all the loss that he'd had in his life, maybe this was one loss he wouldn't allow to happen, pushed out of the life of his son. Maybe it would be important for him to say to the Giacomos, Enough, this you can't take from me.

17

Yesterday, when I got back to the fire tower from my days off, I brought along the plane ticket I'd bought to San Diego. From there I'd take a bus through Mexico to save money. I knew that Michael Guzzo was somewhere in Guatemala. The photo that he'd shown me was of a sacred lake in the district of Huehuetenango, in the western highlands of that country. I'd decided to go find him.

As soon as I got in the door I saw that the cabin was not as I'd left it: my bed had been pushed to the north wall, the chrome-legged chairs had been moved from the east to the west window, my basil plants shuffled along the banister, the cutlery switched in the hutch, the stacked dishes pushed back on the counter. Nothing was where it was and I felt terrified, as if this place were not mine, as if I'd lost my life.

One book was missing from my collection on the east sill, the Catalogue of Unrecovered Items.

Just at dawn, the sound of dripping water. Everywhere I could hear melting snow. Today the cabin is to be boarded up for the winter, plywood nailed over glass, the doors locked. Through the window by my bed, I see snow water flowing over frost on a rock outcrop that looks like strands of a girl's hair. Lightning storms that used to sweep through this valley go on the other side of the foot-hills. Now I see smoke from campfires on Olebar Lake.

Below in the village, people are turning on their breakfast lights.

The logging fires are still smouldering on the Palliser Ridge, a white, drifting smoke that reminds me of washi paper.

When I applied for this job, the Forestry Service questioned my young age, my ability to be alone. That age and loneliness go together is not questioned.

When I was younger, I was more sure of myself, and now I feel porous, less contained, like a sheet of my father's washi. I go out of here in dreams and when I nod off I sometimes can't tell the difference between dream and memory and when I awake I look on myself as a stranger.

There is a squirrel sleeping in the wall; during the day it raids the bird feeders.

The pines below the ridge are singing. I can smell the resin in the swaying trunks. Last night's stars have a scoured midwinter sharpness. Outside the west window, one last star shows its grape petal rays.

There really are so many ways to be a little more gentle in this world.

PART III

SANCTUARY

SANCTUARY

Chiapas, Mexico 198_

1

For two weeks they have waited to cross the border into Guatemala, to return to their village. They number over three hundred men, women and children. School buses have sat for days on the other side of the checkpoint, waiting to take them home. Despite reassurances from the Capital and from the army that they will not be touched, they refuse to cross.

Among them is Bernabe Mateas, a teacher in a one-room school in the highlands of his country. The events that have led him here go way back, to the town of his birth. It is often true that we cannot leave behind where we have been, the events and relationships that have shaped us, because they are already coming toward us, out of the future. Memory is like a beacon that now lights up the past, now the future.

He grew up in Jacaltenango. His parents owned a store in town and his mother was a seamstress. On festival days his family went to Tzisbaj and San Antonio Huista, to set up their stall, their manteado. They sold the blouses his mother made on her old manual Singer sewing machine and typical skirts brought from San Sebastian, Huehuetenango. They were a very religious family and Bernabe loved to go to the festivals, especially the one in San Miguel Acatan, because of the famous marimba. It was a long climb to get across many arroyos and rivers and over many hills that were very steep, and once his father, who was not well, became gravely ill. There was no doctor or clinic in San Miguel. Through great difficulties they managed to return to Jacaltenango, but his father died shortly afterwards. Bernabe was fourteen and his brother Carlos twelve. Their father's death was devastating for their family: they sank into a depression that lasted for months, and eventually their mother had to give up their store in town. In the nearby aldea of El Tablon she had a small plot of land that she tended, and now and then, to keep her sons alive, she'd make blouses to sell to the Jacaltec women. She hardly spoke and spent most of her waking hours alone in the fields or with her medicinal plants — it was her way of dealing with her grief.

Bernabe became angry — at her for her silence, at his father for leaving them so poor. He took up with some kids who were running cocaine from Honduras to the Mexican border. Soon he had money in his pockets, and he left to join a gang in the Capital, where he'd heard there was even more money to be made. The gang was called Barrio 16. Even now he won't say much about that time, except that he was involved in things that still shame him and give him nightmares.

For two years he had almost no news from home. Once he heard that Canadians were planning a gold mine in his Department, and he hoped that the Canadian mine would bring his village some measure of prosperity.

He hung out in the streets of zone 18. Because there really wasn't a lot to do most of the time, he learned to play marimba. He was particularly good at the music of his highland mountains that he'd heard since childhood, and was often called on to take a place beside others at the marimba. Soon he found he loved playing marimba more than the money and prestige that came with being a member of Barrio 16. His dream was to return to San Miguel, to play during the festival there. One morning he got up early, the gang members all lived in a house in the 18th district, quietly gathered his things and left, caught the bus to Huehue. From that city he caught another, regional bus to El Tablon, the village of his birth where his mother lived on her small plot of land.

His mother was overjoyed to see him. She led him into the house to cook some kale and beans for him. She looked much better than he remembered her from two years ago. There was new light in her eyes and she had put on weight. The house was surrounded by tall corn, a healthy green that he'd never seen in the family crops before and her little garden of medicinal plants was flourishing.

He asked about his younger brother Carlos. It turned out that, a year earlier, he'd attended a demonstration against the Canadian mine in their Department.

In order to accommodate the mine's need for land, many people were forced to leave their small farms.

Carlos had received a warning that he had been photographed at the demonstration and that it would be best if he left the country.

He'd gone to Los Estados. He was established in Florida and was sending home money regularly.

Because his mother was alone, Bernabe decided to stay on to help with the crops. The festival in San Miguel was a few months away. Besides, he remembered how his father had loved his milpa, how every year he'd give each plant careful attention, and he wanted to know what it felt like, to really care from day to day for the crops you grew. Besides, he was ashamed at abandoning his mother in her grief and wanted to show her that he was worthy of her love and forgiveness.

He was not prepared for the hard work.

He'd grown soft in the Capital during the many idle hours and days of gang life and his hands soon blistered wielding the azadon. His family didn't have the best soil and his azadon would often strike stone, blunting the blade. Soon he was frustrated and angry. One morning he threw down the hoe and his mother, who was working ahead, looked up at him out of her mild, kind eyes. He'd quickly recalled something of the technique of hoeing from his childhood, but his uncalloused hands resisted what they were once capable of. He realized that even a humble task like hoeing takes patience, a lifetime of patience, and he was hoping to impress her with his willing usefulness.

No land welcomes you right away, she said to him then, smiling. The soil takes its own time to trust you, and it's a long time. She picked up the hoe that he'd tossed, carefully brushing the handle and then she handed it back to him.

She tried to teach him about the medicinal plants that she grew. In their village she would help sick children or poor women with food or natural medicine. She was considered a good curandera with a good heart.

He learned about the use of encino to cure skin infections and el eucalipto for coughs. However he was too impatient to really learn what she wanted to teach him, mainly because he could see no use for such knowledge in his life: he didn't really want to become a curandero. Soon she sensed his boredom and impatience and stopped talking of her precious plants.

One day they got word that a telegram from Los Estados was waiting for them in Huehuetenango, a city four or five hours by bus to the southeast of their village. They knew that it was either from or about his younger brother Carlos and that it was very likely bad news.

Bernabe immediately caught the bus to Huehue. The telegram announced that his brother had been in a car accident in Indiantown, Florida and that he was in hospital. Four others in the car had died, including two young men from their village, Juan Vargas Lopez and Juan Soto.

His mother agreed that Bernabe would leave for Los Estados immediately. To pay for the journey, she mortgaged her land to Pedro Lopez, a store owner in their village. If Bernabe didn't pay off the loan within a year, his mother's land would be forfeited.

In La Trinitaria Mexico he caught a bus to Mexico City. He got off before the bus entered the outlying districts of the city and walked the backroads north, then caught a bus farther on. He'd heard that it was dangerous to go into Mexico City, that he would be easily spotted by the police or the city gangs as an undocumented migrant. He could be robbed, kidnapped or even killed. In a small Sonoran town he waited for the weather to clear to cross the border. The guides who do business there told him when it was safe to cross and how to find his way. He walked toward a mountain peak that he was told was in Los Estados.

He was crossing the Arizona desert at night when it began to rain. In an arroyo, he came to a wooden shelter at the entrance to what looked like an abandoned mine. Some traveller like himself had left a stack of ocote there and there was a well-used fire pit carefully ringed with stones, with some charcoaled pieces of ocote in it. To dry his clothing and warm himself, he made the mistake of lighting a fire. Soon the Border Patrol — La Migra — were on him, flashlight beams stabbing in the dark: they must have been watching from the hills.

They took him to the federal detention centre in Florence, Arizona. There were other captured men and women in the back of the van: from Huehuetenango and San Marcos in the northwestern highlands, K'iche' Maya from Quetzaltenango and Mixteca people from Oaxaca, Mexico. What had been their mistake? In the rain, they had lit fires where the Migra expected them to light fires, had even left caches of ocote for them to use.

In the Detention Centre there were 425 beds, 100 for non-criminal aliens such as himself. Two weeks later, to determine asylum eligibility, he was led into a room where an officer asked him questions:

"What would happen if you were sent home?"

He explained that in his absence the army would assume he'd become a subversive, as they had accused his brother. His life was now in danger.

When he was released with a petition for asylum, he headed for La Huerta, an orchard near Ft. Smith Arizona.

In that orchard Bernabe made a shelter out of a piece of plastic draped over the branches of an orange tree and rags and blankets spread on the ground. Rain had been steady for a week. A woman from El Tumabor in San Marcos gave him the plastic; men from San Juan Ixcoy and San Rafael la Independencia in Huehuetenango gave him the rags and blankets. When the Migra showed up that afternoon, they vanished into rows of orange trees that looked like any other row, under thick foliage. Many in the orchard lacked the appropriate papers and even those who had them feared that their papers would be torn up, that they, too, would be deported.

Church people brought food in the evening: pots and tubs of steaming beans and stew, sandwiches, sweet rolls, coffee and juice. They drove up quickly and just as quickly, forty or fifty men, women and children appeared out of the trees. Bernabe looked around, astonished: these were all people from his country, from Departments that he'd only heard of or sometimes passed through on a bus to the Capital.

He watched a nurse listen to the chest of a sick child, hand out medications to the parents. Six young men from Barillas, speaking softly in Q'anjob'al, lined up before her and she gave them injections.

"What is that for?," he asked.

In Spanish she replied, "Vaccinations against measles, typhoid, diphtheria."

She gave him a black garbage bag to use as a raincoat.

Just as the church people were leaving, vans with Florida or North Carolina plates began to circle the orchard. Bernabe flagged one down. He made a deal with others to get to Indiantown, Florida. They made the trip in two days, the van only stopping for refuelling, the two drivers taking turns sleeping.

Indiantown: El Pueblo de los Indios, easy enough to remember — a town for Indians in Florida.

Early in the morning they let him off on Magnolia St., where men and women were already gathered, to be picked up for work. The air was humid, still, and he could smell the nearby lemon groves. The street was swept clean and reflected the fading lavender light of a Florida night sky.

He wanted to get to the hospital to see his brother immediately. He asked a migrant worker where the Martin Emergency Centre was. This man was talking with others, laughing over some joke they'd shared. Something in his kind, gentle face, in the humour in his eyes, something also in the way the others listened to him with deference made Bernabe think that he was both liked and a man of authority.

The question about the location of the hospital extinguished the smile in the worker's eyes.

He became very grave and took Bernabe aside to ask why he wanted to go there. The others looked on in silence. Bernabe replied that many weeks ago he had received a telegram saying that his brother Carlos Mateas was in a car accident, that he was in Martin Emergency Centre and that he'd travelled thousands of kilometres to find him.

He could see that this man was torn between going to work and helping him: already vans were pulling up to take these men and women to the citrus groves and into the winter vegetable fields.

He spoke to the group he'd been joking with, saying he'd be along later if he could find a ride. Once again they looked on Bernabe in silence, their faces expressionless.

"My name is Andreas Tomas. Come with me," he said, and they walked south down Dr. Martin Luther King Jr. Drive, past the New Bethel Church, past a low, tin-roofed house made of blue-painted bricks. Many of the houses were on scrubland, hardly tended, and south of there Bernabe could see the well-tended lemon groves.

He took Bernabe to an apartment block called Blue Camp, named after an ancient layer of peeling paint.

The walls of Andreas Tomas' room were covered in family photos, pictures of saints and a magazine photo of the local San Miguel festival. On one wall he had carefully hung a child's traditional blouse and sash in the pattern of his region. He opened a closet to show Bernabe rows of audio cassettes that contained messages from friends and relatives back home: news of baptisms and weddings and warnings for people who lived in Indiantown that they should not return home because the army was looking for them.

He showed his guest the rest of the apartment: the tiny kitchen, the living room and the one other bedroom, both of which were divided into many sleeping quarters by blankets hung from the ceiling. The only common area was a large plank table off the kitchen where the people who slept and ate there could visit. He showed Bernabe a place in one of those divided rooms where he could sleep that evening.

Bernabe protested that he had to get to the hospital immediately and that, not knowing how far away the hospital was or his brother's condition, he didn't know if he would return that evening.

"You don't need to go to the hospital," Andreas said.

He took Bernabe outside to show him his brother's grave.

Andreas explained that Carlos had died of his injuries shortly after the telegram was sent and that he himself had sent the telegram. He had founded the Aguacatan burial society, to help pay the funeral expenses of illegal immigrants who died there and, when possible, to send the bodies home.

"We are not permitted to use the local cemetery," Andreas said, "so we bury our people here, under this hickory grove, or we send them home."

Bernabe was beside himself with grief and disappointment.

It felt like he'd come all that way for nothing. Still, when you've suffered such a loss, you're less likely to get confused. He knew he had to accomplish two things: pay off the loan on his mother's land and send his brother's body home for proper burial.

That day he wired a telegram to his mother, saying that Carlos had died and that he would ship his body home soon. He imagined the grief this would cause her and he felt anguish at the thought that he couldn't be there to comfort her.

The next few weeks passed in a blur. He worked long hours in the winter vegetable fields, picking cucumbers and tomatoes that grew on stakes. In the evening he negotiated a loan from the Aguacatan society to send his brother home so that his soul could dwell in their village where it would be properly honoured and remembered. Every waking hour he worked hard to numb his grief and at night when the vans came to take them from the fields when it became too dark to see, he fell into bed, into a sleep of exhaustion. Every day he calculated and worked, calculated and worked, reckoning how he was to pay off the loan on his mother's land before it was forfeited, knowing that she had already suffered too much loss in her life.

That was the winter of 1962. On December 12th, a bitter frost descended on southern Florida. The silence woke him, a silence more silent than he'd ever heard. A sudden night cold that falls on the world absorbs all sounds. Stepping over sleeping bodies, making his way through the hanging blankets that partitioned the room, he went outside to see what was going on. The sky was alight with the harsh glitter of the Southern Cross and the constellation called Gemini. The grass crackled underfoot and the street power lines glittered in the moonlight. He walked to the Becker groves. The oranges that he touched there were as hard as stone. The leaves rattled like glass. All breath had gone out of the silent trees.

Then all of a sudden it began. The whole grove was filled with a muted splintering. Bernabe put his hand on a trunk. He felt it trembling; from inside he could feel the freezing sap tear the heart wood.

After that terrible night in which thousands of trees died, they worked every day and long into the night picking any fruit that could be salvaged for juice.

After that there was nothing – no work.

One day he went down to Magnolia St. with Andreas Tomas and stood there among dozens of others and no vans came to pick them up. They realized then there would be no work for months, till a new crop of winter vegetables ripened.

Bernabe stood by Andreas Tomas, thinking that he would be one to get work, if anyone could. He was desperate: though he had sent down regular payments, he hadn't paid off the loan on his mother's land. Several workers waited long past the time when many others had given up and returned to Blue Camp because Andreas Tomas waited, telling them of his life in Aguacatan.

Finally a van with North Carolina plates drove up. The driver introduced himself as a Mr. Beecher.

"I heard there were people like you here," he said. "I've driven all night to find you."

"Better pay," he said. "Inside work. That's what I'm offering you."

Bernabe climbed into the back of the van with nine others. Andreas Tomas stayed behind. He explained that many people in Blue Camp depended on him and that he couldn't leave on such short notice: he had to ensure that people without work were fed and attended to when they became sick and he had to ensure that the Aguacatan burial society continued to function. He closed the van door, gave it a rap — a kind of blessing I suppose — and they drove away.

Twenty hours later Bernabe stepped out of the van into Morgantown, North Carolina.

He rubbed his eyes, looking around. He saw mountains. On one he recognized oak and pine. Storm clouds were blowing over it, trailing rain.

Those mountains reminded him of the ones that surrounded his home village, though the clouds were different.

Here they were heavy, grey with rain, and they turned like a river pool in summer, muddy and slow. The North Carolina mountains shouldered them and drew them in close and laid them over the forests. To the east he could see the sky clearing. Wind and sunlight and rain.

That night, after he was set up in a trailer on Jefferson St. with three others, Bernabe went out to walk the back streets. On telephone poles he saw flyers telling of work in Athens, work in Cumming, work in Canton: Trabajo. Pollo. Llamada 549-6006. $3.50 par hora. He saw a line of four children with a man trailing behind them, twitching a long stick at their heels.

Something in his walk reminded Bernabe of the men of his Department and he called out in their native language,

"How long have you been here?"

"I don't remember," the man replied. He was wearing rubber boots, corduroy pants and a plastic apron. He wore a capixayes — a black woolen tunic typical of men from their region.

"I'm on my way to work. I work on the Perdue trim line."

"What do they pay you?" Bernabe asked.

"Three dollars an hour."

"You can make $3.50 in Athens," he said, pointing to a flyer.

The Perdue worker laughed. "Sure," he said, "and when they take off money for your apron and your gloves and for housing and your boots, you're lucky if you have anything left."

"Who are you working for?" he asked Bernabe.

"Mr. Beecher," he replied.

"Cargill," he warned. "They're okay. But if you get hurt, they won't stand by you. You'll be out the door in no time. Be careful."

Then he turned to walk away, twitching the stick at the heels of his children.

"What are you doing?" Bernabe called after him.

"Teaching them to walk," he replied.

The next morning at 4 AM a van pulled up outside the trailer Bernabe shared with three others. They were taken to the processing plant. The cold, damp air smelled of rain and of pine. Though it was still dark, he could feel the mountains nearby. He felt they would protect him.

Because he worked hard for long hours and wouldn't turn down any work, no matter how difficult or tiring, he was given many relief jobs in the plant. Sometimes he worked in the blue room, where he pulled live, scratching chickens out of crates to hang them on a line that dipped them into a vat of cold, electrified water, to stun them; sometimes he worked on the trim line, slicing meat from carcasses that went by on metal cones. After a few months of this, his fingers grew numb and his wrists flared with pain.

Still, he would not stop working; he cursed his body for its softness and he grew heartsick at the thought that he would not be able to pay off his mother's loan or the loan he'd taken from the Aguacatan burial society to send his brother home.

Though he was exhausted, he was also restless and could hardly sleep.

At night, so as to not disturb the others in the trailer, he'd go out to walk the back streets of Morgantown, and sometimes he'd walk into the mountains that smelled of pine and oak.

One night he came across the man from his region who was teaching his young children to walk, twitching a stick at their heels. He asked Bernabe how his work at Cargill was going. Under a street lamp Bernabe showed him his swollen hands and wrists.

The Perdue worker said that his condition was serious, that he'd seen many end up like Bernabe, and that soon he'd have to give up work in the plant because he would no longer be able to work at the necessary speed and with the necessary precision.

"You'll see," he told Bernabe. "The pain will become too much. Then they'll replace you with someone else they've picked up on the streets of Indiantown."

He told Bernabe that his name was Claudio Perez and that his eldest daughter had turned fifteen. Perhaps out of pity, Claudio invited him to her quinceanera, her coming-out party.

He went to the Perdue worker's house the next day.

Claudio and his wife lived on King St., in a wooden house that they'd rented. Two blocks away, Bernabe could hear the marimba they'd hired for their daughter's party. The joyful music, a son de entrada, convinced him to go in. He had not heard marimba like that since the festival in San Miguel.

Claudio Perez met him at the open door. In his arms he cradled a plastic tub of soft drinks and cans of beer that he was handing out to his guests. He invited Bernabe in to join them. From the kitchen he could smell the sweet, acrid odour of corn tortillas on a hot plancha, the odour of black beans, kale and epizote. Many men were standing around in small groups, talking softly, and the women were sitting on the sofa and in chairs. Colourful streamers and balloons hung from the ceiling and were taped to the walls. Three men were playing a marimba that stood against the back wall.

Though the music was wonderful, out of shyness no one danced. The men spoke to one another without looking in the direction of the marimba, as if ignoring it. The women, too, speaking to one another and going into the kitchen to help prepare the food, didn't look at the marimba.

The party started at 4 PM and went on till four or five in the morning. When one marimbista grew tired, another would get up to take his place; only then would the tired one smile, talk, go to sit among his friends with a plate of food. The one who took his place immediately assumed the expression of the other players, solemn and grave. Their austerity and restraint were a sign of respect for Claudio Perez and his guests and for the souls of the dead for whom they were also performing.

Bernabe had forgotten this: in his region, this music was accepted like a heartbeat, sacred but never looked upon or singled out for special attention.

Around 1 AM, when he began to hear music of San Miguel Acatan that he knew, music that he loved, Bernabe asked to take a place at the marimba and he played the centre position for awhile.

Fortunately he didn't make a fool of himself by stepping on the feet of the other players or hitting their sticks with his own.

Josephina Perez danced with several men and her comare Rosenda Bravo danced. The few other women who remained looked on the dancers in shyness.

Soon the burning in the wrists made playing impossible and Bernabe reluctantly gave up his place to another.

Claudio Perez took him aside to speak to him.

He said that Bernabe had honoured his daughter, his family and his house with his playing, that he had played the music of San Miguel Acatan in a way that Claudio had not heard since his childhood and that he wanted to do Bernabe a favour.

He said that he ran a small business delivering personal letters recorded on cassettes, videotapes of baptisms and marriages and small goods to their home region. He offered Bernabe a job as a carrier. He said that the work was dangerous because Bernabe would have to cross two borders without the necessary papers, but that it was well-paid and that he had reliable contacts.

Bernabe asked him why he was willing to do this for him.

Claudio said that his music, which was the music of San Miguel Acatan, had touched him deeply, that it had brought back many good memories of his childhood in their region and that he would not let the work in the plant to continue to ruin Bernabe's ability.

He did not fear the work that was offered. His life as a member of Barrio 16 had taught him everything he needed to know about running goods under the eyes of the authorities. He was very familiar with that way of life, the things you had to pay attention to, the tricks, the dress, where to go and where not to go, the expressions and the ways of looking upon others. Within a week he was heading south, his bags loaded with audio cassettes, videotapes, small gifts and envelopes of American dollars for relatives in Huehuetenango. And he returned with cortes, huipiles and pan de festa, a kind of festival bread.

He made that trip several times a year.

He was so reliable that in their home region and among their people in North Carolina he became known as El Cartero, the mailman, and he was often greeted with an open smile.

When Bernabe had paid off his family's debts, he began to save to return home permanently, to live with his mother who was alone. Through relatives that he'd helped with his deliveries he formed contacts in the army, to guage the risk of his returning.

When he got word that he would not be harmed if he returned he went to Xela to study to become a teacher.

After three years, when he'd received his certificate, he returned to El Tablon. His first school, a tin roof goat shed, was in the neighbouring aldea of Lupine. He stayed in El Tablon with his mother and on school days travelled to Lupine. He taught there for a few years and married one of the women of Lupine — Helene is her name, and they had a son, Manuel Mateas. He had just turned seven when they were forced to leave El Tablon and cross the border into Mexico.

The troubles in Bernabe's village began in early 1970, a few months after he'd left Lupine to take a teaching position in Tzibaj, an aldea north of El Tablon. These troubles were marked by the arrival of a young woman. Her arrival itself seemed insignificant at the time, but later he realized that the events that followed her were a mark of things to come.

He was on a bus from La Trinitaria, Mexico, where he'd been to buy notebooks and pencils and coloured markers for his new school, and it was also an excuse to visit his friend Tomas Ortega who, like his brother, had had to leave their country because of his association with people who opposed the mine in their district.

A violent storm that passed through his region cut short Bernabe's visit. He was worried about the safety of his family, his students and his school. The bus he was on crossed the border at night. He was sleeping when he felt the bus gear down. They were on tarmac under a long string of glare lights. Ahead he could see idling trucks, some tarped and some with what looked like stacked fruit or vegetables in open baskets.

As soon as the bus stopped, two soldiers came aboard. One stood by the driver, a rifle cradled in his arms. The other began to herd people out, starting at the rear. Bernabe watched a young girl lift her packsack from the metal overhead rack; she couldn't have been more than seventeen or eighteen, a pale complexion, her eyes wide and anxious. She kept looking at the soldier behind her who was not as tall as she, and not much older. He had the broad forehead and narrow, dark eyes of a campesino from the San Miguel Acatan highlands. Carrying the rifle in one hand, he was rubbing sleep from his eyes as if to stay awake.

Outside, they were directed to unpack their bags on the tarmac.

Bernabe was directly behind the young woman, and he asked her, "Do you know what they are looking for?"

She turned to watch him repack his duffle bag with school notebooks and small boxes of coloured markers and pencils.

"Weapons," Bernabe said.

"You speak English," she said, and he could tell she hadn't heard anyone speak in her own language in days. "Your accent sounds like home!"

She helped him to replace the coloured markers that a soldier had spilled out of their boxes. His wrists had flared up in La Trinitaria. He had no trouble with the notebooks, but the numbness in his fingers and the ache in his wrists prevented him from picking up markers.

"Thank you," he said. "My name is Bernabe Mateas."

"Mine's Lacey."

Back on the bus, he sat with her. "Do you mind?"

They didn't speak for several minutes. She was so quiet Bernabe thought she'd fallen asleep, her arms wrapped around the pack in her lap; then in the light of a passing transport he saw the glint of her eyes staring straight ahead.

She had a look he'd seen many times, from this border to Mexico, to Indiantown and North Carolina. It's the look of someone who has arrived and is looking for someone.

He was hoping that Lacey would talk with him. He hadn't been able to sleep for two days.

He explained that during a particularly difficult financial time in his last year of teacher training, he'd gone to work on the Vancouver construction sites. "I have a good ear for pronunciation," he told her. "To fit in, I'd picked up the accent there."

He thought, those who do not trust enough will not be trusted. He told her about a dream he'd had in Tomas Ortega's house in La Trinitaria. He'd dreamt of a spring bubbling through sand. In the dream he'd stirred the white sand with a finger, just where the cold, bright water was burling in a pocket the size of your fingernail. From such a little spring abundant water flowed in two directions, into a wide gravel and rock bed. He realized then that he had to protect the source from a menace he could feel but not see.

It was this dream that had kept him awake for two nights, and he was talking out of a fear of being alone.

Still, a listener wants something to hope for. He could see the burden in Lacey's strained smile when he glanced at her, and he wanted to ask, What do I need to carry for you?

"Where are you going? Huehuetenango?"

"I'm not sure."

"Do you have a map? Can you show me where you're going? In these times it's best to have destination and know when you'll arrive."

"I don't have a map.

I'm looking for someone, a boy."

"In love?"

"No," she smiled.

"Sometimes," he said, "to find someone in these high-lands, you have to take paths known only to goat-herders.

Why do you want to find him?"

"To give him a message." She had a fine clear voice, with-out assurance.

The light was just growing over the hills, and they could begin to see steep hillsides planted over to corn, a dim light in an adobe farm house, the dark shadow of a copse of trees planted in a hollow.

"Do you know where your boy was going?"

"Some place called Tikru Lake."

Most in these highlands had heard of that sacred lake, though few actually knew the way there. His wife Helene knew the way in because she was a practitioner of the costumbre. He and his family had visited it many times. They would go there during the time of the sacred ceremonies, to remember and honour the soul of his father, of his brother, and to ask for the blessing of their corn. Strangers were not permitted there.

She pointed at a passing bus that was going in the opposite direction: "Yet he could be on that!"

They had come into perhaps the steepest farmland in that country; the fields rose sheer above them and were wreathed in mists.

"Here," he said to her, "they grow mostly corn. Sometimes the volcanic slopes are so steep a farmer has to tie himself to his house before he goes to work, otherwise he'll fall off!"

It was an old joke, but he liked her laugh.

"Is your message for the boy good news or bad news?"

"I've a letter for him," and she touched her shirt pocket. "It says he's a father."

Lacey told him about the mother of the boy's child then, her best friend, and how another wanted to take the child from her.

"It may already be too late. She has no one left to help her."

"She has herself," he said. "And how does this other one plan to take the child?"

"By taking up her time."

He told her then about his brother who was in a car accident in Indiantown. "When I heard, I left to be with him. Distance has no measure. Love draws you on in times of danger. You must try."

"But what if I'm too late?"

"I don't understand time or how we approach each other, but when I heard of my brother's accident, I was with him immediately."

"You had thousands of miles to travel!"

"No, I was already there. And you, the nearer you get to him, the nearer you are to her. You are going to her now, your best friend. Nearer and nearer you approach.

Give up trying to find him. Search for him every day but give up trying to find him. That's the only way to go forward."

Climbing on switchbacks into the hills, the wide sky opening in the early light, they entered a wooded area, and she asked him the names of the trees. Pine and eucalyptus, he pointed out, ceiba and oak, and farther on an avocado orchard on the hillside below.

She settled in, her arms hugging her pack, her eyelids drooping and soon she was asleep.

The bus came to a halt on a cobblestone road among four or five adobe houses.

"Come with me," Bernabe said. "If your boy is around here, we'll help you find him."

"What is this place called?"

"The Department of El Tablon," he said. "In this Department there is also a village called El Tablon."

He pulled a duffle bag off the overhead rack and she stood to follow.

In a yard across the road by a tethered goat, a girl was washing her long hair in a plastic basin, wringing it in her hands. At her feet a four- or five-year-old boy, squatting on his haunches, was chopping corn stalks into kindling. Smoke drifted from under the eaves of their hut.

They went along a path along a ravine. They could smell the remnants of rain in the air and mud in the path from the recent storm clung to their boots. Soon it felt like they were walking with weights strapped to their ankles. Here and there were small apple trees with withered leaves, the beginning of an orchard or the end of a failed one, he couldn't tell which. The girl was tired, and he had taken a shortcut that he didn't often use. A stone's throw below, they saw a man leading a mule, a saddle loaded with firewood on its back.

On a path of crushed pumice, they scraped the mud off their boots with a stick.

Before them was a new valley and a new sky. Small tilled fields bordered by raised grass paths quilted the hillsides. The patter of a one-piston motor echoed through the valley.

Ahead a boy palmed a bicycle wheel down the path, jogging beside it. Below there was an adobe hut with a thatched roof that she touched as they went by, the thatch damp with rain. She looked like a child walking in a dream. Everything here was new to her, and though she was very tired, she had that wide-awake look of someone for whom every impression is not a matter of habit.

She asked about the grove of trees on a far hillside.

"Those are pines," he said. "We grow them for lumber and firewood."

Beyond, to the west, a chalk-white scar in the landscape that was kilometres long, the rim of the open-pit mine.

"A lot of people have been driven off their land to make room for that mine," he said. He tried to control the anger and sorrow in his voice when he spoke of the displacement, but not successfully, because she looked at him more carefully.

On the other side of this valley, he led her into a compound. His mother was washing clothes in a pila, an outdoor sink. She came toward them across the open courtyard, wiping her hands on a length of polythene that she'd tied around her blouse and that reached to her ankles. She touched the girl's outstretched hand, brushing her fingers, then raised her hand to her forehead. She lowered her head, like someone bowing.

"My mother says welcome."

She had a gentle manner, but she was suspicious of anything new that came from outside their Department. Her eyes narrowed, and when she glanced at her son her expression said, So you've brought us home another stray?

Her health was not good: bronchitis from the daily smoke of cooking fires, arthritic fingers and wrists from working the fields and from shelling corn at dawn on cold mornings.

Lately she said little and didn't often smile; sometimes when he saw her in the distance, tilling a field, she looked like someone who sensed that someday — perhaps soon — they would have to leave. She would work the hoe then stand and look around as if she felt something in the air, look across the fields and the valley to the distant hills. She would stand there gazing for a long time, immobile as a startled Kej, a white-tailed deer, and he could sense in her darkening a gathering stubbornness.

At night a week before a helicopter had passed low over their land, and she'd asked him in the morning, 'What do they want?' He shrugged, said I didn't know, but he could still hear the whap whap of the blades, a sound that is meant to stay in your ears and heart, to keep you awake. That sound sours in your chest and creates a hollow of fear. It was their first attempt to uncouple his family from their fields.

Now she was putting the two together, the helicopter and the girl. Momentarily, the shadow of fear in her eyes said she felt a menace she couldn't locate.

Still, they were a friendly, gracious people.

She offered the girl food, drink.

But he could see that the girl's eyelids were drooping. He remembered then that she had crossed the length of Mexico in two days.

"Would you rather sleep first?"

Yes, she nodded.

"I'll show you your room."

She watched the mother return to the outdoor sink. She had felt the old woman's fear and she looked puzzled.

They went over to a small adobe building by some rabbit hutches.

"This is my old room. I share a larger one with my wife and child."

He pushed open the wooden door that had a bird with long tail feathers carved in it. The door smelled of pine and the beams in the room were new pine, the colour of fresh straw.

"The roof was torn off in a storm. We replaced it this spring."

She told him that she used to work as a lookout in a fire tower and that she had seen many powerful storms go by, lightning crashing into the trees.

She unlaced her muddy boots and went in.

Inside there was a double bed with a faded coverlet on it, a small wooden table and a wooden bench. The only light in the room came in through the eaves and the open door. The air in the room felt cool and the light coming in through the eaves spread over the new beams.

"You must be tired," he said. "I'll close the door to give you some peace."

She thanked him for his hospitality, a shy smile in her eyes then.

He said that she was welcome to stay as long as she liked and that his wife would have some breakfast ready for her later, after she had slept.

Later, when Lacey's room was quiet, he slipped a note under the door saying that he was going to visit a student who was sick, perhaps from ground water poisoning, and that he'd make enquiries about the boy Michael Guzzo.

2

She slept for two or three hours stretched out on the faded coverlet. When she awoke, flies were turning in the warm shafts of light that had climbed down the straw and clay walls.

Her mouth felt dry and she had a headache. What was she doing here? She remembered the walk along the crest of the ravine, touched the letter she carried in her pocket.

When she got out of bed, she saw a note tucked under the door. It reassured her that she was welcome. "My wife has breakfast ready for you."

As soon as she opened the door, the light heavy and blinding, children crowded around her. They touched her pale arms, her loose blouse. Off in the distance she could see a volcano ringed by clouds. While she stared around, a young girl took her by the hand to lead her across the court-yard to a doorway.

"Welcome," said a woman at the stove. She was dusting the plancha with lime dust and placed two tortillas on it, moving them around with her fingers. There was a boy at her side who looked to be three or four years old.

"Please sit down."

At the plank table she watched the young woman at the stove pour a drink from a jug into a plastic cup.

"You must be thirsty."

She nodded. The dyed drink was sweet and clear. Children perched on the bench on the other side of the tres-tle table watched her quietly. She could see there were two sets of twin boys and the young girl who had taken her hand.

"Did you sleep?"

Again she nodded, as if not quite awake.

"I'm Helene, Bernabe Mateas' wife."

She brought over a plate of tortillas, kale and beans, sat down beside her.

"My name's Lacey," the girl said.

The boy had followed Helene from the stove and was standing at her side, clutching her dress. He stared up at Lacey wide-eyed.

"Manuel Mateas," she said. "Our son."

She pointed across the table to the girl who was kneeling on a bench. "My niece Petrona Raymundo, daughter of my sister Virginia. The twins," she said indicating the two sets that sat beside the girl and across from Lacey and who were staring at her, "belong to my sister Rosario Lopez: Juan and Sebastian, Martin and Escobar."

The kale and beans tasted salty and the tortillas slightly bitter with lime dust.

"You look worried."

She explained that she was in a hurry to find a friend, that she had something important to tell him.

"You Canadians come a long way to tell people things," she said. "A Canadian bishop was here a month ago, to talk to people about the mine. It's poisoning our water. And now you."

The young woman poured out more of the sweet drink. "You've had a susto," she said, "in your heart. I'll make a special drink for you."

"Did you learn English in Vancouver?"

"No," the young mother smiled. "My husband taught me. I've hardly been out of these hills, only been to the city once."

After breakfast, Lacey and Helene walked through a field of maize to the grass and scrub beyond. Along the footpath they gathered apazote leaves and in a forest they found cypress and oak leaves, Helene reaching with her son at her side to fill woven sacks.

"This is for fever," she said, "Aching bones. This is for machete wounds."

On a hill covered in blue tradescantia they came to a large mound of stones. Helene swept the sacred area clean with a sprig of escoba. She spread pine needles and placed pine branches decorated with sprigs of hydrangea in the four corners of the quadrilateral world. Then she gathered cuttings from a small tree with yellow flowers called chilia.

Lacey had never done this kind of work at home. Her mother used to be a midwife who was trained in the use of anesthetics and she would sometimes brew a special tea or massage a woman's belly with almond oil to help with the contractions, to help her relax. But her mother had quit that work soon after the Giacomo baby died, she had lost confidence in herself attending that birth. Now she cleaned rooms in the Mackenzie Hotel.

Her parents had not wanted her to leave. They said she was too young to travel in such an unsettled country, that if anything happened it would be very hard to get her out.

On the day her plane ticket arrived, on the day she was packing to leave, her father, a papermaker who sold his paper to artists and printmakers, took her down to his one-vat mill.

"You can't repair what's been done," he said, stirring a vat of pulp with a wooden paddle, waiting for it to reach the right temperature and consistency, pulp flecks drying on his hands. "It's not up to you."

"I can't just stay and watch what's going on with Rose."

"This is a small town, Lacey," he'd said then, going to the sink to wash the pulp from his hands. "Everyone knows what Mr. Giacomo is up to. Something will happen."

"No," she'd said then and there was real anger in her seventeen-year-old voice, "I can't wait. You don't know how he looks at her and I see it every day."

"What if you don't find Michael?"

"Then I'll come home."

3

He's on a bus on El Camino Real, heading south to Encinitas, California through the darkening hills by the ocean. Shifting the pack in his arms and rubbing his eyes, he's slept through Oceanside, missed the stop for the hostel and now in the fading light, there's all these new faces, people who must have gotten on in Carlsbad, a woman sitting beside him, her hands resting in her lap, a bucket of cleaning supplies at her feet, gleaming bottles and wet rags draped over the side, a toilet brush sticking out of it, the smell of industrial cleaners.

Spanish and another language he can't make out, the woman beside him quiet till a man across the aisle in a paper painter's cap leans out to say something and she laughs, glances out the window and the boy sees her dark eyes then, gleaming in the fading light.

In some rows there are three men or women sitting in two seats though other seats are empty, shoulders touching, the flare of the quiet talk between them, muscled hands resting on knees, lean, dark faces.

He can't make out what they're saying, and he stays quiet, the weight of the pack on his knees, the thrum of the engine under his sneakers, looks out the window at the passing hills covered in sage. And he looks at his hands, touches a splinter scar under his left thumb, a jagged piece of wood that had caught him on the green chain weeks ago, and now he feels far from that place in the Kootenays, doesn't miss the work he tells himself, the banter on the line, Vince Camozzi going on about the girl he was seeing in Banff and asking him about Rose in that smiling tone that says he knows all, knows all.

He remembers the splinter sliding in and he'd dropped the board on the line, drawing away sickened and dizzy, he'd not noticed the frayed seam in his glove and the splinter had slid in exactly *there*, and when he'd stepped back to pull it out, the blood already flowing down his wrist, he'd felt how fragile he was, fragile and light in his own body.

All of this is new.

He gazes at the passing hills and already the faces around him are in shadow, evening comes quickly here, how quickly the California light fades. The woman beside him makes no sign, staring straight ahead, the cleaning bucket wedged between her white, polished shoes, dark hair braided and coiled in a bun.

He asks her nothing, doesn't know her language.

Eighteen years old and heading south, the places he's travelling through, Oregon, California, he'd only heard about in the talk of the Portuguese and Italian workers who would come up for the harvest back home, but now he's seeing these places, they went by so quickly, Oceanside back there that he's slept through and ahead the sky lit up by Encinitas.

He's heard Encinitas is a rich place, houses of pastel bricks and wide mullioned windows, high, iron gates, as big as palaces some of them, the kind of houses that kept guard dogs, no out of the way places to sleep, no overgrown parks or a strip of beach, the streets well lit-up and neat.

Something carries him along, waiting and watching. Some gleam of light on the horizon, in the way that northern California beach had kept him sheltered last night, dampness ebbing into his sleeping bag, and at 1 AM or so he'd awoken to see three fish-boats gathered in the bay, their mast lights rippling on the water. He's young at this, doesn't know what or who to trust, relying on hunches, dim reassurances, a sheltering beach that will keep you safe for awhile or so it seems.

And now again he has this startled wide-awake feeling.

The bus has pulled over to the highway shoulder.

The woman beside him stands, reaching for her pail.

It makes no sense to stop here.

He looks out at the hills, no houses, just sage and pine and the long pull of evening shadows, and a lot of people are standing to get out, like they've arrived at some station at the end of a line, maybe a dozen or more, gathering up shopping bags, tool kits and pails, the woman with the cleaning pail, a man across the aisle in a spattered painter's cap, a can of brushes in his hand that smells of turpentine, another with a bricklayer's trowel, his bare arms streaked with cement dust.

They are filing out to cross the highway, to walk into the darkening hills.

He shoulders his pack to follow.

And it could be the place, all right, for this night, a wary glance at the traffic, waiting for gaps, darting across, like orchard workers coming in from the trees, shouldering the tiredness in their limbs, the easy talk and laughter at the day's end, walking — where? — to a bed somewhere, and he's cautious and curious now, standing on the side of the highway in the last light and he looks ready to cross till a hand touches his arm, the woman who had sat beside him.

"Wait," she says, "too dangerous." Some big transports roar by, hiding the cars in the far lane.

She doesn't even ask what he's doing here, just smiles and says, Wait.

They could be standing on a street corner back home in New Slocan, a local helping out a stranger. And hasn't he often felt this way lately, wide awake and on the alert? And isn't that what makes what he sees and feels so vivid, the buffeting wind of the passing transports, the way the long shadows pull down the ravines as dusk comes on, a faint pink stain on the sage and the flickering of campfires bright in hills. Light on his feet and ready to dart, yet staying here.

They run through a gap in the traffic into a ravine strewn with aluminum cans and wind-shredded plastic bags, and they climb.

She tells him a story then, as if to apologize for touching his arm, for holding him back. She's talking about the San Clemente checkpoint on some highway called Interstate 5, something about her cousin crossing the border, and he leans in now, her voice so soft, and there's the clatter of footsteps in the arroyo, high chalky walls, sometimes he gets lost in his own thoughts and feelings, doesn't really hear what people are saying. Not that there's really anything interesting in the tug and pull of his own worries — about being welcome, being helpful for instance. Lost in a cloud, his mother said once: You haven't heard a word I've said, and he'd brought himself back then and looked at her and saw she was hurt, she had a need like grief spreading over silence.

"My cousin was running across the highway at night with his suitcase," he heard the woman say, "near the San Clemente checkpoint. And he was hit by this car."

He leaned in as they walked to ask whether her cousin was taken to hospital and how he was, and she said No, he'd died on the side of the road, they'd shipped him home to San Miguel in a box so that his soul could rest in the village. "His name was Martin Merida," she said.

"Every week two or three people die there, trying to get across."

"There are safer places," she said then, as if giving him advice: "Tecate and a place called the Soccer Field."

"I'm sorry," he said, but he didn't know what he was sorry for.

Not sure what he means.

Eighteen.

He'd never heard anything like it, people crossing a border, terrified in the bright glare of highway traffic, misjudging the distance.

They came out of the arroyo into a cleft in the hills lit up by campfires. Tarpaper dwellings, over a dozen of them, small fires ringed by stones.

The woman leads him over to a shack made out of plywood with plastic tacked on the flat roof, an orange box door framed with 2 × 4s, rusty hinges, hardly bigger than a child's play hut he says to himself when she pushes open the door to show him her narrow bed, a row of wooden crates in which she'd folded her clothes, stacked her pots, knives and forks, a few tin plates, some cans, a small watermelon, packages of crackers.

Yesterday, she'd gathered firewood in the hills and left the bundles marked with strips of red cloth by a path. Would he go get the wood for her? He nods and she points out the path with a flashlight, gives it to him to find his way.

On the path he sees a man reach under a bush to pull aside a sheet of polyethylene, and under it there's a hole with a sleeping bag in it and pots and a plate, all this lit up by a flashlight. He sees others walk down a ravine into the dark, vanish. He gathers up the bundled pine and sage branches marked with red cloth, the night rapidly drawing over the hills, the faint scent of the sea, the smell of sage heavy on his hands. The sticks he gathers are light, almost like paper, bleached by heat and light. When he hears the scutter of a lizard in the grainy soil, he stands to look back down the path to the fires, the dark shapes of the tarpaper cantons below.

Here.

She thanks him for the wood he brings in.

"Enough to get a fire going," she says.

She has some scrap 2 × 4s and some pruned orange branches stacked by the wall, and she puts some stones near the fire she builds to heat and carry into the canton later.

"I'll show you where you can sleep."

She starts up a path on the east side of the encampment, carrying blankets.

"Where are you going?"

"Tikru Lake," he says.

She looks surprised. She'd never heard of the place.

Below he can see ribbons of light on El Camino Real, the lights of Encenida to the south.

He doesn't tell her that his going there has to do with water.

All this happened when he was thirteen and he didn't think about it then, try to understand what was going on. There were some fires in his home valley, houses burned and pushed into their cellars, the orchards felled.

Then a quick, whispered argument between his mother and father in the kitchen when he was supposed to be asleep, he couldn't hear the words but in the morning the air in the kitchen still, muffled, held their anger. He saw his mother's drawn face, quiet over the stove and the way the breakfast plates had been set out for himself and his cousin Maren, his father already gone. No one needed to know about that. The sadness and tears in his mother's eyes, the way she hugged herself in her nightgown by the stove, you didn't have to talk about it or even notice.

Things were changing in those days.

Machines came in at night, lit up by glare lamps and in the morning you'd see the smoldering remains of a house, hear the chainsaws in the orchard, the crash of the trees, splintering branches, all that noise ripping through you, and for what? To clear the valley for a reservoir. How could you stop that, stand in the way?

He remembers the land buyer at their kitchen table, a quiet man, almost like a priest.

He was showing his parents some papers, going through the figures, showing where signatures were needed. When his mother rose from the table and shouted "No!," her fists balled in anger, his father who was standing behind her put his hands on her shoulders, gently pressed her back into the seat, was saying, "It's not about *him*, hon.

It's not his fault."

The land buyer kept pushing the white cuffs of his shirt into his jacket sleeves, as if the shirt sleeves were too long and in the end he spoke softly about how this needed to be done, couldn't be avoided, the threat of court action and he looked embarrassed in the end.

And his mother didn't say anything, her nostrils pinched white, fist on the table, her eyes dry with a kind of staring fury.

She'd shrugged off his father's hands, stood and walked away.

Now he and the woman have come to a flat place on the hillside that looked like a section of disused trail or road.

"See?"

She's pointing north towards Oceanside and she says there's apple and orange orchards back there where there might be some work or sometimes the men in construction were looking for help, maybe he could pick up some work in the morning, but he says no, he's planning to move on.

They came up to two women sleeping on the landing, under blankets on plastic bubble wrap and spread newspapers. He could see sneakers carefully placed at the foot of their mats, ball caps and a shirt and a sweater spread on the sage.

She lays out the blanket she's brought for bedding and she tells him to unroll his bag on the blanket, to claim a place for the night.

Beyond the women a man sat up, shielding his eyes from the flashlight.

"He wants to know who you are," she says.

She replies in Spanish and the man shrugs, resettles under his blankets, turning away from the light.

"Are you hungry?"

"Yes," he nods.

After he's unrolled his bag, he follows her into a canyon, to a shack lit up by kerosene lanterns.

A radio is blaring music.

She says this is a restaurant.

When the owner comes out among the trestle tables she orders a bowl of soup for him, "Caldo de pollo," she calls it, and he sits at a table beside a man in his mid-forties who is wearing a paper painter's cap. A kerosene lantern is burning in the middle of the table and a lot of other people are sitting around it, looking and not looking at him, so that he feels every inch of his body, his heart thumping, "Evening," he says and no one replies, propped elbows, people hunched over their bowls, tired and scraping out the last of the soup, and the painter beside him says, "Every morning on Encinitas Boulevard is a morning of hope. That's where we go to be picked up for work. I've got a steady job that will last for a couple of weeks — I'm lucky!" and those sitting near him in the shadows of the lamp smile. "Then I'll be back on the Boulevard. We're all hopeful, and tired and sometimes a little careless."

"If you're careless," he says, turning to the boy, "if you ask for too much or you stay at one job for too long, the Migra will pick you up and take you to the border. Don't stay in one place too long; don't make your face or your walk familiar."

A woman brought the painter some soup from the kitchen, "Maria," he thanks her. From under the bench he lifts two plastic bags filled with bread and melons that he's pulled from an alley dumpster behind a Safeway, to share around the table.

"Even this won't last," he goes on, waving a hand at the shack they called a restaurant and at the smaller ones around it. "We'll have a few more weeks here, maybe a month or two, no more. Our campfires disturb the peace of Garden View suburb. They see our fires in the hills through their living-room window and they feel uneasy. Something must be done, they say. The Health Department will come and declare our living conditions unsafe."

"What will they do," the boy asks, "burn these places down?"

"No, they'll pay us to dismantle them and carry the wood and tarps and tarpaper and nails out of the hills, pay us by the pound!"

"Where are you from?" The painter asks, and he sees many lean forward to listen. That was how these men and women located themselves. Reach back through memory, to the place they called home, bring it *here* so that they and others are held and made to wonder at how far they have travelled and yet they can reach back and be held. They are eager, not just to hear the boy name a place, but to see through to the place in the boy's eyes, a real human light they can understand.

He tells them about the flooded-out valley, that his village was now under water. In the still faces around the table he sees an amazed shock that something like that could happen in Canada, that a place they dreamed of going to could be so horrifying.

"Where are your dead?" a woman across the table asks, "The souls of your ancestors? Where can you go to honour them, to play music for them?"

"The people who agreed to that are ill," the painter says. "There must be something really wrong with them."

Around the table the boy shows a photo torn from a book, a sacred lake somewhere in the Central American highlands. They pass it around. No one knows the place.

He is going there, because he needs a destination. But something else in the photo holds him: the sense that it's a healing place, that maybe there his nightmares will fade.

"You looking for work?"

"No," he says, "going south into Mexico, then Guatemala."

And the painter says he's from southern Mexico, from a village in Oaxaca, naming the place and showing himself in the smile of his memory, where there is no work. He and his family lived on corn planted on a small plot that his father-in-law had owned. But bad business and some poor decisions had ended it all.

"Then," he says, looking at the boy, "we went to work in the citrus fields of Sinola and the tomato fields of Baja California Norte," reciting these names as if they were the lines of a song, and he traces the route with his finger as if the table planks were a map, the rub of his finger measuring out distances and direction, hundreds of kilometres over backroads. In Tecate his wife ironed and washed clothes while he worked in construction.

Last week, to seek a better life for his family, he'd crossed the border at I5, running across the highway in the dark.

The boy looks around the table, others are listening. Some nod.

Some smile and he sees acceptance in their eyes, like it's okay that he's here, to sleep out in these hills like these people, and one of them — a man with the muscled hands of a construction worker — says he'd tried to get into Canada last year because he'd heard there was work on the Vancouver construction sites, was turned back at the border, all that money and time wasted, ended up picking broccoli in eastern Washington, anger in his voice and the boy feels himself stiffen, still on the bench now, still as wood, not knowing where to look, the measured looks on him.

He feels the painter touch his arm, "Where south?" he asks and the boy says Xela.

"Wait," he hears the painter say, rising from the bench, "I'll show you," and he walked up the canyon into the dark.

And he returns with a creased and frayed map that he spreads on the table, thick, crayoned lines leading through Mexico.

"Avoid Mexico City," he says, "the station is full of drug runners and pickpockets. Avoid Nogales, it's controlled by Los Zetas. Cross here," and he points to El Paso. "Take a bus to Camargo and then to Colima," and he traces the route, measuring down secondary roads that lead through Lazaro and Tecpan, along the coast into Oaxaca. "Cross the border here," he says, tapping a place called Tapachula. "You ask for a bus there to take you to San Marcos. In San Marcos you can catch another to Xela."

"Hardly anyone speaks English in those hills," he says then. "You'll have to learn some Spanish and some Mam."

He gets up just before dawn, the bright beacon of Sirius over the hills. There are seven or eight men and women sleeping on the landing, dark shapes under blankets, in bags. A cough, the rustle of fabric, the low cry of a dreamer. A single transport passes below, the rapid patter of a jack brake.

He folds the blanket that the woman lent him, places it outside her door. Walks down to the highway in the dim, grey light, wisps of fog on the trail, dew on the sage.

━━━

Michael Guzzo arrived in Xela in the winter of 1970. He enrolled in a language school just off the Parque Central. After his first two hour lesson, with a few simple exercises and a list of words to memorize, he went to study in a restaurant near the square, at an upstairs table. He was working under street windows grimy with diesel fumes and dust. He looked like a child learning to speak, shaping his lips to make sounds that reminded him of the Italian he used to hear at his grandmother's kitchen table. The woman at the next table smiled, was watching him over her salad.

She said she was a nurse down from a village called Chapel. She was in the city for medical supplies. He couldn't place her accent till she said she was Australian. Her forehead was beaded with sweat and there were shadows under her eyes.

He had decided on the bus ride down to stay away from English-speaking people, to wander on his own till the city began to open out for him, word by word. He'd remembered listening to the Québécois French and the Portuguese of the orchard workers back home, words that drifted out of the trees in the still light of the evening, spread out of the branches. The voices of the workers hidden in the leaf shadows sounded like bird song and even at five he'd wanted to understand what they were saying, eager to enter their laughter, the music of their voices and longing that said where they were from.

The Australian nurse was wearing a shawl of woven cotton, dull browns and greys; she shivered under it, her eyes glazed. She toyed with the salad, chewed on a leaf.

"A touch of the flu," she said, pushed the salad away.

"I'll just sit here awhile," she said, sipped some water, touched her forehead.

She was listening to his whispered pronunciation and laughed. When she stood she flattened her hand on the table to steady herself.

There was a strong glare of light in the street where he walked with her. They kept to the shadows of a store that sold electronics, then a grocery store with a wide stone terrace. A cough rattled deep in her chest and waves of nausea passed across her face.

At the intersection of 12 avenida and 7a calle, she stopped to let a car pass. Up the calle he could see an old stone arch that people walk over when the street floods during spring storms. He was carrying her bag of groceries and a duffel bag of medical supplies.

She had the distant, concentrated look of someone just trying to make it back to bed. She was from the same region that he wanted to travel to, maybe he'd ask her about that when she felt better, but just now he had to see her out of the glare of the streets, and he wondered how old she was then, 25? 26? The pale, hurried way she walked made her seem so young.

They went through a door in a heavy black enamel door that could be swung open to let cars park overnight in the hotel courtyard. He followed her up worn, orange-carpeted stairs to her room on the second floor. She unlocked the door, the key shivering in her hand.

"Thanks," she said, turning to take the bags from him and placing them inside the room. "I'm okay now."

"I've enough meds in that bag to treat a whole village," she smiled.

She looked thin and tired when she closed the door on him. He stood in the hallway, wanting to knock then turned and went away.

She had chatted fluently in Spanish with the patron

while paying for her salad, and she'd told him in the street that she often went to that restaurant for the elaborate salads and pizza when she came down from Chapel.

"It's the only decent place to eat," she'd said, "if you don't eat meat."

He stood at the balcony railing over cars parked in the courtyard below: a couple of Mercedes and a Jeep. The sky over the open courtyard had turned a pale grey. From across the street he could hear the whine of a skill-saw, the clatter of boards, but nothing from her room.

She had closed and locked the door behind her.

In the courtyard below, the concierge, a thin-faced man with a small mustache and a shock of black hair, was watching him from behind a desk near the street doors.

When he went by, the concierge asked, "La muher esta bien?"

He shook his head; he'd only understood one word: bien, bene in Italian. Not understanding the question made him feel ashamed, though the concierge's tone was friendly. A strange feeling of not understanding, like in school when you're asked a question you don't know the answer to and everybody's looking at you, smirking at your silence.

But this you notice: the fewer times you have the right answer, the less you are called on, and soon it's like you're no longer there, which is a way out into the open.

He went into the street, the door in the door pulled shut on a heavy spring behind him.

He walked half a block to the city square. Now that it was late afternoon, couples were strolling by arm in arm, the men in business suits, the women in long, flowing dresses.

School girls in red and black uniforms lined the concrete seats in the rotunda. They were eating slices of watermelon sold from the back of a cart near the taxi stand. Soldiers moved through the crowd, past a woman who was selling painted wooden flutes that she'd laid out on a cloth spread on flagstones. The soldiers looked like boys with rifles slung on their backs, they looked that young. No one seemed to be paying them any attention, and they flowed along with the crowd, their faces composed and distant.

4

The next morning he brought her some bottled water and dry crackers. When she met him at the door, she was wearing a loose T-shirt and baggy sweatpants and her feet were bare. The walls of the room were yellow plaster, the ceiling and floor planks painted a dark brown. There was a lamp fixed to the wall above a bedside table with a paperback on it, opened face down.

She went to sit cross-legged on the bed and placed a bowl between her knees. He sat at the foot of the bed, gazing at her.

"I have to go back to Chapel this afternoon," she said, "It's four hours northwest by bus. Can you help me get to the station?"

Her forearms were pale and mottled, and under her broad dry forehead her cheeks had hollowed, the skin taunt, and her lips were puffy and dry. Waves of nausea passed across her face. She bent over the plastic bowl between her knees, patted her lips with a facecloth and her stomach heaved.

"I have nothing left to throw up," she said.

She agreed to take some Cipro from the supply bag, "They're expensive!" and he brought her water and tinned juices. The next day, when she could begin to eat, a thin tomato soup and dry bread from the restaurant where they had met.

She slept most of the time.

Once, when she was in the shower, he took the sour-smelling sheets and pillow case from her bed down to the concierge for laundering.

When he returned, he opened a window to air the room. The window looked out over a flat concrete roof with re-bar sticking out of it. Clothing hung from a line cinched between two of the iron bars. A dog sniffed through a heap of tin cans, its ribs showing. The grey cloud-cover had broken, and clear daylight had settled over the city, over a pine-covered hill to the east with tall white letters that read Christo Viene on it.

The concierge brought in fresh sheets that he used to remake the bed.

The first night, before the Cipro began to take effect, because it looked like she was getting worse, a hopeless, glazed look in her eyes that wouldn't look at him directly, her hair damp on the pillow, the quick rise and fall of her breath under the sheet like the struggle of a bird caught in vine nets, he got the concierge to help him drag in a mattress and he made up his bed by the door. When he woke up around two AM the bedside lamp was on and she was gazing at him.

"I have to change the dressings," she said.

At first he didn't understand, not sure whether he was awake or dreaming.

"His foot is infected," she said.

She went on gazing at him, her head on the pillow, her face in shadow, the sheet drawn to her chin. A strand of damp hair lay across her forehead.

"I showed his daughter how to change the dressings, but I'm not sure she'll remember.

The aunt!" she added, grimacing.

He sat up, the blanket around his shoulders. She was gazing at him and thinking of her patient. The lamplight showed the ridge of her shoulder under the sheet, the dropped hollow of her belly, the gentle rise of her hip.

"The aunt takes off the dressings and puts epazote on the wound. She's a curandera.

He's a *diabetic*," she said, closing her eyes.

Within minutes she was asleep. Her breathing was shallow and quick and when he went to turn off the bedside lamp her saw that her forehead was creased in a frown, her mouth sad and bitter.

5

To return to Chapel, the village where she ran a nursing clinic, they took an early bus from Minerva station, heading north through the city shrouded in a fog that she said would burn off by mid-morning. By the time they'd left the old town with its cobblestone streets and tall wooden doors, she'd fallen asleep, her head nodding against the window glass. The bus ground to a halt at the stoplights, the metal floor curving under his boots as they climbed Avenida de los Americas, past the tarp and tarpaper stalls of the Maya market.

A little wiry man in a jean jacket and broad stetson got on, his bundle of firewood tossed on the roof. He went to sit and talk with two others crowded onto one seat, perched on the edge with his legs in the aisle. They went by cinder-block works, tire shops and weavers' stalls and shops that sold wicker furniture, till they came into vegetable fields. Again the bus slowed to a halt, hissing air brakes, and out of the mist under some pines, across ground littered with torn plastic and corn husks, a woman got on. She had a sleeping child tied to her back in a broad cloth. When she settled in the seat across the aisle, she brought the child across her lap and spoke to it softly in a language he couldn't understand.

She looked across the aisle at him, startled, then her face went blank and she stroked her child's forehead, its mouth streaked with milk. She was wearing a traditional dress of woven cloth and her loose, short-sleeved blouse was embroi-dered with flowers and birds, a rope sack of melons at her side.

The only acknowledgment he'd seen in the woman's face was a look of momentary surprise.

She spoke again to her child in a language that was not Spanish. Her tone reminded him of his grandmother's voice when the Calabrianne, an orchard worker that his family often employed, used to come to visit. He'd be out on the porch or in the garden because there was no use sitting in the kitchen when those two got together, he could under-stand little of what they were saying, both from southern Italy, and through the screen door he'd hear her talking with the Calabrianne, talking in her childhood language. There'd be snatches of it through the day, pane instead of bread, going back to the place where she was born.

And you could hear it in her voice, like an animal that has come from a long way to rest, back and safe, how her tone softened, it was the music of the place she was from and he could feel that place, the place of her young girlhood. And he wondered, where did his land, his birthplace, rest in his voice? His grandmother used to go back to her own in words and it was like she was a young girl again, in her voice and laughter.

Alana stirred then, looking straight ahead and rubbing her lips. When she reached to pull a shawl through the metal bars of the overhead rack, he felt the heat of her arm on his cheek. She wrapped herself in the shawl, shivering, and rested her head against the glass.

"How are you?" he asked, but she didn't reply, keeping herself still and looking inwardly, licking her dry lips.

Now they were climbing in the hills through cornfields and pine groves.

Here, the bus pulled over and two soldiers got on. One stood near the driver; the second walked the aisle, showing a grainy photo.

When he came to the woman with the child asleep in her lap, he didn't even look at the two gringos across the aisle: this was not their concern. He held the photo up before the woman while she held her child. Alana half-stood to glance at it, an eager look in her eyes.

The woman with the child only shook her head, and the soldier moved on.

The boy could feel her held breath: if you say nothing, keep yourself small, people like these soldiers don't notice you, go away. Except in his valley they'd driven everyone out, and he felt a surge of anger then, went to stand before he knew what he was doing, as if to shake off the burning in his chest, but Alana put her hand on his shoulder, held him down.

After the soldiers had got off and the bus was crawling up to speed, Alana said, "I know the guy in the photo."

Outside he saw a cinder-block church in the mist, blue-painted doors and a cross fixed to the metal roof. The yard was swept bare and there were oleander wreaths fastened to the metal fence.

"He's the patient I was telling you about, the one with the infected foot."

The ayudante crouched beside their seat to collect the fare. She handed him crumpled bills and they whispered for a long time in Spanish. Then he walked to the next seat, folding the bills onto a thick wad.

"The man in the photo, my patient, he's a deserter," she said, "from a civil patrol. Someone is dynamiting the electrical towers that bring power to a mine in Huehue. The army has set up civil patrols to protect the mine. If you don't join, it's assumed that you support the people who are destroying the towers. Or that you're one of them."

"Why are they doing this?"

"Sabotage." she said. "I don't know what's going on. Maybe rival gangs. I don't know what'll happen. These security patrols are a new army invention, and no one knows whether to take them seriously. Anyhow, they're looking in the wrong place for him, he's gone to stay with his daughter," she said smiling, "in my village."

They were on a dirt road bladed under a cliff. The bus passed a car-sized boulder pushed to the side. She said it had fallen from the cliff last week, holding up traffic for hours till a D7 cat could be brought to shoulder it out of the way. He saw a man perched on the boulder, leaning low, searching for fissures with a hammer and a chisel, a scarf wrapped around his mouth.

"I'm already feeling better," she said as they came into the country of her village. She seemed more alert now, looking around with a familiar interest. She said that she always found the trips to the city for supplies exhausting, but that it was good to get away from the daily routine of the clinic. "I don't have a life of my own," she admitted. "There is always something or someone who needs looking after."

Below he could see a village on a plateau wreathed in wood smoke. The surrounding hills were planted over to cornfields and pine groves. A muddy, boulder-filled river went through the valley.

"Maybe you could stay awhile," she said then. "And help out." She looked lonely shivering in her shawl, and he could see that she didn't ask for help easily. He nodded, yes he'd stay for awhile, but he didn't know what he could do here.

The bridge to the village was two hundred yards down the road, and soon they were in a street of one storey cinder-block buildings, all the wooden doors painted faded green or brown. Alana squeezed by him to talk to the driver, and he pulled over by a church. Its doors were flung open and someone inside was playing an electric piano, a tinny voice echoing over the music.

"You can stay here," she said.

Outside, the ayudante was already lifting his pack from the bus roof-rack to the street. A woman led him across a courtyard into a small bare room.

"The driver's sister," Alana said, "their family owns this poseda. You settle in and I'll come find you later."

He stood in the doorway to watch her climb back on the bus as it pulled away.

She hadn't looked back or waved, and when she'd spoken to the woman, her voice was hurried and distracted. She had quickly looked around the room they were shown and nodded, as though she were choosing for him.

She had chosen for him; the ayudante had brought his pack in, set it in a corner. He took a thin sheet from the bed to hang in a window that overlooked the courtyard. He spread a sheet from his pack on the bed. Through the wall he could hear someone sloshing water over the bathroom floor and the electric piano from across the street.

A vine was in bloom outside the window, flower shadows on the sheet. The walls were painted a muddy yellow, and the floor was made of rough-cut planks. There was a double bed on cinder blocks near the far wall.

He folded the clothes from his pack on the shelf above the bed, hanging his jacket on a corner. The plank ceiling vibrated when a truck went by. He heard the sharp report of an explosion that reminded him of fireworks.

Looking around the room, at the makeshift bed, at the one rough wood shelf, the faded sheet hung in the window, he felt that nothing in memory could hold him steady, give bearings, as though a darkness was passing over his eyes. A passing sense of vertigo, almost like terror: in a moment it was gone, but it shook him.

He understood then what had killed a number of old people who had been evicted from the valley: all that had supported them — the orchards, the house, the land, the village, the mountain, had been torn away. In their heart, they were starved to death; then the body followed.

He unfolded the photo of a lake that he'd torn from a book and it hung on a nail in the wall. He could unpack in five minutes and he could pack in five minutes. So this was home, then. He could vanish from here, too, without a trace, unseen. He felt like a ghost here, and except for Alana there was no reason to stay.

When she came to find him two hours later, he was running a thin trickle over his hands to wash his hands and face in the common bathroom.

"You can come with me to Celedonia's." She was carrying a satchel of medical supplies. Her hair was tied back and she had washed the road dust from her face and arms.

She laughed when he complained about the water pressure.

"On Thursdays they fill the municipal pool," she explained. "There's no water pressure anywhere in the village."

He followed her down a path to the river.

In the early evening light, doves were flitting over the valley. The slopes were planted over to corn and to pine copses. The bottom land was planted over to corn and to squash: he could see large striped ayote, a kind of squash, among the stalks.

They followed the path down a hill of cropped grass, through maize stalks that rattled like hollow bone. By the river there was an iron-roofed adobe compound. The light was quickly fading over the hills; the shadows on the path in the maize stalks along the river deepened. The window openings and the doorway in the compound below were dark.

"Maybe she's not home," Alana said.

"Celedonia!" she called out.

Three dogs leapt out of the west wall shadows. Alana stooped to raise a stone, and the dogs backed down the path with their haunches lowered.

"The tanned one will try to nip you," she said.

Frightened and angry, she had a rock in her hand and the satchel ready to swing at them.

The dogs had a cringing wariness in their eyes; one had striped, cat-like markings.

A woman shouted at them from the compound below.

He watched the three lope away, and Alana lowered her arm.

"I hate those dogs," she said. "Two are okay but they act as decoys for the third."

"Buenes noches, vengan aqui!" called the voice from below.

They went through a courtyard of beaten, swept earth into an adobe kitchen. The room was dark, except for a flickering glow in the mouth of a stove and in cracks between the stove bricks. The woman who had called to them — Celedonia — moved as a shadow along the shadow of a wall.

Standing just inside the kitchen doorway, he heard two young voices in the darkness call out Alana's name.

A match flared, and the woman stuck a candle on an angled nail in the adobe wall. She lit another and set it on another nail.

"She says welcome," Alana said, "and that these are her two daughters."

The two girls were at Alana's hair, touching its highlights and smiling. One took up her hand and clasped it in hers.

She had brought them earrings from the city.

Sitting on a wooden bench, each tilted her head to put them on. Candlelight spread over the eldest daughter's broad cheeks and over the shadows under her eyes. Her hair was tied at the nape, and the candle light glowed on her high, broad forehead, her teeth, the curved skin of her nostrils and lips. As she shifted on the bench, tilting her head to tug at an earlobe, her embroidered blouse gleamed.

Her father came in, carrying a chair made of wooden slabs and pine branches.

"Buenes noches," he said, smiling.

He placed the chair between the two benches, sat on it, and began to talk with Alana in a quiet voice, sad or apologetic, his hands on his knees. The two daughters went to stand at the stove with their mother who was stirring something in a pot that smelled sweet and bitter.

"A late frost got most of the corn along the river," she said, "and he's had to replant. To get by, they'll have to go to the coast to pick coffee."

Michael looked at him. He was a little man with a narrow chest and sunken eyes, his arms thin. He was wearing sandals made out of truck tires and his feet and hands were covered with dust. His lips looked dry, parched in the candle light and he would not look at his wife or his daughters.

He went out, shirt-tails flapping at his jeans, to return from the bedroom across the courtyard with an album that he carried in both hands.

"Our wedding pictures," Alana translated.

While he sat between the guests, turning the pages to show the photographs, the two daughters returned to drape their arms over Alana's shoulders, touch her hair, touch their new earrings that flashed when they bent over the album to laugh.

One photo showed the groom's father in a doorway, his arms full of gifts: sweet rolls and coffee, cigarettes and liquor.

Another showed the groom and his friends bringing mule-loads of firewood to the bride's family.

"He moved in with Celedonia's family," Alana said, "bringing his machete and hoe, and he worked for the family for two years before they were allowed to marry."

There was a photo of the couple on their wedding day. The mother was no older than her eldest daughter; she looked embarrassed and awkward in her embroidered blouse and woven skirt, her shoulders held high, chin down, eyes wide with anxiety and her hands clasped behind her back. The groom was dressed in striped black and grey slacks, a plain white shirt under a new stetson hat. His arms were held at his sides and his shoes turned out.

The daughters pointed and laughed. Their mother had come up behind them and they drew her down to see, and their eyes gleamed when she smiled.

From the stove she brought them cups of thin gruel that had the sweet odour of squash, and when Alana put down her cup she said, "Time to see him."

They crossed the courtyard to a low door; before they went in Alana handed him a flashlight from the satchel of medical supplies she'd brought with her.

"I hope you can stomach this," she said.

Celedonia carried in a lit candle, and a man in a bed turned his head to look at her.

"Quien es este?"

"Un amigo de Alana; no se inquiete."

"This is Celedonia's father," Alana said. "He's asking who you are. He's a little afraid of you."

The father was watching them with glazed, fevered eyes.

He tried to smile reassuringly. The room had the smell of crushed herbs and under it a sickly, sweet smell of flesh that had gone off.

"Turn the light down here," Alana said.

She had drawn up the blanket to expose the man's feet, lift a poultice of leaves.

"Jesus," she said.

One foot was swollen and streaked to the ankle, an open wound oozing fluid. He could see the black stub of bones where toes used to be. He drew away from the smell. In the poultice that she'd removed and laid on the bed he recognized oak leaves.

He held the flashlight while she placed a dressing under the heel then bathed the foot in saline water from an IV bag. Crouching at the bedside, she swabbed between the rotted toes and carefully inserted padding between them. Then she dried the foot and wrapped it in a gauze bandage.

She checked the supply of antibiotics at the bedside, then added some to the vial.

"You have to go to hospital," she told him.

"No quiero ir."

"He says he won't go.

275

He's afraid he'll die in the San Marcos hospital."

"You'll die here," she said. "The antibiotics aren't working."

She sat on the bed to place a damp dressing on his forehead, wipe the sweat from his cheeks. His eyes were glazed and still, looking at her.

"Quisiera ver una curandera."

She shook her head, packing up her supplies. "I'll see you tomorrow."

The two girls were waiting outside in the courtyard.

The mother closed the door behind them.

"Tomorrow when we come back," Alana said to him, "the dressings will be off and there'll be an herb poultice on the wound. Useless.

He's seeing a curandera, a plant healer."

By then it was dark. The sky was a wide scattering of stars and he could hear the river murmuring beyond the fields. On far hills he could see the dim lights of farms and villages. The night air smelled of pines and of the kitchen fire.

The two daughters walked them to the compound portal on the hillside. They went by a oleander vine that smelled of rose honey.

She hugged the daughters, saying goodbye to their mother. They stood away from him, shy.

"Where are the dogs?," he asked.

"They don't come out in the dark. They're cowards."

She took the flashlight to lead the way. "It's good to be back here." Her steps were light and their was a cool self-assurance in her voice.

"How do you feel," she added.

"I feel sick."

In the dark she laughed, the beam showing rock ledges in the path. "You get used to it."

"Is he going to lose that foot?"

"Either that or he's going to die."

They went into a pine copse. She walked quickly ahead. The path softened underfoot — a carpet of needles and gritty volcanic dust. In starlight the delimbed trunks looked like cobwebs, the living branches high above them.

"He was out at night on a security patrol," she said, "guarding a mine that the army told them to guard. And he got shot at. He thought he'd make less noise running away barefoot, so he kicked off his sandals. He cut his foot on a sharp stone or something."

They left the trees, climbed into a cobblestone path to the village.

"When the wound didn't heal, he went to a curandera, not to me. He's a *diabetic*."

They turned up an alley that led to the main street. She walked down to a lit-up tienda, a young girl at the back counter. On the sidewalk, stacked flats of canned juice and a table strewn with plastic trinkets and cheap padlocks.

"Do you want something?"

He shook his head. He felt light-headed and his stomach was still in knots.

A can of juice in hand, she came out to sit on the curb and drink.

"Your posada is that way," she said, pointing with the can up the street.

He turned to walk away, through dull, pooled light from a few lamps. He went by green and brown painted doors shut for the night, by an iron stairway that led to a second-storey balcony. At the foot of the stairs a sleeping dog lifted its head to turn its blue eyes on him. He could smell the burning charcoal of cooking fires, and in the hills the single blare of a night bus.

Once again she'd had that cool self-assurance in her voice. As far as he could tell she was the only English speaking person who lived in this village. He felt drawn to the way she seemed to fit in, the way she seemed to be at ease with others. Her Spanish was fluent and she even knew a few words of Mam. Celedonia's father's leaving had angered and saddened her, because she knew what he needed.

People liked her here. He had seen that on the bus in from San Marcos. As soon as she had stepped into this familiar street, people had waved, a fruit seller had called out a greeting from where he was spreading melons on a tarp, a young girl had come out of a tienda to hold her hand and chatter about what he couldn't tell.

When he looked back she was still sitting on the curb in a flood of light from the tienda, the juice can in her hand, staring into the cobblestone street.

Maybe he would stay here with her. The work she was doing was useful and he could help out. Already the dream of the lake was beginning to fade, maybe it wasn't so important that he go there after all.

6

Bernabe heard Lacey stir when he rapped on the pine door. It was still dark outside. Light flickered in the eaves when she lit a candle to dress.

They walked past a tall hydrangea bush, the flowers of which his wife used in her ceremonies. In the pre-dawn air they could smell epazote and laurel as they went down the hill to the village to wait for the bus. He was carrying in a day pack the school supplies that he'd bought in La Trinitaria: markers and pencils, glue and construction paper, a box of blunt-nosed scissors. In a small pack, Lacey carried thirty wide-ruled exercise books that she said were like the ones from her own primary school days.

"Is there anything else I can carry," she'd asked, and he'd given her two water bottles for the trip.

In the village, they went to sit on plastic stools around a charcoal brazier; Maria Telles was stirring canisters of milk, hot chocolate, coffee and mosh. She was wearing a woolen toque and a woolen sweater. A faded pink apron was tied over her skirt, with patch pockets that she put money in from the sale of her drinks and buns.

He bought the girl a cup of milky hot chocolate and a sweet bun.

"It's a long walk," he explained to her.

Across the street dogs were nosing among trestle tables under a tin roof. Up against a wall at the crossroads, two or three drunks were sprawled asleep. Up the street, three unlit, empty buses parked in a row.

"Our bus is coming from another village," he said, sipping from a cup.

"Es usted maestra tambien?" the coffee seller asked.

"She asked if you, too, are a teacher," he translated.

Lacey shook her head, smiled.

"Quiera usted trabajar para mi?"

"She says you can work for her in her commador."

Again she shook her head.

He could tell she felt she had to hurry if she was going to do any good. But how do you hurry when you don't know where you're going?

He emptied his cup, stood to go: he'd heard their bus cresting the hill.

Lacey stood to follow, kicking over the cup that she'd placed at her feet. The coffee seller laughed, stooping to pick up the plastic cup where it clattered on the cobblestones. She floated both in a tub of rinse water that reflected the pearly shimmer of an early morning sky and the dull glimmer of the one street lamp at the crossroads.

While the bus was climbing gravel switchbacks out of the village, she asked about his life in Vancouver.

"It's a common story," he said. "But maybe it will help you to understand our life here."

He said that in his last year of schooling, in a time of serious financial problems, he left with a friend to work in Vancouver.

A contact from his village had found him a room in a house on East Pender Street and a job washing dishes at Felicia's, starting at four and working long past midnight, plate after plate dipped through the soapy water that soon turned grimy and grey, the gleaming cutlery swirled around in handfuls and put to dry in the racks, his hands liking the warmth of the water that spread down his arms into his chest and belly and the simple work, no need to talk, calmed him and the easy stacks of dishes and cups gleaming clean, made him feel he had a place there, just concentrate on what he had to do, listening to the cooks' and waitresses' banter, trying to understand what they were laughing or angry about.

What astonished him was the walk home after work though streets that had a strange, buzzing glitter in them that went on and on, way into the hills, past the lit-up storefronts with barred windows, the stacked cardboard and bags of garbage, a machine that swept the streets, prowling with its whirling brushes.

Once he returned in the morning to find his room stripped. The thorough thief had taken everything — even sheets and hand soap — and he burst out laughing.

You've even stolen the mildew he remembered saying out loud, and he went to buy a clasp that he screwed into the door sash, padlocked the door when he was away. The landlord had said it was too expensive to change the locks, people moving in and out all the time.

Sometimes he walked till dawn in the alleys, to see what people were growing in their back yards: apple trees he saw and sweet corn in the summer, pea vines; he even recognized the dark little flowers of scarlet runner beans that grew on stretched twine.

All the dark windows and people sleeping behind them.

Once he could see into a lit-up kitchen where a man was pulling on his boots to go to work by a woman at a table in her nightgown, smoking and drinking tea.

He knew then that their peaceful life would never be his.

"Now I teach in Tzibaj," he said smiling, "for forty dollars a month."

"What can I do in your school?"

"I'm teaching the grade sixes English. You can help."

"I've never taught anything before."

"Tell them about where you're from," he said. "Tell them about your life. If they feel connected to you, they'll learn something they need, some little thing that you may not even know."

As the bus climbed higher, dawn seeped into the eastern hills, and the higher they climbed the more the highlands spread out before them, a patchwork of cornfields, pine forests and valleys, one long river that wound to the horizon. Stones rattled against the floor panels.

Her eyes, bright and clear, showed an eagerness that settled her and she began to look more carefully at what she saw.

He talked of nights on Commercial Street, sitting in the Napoli café with his friends, sometimes playing a little music, Jose Leal the guitarist, Maximo Rios the violinist and Julio Soto who played the chirima, a strange, breathy instrument that reminded him of the costumbre. They talked of politics back home, of who was the new prayer sayer, for instance, and the news of the ongoing battle between the Catholic priest Father David and the costumbre, how the priest was collecting money to build a hospital for the community though there was no accounting of where the money actually went and of how your family had to donate twenty days labour to the construction of the hospital or they would not be admitted to the sacraments.

"That's how it's always been in our country," he laughed, "you are forced to volunteer your labour while your children go hungry."

On Sunday afternoons they played soccer on the 8th Avenue field, sometimes organized into a game with the Honduran La Bicolor and the barbecues afterwards under a Persian ironwood tree, the babies on spread blankets under the leaves because some had settled in Canada and married there.

"Were you married then?"

"No. I married when I returned. I had big dreams. Move to the city, maybe go back to school to become a lawyer or an architect. All that takes time and money. Now we live with my mother."

A flash flood from the storm that had brought him back from La Trinitaria had torn at the road and at a hillside farm house. Below three or four workers were digging the remains of a house out of a mud slide. Broken adobe bricks, scattered as if by a blow, were strewn across the hill. Men were digging out of the dried mud and rocks pine beams, doors, and metal roofing, pieces of it folded like paper, stacking the wood and metal to the side.

The bus went over a crest and came to a stop by a wood shop.

Under the roof of an open shed a pinewood coffin was laid out on sawhorses. He said it was for a grandmother who had died in the slide. "When the family felt the hill turning to mud they couldn't get her out in time."

That torn and shattered house that they'd seen lay across a steep hill in a scar of dried mud. He spoke of the pounding, driving rain, the winds, it must have happened at night, with rivulets of water running off the road and foaming by the house, cutting channels that became streams that no one could hear because of the rain lashing the metal roof, and when the mud poured in at the door, pushed in the walls, the old woman must not have had the strength to get out.

He saw a shiver go through her at the thought of the woman's terror and hopelessness.

Climbing off the bus Lacey was drawn to the ready-made coffin, her hand brushing over carved figures, lithe cats and intricate flowers on its sides. "Cats and flowers to honour the old woman's life," he said. That were meant to keep her near. The grain was smooth and warm to the touch; it smelled of pine and light oil, maybe linseed.

The sun was clearing the side of Fuego volcano, rising over the slopes and warm light flooded the road and crossed her neck and arms, the hair on her forearms bristling. Here the morning light threw long shadows across the river valley far below. There weren't many forests left — just clumps of pines dotted here and there in the ravines and on the hillsides but on the slopes of the volcano there was a forest and on some nearby hillsides, too, that were too steep to plant.

It looked like she was getting over a long time of worry and indecision, that she was beginning to see and feel again.

Still, Bernabe could tell travelling didn't sit well with

her. The landscape went by too quickly for her to feel she belonged here.

There wasn't time to experience her thoughts or emotions in any particular place, and so recently she'd just travelled through scenery. For the first time since she'd left the Kootenays, she wasn't on a plane or bus: with him, she was actually *walking* somewhere.

Yet there was so much she was missing.

What did she really see and feel here?

Hurried along by the fear of not finding the boy she was looking for, she hardly remembered what had happened the day before yesterday.

They turned off the road to follow a path through trees bearing green peaches, the leaves spotted and rusted. They went along a ravine, the hillside rising at their right hand, to the left the valley dropping below.

"Here," he said, "People eat a simple breakfast: tortillas and salt. The land is — what do you say — depleted?"

In this dusty, pale land, corn was planted everywhere a human hand could reach. They passed a family hauling soil from the bottom of a slope to the top of the slope in fertilizer sacks. A young boy was carrying a sack on his back supported by a head strap: he couldn't have been more than four or five in that tired, vexed look he gave them. Behind him the mother and father gave the traditional greeting as they crossed the footpath; then the mother reset the sack on her back, her mouth a thin bitter line, her neck deeply furrowed as she went straight up the slope.

They watched the father lift the sack from the child's back, place his own at his feet and spread the soil as though it were flour on a baker's table, raking it between the plants with a hoe.

"It's too quiet here," Bernabe said, glancing at his watch. "I don't hear children on the paths."

"Sometimes," he said, "children who go to the fincas on the coast to pick coffee return with open sores on their skin, from sleeping on concrete or dirt floors. But the sores I saw on the student I went to visit yesterday were new. I suspect groundwater poisoning from the mine."

"All around this region people are getting sick. Nothing foreign came to us," he said, "till the mine came."

She spoke of the worry she used to feel when she'd worked as a fire watcher in a forestry tower. First, she'd spot a tendril of smoke rising from a lightning strike: at first disbelief, thinking that she might be seeing things, not trusting herself, wanting to be sure before making the call. Then the disbelief would change to certainty when the column thickened and grew.

At the school, he unlocked the padlocked door. Children of every age crowded around her, the teenagers hanging back, the boys in cast-off American jeans and shirts, the girls in traditional corte.

Toddlers were staring up at her; one was trailing a length of rope tied around her ankle, as if she'd been tethered somewhere.

The children looked and did not look at her: they had this way of gazing around her; they didn't focus on anything in particular, as if looking for a place where she made sense.

"You teach two-year-olds?"

He smiled. "Sometimes the mothers leave them here with their older brothers or sisters. It gives them a break and the little ones like it."

He opened the door and she followed inside. The school children didn't follow and he closed the door behind them. It was cold in the school. There was no stove and the early light had not yet warmed the room.

He laid out exercise books, scissors, rolls of paper and crayons along a table under a cinder-block wall. Charts were taped to the wall with English and Spanish and Mam words on them.

He went to the window and looked out. "Mateo Garcia is missing," he said. "Juan Pascal from Lupine. And seven kids from Chehb'al, a long walk from here. Petrona Raymundo isn't here, I've heard she's ill." He counted slowly. "That makes twenty," he said, "twenty missing."

"Is that unusual?"

"Half the school is missing," he said.

He went down a row of plywood tables, and in front of each chair he laid down a few crayons, a sheet of coloured paper and a pair of scissors.

Before the older students' chairs he carefully placed an exercise book with a sharpened pencil aligned on it, an eraser at its side.

His heart was racing and he could hardly keep himself still. He felt there was something terribly wrong with all this eerie silence and absence, and he didn't know what to do. Later he would learn that, the night before, security patrols had descended on the land, driving many families from their homes and burning their crops.

7

She saw her last patient in the evening. Then she locked the clinic, and they walked to Celedonia's.

She brought along a jump kit to clean and re-bandage the father's foot. They followed a path through a pine copse under a sky of glittering stars. He could see the constellation the village called the scorpion and there, in the western sky, the three hearth stones. At the foot of the hill, he could hear the river that rustled at night like corn leaves. She played the flashlight beam along an adobe wall, looking for the dogs.

Celedonia was standing in the portal when the beam passed that way, her hands at her sides.

She said in an apologetic voice that her father was gone. "Gone where?"

"My husband took him to San Marcos. He's going to stay with my aunt. He says there are powerful curanderas in San Marcos."

The nurse sat on the stool outside the kitchen door.

"He's not going to make it," rubbing her forehead. "I should have come earlier. I could have convinced him to stay." Angry, she clutched the jump kit in her lap.

Celedonia went into the kitchen.

She called them in, stirring atol on the stove.

"Where are the girls?"

"At my sister's," she said.

The kitchen felt empty, cold. When Celedonia added pine branches to the stove fire, the flames lifting, he saw her crouch inside herself, unsteady on her feet.

"Why are your girls at your sister's? Are you going to the coast?"

She sat across from them, and in the candlelight he could see the anger and worry in her eyes.

"My husband helped my father onto the bus," she said. "I went with them to San Marcos. My father was in a fever. I gave him water and I kept his forehead cool with a wet cloth, just like you showed me.

He asked me what was wrong between me and my husband. I said nothing was wrong. We helped him into my aunt's house and my husband stayed with him.

Then I went to a market, to buy some panela to bring home. A man came up to me.

'Are you Jose Cabral's wife?'

'Yes,' I said.

'Jose Cabral has made my daughter pregnant,' he told me. 'Do you know who I am? My name is Bernadino Garcia. I served in the presidential battalion under Arbenz. I've been appointed head of the new civil patrol in our district. I want you to remember my name, you can ask about me. Your husband is Cabral, yes? Word is he's become a subversive. I can bring him in at any time. And I cannot guarantee his safety. Do remember this. If you don't sleep with me,' he said then, 'I'll kill him.' Then he turned and walked away."

"You should tell the police," Alana said.

"The police will laugh at me."

"What are you going to do?"

"I don't know."

Alana went around the table to sit beside her. She took her hand and held it in her lap, gazing quietly at the wife.

"Come and have dinner with us. Don't sit here alone."

"Jose Cabral is coming back tonight," she said. "I want to talk to him alone."

"Are you afraid?"

"No," she smiled bitterly. "I'm not afraid of him. I could kill him myself."

Outside the clinic door, neighborhood children stood in the street.

She reached in through the iron grate in the door to unlock it.

"I'd forgotten," she said. "It's Thursday night."

When he looked at her she explained that every Thursday night she had these children over for crafts, a snack and a kind of play time.

From under the reception desk, she took out a box of scissors and construction paper, glue, crayons and plastic vials of spangles, while neighbourhood girls and boys stood in the doorway. One he was sure he'd seen in a field when he first arrived in the village, the dark-haired one. Now she was watching him, wary and distrustful as if she wished him away, not wanting him to interfere with what was to happen next.

She smelled of wood smoke and looked wan and hungry.

Upstairs, Alana flicked on the terrace light, a single bulb on the wall by the stairs. She spread crayons and construction paper on the open terrace floor. Across the valley he could see the last light dimming behind the hill, a lone avocado tree on the crest, the shadow of a volcano in the distance, bulked above the surrounding hills.

"You can keep them occupied while I cook supper," she said.

The two girls drew on the construction paper. The boys ran through clothing and clinic towels hung on lines to dry, the younger one imitating the older who swung a broom handle like a machete.

One of the girls, the older one, asked, "Como se dise eso en ingles?"

She had drawn a mule or a horse, a dog to its side.

She was salting spangles in the glue-spread face of the mule and in the dog's eyes.

Under each he wrote an English word. And under those he wrote a phonetic approximation in Spanish.

He watched her young mouth pucker as she tried to pronounce the English words.

"Como te llamas?" he asked the girl.

"Maria Sanchez," she said. "This is my sister Ena."

Little Ena looked up from the drawing she was making between her splayed knees. With her palm, she spread glue over the lines she'd drawn.

She brought her hands together, watching the skin of her palms tent when she pulled them apart.

Maria led her sister by the wrist to the terrace sink. She washed Ena's hands, daubed at a glue smear on her blouse.

The boys were charging through the hung laundry.

Watching from the doorway, Alana said, "Time to dance."

Inside he could see that she'd made a skillet of rice flavoured with tomato sauce, chopped peppers and canned tuna.

"You can dance on the bed," she said, "one at a time."

She put on music and the first up was the boy with the broomstick, kicking out his legs in a way that made the others who were sitting on the floor clap and laugh. "One at a time," she'd said, and they'd sat on the floor, used to the ritual.

It was the way she ended the evening.

After the last dancer, after little Ena's hopping with her eyes closed and her arms stiff at her sides, her eyes startling open when she approached the mattress' edge, they filed out the door, carrying their art and small packages of salted crackers.

"See you next Thursday!" she called out.

She set the table with plates and cutlery from market bins kept under the sink. From the skillet she heaped rice on his plate, less on her own. She poured out water for them to drink, her hand trembling when she picked up her fork.

"I'm too tired to talk about anything that's happened today."

So he talked about his family back home. They'd worked half to death trying to shore up their land in terraces. Why had they stayed when many had sold out and gone to West-bank or moved to the new town the Hydro had built at the far end of the reservoir? "We won't abandon this place," his father had said, while the reservoir water seeped into the hills, loosening them, and the trees they'd planted began to tilt toward shore.

When they realized there was nothing they could do about the walking hills, when the terrace walls, some of them made of logs and some of them made of stone, began to split and founder, the heart went out of their work.

He would listen at night to the complaining trees, and he could feel the house strain against the pull of the hill. In the fall, in the down time before the pruning and replanting began, he left.

"Go up to New Slocan," his father suggested, "There's work for you there," laying a cheque on the table to help his son get settled.

"Go and see what's out there."

On shore, they listened to the hiss of a fall rain on the reservoir and watched the grey mist rise from it.

"You can't stay here. There's nothing here for you."

And he wanted to say, There's nothing here for you, either.

But his father had to find out for himself: that in his grief he was just trying to replant on this hillside the orchards that had been taken from him. As if trying to repeat what you once had was enough of a life.

When you work with no hope, he'd learned, there is no richness to the days that blur together, and you push yourself to keep going, sick at heart.

They climbed into the skiff, to pole their way through a mat of wood debris that opened at the bow, thumping the aluminum sides.

"There's no life for you here," his father said, "and I'm sorry to see you go."

Yet already he could feel that his own going would lead to a put-off decision. That his parents would soon board up the windows, lock the doors and walk away.

Soon alders would overtake the orchards, then cedars

and firs. Rain and snows would wear away at the house, the outbuildings, or maybe the whole hillside would calve into the lake, leaving a raw scar for salal to grow over.

It was amazing how quiet the reservoir was.

He told her how it concussed the landscape. You looked out over fretful water to the lip of the dam on the far horizon. Not even the sound of a fish jumping, just the thud of the debris on the bow and a shivering wind. Soon they were skimming through riplets that hissed against the bow like glacier water thick with rock flour, over a drowned forest.

He knew that he was being sent away so that he would be spared the day when his parents moved on. His father was watching the water ahead for drift logs and deadheads, his face lined with habitual worry and grief.

They moored the skiff at the Ames' Landing dock, a wooden float lashed to a couple of tin-capped pilings, and walked up through the mist on the asphalt to the Burton store, its windows still dark. There they waited for the bus. They shared a thermos of coffee, his poured into a tin mug that was kept in the skiff locker. It bore the name of the river ferry his father used to captain and he ran his thumb over the embossed image of the ferry, over and over, as if trying to take the feel of it with him.

He was going up to New Slocan to work in the Odin Mill. Near blind, his uncle had bought into the mill for a retirement income.

He'd set his suitcase down by the unlit gas pumps, ashamed at his eagerness to leave.

His father reached out his hand to take his as the bus came up the road, saying "Thank you for your help," and in his eyes there was a mute appeal that the boy couldn't answer and he flinched away from his father's gaze.

Then he talked of Tikru Lake, of the photograph that he'd found in a second-hand book in the Grizzly Bookstore. He'd dreamt of that lake.

Maybe there was nothing there for him, but he had to go see.

"I'll show you where it is," Alana said. "It's not far," gathering the plates and setting them in a tub to wash later in the sink.

She spread out a map, her forearm brushing his as she traced the route with a finger. "Here it is, you start here," she said.

"You take the bus to El Tablon," she said, "You can go tomorrow if you want. You'll need a guide to show you the way in. A few hours on a bus then a day's walk."

He felt her warm breath when he leaned in to follow the route.

She folded her arms on the map, laid her head down on it, an inward stare of loneliness.

He stood there, gazing at her.

He went to turn up the music, drew her to her feet. She let her head rest on his shoulder, arms draped around his waist. He could feel her heart beating against his chest, the weight of her tired arms on his hips, a slight breath on his neck. And soon he felt her head weigh heavier as sleep began to draw into her. The turn of their dance narrowed till they were turning in one place, her eyes closed.

8

At the end of the school day, on the bus back to El Tablon, they got off in the aldea of Santa Ana. On the western slope, close to this village, they could see pine stumps, the trunks stacked by the roadside.

"I've something to show you," Bernabe said.

They went into a hall with a white painted cross above the door.

"What are these?" Lacey asked. Across the hall floor there were twenty or more stacks of cinder blocks and stovepipe.

"Stoves," he said.

"Fuel efficient stoves. But nobody knows how to put them together. Some American church brought them here. And then they left at the start of the troubles over the mine. Let's take one," he said, "to see if we can make it work."

While he went to hire a truck, Lacey sat outside on the hall steps. Below she could see clothing spread to dry on boulders by a muddy river. A security patrol was passing on the far bank.

The men were walking single file, two carrying rifles. She could see they were looking for someone. She watched them vanish into a pine grove.

She felt that Michael was somewhere in these highlands.

How would the message she had for him enter his heart?

She had written the letter on paper her father had made. That folded piece of washi paper she carried in a buttoned shirt pocket, touched now and then to make sure it was still there, was made to last hundreds of years: paper that could survive immersion in water, mudslides, blood stains, almost anything.

"Let the words dwell in you." She had read that somewhere: Let the words dwell in you. And how will he be changed, if at all?

When she used to work in a fire tower, the dispatcher on the radio phone would ask her, What's your news? What do you have for me?

At first, when she called in a fire, her heart would beat out an emergency rhythm and she'd speak too quickly, jumbling her words. Later, when she got into the habit, she calmed down.

Still, there was always an edge of clairvoyant tension, of sharp seeing, when she walked from the fire finder to the radio desk.

She was remembering helicopters in the air, the smell of burning pine and fir. Words over the radio phone and then action.

She would stand on the fire tower catwalk and watch as the helicopters she'd called in brought firefighters. Whole days and weeks would go by, nothing. Watching, waiting, reading Ryokan or Spinoza. Then a lighting storm would blow up over the Palliser Ridge, and she would watch trees explode into flames.

Those were moments when she felt really alive and even now she remembered some of the fires she'd called in as if it were yesterday.

So often there are signs in this world.

Once, on a second-hand clothing rack at the back of the Grizzly Bookstore, she'd found a paper raincoat from Japan that had been left on a transcontinental train.

When she touched the sleeve that had the luminescence of corn snow she imagined that it was a warning for Mr. Giacomo, a rich man in the village. He had moved there when she was three. Soon he was buying land for orchards and vineyards. He bought Jonny's taxi and the Mallone café and he'd floated a great house across the lake from Burnham for his wife.

There were rumours that he hadn't made his money logging in the Nachako country as he had said, but from the sale of gems and pottery stolen in Japan at the end of the war. His mother was Japanese-Canadian, and he'd worked for the Allied Translator and Interpreter Section in Tokyo.

Once Mr. Giacomo had told her that he'd served as a translator for General Douglas MacArthur. He was there when the gemologist Edward Henderson was brought to Tokyo to appraise the gems that MacArthur had recovered from the ashes of burnt-out buildings. "We got buckets full of sand and gravel with lots of diamonds in it," he told her. "Then we worked down in the vaults of the Bank of Japan where they kept all their gold. 800,000 karets of diamonds stored there shrunk to only 160,000 karets," he'd nodded, looking at her. And now he wanted her best friend's child, Michael's child. She hoped that if and when she found him, Michael would act, but she didn't know what he was capable of, whether he'd even care.

She didn't know him that well. They'd met a few times

in the Grizzly Bookstore and he'd asked her to look after a carton of books before he left.

Once Rose invited her to go swimming with them off Olebar beach. They'd rode down on bicycles, towels rolled and strapped to the carrier over Rose's rear tire. That was in the middle of the summer and a wind storm came up when they were out in the water. The dry wind raised swells on the lake and soon it was frothing with whitecaps. Lacey had gone ashore and was sitting shivering on a towel, watching the two who were still out there. They were laughing and shouting, treading side by side in the swells that hefted and dropped them. He dove and then, through some trick of the wind and a shift in the current, when he came up she was fifty, sixty feet away, drifting downshore. He was laughing at the sudden wildness of the waves, but Rose, frightened, turned to swim in.

Something in his laughter had disturbed Lacey then, a testing recklessness that had no feeling for his girlfriend's fear. Yet she shared a love of books with him, and for that she felt close to him.

Now she could smell the pine smoke of the village kitchen fires. Below in the evening light she could see that women had come to collect dried clothing from the river boulders. She could hear the slap of the current at the boulders in the river, the answering burl of a gravel bed downstream.

Only a messenger, her heart quiet and still.

Then she could go home.

Bernabe came over the bridge in a dented pickup, standing in the bed with his hands on the cab roof.

He leapt out to untie a rope tied in place of a tailgate. Lacey went inside with the driver to bring out a plancha of brushed concrete. Then they carried out cinder blocks and stove pipe, pushing them onto the truck bed.

"If it works, we'll come back for another one," he said.

They rode in the back of the pickup. The driver had a three-year-old child in the seat beside him. Bernabe could tell she liked being outside, the air cool on her forehead and wrists, holding onto the side of the truck and crouching to absorb the shock of the road-stones and ruts.

"I'm not stealing it," he reassured her. "I have permission from the Mission 2 Serve. If I can figure out how it works, I'll give away the rest."

"I think I know where your boy is," he went on. "There's a young gringo in Chapel, on the other side of the San Pedro mountains. If you can wait I'll take you there at the end of the week."

"He's not my boy," she said. "I'm not even sure I'll like him anymore. I'm waiting to see."

9

They don't usually patrol in the afternoon. The men have crops to attend to, a market stall or a job on a bus collecting fares.

But Bernadino Garcia is the leader and he has heard that Jose Cabral is hiding in the village of his birth. This village was also called Los Pinos, The Pines, and he sees that they've cut down many trees near the village, the blind adobe walls turned to the receded forest.

They went from door to door, asking.

No, Jose Cabral has not been seen.

Jose Cabral has gone to San Marcos, to pick coffee.

Jose Cabral has gone to the city, to work in a shoe factory with his cousin.

Jose Cabral has gone to Los Estados, to work on the broccoli farms in eastern Washington.

So they combed the forest around the village and along the river, looking for him.

The search was not authorized. The army had said there was no anti-mining activity in the area. The subversives were elsewhere, in the Huehue lowlands.

Garcia had asked the army commissioner, "Why have you appointed me leader of a security patrol?"

"Because you can write."

He could table reports. An army must have written reports; they were a necessary ritual that distinguished the military from vigilantes.

The goal of the security patrols was to ensure peace, stability. The men of the villages were asked to join.

Not really asked. If you don't volunteer, they were told, you will be considered a subversive.

The government had promised a few coins a month for those who agreed to walk around the Department with a rifle or a stick.

Many had signed up because there were no known subversives in the area.

As long as the subversives were far away in some other Department, there was no question of bringing in a neighbour or a friend.

He was a shopkeeper in la calle des Flores. He sold medicine and other medical supplies, including regulators and bottled oxygen. In the democratic Arbenz era, he had served in the special presidential battalion, and because he could write, the army had made him the leader of this patrol of six men. He had heard that many zone commissioners had been appointed throughout the highlands and that each village was to form its own security patrol.

He asked his zone commander why these patrols were being set up, why the army had taken such an interest in civilians.

"Boredom," the commissioner had replied. "Pure boredom." The commissioner was an army veteran who did not bear arms, did not get paid and was a resident of Lupine.

He had told his men that Jose Cabral was a suspected activist, maybe the first recruited in the region. Before he recruited others they had to bring him in for interrogation.

The truth was that Cabral had gotten his daughter pregnant and vanished. Furious, he'd thought of going to the police, but the police would only laugh at him.

Then he remembered he was his own authority.

They went over the hill and below was the Rancho Viejo river lined with clothing-strewn boulders. Across the muddy water he could see a cinder-block prayer hall, a young gringa sitting on the steps. She looked like she was waiting for someone.

He was surprised to see her there.

Many foreigners, including the American builders of the prayer hall, had left during the start of the unrest last spring.

Garcia told his men to separate when they came to a pine grove. He knew there was no one in the grove and so did the men. But they must make a show of searching. These villagers were his own people; he knew how they thought, how they lied. Cabral was certainly in the village somewhere, well-hidden and protected.

Perhaps he was watching them right now, laughing.

The gringa was watching them. He could see her young age in the way she sat, legs drawn up, chin resting on knees, arms wrapped around her legs. She was surely the age of his own daughter. Young, vulnerable, hugging her knees and unsure. Cabral had certainly seen that open-hearted lack of confidence in his daughter. It was always in her laughter when she brought her friends home to their house on calle des Flores.

But when his daughter stood alone, you sometimes saw a troubled look, bewildered. He had seen that in her and had turned away, preferring her easy laughter.

Now he understood his fault.

He should have asked why, now and then, she had looked so unhappy.

If she saw him gazing at her, she'd immediately smile — a gift which he accepted with relief. Now he recognized that the relief he'd felt was cowardice. Something was troubling her and *he had not wanted to know.*

He recognized the truck that pulled up. It belonged to Pablo Valiente. Standing in the pines, he watched Valiente and the gringa carry a concrete slab to the truck bed, the

303

teacher Bernabe Mateas following with an armful of cinder blocks.

He felt the gringa had appeared at that very moment to give him hope. After their walking through the village under the eyes of others who were perhaps laughing, after hours of misdirection and aimless searching, she was a sign of what could be done.

What if he took her and held her?

Then the laughter would stop. He would be in a position to negotiate. Valiente was from this Department and so was the teacher. Let them care about her, invite her into their homes. With that invitation came an obligation. And when that obligation was strong, he'd use her to find Cabral. At that thought, he felt the single concentration of his hatred.

He watched as they stacked cinder blocks and stove pipe in the truck bed.

She had sat there just like his daughter: vulnerable, alert and shy.

Only his daughter would no longer sit like that.

Cabral had destroyed her capacity for happiness, her life. The gringa's apparition was a sign that God favoured him. He only had to figure out what to do with her, just when he'd almost given up hope. He only had to wait, be patient.

10

Michael awoke to the blat of a finger tapping a microphone.

He rolled over and looked at his watch. He'd slept in again.

Church service was underway across the street: a plaintive voice flapping over the chords of an electric piano. The clinic was closed for the day. He and Alana had agreed to take a bus trip to El Tablon. He'd heard that cortes were woven there and he wanted to see how it was done. He would also ask about the way into Tikru Lake. He might go on to the lake then or he might return with Alana, depending on how she was doing. In the street he bought cellophane packages of sliced watermelon, cantaloupe and pineapple, a half-dozen buns from la tienda Sophia, soft cheese and bottled water. The sky was clear, the light growing warm in the street that was still wet from last night's rain and the air over the hills was sharp and clear. It smelled of wood smoke and the cordite of bombas let off in the fields to awaken the morning gods, the day lord.

When he arrived at the clinic the metal door was locked. He reached in through the grate to unlock it from the inside. He climbed to the third floor terrace. The door was shut, the curtains drawn. Laundry that she was going to wash in the morning was soaking in a plastic basin by the sink.

He had to rap on the door twice to get her to open it. She was in her dressing gown, shielding her eyes from the glare.

He got her back into bed, took the dispensary keys from the table and went downstairs for some Cipro. He brought her a glass of water from the jug on the kitchen counter and the pills.

"You work too hard," he said.

He sat on the bed to place a folded, damp towel on her forehead.

"I don't have time to get sick," she complained. "There's too much to do."

He went to heat some water on the hot plate then brought her tea sweetened with panela. He washed the evening's dishes that were stacked on the counter. From outside he could hear the rattle of a metal shutter raised in the tienda next door, the blaring horns and squealing air brakes of livestock trucks and buses coming in from outlying villages. When he brought her more tea he saw that her eyelids were drooping and that her body under the blankets was like a child's, so small she'd become and curled in herself.

He read to her from Eduardo Galeano till she slept; he changed the sweat-drenched sheets when she got up to pee. He heard her retching into the toilet and went across the terrace to help her back into bed, his hand on her heaving stomach that felt hard and small.

"There is hardly anything of you left!"

"I have to get dressed. I have to make sure Celedonia's okay."

"There's nothing you can do right now."

"I feel like I haven't done enough."

"Back to bed," he said, directing her by the shoulders.

He agreed to take Celedonia a note asking her to come to the apartment. From a low shelf he took out pyjamas and underwear, glanced at her while she changed with her back to him, arms shivering. He buttoned the pyjama top for her, drew a strand of hair off her forehead, helped her into bed, drawing the sheet to her chin and placing a damp cloth on her forehead. She turned on her side, the cloth dropping to the bed, and asked for a pen and a notebook.

She tore the message she'd written out of the notebook, handing it to him. "I'm asking her to come back with you. You could probably say that in Spanish but I want her to know that she's to come *right away*. I'm worried about her."

She settled back and closed her eyes. He left the dispensary keys on the table and pulled the clinic door shut when he went into the street, listening for the click of the lock.

Two women who were sitting on the curb got up and came toward him. Both were wearing traditional corte and huipil, women from an outlying village.

One touched his arm and asked softly if Alana was in, they'd been waiting for hours.

They'd heard that someone was giving away stoves American missionaries had brought into the highlands.

Perhaps Alana could help them get one.

He said he'd heard nothing about these stoves, that Alana knew nothing about them either, that she was ill and could not see them today. He walked away and they stood in the middle of the street, watching him.

He followed the street that skirted the western side of the village to a path down to the river. The late morning light was lying across the hills and he could smell cooking fires. Outside her kitchen, Celedonia was hanging clothes to dry on a rope tied between two ceiba trees. Behind her, a field of tall maize stretched to the river.

She read the note asking her to go to Alana's, and he followed her back up the path.

Turning as she walked, she was trying to tell him something he couldn't make out.

He could understand simple things now — buy fruit in the market, talk with vendors about where he was from, but often when the words were new to him, he was lost.

She was like a dream figure speaking urgent gibberish, her face crossed by waves of irritation. He thought it had something to do with her husband. He saw her shrug her shoulders, resigned.

She began to climb quickly now, up a different and more direct path. They went by a half-finished cinder-block house, rebar sticking out of the bricks. Shredded plastic bags, broken concrete blocks, rotting oranges and melon rinds were scattered across the earthen floor. Passersby were using it as a dump and he felt the sadness of the place, its disuse. He followed her as a child might, chastened and wondering, with the vague sense that he'd done something wrong — was doing something wrong. Not understanding what she was trying to say and her impatience made him feel that he'd become an unwanted burden, someone who was just getting in the way at a time when something needed to be done. But what it was he couldn't tell.

"Celedonia says someone is looking for you," Alana translated from bed. "A young Canadian. Who is she?"

"I don't know."

"Celedonia can stay with me. You go and find her. She's in El Tablon, staying with a teacher. "

He couldn't think of who she'd be. He'd had no news from home, and no one he knew would come this far to find him. He had made no arrangements to meet anyone and had told only a handful of people about his plans, which were uncertain. He had sent only two letters to Rose, both from Mexico.

"Celedonia can look after me," she said. "You go."

When she coughed, he could hear a soppy rattle in her chest, probably pneumonia. If the Cipro didn't work she'd have to go to hospital in San Marcos. In the weeks that he'd been with her, he'd seen how hard she worked, how little she slept or ate.

She would go out of her way to help almost anyone. He'd seen how she couldn't walk down the street without someone stopping to talk with her, a hand on her wrist, sometimes to give her a bag of avocados or a handful of stoney little peaches, or to ask for a favour, a street consultation. He could see that she felt needed then and was of help. He would stand to the side, watching, and sometimes he was introduced as her new friend.

Still, there were things you couldn't say to her. She was always seeing patients, visiting with those who had become friends and who always seemed to want something from her, organizing a playtime for neighbourhood children, trips to the city to buy medical supplies or to arrange for a patient to see a specialist.

She always kept going, hardly taking time to eat or sleep. Once they were walking through a market when he told her this and she'd walked ahead then, ducking under the strung blue tarps over the market stalls and weaving through the close-packed stream of people coming toward them, at a quickened, irritated pace.

When he touched her she'd pull away, get angry. Now that he was leaving, he could see the disappointment in her eyes, the loneliness.

"I'll come back," he promised.

"You don't have to come back. Celedonia will take care of me. I'll be on my feet in no time!"

He could hear her voice waver.

"You can't go on by yourself," he said.

She drew the sheet to her chest. "I have and I will," glaring at him.

"You're always sick," he said.

"Get out," she said.

11

The patrol leader Bernadino Garcia made one, decisive mistake. To find the gringa, he went to the wrong house.

Garcia wasn't from the village and he should have remembered that he would be lied to, had relied on one set of directions. The abuella who opened the door was stirring a pot over a fire ringed by stones on an earthen floor. Smoke was rising through the eaves and through holes in the roof thatch. An open umbrella protected the bed from an afternoon's rain that had just let up. Bent over, hardly taller than a girl, she looked at him out of wizened eyes that shone like wet stones, her face a leathery mass of wrinkles, her hair bound under a pale green bath towel. She smelled of wood smoke and urine.

When he asked where the teacher Bernabe Mateas lived, she seemed to look through him, blind. Then he saw the milky rings around her pupils. She offered her hand for the traditional greeting and show of respect. She pointed down the road the way they'd come and shut the door.

He and another carried a rifle. The others carried sticks.

They were a new authority in the highlands, unwelcomed.

To try to find the teacher's house was like a dream in which every step feels like you're wading through thick syrup. He would not forget this: in a scattering of huts on two hillsides it took an hour to find the teacher's house. In full view, they had wandered like dogs sniffing for market scraps.

By then the teacher and the gringa were gone. Bernadino Garcia insisted on inspecting the compound. An old woman led them into a warm, smokeless kitchen, a small stove of new bricks burning in the corner. It gave off a steady heat, the fire banked low. Two of his men went over to warm their hands.

They watched the old woman feed sticks into the firebox under a concrete plancha dusted with lime.

They looked over the wood at its side: small branches cut to lengths of maybe thirty centimetres, and kindling of the same length.

It looked like a child's stack of wood for a play stove.

"Does it use much wood?"

"Maybe a third of what I used to use."

They looked at each other. The younger one Luis Miralles had to borrow a pack mule to bring in firewood. All the pine forests around his village were young, privately owned. Occasionally he'd get pruned branches, that was all. For firewood he had to go to the San Antonio forest, two kilometres away.

"Where did you get it?"

"From my son. He's giving them away."

They glanced at each other again.

12

Word travels quickly on the highland buses: a boy was on his way to El Tablon, to see how cortes typicas were made and to ask the way into a volcanic lake called Tikru Lake.

Lacey was waiting for him in a street called calle de los Tejedores, street of the weavers. Here cortes typicas were woven, yards of cloth wrapped around the waist and tied with an embroidered belt. One door to the street was open and from inside Michael could hear the clack of the warp lifted and lowered, the hiss of the shuttle skimming over the shed. Standing in the doorway, he couldn't see into the shadows, could barely make out the figure of a man tossing the shuttle back and forth, the curve of his arm. The air felt cool and there was a faint smell of dried oranges and dill and ground water. When he stepped across the threshold into the room, she came up behind to put her arms around him. He felt a shock of fear go through him, so bright and clear that he froze, just like those birds he used to free from the vine-yard nets back home, cupped still in his hands till he lifted them into the air.

At first he couldn't make out who she was, didn't recognize the freckled forearms, but relaxed into an embrace that was gentle and kind.

"It's you!"

He turned in the sound of her voice.

She looked as young as he remembered, on the days when he saw her in the bookstore. She was dressed in jeans and in an embroidered blouse. Something was new in her. She seemed to see him and yet look through him.

She took him by the hand to stand at the weaver's side, "Just watch."

The shuttle flew across the shed, building the cloth thread by thread, mild colours of orange, purple and brown. The weaver's hands had the grace of a temple dancer. The bolts of cloth stacked on shelves behind him smelled of dry straw.

"I've been watching for hours," she said. "I'm beginning to see how it's done. This is for you," fetching out a letter from the back pocket of her jeans.

He unfolded the letter but the writing was too small to read in the dimly lit shop.

He pulled her outside to sit on the raised flagstone sidewalk, his heart pounding.

"You wrote this?"

"Because I couldn't trust myself to say it."

In the long hours when she wrote reports, noted sightings, she had no one to talk to except the radio dispatcher who spoke in code and who avoided chitchat 'to keep the channel open.'

For days on end, she wrote and rewrote, so that he might choose from a place of knowing.

When he bent over the letter, she walked away.

She felt angry, exhilarated and afraid.

Let there be a moment of stillness, let all the silence that she'd gathered come into the words to catch him unawares, open his heart.

This morning I got up in the dark to turn on the light, sweep the cobwebs from the cabin ceiling. I was remembering a dream. In the dream you were floating above me, weightless like a balloon, and I reached to pull you down by the leg.

At dawn I went out on the catwalk. Tendrils of cold air went by, like breath off the glacier. I could see the sky was clear, just a few stars showing, and I knew it was going to be one of those sunny fall days that smell of snow and make you feel you could walk for miles.

Odin Mountain just a shadow, I decided to go see the place you always talked about, where your village used to be. I wanted to see the foundations of the houses and stores you used to talk about: Beruskis and Alfis and the remains of the stone house, all out on the reservoir flats that are planted with fall rye to keep down the dust that sometimes blows through our village in late summer, the stone and concrete foundations scattered in the tall grass.

No one talks about your village anymore, as if we've agreed to forget about it. I think we're all ashamed of what happened, and I feel like we've disappointed you in some way.

Sometimes I feel that if I could just describe for you what is here, you could really feel what you've left behind. I'm dreaming of wandering, too, and yet I feel so unconfident, useless. Sometimes I don't even know what I feel.

This morning I went down to Rose's. She's rented the apartment above the Giacomo café. In the alley I called out to her open bedroom window, and when she didn't answer I went up the outside fire stairs that go past her kitchen window all the way to the flat part of the roof. She was on the dewy roof, hanging out bedsheets and diapers to dry on a line. She's had a baby by you. There's a one-armed rocking chair up there, curved, laminate wood, the varnish worn off, mustard yellow cushions. She sometimes sits in it to read or study or to nurse her baby. She's planted some late summer kale in raised beds up there, the dew jewelled on the leaves and some gangly sunflowers in big pots. A voluntary tomato was growing out of one of those pots in a bloom of little yellow flowers that would never produce any fruit.

Let's go, I said to her. Let's go for a ride somewhere.

The sun was already up and it was already getting warm, you could see from her roof the green glacier water sparkling in the river bed, the sway of the poplar leaves in the morning breeze along the bank, main street swept clean with a few cars in it, people going to work in the sawmill or going to open a store.

I knew it was her day off and I wanted to get her away early because I knew that sometimes Mr. Giacomo would ask her to work anyways, and she often does because she needs the money—she's saving up for her own place.

I've got to study, she told me, draping a sheet over the line, clothes pegs between her teeth that turned her smile into a laughing grimace. I could tell she wanted to go because she was hesitating and thinking about it.

Maybe just for the morning, she said then.

We went down the fire stairs to the apartment, climbing in through the kitchen window.

Hurry! I said because I could hear Mr. Giacomo unlocking the café below.

She made some sandwiches and sliced some apples to take with us, pushing aside the textbooks and work papers on the table. She was taking a first aid course to get a better job, maybe in a logging camp. I got the baby out of his crib and into a jumper that

315

I'd spread on her unmade bed. She showed me her account book, how much she'd saved for her own place, "It's going to take years!"

We went back out through the window onto the fire stairs, because we didn't want to go through the café. I was carrying the baby — Sen is your son's name. She handed me him through the window. In the alley she put him in this bike seat, a grey plastic one with blue padding bolted over the back tire of her bike. The seat was tilted so he could sleep in it and she strapped him in. Then she unchained the bike from the stair railing.

We rode down the alley where Mr. Giacomo couldn't see us to 1st St., crossed the river on the one lane bridge in lower town, the one with planks that rattle under your wheels, and we went by the Cowan St. Mill. I could smell the yew wood they were cutting, drying boards that my father had ordered, the ones he props in the yard outside his mill to dry his paper on, and I saw Mr. Beruski wave at us from the mill yard and I waved back.

We rode south along the river. The air had that cool, damp feel of early fall. The light laid a dusty haze across the peak of Odin Mountain and you could see that fresh snow had fallen up there. Wide gravel bars stretched to the middle of the river, the water was that low, and you could see the deeper channels in the gravel, the water darker and riffled.

The farther we got out of town, the more Rose smiled.

This is wonderful, she said, I haven't felt like this in months!

And she went on weaving down the paved shoulder till she remembered she had a baby behind her. Then she straightened out, and when I pulled up beside her she said, Thank you, Thank you for suggesting this.

Where the river widened out, the reservoir flats were covered in grass.

We parked our bikes under some poplars, and we walked down to the flats. Rose carried your son. Summer grasses were growing through the foundations of your village. We found the graveyard with all the graves covered in concrete, we found the stone foundations of the house you used to call 'the castle,' we found the cellar of Beruski's store silted in. It's all still there: you can walk where the streets were, and find these things. A cold wind was blowing over the grasses and there weren't any birds.

I told Rose then that I was going away.

Where?, she asked.

I don't know yet, I lied. I haven't made up my mind.

I didn't want to tell her where I was going because I didn't know how I'd feel when I saw you again. Maybe I'd just walk away and not say anything, I didn't know. Maybe I wouldn't like you when I saw you. Maybe you'd have changed.

Michael's put the idea into your head! she said angrily. How long will you be gone for?

I don't know. A couple of months, maybe.

She was fighting back tears. She wiped her eyes with her sleeve, looked away. I was the second person to leave her like this.

God, this is a sad place she said, looking around. I could tell that she was angry, even hated me then. She had that determined look she gets when she sits down to study, like she's facing a difficult climb. She was hugging that baby to her chest.

Maybe you're looking for a home in the wrong place. Sometimes I feel my home is just in a longing for faithfulness, and then for a little while the way I touch things, look on them, the way I see and talk to people becomes a little more kind. Have you ever felt that way? Maybe you should come home and meet him. If you could just take him sometimes, so that she doesn't have to feel it's all up to her.

13

They were heading north towards Cero de Fuego, Lacey and Michael sitting on folded blankets in the back of a transport truck, under a lashed tarp. Bernabe was driving, his wife beside him.

He was taking the boy and the girl to a place where he knew they would be safe. He had heard that a civil patrol was looking for the girl, to use her in their efforts to find Jose Cabral. The patrol leader Bernadino Garcia had accused Cabral of dynamiting towers that carried electricity to the mine.

Bernabe had heard that Garcia suspected that he knew where Jose Cabral was, or could find out: they were from the same region of aldeas northwest of Jacaltenango, all within walking distance of each other. Bernabe knew that Garcia wouldn't dare touch him — he was well-respected and still had connections from his days as a carrier. Garcia's plan was to hold the girl, till Bernabe agreed to say something.

You have to leave this country, Bernabe had told the boy, the girl. We have to hurry. No one knows what these civil patrols are capable of. No one can guarantee your safety. These people can do whatever they want because the army is behind them.

While they were walking in the streets of El Tablon, Bernabe had come to find them.

So you have received your news, he said to Michael. Is it good or bad?

He could see a kind of wonder in the boy's eyes then, and a glint of fear.

But there was no time then to talk. The civil patrol was in the village and they had to leave immediately.

Now the boy and the girl were in the back of a transport hidden behind crates of watermelon and oranges, the truck gearing down as they climbed into the Huehue highlands.

What are you going to do, Lacey asked him then. It was late afternoon, and in the diffuse light under the flapping tarp she was hugging her knees, her face in shadow, not looking at him.

He asked what his son was like and she told him about the birth of the child, the mewling cry, how his wrinkled, cupped hand had curled around her finger like a pale water flower, his grip firm and surprisingly strong and gentle. He's getting close to one now, she said, maybe learning to walk, tottering around on his fat little legs.

And Rose is keeping him?

You don't know how difficult that is, she said, and for the first time there was the sharp touch of anger in her voice, and impatience and maybe a sense of irreparable loss.

She told him of how the Giacomos had set up to take the child, having lost a baby of their own, and of how in the end Rose had refused, fleeing on a train to Field, but she never got there because Mr. Giacomo had gotten onto the same train, sat with her and talked, took her courage away with his words of loneliness, a hard life, when he had such a fine, rich life to offer the boy. An easy decision, he'd said then, a necessary one. *You can't do this on your own.*

There are so many people I've met, the boy said then, who are running from loss. He spoke of the painter and of the

woman he'd met north of Encenida who cleaned hospital
rooms, how they lived out in the hills above El Camino Real,
waiting for the day when they would be forced to move on.
Their only protection is to not be seen, to not be singled out
by a word or a look, to not be *there* when the Migra comes
looking for them, to have already vanished, and yet they carried the touch of where they were from in their eyes and in
their look, not often shown, but a real human vulnerability
in the quiet reach of their trust and their willingness to help:
Yes, you can stay here, too. No guard dogs, no electrified
fences, no barred windows, no patrol cars, no one prodding
you in the back in your sleeping bag with a baton in some
park in the middle of the night saying, Move on.

What do you mean?, she asked.

I've been trying to figure out what I feel, where I really
belong. Have you ever felt this, how eager your heart is when
it suddenly, dimly, hears a real voice, how deep the longing?

Say when you read something or someone says something to you that you *know* is true, so true, and so beyond
what you usually feel that you feel a shiver go up your spine?
It's not even a choice, he said then, it's who I *am*. I'm tired of
things being taken from me. I'm tired of loss so that other
people can get what they want. I'm tired of their greed and
thoughtlessness.

She smiled then, nodded.

Night was drawing in, the diffuse blue light under the
tarp fading to darkness. He told her then of something that
had just come to mind, a story his grandmother had told him
in her last days, maybe just to keep talking, maybe so they
could stay awake in that truck:

This took place in the spring of 1967, the spring before she died. At that time the Hydro was buying the village and the valley where she lived, to turn it into a reservoir.

In those days his grandmother didn't answer her door. Often the agents came by, not always the same one, and when she heard the knock, unfamiliar, urgent, she went out through the back screen door into her garden, unlatched the gate and walked away down the alley, walked and wandered, sometimes across the tracks up onto the mountain they call Palliser Mountain, and she asked herself, Am I a coward?

One morning an agent caught her by surprise. She was out back hanging laundry when he came around the house. She was running out sheets and dishcloths that billowed and flapped in the early morning breeze that came off the mountain, smelling of snow and rain-slick rock. He must have heard the shrill of the wheel.

"Good morning Mrs. Murray," he said, and she looked down at him from the porch, a clothes peg between her teeth as she sailed out another sheet, a flash of anger in her eyes.

"You're taking more time than anyone else," he said to her, apologetically smiling.

She would have dismissed him then, except for the voice and the smile in his eyes. His face was all crinkled and closed like a turtle's and his hooded eyes were dark with humour.

She wouldn't let him in the house. She pegged the last sheet and walked down to him.

He was in her garden then, looking at her young plants. "What are you growing here?" There was a soft courtesy in his voice that reminded her of her young husband who had died many years ago.

"Salad greens," she said, "martock peas."

He bent to pluck a feathered, burgundy-streaked leaf. "Tastes like a radish," he said, "hot!"

"Arugula," she said. She'd brought the seeds with her from Italy over fifty years ago.

He didn't talk about deals or land purchases, he talked about visiting. "I've visited the Pradolinis this morning," he said. "The Beruskis."

And suddenly the fear rose in her throat that there would be no spring here again.

She could feel the warm spring sun on the back of her hands that smelled of bleach. She watched a young red-tail soar over the Community Centre across the alley, turn south to the valley truck farms with a flick of its wing, riding the high winds and the clear air.

"Let's walk," she says, and she led him away from her place into the alley.

He had some papers to show her, some numbers, but she didn't appear to be listening. She could hear the hawk's shrill cry from somewhere near the roundhouse, hunting along the tracks to bring mice or rats to its young. There was a flash on the mountain, like that of an opening window, and the ground trembled as a freight train made its way down the tracks on the far side of the Community Centre.

He wanted her signature on an appraisal sheet that listed her property: orchards, house, lot.

"Fair market value," he said, and in his eyes there was that old humour.

"I won't sign this," she told him then sharply. "I won't sign away my life."

He shook his head. "Others are troubled, too," he said. "This is not an easy time for anyone."

He mentioned that he'd be back again, in a week or two — he had others to visit — to see if she had changed her mind, and in his voice there was a shadow of impatience, not much, because he was also kind, but he was really saying that soon there would come a date when this would have to end. Not firm yet, but not indefinite, either, some horizon that she felt coming towards her.

"I won't sign," she said again. "Ever."

"You'll end up in court, and the Authority never loses. They can't appear to lose; it wouldn't look good. And you'll get less than they're offering you now. They'll spend millions to save thousands."

"It's surprising how many of my friends and neighbours who have been forced to leave have died: John Camozzi, Margaret Pradolini, Mary Beruski."

For the first time the humour in his eyes was gone, and for a moment there was a kind of wonder.

When he didn't reply, she said, "I feel like I'm disappointing you."

She'd said too much for his courtesy to bear.

It had never occurred to him that the loss of your home, your land could wear you out utterly, put you in an early grave.

He handed her the papers and turned to go. He had others to visit.

"It's been a pleasure to see you," she said. "Come again."

She went and sat on a bench by the tracks. The freight train that she'd heard was a coal train from Alberta, hamper after hamper rumbling by, the coal piled high and smelling of oil, the metal wheels shrieking. She looked at the papers he has given her. The figures weren't generous, they never were.

Still, was strange to see a price put on everything you are and ever will be.

What are they buying then, these assessors that come from the Hydro Authority? They never send the same one all the time. In two weeks she'd be dealing with another one. What were they getting with their dam? They were getting her young husband furrowing in the grass for wild potatoes, one hand crippled from a fall. That was just a few weeks after he'd arrived on the train from Montreal over fifty years ago, and he hadn't yet found work. They were getting her trees and her garden, the Palliser forest, the river, the mountain and the sky, all of it.

She was trying to understand what was happening to her. She couldn't go anywhere in the village without a memory flaring up, maybe for the last time. It was as though the village and the trees and the mountain were trying to speak through her memory, as if the earth itself were speaking through her before its final submission. It made her feel that her memories were not her own, that they belonged to this land that soon would be underwater, that the final expression of its pain and sorrow was in the voice of her memory. For the earth did suffer, she knew that then, and she often walked barefoot to feel its apprehension and pain.

Though she is sitting on the bench, she was far away from the tracks, the mountain, the receding train. That's all the Authority knows how to do, with its numbers and

figures, assessors and engineers: shape dust. She admitted
to herself that she was deeply wounded, that something
inside her was dying, and that the flare of her memories,
so vivid and real, was the final gift of her life to this land.
She slapped the bench once, hard, as if to give notice to hard
reality: I am still here!, stood and walked home.

This is what his grandmother wanted to say to the assessor,
he told the girl, the one who walked away after handing her
the papers, walked quickly down the alley to some other deal
or court ordered purchase:

Come with me. There is no life where you're going.

Look at my pea vines. Vibrant, green, already in flower!
And the soil around the roots, two feet deep. It's taken me
forty years to build that soil, rich and dark and full of life.
Run your hands into it, smell it, feel how warm it is, how it
invites life.

These are my trees, my vines. I know each of them indi-
vidually. These my husband planted thirty-five years ago.
They're Galloway Pippins from Scotland. He had the scion
wood smuggled in by a friend. Sometimes I walk among
these trees clapping my hands because they make me feel
like I'm four years old. How? I don't know. Something from
them goes through me. I'm pruning the branches, yes, or up
on a ladder looking over them, and I feel a sturdy kindness
and a grace in them that surprises me and that makes me
want to clap my hands.

Now all I can do is wait and see what will happen:
listen to the rain, feel the sun and wind on my skin. A handful of trees and I have enough cash to live on when I sell fruit

at the end of the season. What I don't need to buy I trade for: a little wine, a second-hand sweater.

Once an orchard worker from southern France called me a fainéante.

That's true, I said to her, my joys here are free.

That's our mountain, Palliser Mountain we call it. It watches over us with the eyes of an old cat. I walk into its forests maybe three, four times a week just to feel its breath. At this time of the year if you brush by a young pine its scent will turn you around in your tracks.

And the river. The final thing you want to kill in order to live. So many memories there: the slate in its banks that my husband found, the booming grounds where my husband walked across the logs to find work, the seasons of its currents in full flood now and tearing at the bridge ramparts. You go down there, you can smell mountain snow in the water, oily, impatient water as green as grass.

There is no life where you're going because you're careless.

There is something violent in the way you hurry along, visiting as you call it. Always at the bidding of the Authority, always anxious because of their impatience. Don't you see this is carelessness? Don't you have any feeling for what you are doing? There's a kind of treason against life in those machines you bring to us, to push down our houses and cut down our orchards, our forests. There is no life there in that commotion of iron and fire, and that's what you serve.

Early in the morning, curled up beside each other on blankets, the boy and girl awoke when the truck geared down, pulled over to the side of the road. Through the tarp they heard angry shouts, the slam of a door.

A hand rapped the metal side of the truck box, listening for an echo. Two members of the security patrol stood outside, Luis Miralles and Pedro Real. Miralles was carrying a rifle. The two in the back could hear fear in the teacher's voice as he got out of the cab, they were arguing over something. Then they heard the slap of untied ropes as the tarp was unlashed, starting at the tailgate.

And once again Michael felt terror go through him, the terror of a menace that you don't understand that is whipping you up against the edges of your life. He heard the anger of the two patrolers and what sounded like a placating offer in the teacher's voice, but he didn't understand the words. The girl's hands were trembling in his.

Get ready to run, she whispered.

Then they heard the scrape of cinder blocks and a concrete plancha being pulled from the truck bed, the tinny echo of stove pipe, the clatter of bricks stacked on the roadside. They heard the tarp being relashed, the air once again settling into the musty smell of ripe oranges. They heard the teacher whisper in English through the tarp as he climbed back into the cab, a glint of grim amusement in his voice, "They took the stove."

And in the back they drove on, for an hour or more, not knowing what had happened. Somehow the search was halted, it had something to do with a stove but what that meant they didn't know. The plastic smell of the tarp and the musty smell of the crated oranges in the back grew strong in that morning heat. The truck swayed as they climbed switchbacks high into the hills. For a moment there was an odour of concrete dust as they went by a cinder-block works.

They came to the base of Cerro de Fuego.

Here Bernabe let them out, and his wife began to climb with them.

"I have to take the truck back to El Tablon," he said. "It belongs to my cousin and he needs it to get to market. My wife will explain everything."

While they climbed through the streets and through the cornfields of El Pajal, Helene said, "Two from the Jacaltenango security patrol were looking for you, but they saw the stove and were satisfied with it. My husband is a clever man," she smiled. "He made sure the most tempting thing was right there for them to see when they opened the tarp."

They climbed in a path of volcanic grit. The boy had to turn his shoes out, scuffing the edges of the soles into the dust so as not to slip. It was like he was climbing in ice-crusted snow. Though it was early morning, the sun was warm on the slopes and on the pines. Below a valley of small farms and in the east the blue haze of Huehue. They went by pine logs stacked for trucking. The girl knelt to count the rings on a stump. "These weren't very old," she said, "maybe thirty years." Michael reached for her hand to draw her away. They had to keep moving so as to avoid attention.

Ahead, a young child was sitting by the path, her nose and upper lip smeared with mucous, dark eyes and dusty black hair. When they came near the child, a farmer with a hoe in the field above shouted and Helene Mateas called back.

"He was telling us to go away," my wife said, "to stay away from his child."

"What did you tell him?"

"I gave him the blessing of a curandera." They watched as he descended the slope to put a coin in her hand.

Five hours into the forest they came to the rim of the volcano. They'd walked through pines to the crest; through the trees they could see sparkling water below. They went down wooden steps, hundreds of them, staked into the side of the crater, sometimes stepping sideways to keep their balance.

They came to a beach of white pumice stones. The one Lacey picked up was as light as hollow bone. Sunlight rimmed the crater and the wind-rippled water darkened.

He recognized the stick tripods arranged on the beach in some kind of sacred pattern, ribbons fluttering in the breeze. This was the lake in the photograph. And he saw exactly what the caption said he would see: mists racing across the water as clouds were born.

They set down their packs. They had brought in food, blankets, a tarp that they strung up between bushes for shelter.

Helene stayed with them into the evening, talking about the altars made of fluttering ribbons and stake tripods placed on shore.

"This is a sacred place," she told them. "No one would dare touch you here. And anyway," she smiled, "hardly anyone knows the way in."

Late in the afternoon, she lit a fire and they waited for the sun to go down. At dusk she went to catch fish. The wind had picked up, darkening the lake, and high on the slopes they could hear the pines singing.

"As soon as it's safe we'll take you to the border."

"Why are you looking at me?" the girl asked.

"I don't know, "Helene said. "But there are many, many things these days I don't understand."

She left the boy and the girl by the fire, went to sleep on blankets under the tarp. "Don't be up late!" she called out, "We may have to leave as early as tomorrow morning."

The girl turned to him then, and for the first time he saw a new worry and anger in her eyes. "Maybe this is all for nothing," she said then.

"Maybe Rose won't have anything to do with you, or maybe the Giacomos have convinced her to give up your son."

He felt a familiar sense of drifting then, of not being held in place, but it was beginning to fade. The offer of his return was like a song that drifts in the wind, maybe not understood, maybe not even heard. But the offer didn't depend on some secret want to curb or manipulate or destroy. He wanted to hold the boy, to feel his weight, that was a deep ache in his hands. And maybe Rose would accept him because the offer of his love would last in the grace of his hands and lips. That was how he was changed, he felt then, a change that had begun around the campfires that disturbed the peace of Garden View suburb. There are those who uproot and those who plant, a line from one of his grandmother's songs. But these times were, in a way, different: there are those who learn to sleep out in the open and those who remain and stare from behind curtained glass, afraid to go out, afraid to make an offer of trust and tending care.

Early the next morning the girl drew back a blanket to step out from under the tarp. The boy, the young father, had huddled in beside her, and she drew the blanket over him.

Helena was on the beach, crouched before a tripod of sticks tied with ribbons. The ribbons were fluttering in the breeze. The girl looked across the lake. Clouds born out of thin air rode off the water.

The dawn sky rimmed the crater. To the west she could still see the triad of bright stars in Orion, the three hearth stones.

She crouched beside Helene, whose face was grim and drawn, staring over the water.

"Often back home," the girl said, "I could feel an electric charge in the air before a storm blew over Palliser Ridge. The sky could be perfectly blue and I could feel it bristling on my forearms, like static electricity."

"Yes," the wife said. "Something is coming, I can feel it too. The helicopters that come at night, the civil patrols, the unexplained sicknesses in our children, burnt crops, it's going to get worse, much worse. A darkness is falling," the wife said, turning to the girl. "A darkness that will last a long time."

Michael had come out from under the tarp. He went by them to touch the water, old, archival.

"I had a dream that she was drifting far way," he said then. "I don't know if I'll get there in time."

"No," Lacey said, her gaze steady on him. "You're already there with her. All it takes is a change of heart."

14

A few years after Bernabe and Helene saw the two young Canadians across the border, they, too, had to leave. Because the helicopters came at night, the village couldn't organize itself or resist. One aldea after another was targeted. People were forced out of their homes that were then burned. Rosalina Tacam, who had spoken at a rally against the mine, and who had refused to sell her land, was shot in the face.

The community leaders of Tisbaj, Lupina and El Tablon met in Bernabe's school. No classes were held, and they met for two days. At the end of this, after weighing many options, they decided to leave. They gathered their families, their few remaining healthy stock and walked away on highland footpaths, crossed many arroyos and steep hills to the Mexican border. They left almost everything behind, only taking a few cooking utensils, some precious photographs or letters, some corn meal, eggs and salt and some beans, the few clothes they could carry, tarps for sleeping under. Whole aldeas were emptied in this manner, overnight.

They saw the astonishment of the Mexican border guards who came to find them in the highlands of Chiapas: they had camped out for weeks before anyone official came to look for them. The captain didn't order them back across the border, but he looked angry and perplexed at their number.

They asked for asylum and for the help of the international community in protecting them from the mine's and the army's 'security patrols.' They asked that their right to the health of their land and drinking water be respected. They said they would not return till their safety and their way of life were guaranteed and secured.

Soon international human rights groups and reporters were coming to visit them. To the embarrassment of their government, they were featured in a number of prominent news programs across the world.

Friends and relatives in Canada and in Los Estados persisted in the work of letter-writing campaigns, educational events, media coverage and lobbying politicians. They built an adobe and thatched-roof school in the Chiapas highlands, a makeshift clinic. And they waited for word from the Capital.

The Kootenays, British Columbia 198_

After shift, he drives down to Burton to pick up his son. He's still in uniform, the shoulder patches with the provincial crest on his jacket, the black pants, the polished boots. It's late spring, a weekend, so the boy will still be asleep.

There was only one call last night, to a rancher outside of New Slocan, the driveway under the ambulance headlights, he remembers, was paved in aggregate concrete, and there was a stand of tall firs that hid the road from the house, the porch light on, a woman standing in the doorway in a housecoat.

"He's having trouble breathing," she'd said, and he'd followed her in carrying the jump kit, while his partner Anita Fuscaldo got the cot out of the back of the ambulance, brought it under the roof of the open carport that sheltered the doorway, the pots of geraniums that were just in bloom on the steps, their colours garish in the porch light.

They went down a narrow hallway, all lit up, plastic tubing following the floorboard along the carpet, to an open bedroom door, a man inside sitting hunched over on the bed, breathing through an oxygen canula. His skin looked dark, as if burnt, and he shook off Michael's hand when he went to take his pulse at the wrist.

"He can't stand to be touched," the wife said.

He was drawing in deep breaths, his mouth open, a gleam of fear in his gazing eyes.

Michael asked for the husband's meds, care card, and his partner Anita who had just come in wrote the number on the call sheet. They walked him down the hallway in his housecoat and slippers, the oxygen line curling behind him, and they got him to sit on the cot outside the doorway, put him on portable oxygen, loosely draped a blanket over him when he'd swung up his feet, the wife standing in the doorway, her face lined with worry and grief.

When they'd loaded him into the back of the ambulance he struggled against the cot straps, tearing off the oxygen mask and snarling he couldn't breathe.

Michael spoke quietly to him, saying he'd only make it worse. "Here, this will help you," slipping on a non-rebreather mask that gave him 100% oxygen, his lungs full of cancer.

It was a sixty kilometre drive over the Perry range to the hospital in Nelson. He dimmed the lights, the patient closing his eyes and settling into the relief of pure oxygen, his breathing slowing, sleep coming on him now that he was no longer fighting for breath.

Anita was new to the area, called him forward to ask for directions at a fork in the Perry mountains; they would soon be climbing through Grohman pass, through high cedar woods, and there they'd have to watch out for deer on the roadside, watch for a late spring frost that could lay down black ice on the asphalt.

When Michael went back to sit on the bench, the patient's breathing was easy, his eyes still closed, eyelids flickering, briefly dreaming then. He must be exhausted, who knows how long he'd waited before he got his wife to call, struggling for breath.

He was dying and maybe he'd fought for a day or two against giving in, knowing this was probably his last trip. Michael drew the blanket to his chin, cool in the ambulance now that they were going over the pass.

He wondered at this work he was doing. In the first year or two he took as many shifts as he could, for the experience he told himself, but it was more about the adrenaline and the glory, the self-satisfaction of walking into a house where there was pain and grief and knowing that he could do something about it, that the people there would be grateful. Was he at it, then, to win badges of recognition, to take pride in restoring life or offering comfort when nothing else could be done?

Now he wondered whether it was possible to take care of people without a desire to please one's self.

What would that feel like, to forget yourself and your eye for glory while you went about your work?

He could hear the low, throaty purr of the ambulance's diesel engine as it climbed in the pass, the hiss of the oxygen mask, They must be going by Orange Creek where the cedars opened into a clear-cut on the flank of Perry mountain, the wind buffeting the ambulance. They were following the Kootenay road from New Slocan through Syringa into the Nelson area.

He could hear Anita talking on the radio, responding to a summons from Dispatch, location and expected time of arrival at the hospital. She had forgotten to call in, new at the job, and Michael could hear the anxiety in her voice as she gave their location, somewhere near Perry mountain, speaking in a hurried, clipped tone because she wasn't used to speaking on the radio.

She was a part-timer, just out of the IFA course. She was in her thirties, had taken the job to supplement her income. Her other work had something to do with raptors, using them to chase birds away from airports and garbage dumps.

It was early in the morning when they got to Emergency, and the air would be colder, so he covered the patient with an extra blanket, tucking it in between the cot mattress and the side rails. He slid the portable oxygen cylinder under a strap by the patient's leg, switched the line from the car port to the cylinder. He was saying that they were at the hospital now and that they'd be going in soon and Anita opened the back doors, letting in the sounds and the bright lights of the Emergency entrance, the chatter of an empty cot wheeled by, the cough of a woman in a hospital robe standing by the side entrance and smoking, an IV bag on a wheeled metal pole at her side, under a wall of plywood and scaffolding where the new wing was going in. He touched the patient's shoulder lightly when he heard him try to say something, muffled words in the mask, bent down to listen, but he only shook his head, a tired, frightened look in his eyes, turned away.

Michael got out to help wheel the cot to the Emergency doors. Inside, along a wall that divided the hallway from the ward, two patients in ambulance stretchers were waiting to be admitted. He knew one of the paramedics standing by them, Leah was her name, a friend of Rose's who had just hired on and he nodded to her.

Admitting was backed up: in the waiting room he could see a man with a bruised, bloodied face who looked like he'd come from a bar fight, a friend sitting with him, a young woman comforting a child that had a barking cough, the child turning restlessly in her lap, some chatty teenagers gathered around a pale, quiet young man, being careful not to look at him or at the wrist he was holding in his lap.

They pulled the stretcher behind the other two, and he waited while Anita went back to the ambulance to clean up and restock the jump kit for the next call. He could hear the clatter of some bed rails being put up, the murmur of a doctor's voice at the unit desk, the low wail of someone in pain.

He asked Leah to keep an eye on his patient while he went into a treatment room to wheel out an oxygen tank, switched the patient's line to the hospital tank and turned off the portable. He asked Leah how she was finding the work and she smiled and said she was enjoying it, but he could see by her anxious smile and the way she stared around that this was not what she'd expected and a little more than she could handle. Her patient was an elderly woman who was already in a hospital gown. She was dozing and smelled strongly of alcohol. Sometimes people only did a few shifts and then quit, not liking the confusion, the unpredictability of what you could walk into on a call, the ultimate lack of control. 95% of the time the work was routine; 5% of the time it was pure terror.

"Is it always this crazy?" she asked.

"Every Friday night," he said.

While he waited for the intake nurse, he thought of his son who was living with Rose in Burton, seven years old now. They saw each other on weekends and in the summer they'd go camping or drive down to Butucci's to help out in the orchards.

In a month or so he was flying down to a refugee camp in Chiapas, some people he knew from the Jacaltenango region were going home and he wanted to walk with them when they crossed the border.

He would have to tell his son about this, let him know that he'd be gone for awhile. He wanted to boy to go with him, didn't want to think of being away for so long, weeks, maybe a month or two, but he knew it was too dangerous.

He was going as a witness, an accompanier. They'd walk for hours in the scorching mid-day heat to cross the border, and then they'd travel on crowded buses and sleep in schools, if the authorities could be trusted. Something told him that he had to go, though the military might turn on them at any point, calling his friends subversives and terrorists. Two weeks ago there'd been an incident: an army patrol had opened fire on some returned refugees, killing eleven and wounding over thirty, including several woman and children. He'd talked to Bernabe Mateas about it on the phone, the teacher's voice hushed, frightened.

"There's a presidential election underway in my country," his friend had gone on. "We're being offered the choice between a war criminal and an idiot."

When the intake nurse came up to his patient, he fetched the rolled form from his back pocket, handed it to her and she quickly glanced at it, then took her own readings, blood pressure, pulse, sugar levels in the blood.

"Busy," Michael said, and she nodded impatiently, jotting down a reading from the blood pressure cuff.

She pointed to a bed and she said, "Put him over there," a hallway bed with a pull-around curtain. He rolled the stretcher over and his partner who had come in from cleaning and restocking the car let down the side rails. While he braced the stretcher the patient shifted over to the hospital bed, taking quick breaths and wincing.

They drew a blanket over him and left him then, a nod and a quick goodbye, they'd been tied up in Emergency too long. When he pulled the curtain round Michael could see fear and appeal in the man's eyes, defiance.

But they were moving on, and he never felt he said goodbye in a way that mattered; there was always the next call, Dispatch at your back pushing you along, and sometimes anxiety at the thought that he wasn't *performing* well enough, and he smiled at himself now, his anxious need to please and how he burdened others with it, even his patients, sometimes.

They were driving now back through the New Slocan country to the station. Anita had the radio on low, rustling early morning announcer chatter and he wondered why she liked that station in particular, something about the music and the announcer's voice; he'd have to ask her sometime. The dawn light was growing over Mt. Perry and turning it to shadow, and he also wondered whether he burdened his son.

He and Rose were trying to figure things out, in those early weeks when he'd returned. Rose had this apartment above the Giacomo café and he had a trailer on the Palliser, maybe he should give it up and move in with her. Except for the anger and his inability to connect with her life.

It had started with, "There's no room for a crib in that trailer of yours!" and his refusal to have anything to do with Mr. Giacomo, that bastard who had been after his son. No way he was going to move into an apartment that man owned. And so it was about places and home. Where *can* we live together? But more than that, her trust had gone, that was it.

"How do I know you won't leave again?" she'd asked him once. They were sitting at her table in the upstairs apartment, first aid books and note cards and exercise books spread around her. He hadn't yet found work, the Odin Mill wasn't hiring, so he sat with her in the evening while she studied.

"I won't leave."

"Yes you will. There is nothing for you here, no work. You live in a *trailer*."

"I promise you," he'd said then. "Things will work out."

She only shook her head, went back to her books. Their son awoke then, tossing fitfully in his crib and he got up to walk him, hold him in the crook of his arm and against his chest, the little one settling in, the weight of the baby's head on his shoulder.

When he turned back to the table she was looking at him. "I can't wait. I have to get on with my life."

How could she trust him when he didn't even know himself what he was going to do? It was a question that he ended up living in for months with no clear way out, and in that time any confidence she had in him, any hope for a real relationship in which she could let go of her determined need to get on alone, faded.

So now they lived apart and shared the custody of their son, had for years. Anita was surprised to hear he had a son that was 7 years old.

"You're still young yourself," she said, "a bit like a kid yourself. You must have been really young when he was born."

"Eighteen," he said. Eighteen.

At the station she parked on the tarmac and they washed the car down, spraying mud and gravel out of the wheel wells, scrubbing the sides with long-handled bristle brushes till they gleamed.

And now he was driving to Rose's to pick up their boy. She and Lacey shared a house in Burton. Rose would be off to work herself when he got there, was a paramedic in Station 19, down in Syringa.

She'd gotten him into the Service, helped him practice for the first aid exam and then coached him through the application process and sometimes they got together over coffee to talk about calls and about their son.

When he knocked at the door the boy flung it open and climbed into his arms, still in pyjamas. He smelled of warm bedclothes and of something sweet, like raspberries.

"You're late!" Sen said angrily and happily. "Where are we going?"

Rose walked into the room then. "You're late," she repeated, "Why didn't you call?

I have things to do as well, you know?" He flinched but didn't respond. Of course she was right — he should have called. Easy enough to say something cutting back to her, he could feel an angry response rising in his heart, but he had learned long ago now that that went nowhere.

She was getting ready for work, tucking in the white shirt with the service crests on its shoulders, the black belt hanging loosely at her side.

She looked tired and worn, her forehead puckered in a frown.

"What's the matter?," he asked.

"I'm thinking of applying for a full-time position in Kamloops."

She explained that the position — if she got it — would give her a secure income and more money and that maybe she and Sen could afford to buy their own place. She had ambitions, too, of maybe eventually becoming a unit chief or a dispatcher.

He understood all of this. It was a good move for her and her career, but it felt, unreasonably he knew, like abandonment. Maybe he would follow, find a job nearby so he could be close to her and their son. Maybe he would leave this place, too.

Still, she had no time to talk right now.

She was brushing out her hair to tie it up and he could see she'd put on a little makeup to hide her tiredness.

She gave him a smile that asked, How are you with this?, but there was no time to talk.

He set the boy down. He could see that she was afraid — of the decision, of what he might say.

Kamloops was hundreds of kilometres away. That would mean that they would see less of each other, much less. It would be a journey to see her and his son, and when the boy stayed with him, they would have to travel back here, to his own home.

Rose and his son were going to grow apart from him, through daily memories and routines that would be their own.

Once again he felt that old fear of things he couldn't control, of changes that he'd not foreseen and the effects of which he couldn't say. Maybe he should try to get away from here, out of this country. The habits of his days went round the reservoir: ambulance calls, driving down to Burton to see his son, took him along its shores almost daily. Maybe, after all these years, he should just get over his grief and move on.

When he'd helped Sen to dress for the day, they got into the car, the boy strapped in beside him. He started driving north on the Kootenay highway, along the Arrow shore. He was thinking of a place they could go for breakfast.

They could have breakfast in Nakusp. Lacey was going to meet them there. He asked Sen if he was hungry and he said yes, looking out the window with that dreamy expression of his that reminded him of Rose. Pleased he was and settled and unsure of where they were going, sleepy still, rubbing his eyes.

He tried to put aside last night's call, the pain in the man's eyes, his look of hopelessness. "I don't want to go," he had said, sitting on the bed and his wife's eyes had started with tears then and she had turned quickly away, gone to fumble among the pill bottles on the dresser, packing up his medications in a plastic bag. They didn't even try to pretend, none of that false cheeriness in her voice – Oh, you'll be back soon! – the silence of grief between them, in the look they exchanged at the door, the husband on the cot and the wife standing in the doorway, love and goodbye was in that look, tenderness and grief.

North of New Slocan, the hills rose steeply dark with stands of fir and cedar, a morning mist coming off them and dimpling the windshield. As they rounded a curve, he caught a glimpse of the grey expanse of the reservoir through the trees. About fifty kilometres north they came to an over-grown side road that used to lead down to a farm on the flats, the grass rustling against the underside of the car as they drove down, and the boy looked around.

"Where are we going, daddy?"

He could feel a choking sensation in his throat as they came into an orchard. He parked by some trees with branches twisted or snapped by bears that had climbed after apples.

He went over to touch the stone foundation in the tall orchard grass – his aunt Manice used to live here. Now she lived in a rest home in Naramata. There were two cousins from that time that he often thought about, though now he saw little of them. He remembered when his cousin Anna, a newborn, Manice's child, was first brought to this house. *She will be like a sister to you*, he was told, and he was made to hold her on the porch steps as if to seal the relationship, he a boy of five and the cousin swaddled in a blanket so that she wouldn't scratch her face with her tiny fingernails. He was astonished at how little she weighed then and to protect her, to make sure that she wouldn't just float away, to keep her to earth, with a five-year-old's logic he figured he'd need to gather a sack of bones to put under her crib. Later, he'd often not wanted to have anything to do with her, especially in school. Once, lost, she'd appeared unannounced in his class-room doorway and the teacher had asked,

What is your name, little girl?

An-na es-pisi-to!

Some classmate asked if he knew her and he'd denied that she was his cousin. Mocking laughter. Now he felt a burning shame at that denial. Somehow as a boy he'd made the decision that Anna was from a different life unconnected with his, that she didn't *belong*. He felt the distance between *sister* and what they really had, between the new village that the Hydro had promised and what they'd delivered: uprooted houses and stores set on blocks in a dust-strewn site.

Despite the claim that she was to be like a sister, they had drifted apart. They had watched the village vanish before their eyes and it had not held them together, it had not given them the streets to walk down together, the orchards to climb in, the river in which to toss the burning dill torches of the festa. Between them, they could not make those places stay. So in the end, ungrounded, not kept to earth, they'd drifted apart. Now she sold real estate in Naramata to be close to her mother.

And the other cousin, Maren.

After she'd set the Giacomo house on fire, they'd tried to run away together. She'd set that house on fire because her father Paolo was going to take her away, back to the

Aconcagua in the Argentine, the place of his birth. To pay for the plane tickets he was going to sell the Giacomo house, so she burnt it down. And then he and Maren had gone to hide in a cattle car, to run away to Burton. She had kissed him then, in that cattle car, her lips trembling on his.

Later, as the train climbed through orchards, she fell asleep on burlap sacks, her head resting in his lap. A child of twelve, he felt then a death in his hands and he was no longer able to touch her. He felt then that it was not only houses and orchards that were vanishing, but a tenderness that could no longer be held in a place of its own.

He hadn't seen her in over a year. He'd heard that she was to marry one of the Fuscaldo boys.

And now he remembered one of his uncle Paolo's riddles that Paolo immediately answered himself:

Wait, his uncle once said to him: What does a man have for himself when he has lost himself?

A fist in the mirror!

Now his son was standing in the tall grass, bundled up in a shiny, nylon coat that Rose had bought in a second-hand store, the sleeves too long for his arms. The boy was watching him, uncertain.

"What's that smell daddy?"

It was the odour of windblown, rotten apples and of mouldering leaves on the reservoir shore.

He parted the grass under a tree to show the boy the wrinkled apples and he bit into one to show its white, winter flesh and for the sweet, acrid scent of it.

He said he used to pick these when he was a boy, that the unpruned trees were going back to the wild.

"I'm going away for awhile," he said then, "to Chiapas to help some friends."

"Can I go with you?"

He spoke of Bernabe Mateas who had a child a little older than Sen. A teacher he'd met in El Tablon and who had got him and Lacey out of the country at the start of la violencia. "Maybe you'll meet him someday. His son doesn't speak English. You'll have to learn some Spanish."

He started naming things around them in the language, the words strange on his tongue and in this place and the boy looked at him.

"Stop saying those sounds, daddy," he said. "Stop it. You're just trying to trick me!"

There was anger and bewilderment in the boy's look.

"I'm not trying to trick you," he said, crouching down and pressing his knee into the grass by his son.

"Yes you are!"

And then he said, "Can I go with you?"

"Where?"

"To that place you said."

How is it that words, especially in a language we don't understand, can make us feel angry, displaced or even afraid, unweighed to the earth? He remembered then a story he'd heard of his grandfather pedalling south from Dundee, Scotland to Roca D'Avola, Italy in 1920, a bag of slater's tools strapped to the carriage over the bicycle's rear wheel and of his using his slater's hammer to break up a boulder uncovered in front of the Roca church to impress a young pregnant woman who would later become his wife. He knew then, so the story goes, that he would follow her anywhere, even to Canada.

You speak like us, she'd said.

You have our accent, because his own mother was from that village and had taught him the language in Dundee.

Wasn't it true, he thought then, that only one language, the language of your birth and childhood, could connect you to your heart, that when you speak that language, even after years of its having gone silent, you are back home?

In another world, in another life, he could have brought his son here and his aunt Manice — the baby that his grandfather once helped to rescue in southern Italy, now an old woman who live in a rest home in Naramata — would have come to the door to greet them, take the boy in her arms. She would have led the boy by the hand through her orchard, shown him her trees, always well-pruned in a way that was like an easily identifiable signature.

Let's go, he imagines her saying. I know others who want to meet you, and they take the gravel river road by a grey expanse that was once the river. In the village, in a late, slant autumn light, on a café terrace, the two are waiting, Maren with her bushy eyebrows, narrow chin, green eyes of a girl from Roca, Anna with her wide smile and a dancing light in her eyes. They are sitting at a table drinking lemonade, both in dresses that look almost identical and when Manice and his son approach, they stoop down to say,

What a wonderful little boy! We're your aunts!

"It's cold here, daddy," the boy said then, looking over the reservoir. "Let's go!" His cheeks looked pinched raw from the wind, his nose running.

"Here, take this," and he fished in his jacket pocket for some tissue the boy could use. His son had no connection here, no memory. All he saw was dead grey water and all he could feel was the chill of that shrill wind.

Somewhere on the drive to Nakusp, he made a decision. He was too connected to loss here; this is where he'd stand. But not only loss. Just as with the undocumented migrants who camped out in the hills north of Encinitas, he could reach back and be held, at every turn here there were memories that held him and made him who he was, offered him the possibility of making the choices of a good man, of a real human light in his eyes and touch.

At a café in the town he spread a few photos across the table to show the boy his friends in Chiapas, Bernabe Mateas and his son Manuel, Helene and Andreas Tomas, but the boy was not interested in those faces: the plate of waffles had arrived and he was too hungry to pay attention.

Then he looked up from his plate and smiled.

Lacey had come in to sit with them. She worked in a hardware store across the street, had come to sit with them on her break.

"These are for you," Michael said, gathering up the photos and handing them to her. "Bernabe sent them."

"Look at Manuel," she said then, a bright light in her eyes, "he's become a big boy!

Just like you, Sen," she said to his son and the boy, cutting the waffles, nodded thoughtfully.

"Are you coming with me?" Michael asked her then.

"I don't know," she said. "I don't think Rose would like it. We've already left her once, and I don't think I could do that again, even for our friends. It's dangerous, Michael. And she needs one of us to stay."

"You go," she said then, touching his hand. "One of us has to," and he nodded.

"Better get back. We're always busy on a Saturday morning! People in to buy lumber for some shed they're building, paint, plumbing supplies, you know: weekend jobs. It's always good to see the two of you together," she said then, standing and smiling. "Always."

After breakfast, Michael and his son drove to his trailer on the Palliser where he changed into street clothes, and there, at the table he wrote out a cheque for two thousand dollars. It was a deposit on a property he'd walked a few times and was thinking about buying, part of a farm in the Bearpaw Valley.

The road to Pinnacle Creek followed the base of Mt. Odin. The mountain was one of the tallest in the region, over 2,100 metres, its steep flanks covered in fir and pine. This used to be a logging road that was made public when Timberlands sold its concessions in the Bearpaw Valley to farmers who moved in to tear out the stumps to plant hay and grain fields and orchards and Christmas trees. He wouldn't know much about the valley except for a call that had taken him there, a farmer who was pinned by a tree he was felling. By the time they got there the farmer was dead, volunteer firefighters standing around waiting to cut away the tree so that the body could be removed to the RCMP station in New Slocan, where the coroner would examine it.

Now there was a homemade For Sale sign at the foot of the driveway.

He knew the widow: she used to be a train dispatcher in R. Years ago when he was ten or eleven he'd see her on

5th street, sometimes early in the morning or late at night coming back from shift work; he'd see her from his bedroom window, and sometimes she'd look up, smile and wave as she walked by, but he never got to know her, she wasn't part of his family's circle of friends.

She was Mrs. Palladino from Enderby, who had gotten a job as a train dispatcher, that's all he knew. And he'd heard that she often walked alone, didn't have many friends in town.

She was waiting for them on the porch when they drove into the yard; he'd phoned ahead to make sure that she was at home and to ensure that they would be welcome. The spring sun had broken through, and she was warming herself on the steps, a cane at her side.

He'd been by a few times to walk the property, and now he wanted to show it to his son.

"You go on ahead," she smiled, "That's a fine boy you've got there!" and his son looked at her shyly then, taking his father's hand.

They walked up the fence along the property line to a gate that led to a mined out gravel pit. On the north face of the pit a grove of alders had rooted, dense light, milky air, alder pollen sifting through the branches. In the hollow a pond, dark, sifting water, otherwise mounds of sand and gravel, tufts of bracken.

This is what he was proposing to buy, all he could afford, really. It would take years to build soil here. Already, though, the alders had started. He and the boy walked to the grove and he knelt to scrape away last year's leaves: under them, handfuls of dark humus.

Years of work, that's what he was proposing: build soil, plant trees and vines, a vegetable garden, let that grove go back to the wild.

"I'm going to buy this," he said to his son.

"What for?"

"So we can have a home here."

"There's no place to sleep, daddy!"

He felt the boy's hand tighten in his, and he was looking up at him, wide-eyed.

How strange must be the ways of grown-ups to him. What they propose must often seem ludicrous and without sense. They must seem like wild dreamers in need of much correction. The boy had Rose's practical sense of purpose and he wanted to know how, really, this was supposed to work.

"We'll move the trailer here," he said then, "and we'll build a house when we can afford it."

"This will be your room." They gathered stones to mark out the lay of the foundation, the division of rooms, the entrances and where the windows would be, and the boy stood in his room and looked south toward the water.

"Can you see it?"

"Yes," he nodded. "But there will have to be real walls."

"Yes," he laughed, "there will have to be walls."

Later that evening, he returned. He and the widow sat at the kitchen table, more formally now that he has laid out the cheque between them. He saw that she was reluctant to accept it, that it would mean so much change in her life. He was not buying the whole farm, just the gravel pit, but it was already a step in a direction that she was reluctant to take. The two thousand dollars was a deposit, and the price he was offering was generous. The pit was practically worthless. Subdividing it from the rest of the property would make her farm more saleable. She knew this, and yet she was quiet, withdrawn.

You were one of the paramedics who came when my husband was killed by a tree he'd felled, she said.

Yes, he nodded.

I'll tell you how we ended up here and how he died, she said. I'm telling you this because I want to warn you about something.

My husband's name was Hector Palladino, He used to be a fireman on the railroad and I was a dispatcher. I met him in Field.

He was walking along the platform when I stepped off the train for some fresh air. I'd been in Banff for a weekend holiday.

"Don't wander away," he warned me. "We're only here for five minutes!"

I explained that I knew the precise time the train would leave, that I was familiar with this route as I was a train dispatcher in this division.

He swept off his striped trainman's cap and bowed low, saying, "I didn't know I was in the presence of royalty!"

His ears stuck out from under his short-cropped hair and he had a thin, nasally voice, like that of a tin whistle. I'd sworn I'd have nothing to do with a railroad man.

Soon he was calling me at work from the station in Field. Once in the fall, without a word, he held the phone to an open window: I could hear snow falling.

We bought a two-bedroom bungalow on 2nd street and tried to save for a few years, to buy land to get away from the railroad. He only worked within our division. Sometimes he'd get work in town, sometimes as far away as Enderby. He could be gone for weeks at a time, at a moment's notice. He hated shift work, always being at the beck and call of the telephone, the weeks that sometimes went by without a call and the bills piling up, his hands idle.

We put off having children because he didn't want to be away or asleep for most of their home life.

Then one day he came banging in through the door, saying that he'd got a job on one of the tugs the Hydro had hired to help clear the forests north of Burton. He'd be gone for ten days in camp, home for four. The pay was good and meant that we could start to save for the farm we always talked about buying.

So that fall, the fall of 1968, he was gone most of the time.

Finally, after a few years of this we had enough saved to make a down payment on land we hoped to own. I don't know what was in us. As we got close to our dream, something in us began to change. Maybe it was because of the money we were using, the way it had been made; grief money, I called it to myself, cutting down all those forests. It made us impetuous and even a little giddy, so that we didn't see the things we should. We saw the pretty little house, the gardens, the well-tended orchard and didn't see that the mountain would cast a long shadow in winter and early spring, making it a cold dark place. The soil was mostly grey clay that had no odour and every February a spring welled up under the basement floor, flooding it.

I wondered why the orchard was planted to the northeast till I realized it was a windbreak for the winter winds that come through here, funneled by Mt. Odin and the flank of Mt. Burnham.

Because we heated with wood, every winter we needed five cords to keep this place warm. At first wood was cheap or even free for the taking because of the clearing of the reservoir, then the price began to climb after the Hydro crews left and the reservoir was flooded.

We have a grove of second growth fir in the northwest corner of the property, and one morning last spring Hector said to me that he was going to cut down a few for firewood, just thin the grove out a little, "to get ahead of the game."

I didn't know then, that with all his experience on the river, he had never felled a tree.

I was outside spading over some hard clay for a garden when I heard the roar of the chainsaw, a tree crashing into some branches and then, after a few minutes, a brief scream.

He had dropped a tree onto another, angled like this, and she showed him with her hand propped on the table, the butt resting on the ground. He cut away the butt and the rest of the tree slid down and pinned him to the ground.

The firefighters and you paramedics came, and they took him to the police station in New Slocan, laid him out on a table there. That's where I said goodbye. His eyes still showed a look of pain and surprise. He'd tried so hard to breath that the capillaries in his face had burst, turning his cheeks a dusky red.

I touched his hand, gave him a kiss on the forehead, then they covered him with a sheet.

That is my life here now, she said, spreading her fingers on the table as if to rise. Twilight had come, and in the mountain's shadow there was little light left in the room.

I keep feeling that through failure I have something to contribute here, she said. Still, these days I have one medical complaint after the other, the old hurts are in the way.

There is a limit but it varies from day to day. A good plate of fresh peas and a good night's rest and I can go a little farther. This morning my ankles were so swollen I hardly recognized them.

We made mistakes, I have failed. And perhaps my failures are my greatest contribution to life, to something beyond me.

We had a good family, you know what I mean?

I have one more story to tell you before you go:

Peter Camozzi came to see me, do you remember him from the old town? That man can fix anything. He built us our first house on 2nd St. and later, when we could afford it, he helped us build our barn and a shed for hay storage here. I liked the men and women he worked with, his crew. Once he told me that he always hired the same people, though they never came in with the lowest bids on his projects. He knew he could rely on the quality of their work and on them. He knew they would be there when he needed them.

Once he brought a load of hay for our cows on a flatbed trailer. The electrician Mary Williams had come along to help him. They were talking about a project they were working on, the laying out of street lights in a subdivision. And when the hay was in the shed, while they were still talking in that low considerate voice that I often heard among his tradespeople, and because they didn't have a broom, they gathered the straw wisps on the trailer with their boots and pushed it clean, side by side. At that moment I heard myself say, I love these people.

I'll think about it, she said, tapping the cheque on the table. And you think about it, too. Don't make the same mistake we made.

It gets to us all in the end, she said, as he put on his coat. We all fail. Just make sure you don't fail far from yourself.

Chiapas, Mexico

He takes down and folds the blue tarp that has been their home for several months. The rain has stopped, the clouds have drifted away. There is a scent of pine on the wind.

Down at the checkpoint, a marimba orchestra is rehearsing traditional tunes. Already some of Bernabe's people have gathered there, their belongings in carts or tied to their back. Across the border, the school bus engines are starting up.

He sees his wife and son squatting to fold their bedding. A few tendrils of smoke rise from a cooking fire that he's doused for the final time with a can of water. Though they'd only been here for a few months, he feels affection for this place that has taken care of them and offered shelter, and in his heart he gives thanks.

They are waiting for the witnesses to arrive.

Two Canadians, an Australian nurse, an Irish woman, a German filmmaker, and two women from Mumbai in India. They slept last night in the school in Lagos de Colon.

He has spent so much of his life crossing and recrossing this border. And, as always, there was a little fear.

No, a lot of fear.

He has never got over the fear, but he's beginning to feel a border is a kind of sanctuary. At the border the Capital is afraid of its own shadow. Here it must acknowledge that what it can't see or touch easily slips by, can't be controlled, and that is why the soldiers of the border patrol always have a nervous fear in their eyes: their task is impossible. They have been pushed up against the limits of their own understanding, and they feel there's a vast beyond that is more powerful than they are. The vast beyond, that which they cannot exploit or measure or control, is actually quite small; a hidden package of love letters, for instance, the videotape of a marriage or a funeral, a piece of sacred bread or the traditional clothing of a young girl. These pass through the sanctuary of border like corn meal through a sieve. The Capital is always looking behind itself for what has already gone by, on a foot track or a goat path that it cannot see. Border is sanctuary because it gathers all these unobtrusive paths that recognize each other.

He's heard there's talk of raising a metal fence here, financed by the Americans. If they do, this border will become even more of a sanctuary. A fence is not a border. It will be the last expression of the Capital's fear, now that it has lost touch with the land and become memoryless.

The witnesses will bring cameras. They will photograph not only Bernabe's people and their joyful crossing, but the soldiers who impassively line the road on the other side. They will photograph and photograph and send dispatches, the only protection against a possible ferocity.

The Capital has reassured them that they will be safe. However Bernabe doesn't trust them. Somehow it is now in their interest to allow his people to go home, but he doesn't know their reasoning. What has changed all of a sudden? Why this posturing of welcome?

A month ago they'd received a document from the Minister of Justice stating that they could return to their land — as long as they agreed to live peacefully, as long as they did not to raise their voice against the mine in any way or to interfere with its rights. Of course they refused. Such rights could only mean, as the mine continues to devour earth, the ongoing poisoning of their water and more forced evictions.

And now this: a statement that they were free to return, with no imposed conditions.

Bernabe holds the letter in his hand, signed not by the Minister of Justice, but by the President himself. He can't imagine why this is so. Perhaps the signature is a forgery. Still, news of the letter has spread across the world.

Alana is the first of the witnesses to arrive. Her hair is tied at the nape and she is wearing a shawl of woven cotton, a jump kit and a camera slung on her shoulder as she climbs the hill to Bernabe's dismantled camp. He hands her the letter and she reads it and smiles.

"Do you believe this?" she asks.

"No denial has come from the Capital."

She turns and indicates the road across the border. "Soldiers have been sent," she says, "and school buses. What is being prepared for us?"

At first he thinks, against the soldiers all we have are our hands and our hoes. But then he realizes they have more.

We walk in truth and justice, he realizes, and even if we are destroyed we will have added our grain of sand. He takes the letter from her hand. The path is long and you go along it walking.

"What's that sound, daddy?"

I've rolled down the window so that he can hear.

We are driving into the Butucci orchards. Already a number of cars and trucks are parked on a grassy expanse outside the main gate. There's a sign nailed to a stake that says, This way to the wedding. Beyond in the trees, a white canopy, trestle tables, streamers and balloons tied in the branches.

"It's a marimba," I tell my son. He's smiling and his eyes are shining as he leans forward to listen. He feels the joy in the music, a son de entrada.

"That's real bouncy music," he says, and he's eager to get out to find its source.

We park at the gate, walk in among the trees. It's a widely spaced apple orchard and the trees are old, nowhere near the takeline.

We've come early because I've heard that Bernabe is to be here. He's on a tour with a marimba band, to raise awareness about Canadian mining practices in his country and in Central America.

No one wants to hear about a mine, he told me over the phone. But everyone will come to hear marimba!

He's agreed to play at this wedding because I've asked him. It's my gift to Maren.

Long ago I climbed into these trees during a festa to kiss her and she pushed me then, not trusting the kiss, hating that I'd jumped to the doctor's order that I hold down her knees while he stitched her chin. Even then, as a boy of fifteen, by that act I felt that I'd become less than I was and even now though memory and through what I write of those days and days afterwards, I'm searching in memory for a healing and tending way to the ones I love and to this land that I love.

Chairs have been set up under the white canopy. There guests will gather for the ceremony. Not until then will I see her, see how she is dressed, see the flash of her green eyes, her smile, how her hair is tied up, see her from a distance among others who love her, maybe have an opportunity to exchange a few words of congratulations in passing.

People are gathered around the marimba, and I recognize some from the old village: Mr. Beruski who now works in the Cowan St. Mill, Maren's godmother Mrs. Canetti and the groom's mother Jean Fuscaldo. Under the white canopy I see my uncle Paolo sitting alone, his shoulders lowered and his head bent as if asleep, listening.

And then I see Maren walking away through the old trees with the groom, hand in hand. They've been to greet the arriving guests and now they are retiring, to dress for the wedding. She is wearing a light brown dress, her hair loose at the shoulders. He is in light cotton pants and a white shirt, and he stops her. He slips something on her wrist that looks like a band of gold and she laughs then, drawn into his arms. And then they turn and walk away through the trees.

The music is wonderful, it puts a dance in your step. Bernabe has taken the middle position. He stands there, solemn and grave, the blur of the sticks in his hands. All three players, expressionless, look over and beyond the crowd into the distance. Their austerity is a sign of respect for the bride, the groom and for the guests that have gathered for the ceremony. Not only that — the music honours the dead of this land and the land they served, brings them close in heart and mind, and they give us the strength to go on.

Acknowledgements

The song on page 84 is from Danilo Dolci's *Sicilian Lives*. The songs on pages 39 and 66 are excerpts from a Sicilian harvest song published in *The Journal of Peasant Studies*.

Excerpts from this trilogy have been previously published in *Writing Beyond History* (Montreal: Cusmano Communications, 2006), as a chapbook entitled *Mio Zio* (Toronto: Flat Singles Press, 1999) and in *Venue* and in *Queen's Quarterly*. *The Wheel Keeper* and *House of Spells* were previously published as separate volumes by NeWest Press, and have been newly revised for this edition.

Thanks to Dr. Rebekah Shoop. We have travelled many of these paths together. For their enduring friendship and support, thanks also to Kegan, Adrian, Dion, Katie, Wes, Laurie, Drew, Les, Christle and Floyd; to John Taylor, Sylvie Nicolas, K. Louise Vincent and especially to Claire Kelly, Matt Bowes and Natalie Olsen at NeWest Press.

The author expresses his deepest gratitude to Tom Wharton, editor at NeWest. It has been a joy to work with you.

Thanks also to Vancouver Island University and to the Banff Centre's Writing Studio for the time and place to complete early drafts of the manuscript.

Robert Pepper-Smith was born in Revelstoke, BC. He currently lives on a farm in the Cinnabar Valley with his wife Anna and teaches philosophy at Vancouver Island University. His childhood in Revelstoke and his experience as a volunteer paramedic with the NGO Alianza in Guatemala have inspired this work.